# THE TORRID WEB

# THE TORRID WEB

Averil Kathan

The Book Guild Ltd
Sussex, England

First published in Great Britain in 2005 by
The Book Guild Ltd
25 High Street
Lewes, East Sussex
BN7 2LU



Typesetting in Baskerville by
Keyboard Services, Luton, Bedfordshire

Printed in Great Britain by
Antony Rowe Ltd, Chippenham, Wiltshire

A catalogue record for this book is available from
The British Library

ISBN 1 85776 869 8

# *Chapter One*

April Ross sat impatiently swinging her long, shapely legs in the comfortable foyer of Beckensuds Hygiene Services firm. She was a tall, well-proportioned girl with short curly brown hair offset by her pale grey eyes that were the main feature of her face.

She lit up her third cigarette in 25 minutes and glanced repeatedly at the glass doorway through which she was hoping to see Jack Nathan come striding. She despised tardiness in any person, and being only 21 years old, this was compounded by her desire to conquer the world as quickly and effectively as possible. She picked up a copy of *Time* magazine in a vain attempt to occupy her mind with thoughts other than what the forthcoming meeting portended.

'I'm terribly sorry that you have been kept waiting Miss Ross. Normally, Mr Nathan is very punctual.' April smiled vacantly and insincerely at the attractive receptionist who was obviously trying to defend her boss.

April had qualified as a social worker the previous year at Stellenbosch University, and had accepted a post 1,000 kilometres away from her home in Cape Town. It was not that she did not like her parents. On the contrary, as an only child she had a very special relationship with them. And that was the main reason why she had decided to move to Durban. She was going to spread her wings and soar fully independently. She smiled to herself when she remembered the chagrin that her decision had caused her fiancé, Parker Rodman, who had fully expected her to move into his home in Port Edward until they could set a wedding date at his convenience. Well, she had rationalized to herself, she had not been cruel and totally heartless. After all, Port Edward was only a three-hour drive away from Durban.

Besides, none of the available social work posts in Port Edward had appealed to her sense of adventure. They all lacked intrigue and the opportunity to experience something new. But her present job seemed very exciting. April had been interviewed in Cape Town by an intelligent and well-spoken Indian gentleman who had flown down from Johannesburg to meet with her, and that same day she had been informed that she was just what the Indian community in Durban needed. She had drive, energy, spirit and an openness to other cultures that transcended guilt or patronization. April may have been a white girl to look at, but under her skin, she was fully multiracial – an unusual quality in Apartheid South Africa in 1985.

Her arrival in Durban had been a nerve-racking experience. With the help of a cousin, she had quickly found a suitable furnished apartment that was centrally situated. What she loved most about Durban was the fact that most of the suburbs were built very close to the sea, so consequently she had a magnificent view of the bay from her bedroom window. It was like living in San Francisco, and so far the people had been friendly and very hospitable.

On Monday, she had met up with the outgoing social worker who had been transferred to Pietermaritzburg. She was taken aback when she saw Yusef Seedat face to face. Strange how often people's voices sounded so different on the telephone, and conjured up inaccurate images of their actual appearance. She had imagined a tall and stately man, as his voice had sounded warm and supremely confident. The reality was something quite different. Yusef was in his mid-thirties and was a full head shorter than April, who at five foot ten inches had regarded herself a fairly average height, although of late, she had heard that same refrain over and over again: 'You are so lucky to be tall.'

Sure. Who needed tall when all she had ever wanted to be was petite, pale and interesting-looking. Instead, April had been endowed with generous proportions, was tall and stately, and always tanned from the perpetual South African sunshine. Her irrepressible sense of humour was always lurking at the corners of her generous mouth, and a liberal sprinkling of freckles across her small up-tilted nose detracted from any semblance that she had hoped to uphold with regards to being small, pale and interesting. Her most endearing quality was the fact that she was completely unaware of the fact that she was stunning, and having never been vain, she did not see that people in the street often stopped and stared after her as she walked by. In her own mind, she was not hideous, but saw herself as the average girl-next-door type. A far cry from reality indeed.

Yusef stared up at April in fascination, and with an ironic quirk of fate, echoed her thoughts. 'Gosh April, you do not look anything like I had expected.'

April almost burst out laughing at his comment, but maintained her poise and smiled warmly at him. 'Well Yusef, I guess that makes two of us then.'

She stood, regarding him coolly, waiting for his next comment. He was struggling to regain his train of thought, so stunned had he been at April's unexpected loveliness. Most social workers that he had known through the years had been plain, salt-of-the-earth types. This exotic creature before him was an exception to every rule that he had ever known, and he found himself sucking in his slight paunch and standing taller in the vain hope that she would not notice the bald spot on the dome of his head.

'Welcome to the sunny city. We are indeed lucky to have you join us at Indian Affairs. It is not often that we get new blood … er, what I mean to say is that we do not often have graduates with your high qualifications interested in cross-cultural social work.' He could hear himself babbling on whilst he led her to the incredibly battered Volkswagen Beetle that was to be hers to use for business when he left in two days' time. Yusef had to concentrate very hard on not making a total fool of himself in the presence of this self-assured young woman, when all he felt like doing was declaring his undying devotion to her despite the Islamic laws that bound him to his religion and his family.

He struggled to open the passenger door for April, and finally had to resort to kicking it, grinning sheepishly at her. April stepped graciously into the little car with the solemnity that she would have afforded a limousine. Yusef then had to slam the door repeatedly to close it, blushing a deep embarrassed red under his pale brown skin. She looked diplomatically away until she could control her mirth. It was a hot, humid January day in Durban, and his white safari suit was already drenched with sweat between his shoulder blades and under his arms. He sniffed surreptitiously at his armpits to ensure that he had sprayed on sufficient Old Spice deodorant. Happily, from his perspective, he had. He jumped into the driver's seat, and with a series of splutters and jerks, managed to leave the Government Garage without doing any real damage.

Never in her life had April driven with a worse driver than Yusef. He drove recklessly and overtook everything in sight in his desperate efforts to compensate for the little vehicle. He hooted the horn and flung vile curses out of his window at anything that happened to be moving insufficiently quickly for his liking. On top of that, he kept taking his eyes off the road to look directly at April, whilst talking non-stop about the nature of the Indian community and their incredible propensity for gossip. April kept her eyes firmly on the road and found herself shutting them when ever he veered too close to other vehicles for comfort.

Finally, the car screeched to a halt, and Yusef proudly announced, 'Well, here we are. Your office. And you won't get lost either because I showed you the easy short cut and this is it!'

April opened her eyes, glad to be alive, and had to resist the impulse to throw herself out of the car and kiss the ground with relief on being safely delivered. Yusef rushed around the car to be the gallant gentleman and had to kick the door again to get it open. Finally however, he was rewarded by a glimpse of April's shapely thigh as she shakily slipped her legs out of the confines of the car. Her frazzled nerves caused her to miss her footing in her escape from the car, and to Yusef's intense delight, he had to grab hold of her to prevent her from falling on the rough ground. His hand lingered on her arm, and he was surprised at the silky feel of the fine soft blonde hairs that were invisible until one got as close as he was now. He swallowed and proudly turned around to point out a building to her.

April twisted around and stared in dismay at the sight of a dilapidated two-storey building that was sorely in need of major repair work, let alone repainting. 'Great! My first very own office and I get to share it with a troop of cockroaches,' she thought to herself.

The car was parked at a dizzy angle on the edge of a ditch. The terrain was rough and rocky with plastic bags flapping forlornly, trapped against a broken barbed wire fence. April watched carefully where she put her delicately sandalled feet as the area was strewn with broken bottles.

'Welcome to Riverways Estate,' announced Yusef proudly

in the same reverent tones that one would use for an introduction to the Notre Dame cathedral.

'Thank you,' said April as graciously as she could under the circumstances. First this fat bald little egomaniac had tried to kill her on the perilous journey, now he was leaving her in this uncouth wilderness. She felt the pricking of tears. Sharply, she pulled herself together and forced herself to smile.

'I'd like to take a look inside the building if I may,' she said brightly, regaining her dignity and composure very quickly.

'Sure, of course, with the greatest of pleasure, it would be my honour and privilege to show you my modest working place ... er ... I mean YOUR modest place,' Yusef gushed enthusiastically, sure that April could see the beauty and splendour of the building and what it represented.

April smoothed down her skirt which persisted in misbehaving in the wind of Durban, squared her shoulders and set off determinedly to Baboos Building perched precariously above a petrol station.

Yusef set after her with quick little steps as he tried to match her stride. In the end, he was forced to abandon his dignity and had to trot to keep up with her, and a little in front of her. After all, in his community, the woman always had to be at least one step behind the man, an attitude that April would challenge repeatedly in the ensuing months.

Yusef led the way up a dark and musty flight of steep stairs, and seemed to disappear in the gloom.

Resolutely, prepared for the worst, April followed. She turned right after Yusef's scurrying figure, and followed him down a surprisingly clean tiled corridor. Suddenly, she came to a sharp corner, and turned left into a pool of sunlight that was streaming in from the open fire escape door.

'Here we are then,' said Yusef, fumbling in his trousers pocket for his keys. He unlocked the solid wooden door, and April followed him into a large waiting room area. The one wall was windows from the ceiling to the floor, and the light beige sun-filter curtains moved gently in the early morning breeze. April felt her spirits lifting in the sun-drenched room.

'This way,' said Yusef, impatiently waving her towards another door that she had not seen on entering the room. The door led into the largest office she had ever seen in any welfare organisation in her life. The big wooden desk shone with polish and seemed to welcome her into the embrace of the room. Potted plants adorned all the corners, and a pretty pink African violet perched cheerfully on the desk, adding a strangely feminine touch to the otherwise masculine room. Watching her gaze light up when she saw the violet, Yusef made an impulsive decision that he would later regret when he returned home to his domineering wife later that afternoon.

'The plants are all for you,' he said softly. 'Welcome to Indian Affairs, April. I know that my people will love you and take you into their hearts when they meet you.' April noticed the tremor in Yusef's voice and intuitively noted that he was leaving an important part of his life behind him here. She smiled at him and patted his arm sympathetically. She was amazed at the flood of colour that her gesture evoked.

'Okay, let's get down to business,' he said quickly.

For the next five hours, April listened as Yusef filled her in on the details of projects that he had been involved in the community of Bloomsbury. As he spoke, she made copious notes in her file, a habit that she was never to grow out of, and one that had driven her lecturers to distraction at university.

'Miss Ross, please do not write down everything I say,'

they would all tell her. 'Just write down the essence.' Well, she had taken no notice, and consequently, she had always had the highest marks in the class when examinations had to be written. 'Such detail,' they would comment on her papers.

Well here she was, in her first position, in a one-man office. And she was still taking copious notes.

'One of the most important people dealing with the community is Jack Nathan,' Yusef said. 'He is respected and well liked by most of the people of Bloomsbury. He must be the first person that you meet with professionally as he will be able to guide you in important matters.'

'Where can I get hold of this man?' April asked.

'He is the operational manager at Beckensuds Services in Durban. You know them?'

'Well, I've seen their blue vans driving around like maniacs in Cape Town. A hygiene services company, aren't they?' replied April.

'Yes. Anyway, phone him for an appointment as soon as you can,' said Yusef. 'Here are several of the important and urgent case files. Read them whilst I make a few last-minute calls at the expense of Indian Affairs,' he chuckled shrewdly.

While Yusef made umpteen dozen calls all over the country, April settled herself down comfortably in a chair in the corner, slipped her sandals off and lit up her first cigarette of the day whilst she picked up the files at random. She stared at the strange names that presented themselves on the face sheets of the files. Names like Mooljee, Mukerjee, Pillay, Cooposamy, Ramdass, Naicker, Poovalingam. Unconsciously, she tried to pronounce them aloud under her breath, and was very embarrassed when she looked up and found Yusef staring at her in amazement.

'Oh gosh, I am sorry,' she muttered hastily. 'Was I disturbing you? I didn't even realise that I was talking out loud.'

Yusef stared at her. 'Disturbing me? Never! I am just surprised at your command of the names. You have been pronouncing everyone of them correctly. That is incredible.'

April noticed that as Yusef became excited his voice lost its polished tones and reverted to the sing-song type of refrain that she had grown used to in Cape Town, where many Indian people used to peddle their wares on the Grand Parade at the flea market.

'Okay, let's go,' he said, jumping up so fast that the swivel tilt chair that he had been occupying crashed over backwards. 'I have an appointment with my lawyer at one o'clock, and I would like you to meet her. She is a very cultured lady and can introduce you to many of the upstanding citizens in Bloomsbury.'

'Could I ask you a tremendous favour, Yusef?' said April haltingly.

'Anything,' Yusef recklessly promised.

'The only way for a driver to get to know a strange city is to drive herself,' said April, 'and I was wondering if you would let me drive so that I can get used to the car and the town.'

'Well, okay,' said Yusef, surprisingly hesitant. Then he brightened, and beamed at April. 'Sure, I would love to be chauffeured around by a beautiful woman.'

April let the sexist remark pass in her relief that she would at least be the mistress of her own destiny behind the wheel. She slung on her sandals and grabbed her handbag. With a swift swoop, she picked up the car keys from the table before Yusef could change his mind.

'Lead on, Macduff,' she teasingly stated.

'Well okay, as long as you do not turn into one of Macbeth's hags or Lady Macbeth,' responded Yusef astutely. April was delighted that she had found another Shakespeare follower. In her profession the talk would mostly revolve around pseudo-intellectual discussions on impossible theories, and to find another arts buff in the helping profession was very pleasing.

April was introduced to Sitha Mooljee by a possessive and very proud Yusef 20 minutes later. From the warmth of his introduction, April sensed that there was far more going on than just a business relationship. Sitha was a small, very attractive Gujurati lady who had impeccable taste in saris and questionable taste in men. She put out a perfectly manicured hand, and spoke with a surprisingly deep and husky voice for such a small person.

'How do you do April,' she said in flawless Oxford English. 'Yusef has done little else but talk about the new social worker that would be coming to Durban, but I must say that you are nothing like the way he imagined you would be.'

April laughed. 'I hope that is a compliment,' she said.

'Oh most definitely, my dear. Now if you will excuse us...'

'Of course,' said April, admiring the manner in which Sitha had diplomatically told her to leave the two of them alone.

April sat on a comfortable couch outside the office for 15 minutes before a calm but puff-eyed Sitha opened the door, and Yusef solemnly took his leave of her, shaking her hand very properly and professionally.

He was very quiet on the return to the car. After April had managed to kick her door open herself, she sank down onto the hot seat next to Yusef.

'Where to?' she enquired.

'Hmmmm?' Yusef was deep in his own thoughts of Sitha's soft head on his shoulder, as she sobbed out a final goodbye.

'I said, "where to now?"' she repeated.

'I think we should pop in to see Jack Nathan. He's very close to the office,' replied Yusef.

'I thought you said we would have to make an appointment,' said April, suddenly a little puzzled by Yusef's suggestion.

'We are very important people,' he snapped, 'so he will just have to make time for us.'

April detected an undercurrent in his tone of voice that she had not been aware of earlier. She followed Yusef's directions mechanically as her quick mind toyed with possibilities that might explain his sudden urge to see a businessman without an appointment.

April drove through semi-industrial areas and inhaled with delight as they passed the Sweet's chocolate factory. April had a very sweet tooth, and was true to her Taurean character by being a lover of good food and beverages. She was by no means a glutton, but her idea of a perfect date had always been a romantic candle-light dinner without the physical exertion of dancing.

As she drove, she found herself thinking about her fiancé, Parker. Parker was much older than April, and had come into her life straight after she had experienced her first heartbreak with Larry, a man she had firmly believed was Mr Right. She had been hurt, betrayed, and was very vulnerable. April had lost all of her self-confidence when Larry Ireland had calmly informed her that he had weighed her in the balance as a potential wife, and found her wanting, so he had found himself someone eminently more suitable. April had been dismissed like an unwanted shoe, and the scars still ran very deep.

Parker had come along like a godsend. Ironically enough, he had been introduced by mutual friends of her and Larry, who felt that she needed a little fun in her life. Parker was divorced with three children in High School, he was 41 years old, and was built like an amiable teddy bear. He had been a harbour in her very choppy emotional waters. She felt safe with him, but had never felt a twinge of passion or desire for him. She attributed this to the state of emotional inertia that Larry had created in her. In fact the only feelings that she was capable of mustering were connected to her fantasies of diabolical plots of revenge aimed at crippling Larry emotionally.

Parker professed to having fallen head over heels in love with April the moment he met her. She was beautiful in an unconventional way, and her intelligence blazed from her eyes.

He knew the story of her broken love affair in detail from Rosalind and Lucky Albany, and was always aware of the sadness lurking round the parameters of April's forced gaiety. Parker was short and rotund, and looked older than 41. He had also experienced an unfortunate relationship prior to meeting her. He had told April that his ex-wife had not divorced him for another man, but simply because she could no longer bear the man he was, so she chose to be alone rather than spend her life with him. He had said this had dealt a shattering blow to his self-esteem.

He and April found comfort in dealing with one another's fragilities. When Parker proposed, she had heard no bells, but had seen a calm pain-free future stretching out before her.

In this frame of mind she had agreed to become his wife, but she could not bring herself to set a wedding date. Something buried deep in her subconscious was warning her not to rush into such a serious commitment.

Parker lived in a three-bedroomed house out at Port Edward, which was a three-hour drive away from the city of Durban. Although April loved vacationing there, she could not imagine the practicalities of having to drive into central Port Edward every day to go to work in a boring welfare organization setting. Consequently, when she was offered the post at Indian Affairs, she had leaped at the opportunity. Living in Durban would also keep a little distance between her and the realities of her life to be, and she would be able to see Parker every weekend. In her mind, this arrangement made perfect sense. She was not prepared to live with Parker, and she was not yet ready to be married to a man who was going to be away from home most of the time. Parker was a sales representative for farming equipment, and his area comprised the entire Natal region, Eastern Cape and Transkei which meant that he would be travelling extensively during the week. And so, she came to be living in Durban and for the first time in her life she was completely alone, fully independent, and loving the feeling.

'Here we are,' said Yusef, pulling April back to the present. 'Turn right into this side street,' he instructed.

April looked around her. They were in the heart of a factory area that bordered on Riverways Estate, and she still did not have the faintest idea how she had got here. She was determined to go and buy a map first thing tomorrow morning.

She turned into a driveway and pulled up at the large security gates. Yusef leaned across her to speak to the guard. April was suddenly aware of how he reeked of Old Spice, and curry. The guard waved them through after April had signed the register and she cheekily parked the little car in the spot designated for the branch manager. Yusef led her up a small flight of stairs to the imposing glassed entrance of Beckensuds foyer. A luxurious, icy air-conditioned blast enveloped them as they entered the plushly carpeted reception area. It was a pleasant respite from the clammy stickiness of the blisteringly hot Durban day.

As Yusef asked for Jack Nathan, April stared around at the original watercolours of veld scenes that lined the walls of the reception area. It was obvious that the owners of Beckensuds were wealthy, and Jewish. April considered the surname of Nathan, and concluded that this Jack person must also be Jewish. She wondered why he was so involved in the Indian community. Perhaps he had a large Indian staff and was showing a concern for their well-being that would lead to greater productivity and more money for the company. April's grandfather had been Jewish, and she was accustomed to them being a very hard-working and industrious people, which naturally led to success on many levels. This made the Jewish people despised by jealous individuals that were incapable of making similar strides of progress. April had a strong aversion to people with any prejudices of any description, and lived out her motto of 'live and let live' to the fullest. She had always defended the underdog in often impossible situations, and had frequently scored victories on their behalf through her sheer strength of character.

'He's out to lunch,' said Yusef, irritable at this unexpected development.

'Well, a man's got to eat. Speaking of which, I'm hungry too,' replied April, who was never one to miss a meal.

'I don't know who he thinks he is,' spluttered Yusef furiously on the way to the car.

'Who?' asked April in surprise.

'Nathan,' he spat venomously. April looked at Yusef quizzically. He really doesn't like this Mr Nathan, she thought to herself. Perhaps the man was a racist, or worse – a patronizing white pseudo-liberal that tolerated the darker people for what he could gain. April discovered the seeds of dislike beginning to grow at this thought.

'The man acts like he's God,' continued Yusef, 'when all he is in reality is a pompous lush!'

'He's a drinker?' asked April, surprised that someone with an alcohol problem was a prominent businessman and community leader. Yusef, as a Moslem, did not touch alcohol, and incorrectly assumed that those who did were decadent lushes.

'Yes, he's a drinker, and a skirt-chaser too,' he sneered.

Well, April thought to herself, quite a little picture I'm forming in my mind of Jack Nathan. He's a rich alcoholic who exploits people for work and women for sex. In other words, a typical warm-blooded South African male.

Suddenly, to her horror, April realized Yusef had climbed back into the driver's seat. Having been correctly brought up, she was too polite to submit to the temptation of bodily removing him.

'Hop in,' he said cheerfully, his black mood of a few moments ago seemed to have passed. 'It's time to introduce you to Bloomsbury.'

Yusef screeched to a halt in front of a comfortable-looking home in Enez Avenue, Bloomsbury.

'This is it,' he proudly announced. 'Come in and meet my wife, Latiefa. She's busy organising the packers and the furniture removal.'

As soon as April stepped out of the car, she became aware of a terrific noise coming from the house. A woman was screaming hysterically.

'Oh, quick!' she said. 'It sounds like someone is attacking your wife!'

'I think it's the other way around,' said Yusef grinning sheepishly. 'Let us go and rescue the poor packers from her wrath.'

As they entered the house, April could hear a tirade coming from one of the bedrooms.

'You stupid idiots, I can pack better myself. Give me that. This is how you do it ... No ... leave that alone. Stop it! Yusef, you good for nothing, is that you?'

A short very fat little woman in an overall stuck her

head around the corner. Her hair was being held flat by a piece of old nylon stocking. Her brown skin had a yellow tinge, and her flat large nose was covered with freckles. Her mouth fell open as she saw April standing in the doorway at the end of the passage.

'Oh goodness. Hello,' she quickly said in the sweetest tones, patting her head self-consciously. 'You must be April. Yusef told me that he was bringing you around for lunch. Is it that time already?'

'Hello my little dove,' said Yusef, embarrassed to the tips of his toes by his wife's rude remarks to him. April could not resist smiling as she heard the term of endearment. More like a hawk than a dove, she found herself thinking.

'Hello Mrs Seedat. I am very pleased to meet you,' April said politely, walking towards Latiefa with her hand extended.

Latiefa quickly wiped her hands on her dusty overall, and shook April's hand limply. April had the firm cool grip of a confident person, and disliked the hot soft grip that most women had when they shook hands. When Latiefa turned away to scream obscenities in Xhosa at the black packers, April surreptitiously wiped her hand on her floral skirt to remove the woman's sweat.

Yusef led April to the lounge, which was stacked full of sealed cardboard boxes. This was the very first time that April had been inside an Indian's home, and she was fascinated at the sight of a hand basin in the dining area. Yusef noticed her puzzled expression.

'Most Indian people do not eat with knives and forks, unless they go out in mixed company,' he explained.

'Really?' asked April, fascinated at the prospect of eating without using the usual utensils.

'Yes, we use our right hand only when we eat.'

'Why only the one hand?' asked April, and was intrigued

by the blush that had started in Yusef's neck and was rapidly enveloping his entire head.

'Well ... um ... well...'

Just then, the doorbell rang, and Yusef looked comically relieved at the interruption. Approximately 15 Indian people flooded into the small lounge and April found herself crushed between two boxes and a window. The noise level had risen considerably, and above it all, she could hear Latiefa still hurling abuse at the packers. Well, I did want to experience something different, she thought.

'April, I'd like you to meet Manilal Mooljee. He's Sitha's husband,' said Yusef smoothly.

'How do you do,' said Manilal, softly taking April's hand in his and kissing the top of her fingers lightly. He squeezed her hand meaningfully and winked at her. 'I am sure that we will be good friends.'

'Yes, I'm sure. Please excuse me,' said April, trying to move away from the boxes without touching Manilal, 'I hear Latiefa calling me.'

As she brushed past him, she felt his hand distinctly touch her left breast, and had to resist the temptation not to knee him painfully in the groin.

Poor Sitha, she thought, what a husband. No wonder she sought comfort in safe little Yusef with all his faults.

April had grown up in a country where friendships did not easily form across cultural lines, due to all the barriers placed in their way by paranoid government officials holding on to the concepts of separate development that had been so fashionable in the days of the Voortrekkers, but had no place whatsoever in a modern and humane society.

Consequently, no person of colour had ever made a pass at her like Manilal had just done, and she was completely baffled as to how to handle it. The South African Government had even gone so far as to forbid sex across the colour line if you were white. It all formed part of the Immorality Act, and although April could not condone this type of forced segregation, she had simply never given any thought to relationships across the colour line. It had never seemed real or relevant before. It was clear to her that this post was going to stretch her limits considerably, and challenge her ideals. And she was looking forward to the experience.

April moved rapidly down the corridor of the near-empty house, and slipped into one of the rooms. She moved over to the large picture window and looked out over Bloomsbury. The suburb was situated in a valley, and the houses were built one on top of the other. The very wealthy co-existed with the middle class and the very poor all in one street. There was no economic segregation in South Africa, only racial division. As all of these people were Indian, they were forced to stay in the areas designated for non-whites by the terms of the Separate Land Act and the Group Areas Act which enforced their partition. Many of the landowners in Bloomsbury could have bought the whole of the white elite suburbs without blinking, but because of their race, they had to remain in the valley, and built their mansions on one another's doorsteps.

April detected the smells of freshly cut grass, petrol fumes, and jasmine from some of the gardens.

'April, it's time for lunch. Our friends have brought us food because all of our wares are packed away. Come through to the front garden,' said Yusef from the doorway. April turned and followed him obediently, relieved that she would be eating at last. She walked out of the lounge doors into the neat little garden that Latiefa had created. She was relieved to see that Manilal had left. Latiefa came waddling over to her and took her by the arm.

'Come and sit in the shade dear. With your fair skin, you will burn away to a crisp!'

April sat on a chair under the beautiful orange bougainvillea that trailed its cool green leaves around the poles that held up a wooden roof, providing shade and a cool respite from the day's heat. She was handed a paper plate and a fork, and one of the other women brought a large dish full of steaming yellow rice over to her. She noticed that despite the heat, all the women had their heads covered with scarves, and once they had served her and the men, they moved inside like a flock of twittering birds.

April had never eaten curry made by Indians before, and was nervous to try the first mouthful, but her appetite got the better of her fear of setting her mouth on fire. Carefully, she filled her fork with the deliciously pungent aromatic curry and took her first mouthful. This was a flavour that she felt she could quite easily become addicted to. She had never tasted anything so perfect, and it did not burn at all.

After lunch, Yusef hurried her back to the car.

'Get in, I've forgotten something,' he said. April took full advantage of the situation, and got behind the wheel of the Beetle. When Yusef returned, he did not bat an eyelid, but instructed her to drive back to Jack Nathan's office.

'Now? Is he expecting us?' she asked.

'I called his secretary and she said that he should be back any minute now. Come on, let's get it over with.'

April started the car, and drove straight to Beckensuds without needing directions once. Yusef was suitably impressed. They walked into the reception area again and April took the same seat she had occupied earlier that day. Yusef had a quiet word with the receptionist and joined her. 'He's not back yet. We'll wait for a few minutes,' he murmured.

What was it about reception areas that made one whisper? she thought.

After twenty minutes, the receptionist came over to them. 'I'm sorry Madam and Sir, Mr Nathan just called to say that he had to go out to Pietermaritzburg on Union business. You won't be able to see him at all today. Would you care to make an appointment for tomorrow?'

Yusef looked furious enough to kill.

'It's easier to see God than to get to see this guy,' he snapped rudely. The perfectly groomed woman smiled politely and agreed diplomatically with him. April giggled uncontrollably and returned her conspirational wink.

'Come on, April, let's go. Mr Big Stuff will have to miss us.'

There was nothing more amusing than a short man being indignant, and Yusef certainly fitted both categories. His brow was furrowed by his ill-humour, and his short steps were so fast that not even April's long legs could keep up with him.

'Yusef, why don't you like this man?' she asked, unable to contain her curiosity a moment longer.

'Who says that I don't like him?' he asked, appearing genuinely surprised by her question. 'I like him just fine. It's just that … well, he's arrogant.'

'Arrogant?'

'Yes, keeps himself important, you know?'

'Actually, I don't. That's why I'm asking you,' April said. 'I mean, surely he can't be that bad? You told me yourself this morning that he was important in the community affairs. An arrogant man would never have the trust of a people as diverse as yourselves if he were arrogant, surely?'

'Look, April, you haven't even met the guy. Why don't you decide for yourself?' he retorted.

'Oh, I fully intend forming my own opinions, Yusef. But it always helps to have the advantage in knowing something about a person when you are meeting them for the first time.'

Yusef had a spiteful glint in his eye. 'I'll tell you one thing about Jack Nathan, April. Whatever you do, don't bend over in front of him. He has a thing for women with nice long legs, and let's be honest, yours go a long way up.'

April stared at Yusef in amazement. She had thought cattiness was strictly a woman's quality, but here was an educated middle-aged man acting like a teenage gossip artist. Abruptly, she changed the subject.

'When exactly are you leaving?' she asked.

'Officially, I'm supposed to stick around and show you the ropes for the rest of the week, but I can see that Indian Affairs is in capable hands.'

'So?' prompted April.

'So, Latiefa and I thought that we would leave early on Tuesday morning.'

'Tuesday? That's tomorrow,' she said, with an edge of panic to her voice.

'Yes, don't worry. Nothing serious is scheduled for the rest of the week,' said Yusef patronizingly. 'You'll be just fine.'

April felt the panic welling up inside of her and had to bite her bottom lip to prevent it from quivering. This was so stupid. She had all the qualifications, she definitely had the ability, but now that reality was only 24 hours away, she felt very young and insecure again. She nodded mutely at Yusef, who had for once driven sedately. They pulled in to the government car pool.

Yusef stopped the car and let April clamber out onto the grass verge where she had parked her car that morning. 'Here are the keys to the office,' he smilingly said and tossed them to her. 'You can pick up the car here tomorrow morning. Good luck, April, and goodbye. It was great meeting you. Now I really must fly.'

Yusef took off in an awe-inspiring cloud of dust and pebbles that stung April's bare legs. He hooted raucously, and disappeared around a corner with a blare of obscenity at a truck driver who had pulled out in front of him.

April looked at her watch. It was only 3 p.m. She turned, and walked resolutely into the main office at the Government Garage.

'Hello, I'm April Ross, the new social worker from Indian Affairs. Is there something we could do about that car?' she innocently inquired.

The bored-looking, gum-chewing woman behind the desk began to shake her head. Just then, a handsome mechanic came up to her.

'Hello. I'm Tony. Gee, you're sure an improvement on old Yusef!'

'Thank you, Tony. Maybe you can help me with my little problem. That Beetle is really not performing very well. I couldn't take a corner properly and I'm worried about the steering. Do you think that we could exchange it for something else in the car pool?'

'Sure, no sweat. What do you fancy? A limo? A Honda?'

'Are you serious?' she asked. 'Do you mean that I can change the car?'

'Absolutely, honey. Anyone with style like you deserves a decent set of wheels.'

'Tony, my thoughts exactly,' April replied.

'Come on, let's go take a look-see at what we've got.'

April followed him into the huge shed that housed all the government vehicles. It looked like a parking garage at any shopping mall. With one exception – all the cars were white.

'Okay, let's see what we've got,' Tony said, frowning as he consulted his list. He nodded and walked towards one of the vehicles in the gloom.

'Are you sure that you can do this?' asked April. 'Won't

your boss object to you handing out cars like watermelons in the market place?'

Tony smiled enigmatically at her. 'Don't you worry your pretty little head about the boss. I can handle him any time. Right, I think we've found the car for you,' he said, stopping and beaming mischievously at her expression of surprise.

'A BMW? Are you crazy?' spluttered April. 'I'm a social worker, not the Minister of Social Services!'

'If you were the Minister, honey, I certainly wouldn't be hanging around with you in a parking garage,' said Tony, laughing at the outraged expression on April's face.

'Okay, so you don't want the BMW. How about this little beauty then?' he said, pointing at a Honda Ballade.

'I'll take it,' said April without a moment's hesitation.

'We'll retire the Beetle when Yusef returns it later tonight. See you tomorrow, April. I'll personally bring the Honda down for you.'

'Good-bye, Tony. Thank you for everything.'

Tony watched April walk away into the late afternoon sunlight. She was completely unaware of the effect of the sun shining through her summery floral skirt. The late afternoon glow outlined April's body in all its glory, despite her modest petticoat. Her short-sleeved white cotton blouse turned completely transparent, and Tony smiled as April turned around for a final wave, and her entire body was thrown into sharp relief. God bless sunlight, thought Tony irreverently.

April climbed into her red Mazda sports car, a parting gift from dear old Daddy, and pensively started the engine. Well, here she was, all alone in a strange town, the only person that she knew being a busy cousin 60 miles away. She drove slowly back to her apartment, and entered from the back of the ugly brick building to avoid the lecherous and decidedly mental superintendent. She let herself into the lounge, and walked over to the desk beside the window. April kicked off her sandals untidily and flopped down into her desk chair with a sigh of relief. It had been quite a day indeed, and she suddenly felt exhausted. She reached sideways to the bar fridge and helped herself to a cold bottle of soda water, her favourite restorative. She tilted her chair backwards at an angle that would have made her mother hysterical with fear that she would topple over backwards, and placed her long legs on the desk to balance herself. She was startled by a sudden hard knocking upon her door. With a groan, April righted herself and walked lissomly over to the door. Through the frosted glass, she could make out the figure of a man holding a peculiar object.

'Who is it?' asked April, ever mindful of the attacks on women who simply opened their doors to strangers.

A fawning voice replied in nasal tones, 'Open up dear, it's your friendly delivery man.'

April groaned in exasperation as she recognized the voice of the building superintendent. 'Just a moment, Mr Sherwitz,' she replied as she slipped back the safety chain and unlocked the door. Julius Sherwitz stood holding a large white box tied up with a red ribbon.

'These came for you at 4 p.m.,' he explained. 'So I took the liberty of signing acceptance for you. A secret admirer so soon?' The curiosity in his whining tone was unmistakable.

'How did you know that I was home?' asked April sweetly, ignoring his implied question.

'I saw your little red sports car turn the corner, dear. I love women with fast cars, so I tend to notice when a lovely young thing like yourself arrives home from a hard day,' he replied ingratiatingly.

'Thank you for your trouble, Mr Sherwitz. Now if you'll excuse me, I have to get ready to go out,' April lied unashamedly.

'Going to dinner, are you?' asked Julius Sherwitz. 'Maybe you would like to have dinner with me sometime?' he said, openly leering.

April smiled sweetly. 'I really don't think my fiancé would approve. Now goodbye,' she said, deftly shutting the door in his crestfallen face. What a nerve, she thought. The man must be 60 years old at least. She wrinkled her nose in distaste at the prospect of dining with the gross little man and his ill-fitting toupee.

April placed the box on her coffee table and picked up her soda water from where it was making a ring of condensation on the desk. She smiled as she looked at the box. How sweet, Parker must have sent her a little gift on her first night in a new place. He must have recovered from his sulks and seen the wisdom of her decision. She sank onto the uncomfortable couch and lifted the lid off the box. Inside were the most perfect long-stemmed roses she had ever seen. She picked them up carefully to avoid the thorns, and counted an even dozen. A card fell out of the stems and landed face down on the ugly gold and brown carpet. April leant forward and picked it up.

'Red roses for the passion that you have awoken in me,' read April out aloud. Parker would never have written a message like that. Not in a million years. His idea of romance was buying her a slab of his favourite chocolate, and then eating it himself.

April stared at the card in utter amazement. Who on earth could have written such an intimate and unmistakable message, and why on earth hadn't they signed their name?

Oh yes, this day had definitely been interesting.

# *Chapter Two*

The early morning sun filtered through the flimsy blue curtains of the cool bedroom and caressed April into wakefulness.

She stretched, luxuriating in the sensation of being young, healthy and alive on such a perfect day. She turned her sleep-tousled head sideways and peered at her alarm clock on the bedside table. Its face registered 5.30 a.m. With a sigh, April closed her eyes, willing herself to go back to sleep. She had fully intended to sleep until at least 6.30 this morning. Suddenly, she sat up. Of course, today was her first real day at doing the job she had spent four years training for.

She energetically leaped out of bed and raced into the en-suite bathroom. The tiles were all white, and she felt as though she had stepped into an operating theatre. She bent over the ancient bathtub, put the plug in and turned on the hot water tap. The pipes creaked and groaned in protestation, but finally rewarded her with a stream of scalding hot water. She poured her customary capful of green bubble bath liquid into the stream, and inhaled in pleasure as the delicious aroma of pine needles and green forests pervaded the steamy atmosphere.

April left the bath to fill, and walked back into the bedroom towards her wardrobe. Today was very important, so she had to choose her outfit carefully. Today was the day that she fully intended bearding this lion, Jack Nathan, in his den so that she could finally form her own opinions on the enigmatic figure that Yusef had presented.

'Let's see. Professional yet feminine, alluring yet

conservative ... bold yet reticent,' April muttered as she rifled through her clothes. Her hands hesitated as she touched her favourite black and white dress.

'Nope! Too darn short for this occasion, that's for sure,' she scolded herself laughingly as the words of her scandalized mother echoed through her mind. 'Perfect!' she shouted out joyously, startling the pigeons that had been resting on her bedroom windowsill. She ceremoniously dragged out her cream linen two-piece suit, and threw it on the bed as she raced back to switch off the water that was frothing in the bath. April slipped her shimmering satin white nightgown off her sun-dappled shoulders to the floor, and felt the temperature of the water with a tentative toe. It was scalding, and just to her liking. She sighed with pleasure as she eased her suntanned body into the welcoming embrace of the swirling bubbles.

April let her body relax as her mind formulated the plan of action for today. She absent-mindedly soaped herself as she put all the impressions together that she had gleaned the day before. Her main objective was to set up a suitable work schedule that could be followed on a daily basis. And naturally, she would need to set up interviews with all the important members of the community in order to form a solid foundation of mutual trust. How could she even begin to perform her function effectively if the powerful people were against her?

Finally content with her plan of action, April pulled the plug out of the bath with her toe and briskly towelled herself dry. Her chestnut brown hair curled about her head and neck, encouraged by the steam from the bath.

'Darn this hair,' she cursed in vain. Her curly and very unruly hair was the bane of her life. All she had dreamed of as a little girl was having long, straight, flowing black tresses. She threw the hairbrush down in disgust as she gave up the struggle to tame her tawny mane.

There was a sudden wild barrage of knocking at her door. Frowning as she peered at her clock which was now registering 6.00 a.m., April hastily pulled her robe over her naked body, and walked briskly to her front door. Through the frosted glass, she could make out the squat figure of her over-amorous landlord. Slipping the safety chain into place, April opened the door a crack and brusquely greeted the fawning man.

'Hello, Mr Sherwitz. You're certainly up early,' she stated.

'Please call me Julius, my dear, and might I say that you are looking particularly lovely this morning. I can see that you are a morning person,' he babbled, whilst running his hungry little pig eyes up and down the part of April's anatomy that was not hidden by the door.

'Thank you, Mr Sherwitz,' April replied, placing a light but unmistakable emphasis upon his surname. 'What can I do for you so early? Er ... I mean, why are you knocking on my door?' she hastily amended as she saw the unmistakable leer spread across his face.

'Well, you have a phone call on the pay phone downstairs. The gentleman said to tell you that it's long distance.'

'Thanks. Please tell him that I'll be down in a minute.'

April slammed the door on his startled expression as she wheeled around and ran across the lounge to the bedroom. She pulled an old and tatty black track suit out of the wardrobe and pulled it on over her gown in her haste. She hastily grabbed her bunch of keys and ran out of the apartment. To her horror, she ran straight into the arms of the revolting Julius who had not budged from her door. The two of them went sprawling across the floor in an ungainly heap. April leaped up as soon as she hit the ground, avoiding the feeble assistive gropings of the landlord, and took off down the stairs like a prize athlete leaving the starting blocks at the Olympic Games.

'Hello,' she gasped breathlessly into the old-fashioned black plastic telephone receiver.

'Hello darling,' boomed a familiar chirpy voice. 'How's my lady this morning? I miss you and I love you madly.'

'Oh hello, Parker,' April mumbled, startled at her lack of enthusiasm. This was the man she was supposed to be spending the rest of her life with, yet she felt no excitement at this prospect. Surely she should feel a little more excited by his early morning call?

'Why are you calling me this early?' she snapped. 'Thanks to you, I just got groped by the pervert that runs this building. In future, please call me at the office until I get my own phone.'

'Oh sorry, darling, it won't happen again. I certainly don't want my lady groped by perverts,' he chuckled.

This silly side of Parker irritated April with a passion that sometimes took her by surprise. He was always so quick to apologize, especially when it wasn't his fault. April took this as a sign of weakness that she had originally mistaken for a gentleness of spirit. In fact, it had turned out to be a total lack of spirit that had been very soothing in the beginning, but had certainly palled as the weeks had gone by. Parker seemed to stir the beast in April, and she could not seem to control the nasty side of her nature. She blamed Parker for this, as she hated not being happy and in control.

'Parker, dear,' she said, the exaggerated patience in her voice apparent to all except Parker, 'please do not refer to me as your lady. I am not a possession now, nor have I ever been. Is that clear?'

'Yes April, sweet, I am sorry.'

'And stop your incessant apologizing for living, for goodness sake!' she exploded.

'Sorry … er … I didn't mean sorry … I … er … so how was the first day?' Parker ended lamely.

April felt the guilt wash over her. 'Thank you for the flowers, Parker. That was very thoughtful of you,' she said.

'Flowers? Oh, a pleasure dearest. I know carnations are your favourite.'

'Carnations, Parker? These were roses. A full-blooded dozen of the most exquisite red roses that I have ever seen. And the card was very romantic.'

There was silence on the other end of the line. 'Parker, are you still there?' April asked, concerned that the connection may have been broken.

'I'm here, April.' His voice was strangely subdued. The realization hit April – her original suspicions had been confirmed. Parker had not sent the flowers after all. But who on earth ... her mind raced wildly. April did not always like herself and the way that she treated Parker, but she would never have been unfaithful to him. The mysterious admirer was obviously a stranger.

'Parker, I was only joking. I'm teasing you, you beast, because you didn't send me flowers on my first day.' April could not explain why she felt the need to deceive him in this fashion. She did not want to hurt him, and in her own peculiar way, she was fond of him.

'Oh, I see,' said Parker, the reassurance obvious in his voice. He giggled, delighted that she had teased him. This proved that she must care for him.

'Don't worry, pet. I'll send you some tomorrow. Anyway, have a nice day. Love you, cheery bye doll.'

'Bye, Parker, thanks for the call,' said April pensively as she replaced the receiver, too deep in thought to be angered by being called 'doll'.

So there really was a secret admirer. April was worried. She had only been in town a few days, certainly not long enough to make any romantic conquests. Her fertile imagination began to run riot. Maybe a psychotic killer was stalking her. No one except her immediate family knew where she was staying.

April glanced at her wrist watch. Good grief. It was already close to 6.30, and she had to collect the car at Government Garage by 7 o'clock. She raced upstairs and let herself into her apartment, relieved that she had avoided Julius. The last thing she needed right now was a confrontation with an over-amorous landlord. A nauseating thought crossed her mind. What if Julius were the admirer? Immediately she dismissed this possibility. He was too cheap for that.

April set about readying herself for the long day ahead. Already, she could feel the heat of the day nestling outside her balcony. She rapidly drew on her silken undergarments – her one concession to her champagne taste on a ginger beer budget. She selected an apricot cotton sleeveless top, and slipped into the pencil line cream linen skirt. Her outfit complemented her golden suntanned skin. April used very little make-up. She had been brought up on a regimen of good cleansing and moisturizing, and this care showed in the excellence of her complexion. She lightly outlined her almond-shaped grey eyes with a grey Kohl pencil. Her lashes were naturally thick, not requiring the assistance of mascara. She scrabbled around in her small cosmetic bag until she found the lipstick that perfectly complemented her apricot top. Slipping her feet into low-heeled apricot sandals, she grabbed her handbag and briefcase, and left the apartment, blowing a kiss to the blue ocean beckoning her from the balcony.

* * *

April roared into the parking lot at Government Garage at precisely 7 a.m. She prided herself on her punctuality, and could not tolerate tardiness in others.

'Well, good morning Legs. You're looking totally gorgeous,' said Tony, opening her door with an exaggeratedly gallant bow.

'Hello Tony, you old flatterer you,' April smiled at Tony's banter.

'Well, where are my wheels? You promised me the best set in the garage,' she teased, as they walked towards the administration building.

'Phil, fetch number 823. Quickly man, Legs is in a hurry,' boomed Tony. The little mechanic scurried off to do his bidding.

'I'm impressed,' teased April lightly. 'The little people listen to you like you're the boss.' Her laughter echoed across the apron, and Tony joined in with his hearty chuckle.

'Maybe I am the boss, Legs,' he laughingly said, winking broadly at her.

'Sure, Tony, and I'm Miss Universe,' April retorted.

Just then Phil arrived in the Honda. With a screech of tyres he pulled the car to an impressive halt in front of April.

'Got to run, Legs – boring old staff meeting to attend. The boss is a real stickler for meetings. Enjoy your day,' Tony said with a cheery wave.

Phil cleared his throat and opened the driver's door for April. She gracefully settled into the car, breathing in the aroma of new upholstery.

'Thanks, Phil, you're a star,' she said as she started the engine.

'Oh don't thank me, Mam. Thank the boss. You must be someone really special to be allocated this baby,' said Phil, rocking backwards and forwards on his rubber-soled heels.

'The boss?' April enquired.

'Yeah, Tony. Bye Mam, Safe motoring.'

April stared at Phil in amazement as he sauntered away in his blue overalls. She felt a blush start creeping up her neck until her face flamed red with embarrassment. She quickly gunned the engine and eased the Honda out into the traffic.

'Lesson One in the real world, April,' she chided herself. 'Never judge a book by its cover.'

One of April's fears had been driving aimlessly around for days whilst she tried to find her office. Yusef had certainly taken her on the scenic route via everything else, but to her amazement, her keen sense of direction triumphed and she found herself parking in front of Baboos building effortlessly. She glanced at her wristwatch. Good. She had a full half hour before her day officially began. She sighed as she looked up at the dilapidated building, but then she made a conscious decision not to let her environment get her down. After all, she was technically her own boss, and only had to answer to a supervisor in Johannesburg once every six months.

She swung her long legs gracefully out of the Honda, smiling to herself as she thought of Tony, who had really pulled the wool over her eyes. April picked up her briefcase, and made sure that she had locked the car. She would hate to have to face Tony and admit the new car had been stolen on its first day out of the garage.

April entered the gloomy stairwell and bounded effortlessly up the stairs. The dust motes hung suspended in the early morning rays of sun coming from the end of the corridor. Suddenly, she stopped dead in her tracks. It was too early for anyone else to be there, but someone had obviously opened the door to her office suite, as the sun was streaming into the corridor. April froze, conscious of the silence in the darkened building. She cocked her head to one side while she strained to hear any noises that might alert her as to the reason for her office door being open. A puzzled frown creased her brow as she caught the sound of someone treading softly inside. April grasped her briefcase firmly in her hand, prepared to bring it crashing down on the intruder's head if he tried anything. She inched stealthily towards the door on tiptoes. April stretched her neck until she could see around the corner of the door jamb. Bending over the desk in the outer office was an unmistakably female figure swathed in voluminous folds of an exotically colourful material. Feeling very sheepish, April straightened up. Clearing her throat, she walked into the office.

'Hello, can I help you?' she enquired imperiously. The figure behind the desk straightened with a little shriek. April found herself looking at a small, well-proportioned Indian lady who was struggling to regain her composure.

'Forgive me for screaming, Mam, I didn't expect you in so early.'

'Didn't expect me...? How did you get into my office?' April asked, nonplussed by the whole situation.

'Oh Miss Ross, did Yusef not tell you that I would be here this morning?' the stranger replied, the quiver in her voice becoming more apparent with each word.

'No. Who are you?' asked April.

'I'm Aneesa, your secretary. Today is my first day too,' she replied. 'I am really looking forward to working for you.' A proud smile spread across her face.

'Your first day?' April repeated, rather unnecessarily.

'Yes,' replied Aneesa, becoming confused by April's ignorance.

'Oh, please do not say that you have hired another

secretary, Miss Ross,' she wailed. To April's horror, Aneesa's face dissolved into a flood of tears.

'Please stop crying, Aneesa. Of course I haven't hired another secretary. I just assumed that Yusef's secretary would be saying on with me, that's all. I am delighted to have you.' April reached into her bag and produced a handful of tissues. Aneesa gratefully accepted them and blew her nose resoundingly.

'Forgive my silliness, Miss Ross. I really needed this job and thought that all was lost.'

April smiled at the woman reassuringly. 'Well, if we're going to be working together, we will have to get a few things straight,' she said. 'Firstly, it's April, not Miss Ross, and secondly, you will not be working for me, but *with* me, understand?'

Aneesa's brown eyes were very large in her startled face. 'Yes ... understood, Miss ... I mean, April.' She blushed deeply beneath her tan skin.

'Hey, you're a freckle face too,' laughed April.

Aneesa looked at this independent creature in amazement. A smile spread across her face, and April had made her first and most loyal friend.

April walked through into her office and put her briefcase down on the desk with a sigh of relief. She turned around to call Aneesa through, and checked in amazement. On a table near the door was a vase with a dozen red roses.

'Aneesa,' she called. Aneesa came running through into April's office and her eyes followed April's gaze.

'Oh, you found your flowers,' she stated. 'They were outside the office door when I arrived at seven this morning.'

'Was there a card with them?' asked April, casually.

'Yes. I left it on your desk unopened. The envelope said Miss Ross.'

April rushed to the desk and tore open the small envelope. The words swam in front of her eyes.

'Well?' said Aneesa, overcome with curiosity at the effect these flowers were having on April.

'It's too silly to read out loud,' said April.

'Read it. Nothing could be too silly for you to read,' said Aneesa, her devotion to April already apparent.

'Well, okay. It says, "You are the dew that adorns these roses".' She smiled self-consciously, blushing becomingly.

'How lovely those words are,' breathed Aneesa, lost in the images that her mind was conjuring of April's boyfriend.

Aneesa became aware of April's silence and looked at her in astonishment, for April's expression was utterly perplexed.

'What's wrong?' asked Aneesa with concern.

'This is so peculiar,' replied April. 'Yesterday, I also received a dozen red roses from ... a secret admirer,' she finished off rather sheepishly. 'These flowers are identical, and this is the second time that the card has been left unsigned. Really peculiar.'

Aneesa stared at April, at a loss for words. This was an alien situation in her culture. Flowers were rarely sent from close lovers, let alone secret admirers. April certainly had to be an extraordinary woman to evoke this response from a man.

April gave the characteristic shrug that Aneesa would become very familiar with. Whenever a task had to be performed that appeared insurmountable, April would shrug as though flinging a challenge at the world.

'Okay, Aneesa, have you got a diary?' she asked briskly, sitting down behind the large lightwood desk.

'No, I'm afraid not,' Aneesa replied. 'Latiefa must have taken it with her.'

'Latiefa?'

'Yes. She was Yusef's secretary. Didn't you know?' replied

Aneesa in astonishment that Yusef had never bothered to put April in the picture.

'Well, that certainly explains why I needed a new secretary,' chuckled April, her mind filling with pictures of poor hen-pecked Yusef at home and at the office. Life must really have been unbearable some days.

'Aneesa, all I can say is that I'm very pleased that I have a new secretary.' She winked conspiratorially, and Aneesa smiled knowingly.

'Right. Let's get to work. I'll prepare you a list of stationery that we must have today, then it's up to you to ensure that the office supplies are kept in good order and up to standard. Fair enough?'

'Fair enough,' replied Aneesa, pleased at the responsibility that was being placed on her shoulders. She scurried away to fetch her pen and notepad.

For the next hour, Aneesa hurriedly scribbled down everything that April was saying, impressed by this young woman's knowledge of office requirements. April had opened every cupboard and was briskly calculating what was missing, and what was essential.

'Right, that should do it,' stated April, collapsing in her chair with a sigh. She leant over sideways to pick up the telephone directory, and pushed it across the desk towards Aneesa.

'Phone three reputable stationers, and get them to deliver the order within the hour. Choose the middle price range,' she instructed. Aneesa stood up and prepared to move to her office.

'First, coffee,' said April. 'Would you like some, Aneesa?' she enquired.

Aneesa stared at her, horrified. 'But you can't make coffee,' she spluttered. 'That's my job.'

'Nonsense,' retorted April. 'I don't expect you to be my servant, Aneesa. If you are making coffee for yourself, then I might appreciate a cup, and if I'm making some, then I'll make you a cup. Agreed?'

'Agreed...' replied Aneesa hesitantly.

A short while later, over steaming aromatic cups of coffee, April reached into her briefcase and drew out a large page-a-day diary.

'I want you to use this as my appointment book,' she instructed Aneesa. 'All clients or other people that phone me will have to go through you first, and then you will let them have appointments. Furthermore, Tuesdays will be my day to be out of the office and in the community, so no appointments for those days. Understood?'

Aneesa nodded vigorously. 'But what if you make independent appointments?' she asked.

'Well, that's simple enough to overcome. We'll compare appointments at the beginning and end of every day. Okay?'

'Okay,' replied Aneesa, delighting in the unaccustomed colloquialism.

'Now the first appointment I'd like you to set up for me will be with Jack Nathan from Beckensuds. Preferably some time today, as soon as possible. Yusef mentioned that he was a valuable contact.'

'Oh indeed,' agreed Aneesa. 'He is loved by many in the community, although he has made some powerful enemies too,' she added.

'Enemies?' inquired April, her curiosity piqued further by this mysterious man.

'He is very outspoken you see,' said Aneesa. 'Some people do not like this.'

'Like what people?' persisted April, determined to get to the bottom of the man's character.

'Oh, like some political leaders who don't agree

with his politics,' Aneesa casually replied.

'What is it about his politics that they don't like?' asked April determinedly.

'He is against exploitation, and he makes no secret of this.'

'But surely that's good?' asked April, perplexed by the expression on Aneesa's face. She looked almost furtive.

'Yes, it is good, but I am in an awkward position, because my father is one of the men that he has come up against.'

'Your father? Is he in politics, then?' asked April, realizing there was still much to learn about her secretary.

'My father is Abdul Hussein.'

'Yes ... so...' prompted April blankly.

'You mean, you haven't heard about him?' asked Aneesa, sincerely surprised at April's ignorance.

'No, obviously not,' replied April somewhat more tartly than she had intended.

'My father is the member of parliament for the Natal region, and he represents the Indian population in parliament.' Aneesa stopped, and flushed deeply. 'I am afraid that we do not speak to one another at all. For our people, grudges run very deep and can last for generations, even between parents and children if it is necessary. And in this case, it is very necessary,' she stated adamantly.

April thought about the good relationship that she enjoyed with her parents. She could not even begin to conceive the depths of a problem that could lead to the alienation of her family.

'Aneesa, what could possibly have happened to drive such a wedge between you?' she asked gently.

'Because you are my friend, April, I will tell you, but this is for your ears alone as it is a cause of great shame to me.'

'All right. I promise not to breathe a word to anyone.' April leaned back and lit up a long slim cigarette, while

Aneesa straightened herself in the chair opposite her and slowly began to talk.

'My father is a very wealthy man. His father before him started a small business that did very well, and as my father was the only son, he inherited all his riches when my grandfather died. My grandfather was a modern thinker for his generation, and had insured his life and the premises where his shop was. He died under very mysterious circumstances in a fire that destroyed his business as well as his home above the shop. The police suspected arson, but because he was just another "coolie", their investigation was very short. Nothing could be proven, and the insurance company paid out double what his policy was worth because he died as the result of an accident. My father was then in his early thirties, and had a wife and two children to support. All his sisters were married and well looked after, and he sent his mother to stay with her sister in Johannesburg. Anyway, to cut a long story short, my father took the insurance money and bought a great deal of property with it, most of it in the non-white areas. He bought a shopping centre in Durban by using a white man as a front, and within a year he was a millionaire. As the years passed by, his wealth increased immensely, to the point where he could afford to take two more wives. He set them up independently and had many more children. My mother was the original wife. This is not a strange custom amongst my people, and even though I felt sorry for my mother, I understood that this was his right according to the Koran.

'The trouble between me and my father began when I reached my eighteenth birthday. He had chosen a husband for me who was wealthy and willing to merge his businesses with my father's. Unfortunately, I had already fallen in love with a good man of simple means. He worked as a salesman in the Pillay's general store and although his salary was a pittance, I was quite prepared to live the simple life.' Her voice faltered and her eyes filled with tears. Impatiently, she brushed at her eyes with the back of her hand.

'Aneesa, don't go on if this story gives you so much pain,' said April gently, moved by the emotions playing across Aneesa's face.

'I'm all right,' said Aneesa. 'Besides, it's best that you know the truth of the whole story, before you hear a twisted tale from elsewhere. If there is one thing that my people love to do, it's to regale new ears with other people's old scandals.'

April smiled, remembering that these people loved to tell tales as Yusef had been quick to point out.

'Let me continue. You must know these things about the community if you are to be working here for any amount of time, and you need to know who you can trust and who you must avoid.'

'That brings me back to my original thoughts about Mr Nathan,' April said. 'Is he to be trusted?'

Aneesa stared at April wide-eyed for a long moment. April could not guess at the hidden messages that resided deep in Aneesa's eyes. They remained implacable pools of mystery that echoed the philosophies of millions of Easterners.

'Well?' April persisted.

'He is a man, and as such, we can only trust a man for the time that we are in his presence. We can trust as a gesture of faith, just as we trust that the sun will rise in the East every day, and yet whilst the sun is not in the sky, we do not know where it is travelling or what havoc it may be wreaking elsewhere in the world.'

April stared at Aneesa in astonishment. Such a complicated and evasive reply to such a simple question. This man was fast becoming an enigma that she had to resolve for herself.

'So, carry on telling me about your father,' April insisted.

'My father approached me one day and told me that I had to marry Goolam Salie. He didn't ask me, he simply informed me that the time had come to marry. I told him that Goolam was too old and already had a wife. I was not prepared to be a second wife to a dirty and disgusting old man who made my flesh crawl with revulsion. His first wife was kept away from the rest of the world and was always dressed as though she was in Purdah.'

'Purdah? What on earth is that?' asked April, alarmed at the depth of her ignorance about such matters that she might be dealing with on a daily basis.

'She does not show her face or body to anyone when she goes out. She wears a long black dress with a head covering to match. There is a slit for her eyes so that she can see where she is walking.'

'Sounds like hell to me,' said April with a shudder of sympathy for any woman who was forced to wear such hot garments in a hot climate.

'I told my father that I could never subject myself to this type of life, and could not marry a man that I did not love. Well, he did not even shout at me. He looked at me coldly, like a snake would watch a mongoose, then he quietly told me that he knew about my interest in Jusef Johaar, and would see him dead before he would let a loser like that interrupt his plans.'

'And so…' prompted April, fascinated by the unfolding tragedy.

'And so, I left my father's house that night, which was a shameful and scandalous thing to do, and I went to Jusef for help. He was very kind and let me stay with his mother while he went to see my father to attempt to placate him. He came home two hours later, beaten to a pulp. My father had listened to him, then told two of his goons to remove him from the face of the earth as he was an abomination before Allah because he was coming between a father and a daughter. I stayed with Jusef's mother and we were married shortly after that. My father had now become the most powerful man in Bloomsbury and the entire region. He was elected to parliament through fear and intimidation, and only ten per cent of the people even voted at all. But he had made sure that those who voted were casting their ballots in favour of him.'

'And what did he do to you and Jusef?' asked April, the concern for Aneesa's welfare apparent on her face.

'He had Jusef fired, because he owned the building in which he worked, and he threatened Mr Pillay, Jusef's boss, with eviction if he did not fire Jusef. As an added incentive, he lowered Pillay's rent. So naturally Jusef had to go.'

'But surely Jusef found another job?'

'Oh April, it is never so simple in matters like these. I was his defiant daughter who had shamed him in front of the community, and who had upset his business arrangement with the horrible old Goolam. I had to be taught a lesson in humility. And teach me he did, but my spirit was never broken even though it felt like I would tear in two sometimes.'

Aneesa sat twisting her wedding ring as she spoke. It was obvious that she had paid a great price for her freedom of choice. April noticed the lines etched on her secretary's face – lines of character and suffering. Oh yes, the price for her happiness had been worries and sadness.

'So what have you and Jusef done for the past … what … twenty years?' asked April, trying to estimate Aneesa's age.

'This all started fifteen years ago,' said Aneesa. 'Jusef drifted from job to job in the non-white areas, but wherever he went, my father's curse followed him. The people were afraid of my father and so they dispensed with an unimportant person like Jusef. Even when my first child arrived, my mother was forbidden to attend to me. I have only seen her on the street at a distance. We are permitted no contact. She is very afraid of my father's anger. She has seen him kill a pet in a rage against her, so she lives in fear that he will kill her too.'

'This sounds like a real horror story,' said April in a hushed tone. It was nearly unbelievable to hear of such suffering being inflicted by one monster of a man.

'The final blow came very unexpectedly,' continued Aneesa. 'Jusef received a telephone call one day when he had just been fired again. It was a white man who told him that he had heard of his problem and wanted to help him. He needed someone to help him with his computer company. Jusef explained that he knew nothing about computers, but this man was insistent, and said that he would provide him with on the job training. He offered him an immediate salary of fifteen hundred rand, a princely sum five years ago. We were overjoyed. Finally I thought that Allah had heard our prayers. I was pregnant with our second child, and we were still living with Jusef's mother, who was elderly and sickly. We had to live in one room as she only had a two-bedroomed house. Jusef started this job with high hopes, and within six months he was promoted to a managerial position. We were elated and could afford to buy a small home of our own. We moved into our new home a week before my son was born, and our lives had never been better.

'This went on for another year, then one night, Jusef was working late. I got a telephone call. Jusef had been late coming home and I was beside myself with worry. It was a policeman. He told me that there had been an accident, and he needed me to identify a body. My mind went blank. My brother-in-law drove me to the King Edward Hospital. I walked into the emergency room, and a doctor came over to speak with me. She was very kind and told me that she was sorry to have to meet me under such tragic circumstances, but a burnt body had been brought in, and they had reason to believe that it was Jusef. I was cold right through to my soul, and kept saying that it was a silly mistake. They led me through to another room where a figure lay on a stretcher lay, covered in a sheet. There was a terrible acrid stench in the room. The doctor took me over to the stretcher and pulled the sheet back. This horrible monster could never have been my Jusef.' Tears coursed down Aneesa's cheeks.

'Oh please stop, Aneesa. This is hurting you so much,' said April, her composure shattered as she watched this woman opposite her suffer.

'No, I must tell it to the end so that you can understand. I'm fine,' said Aneesa, her voice quivering with the effort of staying calm. 'It was Jusef. He was badly burned, but half of his face was unharmed and untouched. They told me that he had been working alone at the company on his boss's instructions, when suddenly there had been an explosion and a fire right in the area where he was sitting. They discovered that it had been deliberately set, but never could find out who was responsible. Naturally the owner received a large insurance settlement, but Jusef got nothing. He had never been put onto the company provident fund, and had not yet got around to insuring himself. So I was left penniless in a mortgaged home and I had two small children to look after. A month after his death, I discovered that I was pregnant again.'

'Hold on a minute. A fire?' asked April. 'But this is basically the same as the story about your grandfather,' she added, horrified at the implications of her deductions.

'Exactly,' said Aneesa expressionlessly. 'My father killed

his own father for money, and he killed my husband for revenge.'

'Why isn't he in jail?' exclaimed April.

'Because there is no proof, and he is too clever to be found guilty for anything. He always gets others to do his dirty work, and then rewards them so that they remain loyal.'

April stared at Aneesa in horror. Images of her own kindly and harmless father filled her mind. Having grown up in a household of unconditional love and security, it was virtually impossible to imagine the type of spite and malice that Aneesa had just described.

'And why does Jack Nathan concern himself with your father, who, by the way, sounds like a cross between Hitler and Satan?'

'You asked me earlier if I trusted him. I think you can understand now why I am so suspicious of every person if my own father is capable of such treachery. But April, regardless of my suspicions, it is generally accepted that Mr Nathan is a good and caring man for the downtrodden, and he is merciless with those that exploit others,' replied Aneesa.

'That's all good and well, but if he is as marvellous as you say he is, why the hell doesn't he crush your father?' exploded April.

'Because you do not kill the snake by standing on his tail,' replied Aneesa enigmatically.

April stared at Aneesa, dumbfounded. This was no Simple Simon. She would be an obvious asset in the workplace.

'Now I must get on with my work. Please excuse me,' said Aneesa as she left April's office.

April sat pensively at her desk, digesting the information that she had been bombarded with. So much intrigue and discord in such a sleepy place. It was unbelievable.

*   *   *

'April,' Aneesa called softly a few minutes later, aware that she was interrupting her senior's thoughts.

'Yes,' said April smiling vacantly at her.

'That appointment you requested is for eleven o'clock this morning.'

'Appointment?' said April blankly.

'Yes, with Jack Nathan as you requested. His secretary said that he will see you this morning.'

'Good grief, that's in thirty minutes,' gasped April glancing at her watch.

'His secretary also said that he was looking forward to meeting you,' teased Aneesa lightly, aware that April had heard that he was a skirt-chaser. She smiled as April coloured. 'Only teasing. You mustn't believe everything that you have heard about him. There are many jealous men around who cannot bear his magnetism and the unconscious effect he has on the ladies. Judge for yourself.'

'That is good advice which I fully intend taking. Now I must get ready for this encounter,' replied April as she grabbed her briefcase and handbag.

Aneesa watched April leave the office with a smile. Suddenly she shivered with foreboding. There was danger and a great deal of trouble ahead. Aneesa shook her head, and the feeling passed, but her premonitions had never been wrong before. Her forehead creased in a frown as she worried about how she was going to tell April about the dangers without sounding silly and hysterical. She would just wait and see what transpired over the next few weeks, and would intervene where she could.

# *Chapter Three*

'Mr Nathan will see you now,' said the receptionist in her professionally clipped and emotionless tone.

April glanced at her watch irritably. It was 11.30 and she was steaming with impatience at this man's lack of punctuality. She flung her magazine down and stood up.

'Miss Ross?' enquired an attractive and willowy young woman in a blue uniform.

'Yes,' replied April with a sweetness of tone that belied her agitation.

'I'm Catlin, Mr Nathan's secretary. I'm terribly sorry that we had to keep you waiting. There was a serious breakdown in the factory. The calendar jammed,' she explained in her nasal voice.

'Calendar?' queried April, puzzled as to how a calendar could cause havoc in a factory.

Catlin laughed pleasantly enough, but there was an element of falseness jangling in the mirth. 'When I first started here, I was also confused about things,' she said, patronizingly. 'The calendar is a big machine that is used to iron the continuous roller towels that you find in cloakrooms to dry your hands on. We've only got one of these machines, so when it jams, all hell breaks loose to get it repaired in time to meet delivery deadlines.'

'Does Mr Nathan fix the machine?' asked April, perplexed by the situation.

'Oh good heavens, no!' exclaimed Catlin. 'He is the operations manager, not the maintenance man, although he does have a way with machines. He sees to it that all systems run smoothly and he organizes the staff to work efficiently. He's also the 2IC, which places great demands on his time,' she stated, importantly, as though she was describing the king to the village idiot.

'"Too I see"? What on earth is that?' asked April, feeling like the village idiot for not knowing.

'Second in charge,' supplied Catlin helpfully. 'Our current branch manager is always away on all sorts of business including monkey business, so he is effectively the manager of the entire operation.'

'Why do they keep a manager who doesn't do his job?' asked April, conversationally.

'Simple. He's the group managing director's brother-in-law,' replied Catlin sweetly. 'Right, let's go through. Jack is looking forward to meeting you. He is very welfare orientated you know – remarkable in a man with such a flair for business.' She sighed gently.

April looked sharply at Catlin. The expression on her face was one of worship and adoration. April's eyes moved sharply to the ring finger on Catlin's left hand, and sure enough, there was the wedding ring.

'Are you married?' asked April innocently.

Catlin's face clouded over. 'Unfortunately, yes. And you?' she asked sharply, her possessiveness of Jack Nathan transparently obvious.

'Engaged,' replied April reassuringly. She smiled to herself as she saw Catlin visibly relax, and disregard her as competition.

'Take some good advice from an old married lady. Don't,' said Catlin bitterly, her expression indecipherable.

'Don't what?'

'Don't get married.'

Catlin turned away and started walking towards a door that April had not noticed before. As she opened it, the reception area was filled with the deafening roar of machines. Unable to pursue any further conversation, April followed Catlin's beckoning figure into the factory. She was fascinated by the huge bright blue machines.

'These are the tumblers,' shouted Catlin above the noise, pointing at gigantic machines against the wall. 'They are large industrial tumble dryers,' she explained. April nodded mutely. 'This is the calendar that I was telling you about.' She stopped at a complicated-looking piece of equipment that had bands of fabric strapping stretching on intermittently.

April watched as the ladies in overalls fed a 40-metre roller towel through the convolutions and huge rollers until it came out wrinkle-free on the other side.

Catlin tugged at her sleeve and led her past gigantic washing machines. April felt like a Lilliputian in Gulliver's world. The heat in the factory was oppressive and she slipped her linen jacket off her shoulders in an unconsciously elegant movement. She followed Catlin through a maze of roaring machinery and sweating workmen and women who all grinned happily at her.

Towards the back of the factory, things became a little quieter and cooler, and Catlin slid open a door for April to enter. They were in a carpeted, air-conditioned administration block. Goosebumps rose quickly on April's bare arms at the sudden and very welcome drop in temperature.

At the end of the corridor, they turned sharply left and climbed an elegant flight of stairs. At the top of the stairs, there was another small reception area flanked by floor-to-ceiling one-way glass on the right, and two doors on the left. April looked through the darkened glass and watched the factory operating below. From this vantage point, one could see every corner, and every move made by the machine operators. She couldn't resist smiling as she thought of the unsuspecting shirkers who would be surprised by their discovery.

'This way,' said Catlin as she led April to the furthest door. April entered the large office with great curiosity.

'Take a seat, April. He's just on the phone to Head Office.' April looked around at the L-shaped room. The short arm of the 'L' was where she was sitting while the large arm was obviously Jack Nathan's inner sanctum. She could hear the deep tones of a male voice from around the corner. Catlin sat down behind a small light oak desk next to April's couch. This office area was carpeted in blue, and two wildlife watercolours hung upon the wall.

'I don't give continental dickens about what Tom says,' exploded an extremely irritated voice from around the corner. April gave a start at the unexpected vehemence of the outburst. Catlin caught her eye and gave her a reassuring smile. The voice dropped down again to a pleasant bass hum that was indecipherable and strangely soothing.

'No flies on Jack,' laughed Catlin conspiratorially. 'He gives Head Office utter tonk from morning until night to get things done. No one has the nerve to speak to them like that. Except Jack,' she hastily added.

'Why?'

'Why what?'

'Why does he give them "tonk" as you put it?' enquired April.

'Well, they're a penny-pinching bunch of morons that are only interested in the bottom line and what it means to their pocket,' supplied Catlin helpfully.

'At the risk of sounding really ignorant, I still don't understand,' said April.

'The bottom line is the profit that they glean at month end, and they have given the Durban branch a ridiculous budget to try and stick to. We have been saddled with all the old equipment and vans so we have twice as many breakdowns as the other branches, and Head Office squeals like a stuck pig when we apply for new equipment to be bought. Jack tells them their fortune in no uncertain terms, because Barry is too big a wimp to do it. Jack effectively runs this branch, and despite all the inconveniences and breakdowns, he has still got the best profit figures in the whole country.'

Catlin was positively beaming by the end of her monologue. April was aware of the deeper unspoken feelings that were clearly written on the secretary's face. Here was a woman so obviously in love with her boss that it was pathetic to behold.

'I presume Barry is the useless general manager?' said April rather redundantly.

'Catlin,' came the deep imperious voice from around the corner. 'Come here, please, and bring the file on the profit and loss runs from December last year.'

Catlin positively catapulted out from behind her desk. 'Coming, Mr Nathan.'

Mr Nathan? What happened to comfortable old 'Jack' thought April uncharitably.

'We won't be long,' said Catlin as she disappeared around the corner with the file grasped tightly in her well-manicured hands.

April rummaged in her briefcase for her diary and notebook. She had better be well prepared to beard this lion in his den. If he had the top brass at the Head Office dancing through hoops, she had no illusions as to how he would treat her, a lowly little social worker. April pulled the top off her pen with her teeth as she flicked the pages of her diary open to today's date. Her eyes widened in disbelief as she read an entry that Aneesa had obviously made. She was due at an important strategy planning meeting at the opposite end of town in precisely five minutes. She leaped up, unsure of what to do. Damn. The man had wasted so much of her time and he still wasn't ready to see her. Her eyes quickly scanned Catlin's desk. Sure enough, there was a message pad next to the telephone. Hastily, April scribbled down a message about her prior commitment with a cursory apology, and stuck the note onto the telephone receiver where Catlin was bound to see it. She cocked her head to hear if there was a lull in the conversation, but Catlin and Mr Nathan were still very much engrossed in their discussion. April put her diary back in her briefcase and softly left the office. As the door closed behind her, she took off like a sprinter from the starting blocks and agilely bolted down the steps three at a time. She raced through the hot factory and couldn't help smiling at the consternation she was creating. By the time April reached the parking area, she was scarcely out of breath. Her gym and jogging had stood her in good stead.

She reached the destination of the meeting within ten minutes and was rather proud that she had not got lost. April parked the car under the nose of another driver who had been about to take the last space in the area. Jumping out of the car with her skirt flying upwards in the wind, she called out a musical apology to the seething and wildly gesticulating male driver. His rage turned instantly to delight at being able to oblige as April's long legs flashed by.

April entered the committee room in a breathless rush. The meeting had already begun and 30 heads turned to witness her late arrival with frigid disapproval. She opened her mouth to apologize for her tardiness, but was interrupted by the chairlady who snapped at her.

'Who are you and what do you want?'

Flabbergasted by this frontal assault, April found herself at an uncharacteristic loss for words.

'I believe this is Miss Ross, our new social worker,' came an unexpected voice from the end of the table. She stared into the leering eyes of Manilal Mooljee. Damn. And the only unoccupied seat was next to his.

Recovering quickly, April said, 'Thank you, Mr Mooljee. Madam Chair, I'm April Ross, the new social worker for Indian Affairs. I must apologize profusely for my tardiness, but I was unavoidably detained by a previous commitment.'

The old dragon visibly softened at this humble approach, and she twinkled at April. 'Don't let it bother you, dear. Welcome, and do join us. You are, after all, our most important committee member you know.'

Well, actually, I didn't know, thought April. 'Oh?' she enquired suspiciously. What had Yusef got her into?

'Let me introduce you to all the members of this steering committee.'

April sat down resignedly next to Manilal, and gave him a lukewarm smile to acknowledge his presence. For the next half-hour, April was introduced to 29 of Durban's most important people in the field of welfare. All of them had a vital role to play in the continuation of projects in the Indian areas of Natal. Manilal was the last to be introduced, and April was surprised to learn that he was the headmaster of the Kashmir High School for girls in Bloomsbury. Kind of like letting the wolf look after the sheep. She had been aware of his hot eyes running over her body throughout the introductions, and she flinched visibly as he announced to the meeting that he and April were already good friends. April was aware of a couple of eyebrows being raised – Manilal's reputation for fast talk and faster women was obviously legendary. She tried to look as innocent as possible under the circumstances.

The meeting continued well into the afternoon and by 4 p.m. April was well and truly exhausted, thirsty and hungry. But at least she was aware of the central role she would be playing in the coordination of welfare projects for the Indian community. April started as Dr Porter from the Department of Social Work at Durban University brought down her gavel on the table.

'Right, people. This has been a long but fruitful meeting. Let's adjourn for now, and I'll see you all back here at 7 p.m.'

Used to strange hours from her tutorials at university, April didn't flinch. She rose and smiled at Dr Porter absently as her thoughts turned to a nice refreshing bath, cool white wine and a huge pizza.

'Why don't we go and have a drink together?' whispered Manilal into her ear as he grabbed her elbow with a sweaty hand. Because you're married, because I don't like you, because I'm engaged ... the thoughts flew around in April's head.

'Thank you so much for the kind invitation, Manilal, but I'm afraid that I have made other plans,' she replied politely, slipping her elbow deftly out of his grasp.

With that, April bid the others a temporary farewell and left the room. She strode purposefully to the lift, her mind full of thoughts of relaxing.

'April, wait up. I'll ride down with you,' came the loud voice of the persistent Manilal.

As they were on the thirty-first floor, April was not prepared to walk for her principles. She did not reply as the doors of the lift opened before them. To her dismay, the lift was empty.

'Let's hold on for the others,' she said determinedly. Just as determinedly, Manilal managed to manoeuvre her inside. The doors snapped shut and she was trapped.

April retreated to the far corner of the fortunately large lift and held her briefcase tightly in case she would need it as a weapon. Smiling inwardly, she cursed herself for having watched too many bad movies. There was no way that this man would make a move on her, even if she wanted him to. He was Indian and she was white, so that made it a matter of breaking the law. And a damn silly law, but it serves my purposes right now.

'Do you realise how breathtaking you are?' said Manilal in a normal tone of voice.

'I beg your pardon?' stammered April in disbelief.

'I said that you are beautiful. You're statuesque – a magnificent De Milo with arms.'

'Please, get serious,' snorted April dismissively, blushing furiously at this avalanche of flowery compliments.

'I am very serious, my dear. And whether you like it or not, I have every intention of pursuing you.'

April stared at Manilal's impassive face. She could see that he meant every word.

'Look, Mr Mooljee, thank you for your kind words but...'

'The name is Manilal,' he interrupted.

'Manilal, I'm sorry, but I'm just not interested. I have no time for women who get involved with other women's husbands, and I am certainly not about to break my golden rule at this stage of my life,' she ended with a decisive nod of her head.

'I applaud your principles my dear, but it is time for you to join the real world and play the game with the rest of us players. Now, let's be grown up about this, shall we?' he snapped, moving purposefully towards her.

April was about to react by thrusting her briefcase into his crotch when the lift doors opened on the ground floor. She gave Manilal a withering glance and flounced disdainfully past him and out into the foyer. Many people were milling about as it was going-home time, so April quickly lost him in the bustling throng.

Still fuming with indignation, she marched resolutely towards where she had left the car. Fluttering triumphantly on her front window was a pink parking ticket. In her haste to reach the meeting, April had overlooked the parking meter, and now had to suffer the consequences of her oversight. Irritably, she snatched the ticket off the window and then glared resolutely around to see if she could spy the traffic warden who had been so efficient. April caught sight of her own reflection in the side mirror of the car and despite her annoyance burst out laughing at her grumpy expression.

It had not been a very good day. Slipping the parking ticket into her handbag, she unlocked the car and threw her briefcase untidily onto the back seat. There was no point in returning to Government Garage now that she was one street away from home, and she felt almost desperate for a long soak in her bath.

April glanced warily around as she parked in front of her apartment building. All she needed now was to bump into Julius Sherwitz after a day like today. What was wrong with these people? As April alighted from the car, a passing white Mercedes hooted raucously. Turning around curiously, April caught a glimpse of Manilal's leering face and his waving hand as he cruised deliberately past. April cursed herself for not having thought that this man would stoop so low as to follow her home. With a final suggestive licking motion of his tongue, Manilal turned the corner and disappeared from sight.

April trudged wearily up the stairs and let herself into the apartment. She really would have to move soon. The garish and uncoordinated colour scheme was too much to deal with at the best of times, and today it made her feel even worse. She sighed as she moved over to the window. The view was spectacular, and would be one feature of this apartment that she would miss.

* * *

April jumped as the doorbell chimed loudly. She moved cautiously to the door, thoughts of Manilal tearing around in her head. For the first time in her life, April felt a genuine stab of fear.

'Who is it?' she asked cautiously.

'Mercury Flowers, Mam. A delivery for you,' answered a cheerful and unfamiliar male voice.

April slid back the safety chain with relief and opened the door. A very pleasant-faced black gentleman in a white dust coat held out a now familiar white box tied with red ribbon.

'Please sign receipt of delivery, madame,' he said as April took the box from him. April signed the note and handed him a 10-rand tip for his trouble. His perfect white teeth gleamed in his ebony face at the delight of this unexpected and very generous tip.

'Thank you Mam! God bless you, Mam, and your whole family! Thank you!'

'You're welcome,' said April laughing as she closed the door on his embarrassing display of gratitude.

She laid the box down on the couch and ran lightly through to the bathroom to start running her bath. She poured bubble bath into the swirling water and sniffed appreciatively as the room filled with the aroma of ripe peach orchards on a hot summer's day. She walked back into the bedroom and rooted around in her handbag for her cigarettes and lighter. Lighting up, she watched the smoke curl lazily upwards. April picked up her crystal ashtray from next to her bed and returned to the lounge to view the contents of the box. She sat down gracefully and crossed her trim ankles as her long fingers tugged at the red ribbon. Underneath the tissue paper were a dozen long-stemmed perfect red roses, water droplets still clinging to the delicate petals. These, like all the others, were export-quality roses and April was well aware of current market values and how difficult it was to get these roses. This admirer not only had good taste, but he also had influence and money. She scratched Manilal off her list of possible suspects immediately.

Attached to the red roses was a plain white card. She picked it up and peered closely at the writing. The message read: 'Today my heart took flight with you.' April's smile froze on her face. As unlikely as it seemed, these roses had to have come from Manilal. It was since she had met him that the roses had started arriving. So he had known all along where she was staying, but why was this man being so very persistent? April looked at the roses distastefully. Her first impulse was to throw them away, but the practical and aesthetic side of her nature prevailed. It would be a terrible waste to destroy such beauty on a whim.

She stood up and took the roses into the kitchen where she found her last vase. She smiled to herself. 'If this continues, I'll have to order a million vases to keep up with the demand,' she said out loud. She ran the cold water and filled the old glass vase with the roses. Sniffing them appreciatively, she took them into the lounge.

As April lay daydreaming in her scalding hot bath water, her thoughts unwillingly returned to Manilal and the nuisance that he was making of himself. There was no way she could allow this situation to continue. She resolved to speak to him at the meeting later that evening. Her mind made up, she closed her eyes and let the therapeutic bubbles soothe away the worries of the day.

Presently, she unwillingly stood up and towelled herself dry in the bath. Wrapping the towel around her body sarong-fashion, she stepped out of the bath before letting the water out. She was superstitious about standing in a bath of water whilst the water drained away, as she felt that her luck would drain away with the swirling stream. She glanced at the old alarm clock next to her bed. It was already 5.30 p.m., and she still had to dress, and more importantly, eat.

She padded, still barefoot and clad in the skimpy towel, into the small kitchen and looked inside the refrigerator, to see the uninviting remains of a cold pizza.

April whisked the leftovers into the microwave and set the machine humming. She poured herself a glass of fruity white wine, picked up the glass and licked away the small beads of condensation from the sides. The day had been long and hot, and the coolness of the glass in her hand was a welcome relief. She walked into the lounge and flung herself down onto the couch to wait. Automatically, her hand reached for a cigarette to enjoy with the wine.

Leaning precariously sideways, she flicked on the television and watched idly as the images flickered onto the screen. Suddenly she sat bolt upright, spilling her wine on her towel, her attention riveted to the screen. She turned up the volume to catch the commentary of the newsreader.

> 'And now we cross to our parliamentary correspondent in Cape Town for the latest details on ongoing talks pertaining to the Immorality Act,' informed the nasal anchor man.
>
> 'Thank you, Michael. Pandemonium erupted in Parliament today as the debate about the scrapping of the Immorality Act continued. Loud criticisms were heard from the leader of the Conservative Party as the motion of doing away with the Mixed Marriages

Act was discussed. There is still a long way to go, but it appears that by the end of this parliamentary sitting in June, the Mixed Marriages Act banning marriage or any form of intimacy between whites and people of colour will be another memory in the history books of Apartheid.'

April was stunned. It was almost inconceivable that after so many decades of enforcing this cruel law in often humiliating circumstances, the very political party that had created this system was propagating its removal. This would have far-reaching repercussions for future development, and she silently toasted this bold new step in the right direction.

She turned down the volume and went back into the kitchen, unable to wait for the summons of the microwave. Flinging the lukewarm pizza onto a plate, she hummed happily to herself. Her reverie was interrupted by the chimes of her doorbell for the second time that evening. Apprehensively, April approached the front door.

'Who's there?' she enquired.

'Your friendly landlord,' came the sickening reply. 'Phone call for you downstairs, my dear.'

'Thanks, Mr Sherwitz. I'll be right down,' she hastily replied.

Rushing into the bedroom, April hastily pulled on a track suit over her still damp body, and grabbed her keys as she ran towards the door. The corridor was empty and she sighed a small sigh of relief that Julius had made himself scarce. She ran nimbly down the stairs and turned into the small telephone booth.

'Hello, sorry to keep you waiting,' said April cheerfully.

'Darling, how was your day?'

'Hello, Parker. Fine, thank you, and yours?' asked April politely, surprised at the disappointment she felt at hearing her fiancé's voice. It was somehow ridiculous to think of him in those terms – he was too old to suit this frivolous title.

'Great until now, honey. Did you watch the news?'

'No, not really, why?'

'Looks like this stupid government is going to let black men paw white women legally now,' sneered Parker. 'The thought makes my flesh crawl.'

'Well, with the drastic shortage of real men in this country, at least our options can broaden considerably now,' retorted April, furious at his lack of insight and compassion.

'Are you mad?' shouted Parker, causing April to nearly drop the telephone receiver at his vehemence. 'You can't expect any decent white girl to hook up with these stinking vermin. They'll catch all sorts of diseases. You can take the black out of the bush, but not the bush out of the black. Come on doll, surely you realise that? I should know, I have to work with them every day, and I understand the way their minds work. They're just not like us.'

'No, I guess they're not, Parker. How can anyone that had been subjected to a substandard education and intense social and economic deprivation be "like us"? You smug, bigoted bastard.'

There was a shocked silence from the other end of the line. Parker could hardly believe his ears. He had never heard April use such strong language, and politics had just never been discussed.

'Gee, your day must have been worse than you said,' he replied lightly, trying to appease her.

'Well, it certainly wasn't that bad. Do you realise that over three-quarters of our population is going to bed hungry tonight? And half of them don't even have a roof over their heads? Doesn't it bother you at all that there are better-educated black, Indian and coloured men and women out there than you, but they are forced to live in segregated areas which have mansions next to ghettos because of the colour of their skin? They have no freedom of association like you and I, Parker, and their children have to go to expensive private schools for a decent education. Doesn't that bother you just a tad?' she finished sarcastically.

'Gee, love, don't get so hot and bothered,' replied Parker placatingly, horrified by the effect his words were having on April.

'Oh, I'm not hot and bothered, Parker. That would be a waste of good emotion. However, what is becoming apparent to me is our increasing incompatibility. We will have to have a very serious talk sometime soon about our future,' she said wearily.

'I think that you're blowing this out of proportion. I love you, April. We'll work this out. Hey, I'm flexible,' he ended lamely, chuckling hopefully.

'Flexible is not quite the right word, Parker. Anyway, I have to go to a meeting in a little while and I still have to get ready. Thanks for calling...'

'Hey, wait. Don't be in such a hurry. I've got news for you,' he interjected.

'Sorry, the news will have to wait. I've got to run. Bye,' said April firmly, replacing the receiver quickly. She turned sadly away from the phone. The whole situation was falling apart and there was nothing she could do to stop it. She was planning a trip to Port Edward on Friday, so she determinedly put the matter to the back of her mind for later. Right now, she had other priorities.

April glanced at her watch. It was nearly 6.15 p.m. She bolted up the stairs in a hurry to reach the apartment. Cursing herself for not having checked up in her diary, she struggled with the still unaccustomed lock. April was a very methodical professional, and disliked being at a disadvantage in a meeting like the strategic planning session. Guiltily, she thought of Catlin and Jack Nathan. Doing a disappearing act like that would certainly not have endeared her to them. Oh well, at least her reasons for running out on them were valid, she reflected a little defensively.

April gulped down the remainder of the cold pizza and threw the rest of the wine down the sink. No time for the pleasure of slowly sipping her drink. She strode purposefully into the bedroom to ready herself. Her damp hair was springing lightly around her face as it dried in the summer heat. She reached into the wardrobe and pulled out a sea-green short-sleeved dress of a gossamer material that softly clung to her contours, showing her full figure off to its best. For a person of average height, the length of the dress was quite modest, but on April the hemline sat stubbornly above her slim knees, giving her the appearance of an ethereal sea sprite. The dress brought out the green tones in her grey eyes, and was a favourite standby of hers when she did not have time to think of what she could wear. Slipping on her satin camisole, she sighed at the pleasant feeling of the silken material on her warm naked flesh. Suddenly and unaccountably, she was overcome with nostalgia at the thought of having no one to share these moments with. She felt lonely, lost and vulnerable. She slipped the dress over her head and let it fall into place with the softest whisper. Reaching into the bottom of the wardrobe, she drew out a pair of open low-heeled sandals in the precise shade of the dress and slipped her feet into them. Walking over to the dressing-room table, she rummaged through her meagre supply of cosmetics. If she wanted to look the suave sophisticate, she had better spruce up this department of her life she thought fleetingly. Grabbing her old reliable brand of apricot lipstick, she quickly applied it. She applied a little eyeliner, and added a touch of mascara for deepening.

She did not bother with blusher as her suntanned face needed no artificial colour. Taking one final look at herself in the full-length mirror, she nodded in satisfaction at the trim picture that she presented, slung her handbag nonchalantly over her shoulder and walked into the lounge. She found her briefcase at the door and sweeping it up into her arms, she let herself out of the apartment.

'This place definitely needs a dog,' she thought to herself in the corridor. Oh, she definitely had to move to a place that she could call her own, and she was longing for the pets that she had left behind.

'First thing tomorrow,' she announced loudly to herself.

April crossed the busy street to the car, unlocked the door and flung her bag and briefcase into the back. Climbing in, she revelled at the comfort in comparison to the old Beetle. Absorbed in thought, April didn't notice the large expensive car parked in the shadows, which started up and pulled in behind her as she drove down the hill to the meeting.

'Right, people, let's begin shall we?' Only half the members were present and April was thrilled that Manilal had not made it back to the second session. At least she could concentrate, without having to wonder if her underwear was showing. For the next three hours, she became totally absorbed in the projects and programmes that were envisaged for the Indian people of her region. She could hardly believe that it was so late when Dr Porter declared the meeting closed.

'Would you like me to see you to your car, dear?' kindly enquired Dr Lazarus, the medical officer for the district of Durban.

Smiling sweetly at the old and wrinkled grey-haired man, April graciously declined. 'Thank you, but don't worry. Muggers are scared of women with briefcases,' she laughingly teased.

'Maybe where you come from,' he replied, 'but here, they are very indiscriminate. You pretty young things should be locked away in your parents' homes until you are safely married.'

April's smile grew a little thinner, and she bit her lip in an effort not to retort at this blatantly sexist but well-meaning remark.

'Well, I guess I'll just have to take my chances, Dr Lazarus. Good night all,' she flung over her shoulder as she left the room.

As she reached the dark well where the lifts were waiting, she began to feel nervous.

'Mmmnn, Ghost Busters, Mmmnnn,' she tunelessly hummed aloud as she stepped into the waiting lift. Turning quickly, she scanned the area to make sure that she was alone.

'Darn that old goat,' she said aloud to herself, 'He's gone and made me all jumpy for nothing.' The lift seemed to take forever to reach the ground floor. She cautiously stuck her head out of the open doors to make sure that no Norman Bates was lurking about with a big knife.

'Stop it, you silly goose!' she fiercely admonished herself. Determined not to be a sissy, she walked confidently out into the night air. The streets were deserted, and she found herself feeling very grateful that she had parked the car under a street light just across the road. Looking about her carefully, she noticed a large car parked a little way away from hers. Suspiciously, she watched it carefully. She could see no one in the car. Shrugging her shoulders she quickly unlocked the driver's door of the Honda and threw her bags inside, not even aiming for the back seat in her haste to get going. She started the car and drove in the direction of Government Garage. She did not notice the large car start up and follow her.

April drove rapidly through the empty streets of Durban, her hair flying about her face as the air blew in through the open window. All the traffic lights were in her favour and she took full advantage by increasing her speed. She had been driving since the age of eleven, quite illegally, and her skill was apparent in the manner in which she handled the car. The Honda responded well to her sure hand, and she soon pulled up in front of the Government Garage. April gave a short blast on the horn, and almost instantaneously the large gates swung open. The cheerful old night attendant quickly signed her in and took the car to park it for her. Within five minutes, April was in her small sports car and racing back towards her flat.

The night felt oppressively hot, and April was in no mood to return to her apartment yet. She felt alive and keyed up from the meeting. Impulsively, she took the beachfront turn-off and drove up onto the freeway. Grinning, she put her foot flat down on the accelerator and the little car leapt eagerly forward to do her bidding. April was totally unaware of the large car still following her at a discreet distance, its lights reflecting unwaveringly in her rear-view mirror.

The freeway ran parallel to the harbour and the sea, the large tankers casting eerie shapes in the still waters of the docks. The silver sliver of the new moon reflected valiantly across the ocean. April licked her lips, appreciating the slightly salty taste that one could only experience when living so close to the sea.

Her car windows were rolled completely down, and the motion of the car had her curly hair whipping frenziedly about her face. She impatiently brushed the straying tendrils away with her left hand. Out of the corner of her eye, she caught sight of a sign advertising a drive-in-restaurant only metres away.

Well, I might as well have my first of many ice-creams in Durban, she impishly said to herself. April put on her indicator and turned sharply into the drive-in-restaurant.

She gasped with delight at the scene before her. The entire parking area was fringed by colourful fairy lights, with the kitchen facility being in the middle of the semi-circular surface. The parking area was built out above the ocean, and she glided smoothly to a stop in a space facing the sea in front of her, with the waves lapping up against rocks to the left of her. Very few cars were there as the hour was late for the average working person, but then, there was nothing average about April. She got out of the car and walked over to the building.

'Evening, Mam,' said the pleasant Portuguese owner from behind the glass screen. 'There was no need to come to the window you know. I was about to send one of the waiters to your car.'

'I know, but I need the exercise,' she smilingly retorted. 'Anyway, on such a beautiful evening with such incredible surroundings, it would be a crime to stay in a hot motor car. One of your hugest, coldest chocolate twirly-whirly ice-creams, please.'

'Coming up. Sophie, one jumbo choc 99 for the lady, please,' he bellowed across the kitchen. A slow lethargic black lady moved to do his bidding. April had never seen such a large person in her life, and couldn't help staring.

'She eats more ice-cream than she serves,' stated the owner, smiling at the incredulous expression on April's face. 'She's my most reliable staff member, and I have had her for years, so I turn a blind eye to her addiction for ice-cream. It's a small price to pay for her loyalty.'

'That's really nice,' said April softly, touched by the man's sensitivity to a staff member. In times where exploitation was the name of the game, it was refreshing to come across someone who clearly put the needs of their staff first.

April paid for her ice cream and walked towards her car. Mesmerized by the sounds of the pounding surf, she walked past the car and went and sat on the small stone wall separating the land from the sea. She slipped her sandals off, worried that they might slip off into the sea, and swung her legs over the edge. She was delighted to discover that each breaking wave covered her in a fine sea spray. She breathed deeply, appreciative of the salty smells that assailed her senses. April looked out across the bay, back towards the lights of the city she had just travelled from. Now, this was the life. If only she could get an apartment close to this sort of environment, her life would be perfect, she thought wistfully. Well, except for Parker, of course, she corrected herself. The ice-cream was delicious and April sat quite still and relaxed for the first time in weeks as she gave herself up to her senses. She let her mind soar on the evening breeze.

'Sorry to disturb you, love, but I'm closing up and I'd hate to leave you sitting alone in the dark.'

April jumped as the owner's voice penetrated her senses. 'No problem, I'm on my way,' she responded. True to her word, she turned around and slipped her sandals reluctantly onto her feet.

'Goodnight,' she cheerily called as she got into the car. Suddenly, she felt exhausted and ready to head home. The fresh air and change of scene had relaxed her completely.

April reversed out of the space and roared off back towards the city. She could feel her bed beckoning her, and within ten minutes, she was letting herself into her apartment.

The man in the large car smiled as her apartment lights snapped on. He started the engine of his car and cruised off slowly into the night, his mission accomplished.

# *Chapter Four*

'Good morning, Aneesa,' trilled April merrily. 'Today I've got something interesting for you to do. By the way, why didn't you remind me that I had those long meetings yesterday? I belted out of Nathan's factory like a scalded cat.'

'Hello, April. Yes, I heard.'

'You did?'

'Mmm,' nodded Aneesa, engrossed in arranging her desk stationery.

'Be a little more specific, why don't you?' said April, a curious frown wrinkling her forehead.

'Why don't you go and look on your desk?' said Aneesa sweetly.

'Why are you being so darn mysterious?' asked April a little testily.

'Run along and see for yourself,' said Aneesa, a mischievous twinkle lighting up her eyes. April stared at Aneesa in astonishment. Where was the shy retiring little wallflower of yesterday? She decided this self-confident and humorous creature was infinitely more interesting.

'Okay, here I go. See me go? I'm walking into my...' April stopped dead in her tracks as she entered her office, her words faltering. 'What on earth...' she spluttered. Aneesa stood in the doorway smiling.

'Just what did you do yesterday, April?' she teased. April's entire office was filled with flowers. There were bouquets on every inch of her desk, on the filing cabinet, on the telephone table, on the floor. The air was filled with the fragrance of a million blossoms, the room a riot of colours. April stood dumbfounded in the doorway.

'Well, go on,' said Aneesa softly, nudging April into the room. 'Read the messages. I'm dying to know who is this crazy about you.'

'Don't you know who they're from?' asked April, still a little overcome by the excesses before her.

'Of course not. I won't read your messages. That's just not right,' said Aneesa primly. April strode purposefully to her chair. She sat down heavily, and reached into her handbag for her cigarettes. Inhaling deeply, she leaned back and closed her eyes. The day had not begun the way she had envisaged at all.

'Right. Let's get to work,' she said, her eyes snapping open, purpose and determination written all over her face. She reached for the first bouquet's envelope. The flowers were a mass of yellows and oranges, giving a very exotic showing. Aneesa sat down with her note-pad and pen and prepared to take down the name of the generous benefactor for thanking purposes. April tore the envelope open and silently read the message. Her face suffused with a deep red flush that crept rapidly up from her neck.

'Of all the damn nerve!' she exploded. 'Send these flowers to the hospital, Aneesa. I won't have them in the same room with me!'

'What's the matter?' asked Aneesa in astonishment. She had only seen April pleasant and happy, and this anger was quite alarming in its intensity.

'These are from that pig Manilal! Listen to this … ugh! I can't even read it aloud. Here, you read this,' she said, flinging the offending card at Aneesa.

'Soon you will be mine. I caress you in my mind and hope to hold you in my arms. All my passionate devotion. Manilal,' Aneesa stopped reading, and burst out laughing. April's head snapped up in surprise.

'And just what is so hilarious, may I ask?' she asked Aneesa brusquely.

'It's just too much,' spluttered Aneesa, laughing even more uncontrollably.

'Oh no, here's another one from him,' said April, the second card in her hand. She quickly picked all the cards off the bouquets on her desk and gave Aneesa a handful to open. Each message was soppier than the one before, and all were from Manilal.

'Don't let him worry you, April,' assured Aneesa. 'He's quite harmless, you know. He does this to every new feminine arrival in Bloomsbury that isn't over fifty or hideously scarred. He's just never gone quite so wild before. He must really love you.' Aneesa guffawed with delight at her own little joke. April stared at her in amazement, then threw her head back and joined her in hearty laughter.

'Right, this is what we do. Take all the messages from him and put them into an envelope. Send it to the school address with my message which will read as follows: "Go fly a kite!" '

'And must I send all of these flowers to the hospital?'

'Yes, and tell them that they are all from Manilal Mooljee.' Aneesa stood up and started moving all the arrangements from April's desk into the front office.

'April, hadn't we better check that all of these are from Manilal? What if some aren't?'

'That's highly unlikely, but all right.' April busied herself with checking all the cards, and flung all those that were from Manilal into a pile. There was one more arrangement to check. A dozen red roses sat quietly in a crystal vase. This was the only tasteful and expensive bouquet in the room. April's hand shook as she reached for the card attached, every instinct telling her that these were different. She blinked to clear her vision, her heart racing in her throat. Slowly, she opened the envelope. She paled as she read the message: 'Hope you enjoyed the ice-cream You should be more careful and less impulsive.'

The card fell from April's hand. The realization that she had been followed was frightening, yet the message was not threatening. It actually seemed to show concern. Frowning, April went and sat down behind her desk, absent-mindedly crushing the still smouldering cigarette in the ashtray.

'Are these going too?' asked Aneesa, picking up the vase of roses.

'No!' exclaimed April, startling Aneesa and herself with her vehemence. 'I mean, no, please leave them there. They brighten up the office.'

'Anything you say. Have you read your messages? They're next to the telephone.'

April turned in her chair and noticed a pile of yellow telephone message notices on top of the directory. She picked them up and leafed swiftly through them, her mind filled with images of the secret rose-lover. Her last message was the only important one. She quickly called Catlin and made a new appointment to see Jack Nathan later on in the morning.

Aneesa brought her a cup of spicy tea and sat down. 'Now, what was it that you wanted to ask me to do today?'

'Oh yes. Well, besides humiliate Manilal, will you help me to look for an apartment on the beachfront? I'm miserable with the present set-up. And I'd like one that takes pets. And it must be unfurnished, one bedroom with ensuite bathroom, garage parking, safe, pretty, great view, small kitchen and a lounge.'

'You don't want much do you?' said Aneesa, a sarcastically teasing note in her voice.

'And privacy, and a garden,' added April.

'I'll see what I can do,' said Aneesa, standing up.

'Wait. I've got a ten o'clock appointment with Jack Nathan this morning, unless you have already scheduled me for performing major heart surgery?'

'Nope. Not today,' rejoindered Aneesa smiling. 'The day is yours to plan for a change. Just let me know what and where so that I can make a note in case you're urgently required in surgery.' April nodded in approval. Aneesa was learning fast, and the sense of humour was definitely developing.

'Hello, April,' said Catlin coolly as she entered the foyer at Beckensuds. 'And just where did you run off to in such a rush, dear? Mr Nathan's head is still spinning. You know, he really doesn't like to be kept waiting and then made a fool of.' A slight note of hysteria was creeping into Catlin's voice. April sensed instinctively that Jack Nathan had most likely not even noticed her absence, and Catlin was making liberal use of the royal plural to show her own mastery of the situation.

'Catlin, dear,' said April sweetly and softly. 'Hello to you too. Firstly, I was on time for my appointment with Mr Nathan, secondly, *he* kept *me* waiting, and thirdly, I left you a note explaining my haste. Would you prefer I give it to you in blood with my head served on a silver platter?'

Catlin stared at April in astonishment. She had clearly underestimated her adversary. April was far from defenceless and harmless. Catlin plastered an insincere smile on her heavily made-up face, and then laughed shrilly.

'Oh, you're so funny,' she said. April smiled back at her, all wide-eyed innocence. She was puzzled about Catlin's obvious dislike of her, and a little taken aback by her hostility. But she shrugged good-naturedly, and stored this revelation in the back of her mind for future reference.

Once again, April was led through the factory. It seemed

even hotter and more oppressive than the day before. The steam gushed out of several large machines, and April stepped carefully over large puddles of water. The men and woman handling the machines were intent on their tasks, their brown and black faces shining with perspiration that did not seem to bother them in their heavy overalls. April felt quite faint at the thought of having to spend every working day in this blast furnace, and marvelled at their ability to be totally unaffected by the extreme heat.

It was a relief to reach the air-conditioned corridors of power at the back of the factory. The blast of cold air revived April. Catlin politely held the door open for her, and then left with a casual wave. 'You know your way. I have to go back to the administration block.'

April turned to the already closing door, her mouth open to protest that she was quite likely to get lost, having only traversed these corridors once before. Her jaw snapped determinedly shut. She would never give Catlin the satisfaction of begging for her support and guidance. Squaring her shoulders. April turned and faced the corridor. Without hesitation, she managed her way admirably, and soon found herself at Jack Nathan's door.

She knocked timidly on the moranti wood door and listened intently for a reaction. Hearing nothing but the hum of the air-conditioners, she knocked again.

'I said come in, dammit!' bellowed a deep masculine voice from within.

'Geez ... how rude. Okay, okay...' muttered April, opening the door rapidly. 'Hello, Mr Nathan,' she called from Catlin's office.

'Get in here, Catlin,' bellowed the man's voice again. 'I'm dying of thirst. I asked you to please bring me that iced tea ages ago. Being polite really doesn't help in this place.'

April was about to enter his office, when her eye caught

sight of the glass making rings of condensation on Catlin's desk blotter. Impishly, she picked up the glass of iced tea, and walked into his office.

'Your drink, Sir. Will there be anything else?' she enquired cheekily, watching the glass carefully to make sure that she didn't spill it or trip on the long journey to his desk. She smiled as she remembered that Mussolini had used a long distance from his door to his desk as a strategy to make all potential enemies intimidated.

'Well, well. The elusive Miss Ross, I presume?' came his quiet and well-modulated voice.

April looked up at him as she put the glass down on his desk. Jack Nathan was standing with his back to the large window. This gave the impression that he was suspended in air with the factory at his feet. April found herself looking into the deepest brown eyes that she had ever seen. They were framed by long thick lashes, creases of laughter crinkling the corners. He was very tall, and his broad shoulders strained at the seams of his crisp short-sleeved white cotton shirt. His waist was narrow and his stomach was flat.

'Miss Ross. Are you always speechless when someone introduces themself to you?' he asked her, amused by her obvious confusion.

'No … yes … I mean, hello Mr Nathan, pleased to meet you. I've certainly heard a lot about you,' she spluttered, holding out her hand to greet him.

'All bad, I should imagine,' he said, extending his large hand towards her. His grasp was firm and cool. April was relieved. She detested hot, sticky, soft hands. If this man could be judged by a handshake, then the firmness and solidity of his grasp boded well.

'Well, I could say that it was all good, but then I'd be lying, Mr Nathan,' April responded teasingly, recovering herself from the initial impact of this man's personality and physique on her senses. She returned his firm handshake with energy and vigour.

'Let's not be so formal, shall we?' he said, smiling at her. 'The name is Jack, and I'll call you April.'

April felt inexplicably resentful. She was not used to people being so direct in professional circles, and although she tried to get on a first-name basis with people that she would be dealing with long term, it was usually she who would request that they call her April. This man was obviously accustomed to being in control of all situations at all times.

'Please sit down, April. Won't you join me in an iced tea?' he politely enquired.

'No, thank you, all the same. I'm a fruit juice and coffee lady.'

'Oh? But aren't your roots Scottish, and doesn't that make you a tea drinker?' he asked lightly, his eyebrows raised in mock consternation.

'How did you know that?' asked April in amazement.

'I make it my business to know everything about the people that I will be working with,' he replied casually. April felt her face begin to burn with a flush of annoyance. This man was the limit.

'Is that so?' she responded spiritedly. 'Let's see how good you are, Mr Nathan.'

'Jack,' he firmly interjected.

'Jack. Yes. What star sign am I? I'll bet that you didn't go into those sort of details.'

'Taurus,' he replied quietly. 'Anything else that you would like to know about yourself?'

'No, but seeing that you are so good at this, maybe you could tell me which horse will be winning the main race on Saturday?' she quipped.

'Ah,' he said, leaning perilously backwards in his large executive chair. 'I see I have struck a little nerve of annoyance. Now why is that? Is it because you have some deep secret to hide?'

'No,' she snapped. 'It's because I find an invasion of my privacy annoying.'

Jack swung sharply around in the swivel chair and turned away from April to look out of the window at the factory below. She was annoyed with herself for noticing that his thick black hair curled over his collar like a schoolboy's. The silence between them lengthened. April cleared her throat uncomfortably, and shifted in her chair.

'I see that you are not happy with silences in conversations,' he said, his back still turned towards her. 'What you must learn is that those silences often give you psychological advantages as you wait for the next person to speak. People often force their speech in these intervals, and say things that they might not realize they were going to say. This provides you with vital information that you would otherwise have missed.'

April sat mesmerised by his deep voice, then jumped as he suddenly turned his chair towards her.

'Forgive me for waxing lyrical. I'm afraid that it is part of my Hindu philosophy. It has been bred into me from a small boy to always look for the focus of a situation, and to then philosophize about it.'

'Hindu philosophy?' echoed April. 'But I thought you were Jewish?' she ended lamely.

'Ah, April. I am cut to the quick that you make such wild assumptions about me. Didn't you say that you had heard so much about me? And yet you didn't know I was a Hindu Indian. Did you perhaps think I had a remarkable tan?' He was smiling at her quizzically.

'Well, to tell you the truth, I thought that you might have developed it on a kibbutz, toiling in the sun,' she said, laughing a little embarrassedly at her faux pas.

His deep bellow of laughter startled her. His face looked

as though it had been chiselled in granite, his firm chin indicative of his determination. His mouth was full and generous, and a dimple cut deeply into his left cheek when he laughed. Instead of detracting from his manliness, this softening feature brought out the sheer masculinity of his features in sharp contrast. April felt herself responding to this man at a level so deep inside of herself that she felt as if she had met him before, and knew him well.

'Do you mind if I smoke?' she asked a little shakily, her fingers reaching instinctively for her cigarettes and lighter.

'Actually, I do. You are too young to be developing such bad and life-threatening habits,' he replied, his tone earnest.

April looked up at him in amazement. She had asked people this question hundreds of times, and this was the first time that anyone had said no.

'But there's an ashtray on Catlin's desk,' she said, struggling to come to terms with this man's essence.

'I don't care if there is an entire cigar factory on Catlin's desk. She can smoke as much as she likes. She is married, much older than you, and doesn't have your class. Therefore, I would very much appreciate it if you would refrain from smoking and act like the lady that I am sure you are.'

'But what difference could it possibly make to you whether or not I smoke? Surely it is my choice to die of lung cancer if I want to?' Even to her own ears, she sounded petulant.

'Did I hear my name being taken in vain?' Catlin stood in the doorway behind April, her hands provocatively on her slim hips.

'Catlin, where have you been? Please bring Miss Ross a glass of cold orange juice, and leave the reports that I asked you to get ages ago on the tray when you send it in.'

April was astounded at the difference in this man's demeanour as he spoke to Catlin. His tone was as cold as steel, and his face seemed to close down. April turned around to see Catlin's reaction, and felt a vicarious thrill of spiteful pleasure at her crushed expression. Instantly, she felt guilty about this mean-spirited feeling, and smiled reassuringly at Catlin. She was rewarded by a murderous glower before Catlin swung around on her heels and stormed out of the office.

'Incidentally, Jack, were you furious at me rushing off yesterday?' asked April on impulse.

'Good grief, no! Whatever gave you that idea? I had kept you waiting much too long and it was quite logical that you would have other appointments.'

'I see.'

'Why do you ask?'

'Oh, no special reason,' said April casually, mentally notching up points against Catlin. She was obviously no friend, and a person to be wary of.

'I'm sure you never say anything without a reason, April,' stated Jack emphatically, determined to get to the bottom of the matter.

'Let's just say that a little bird told me how I had infuriated you, and what a bad impression I had created.'

'I know just the bird,' he replied. 'For the record, never take anything that Catlin says too seriously. She tends to be a little over-protective at times. Sometimes she acts just like a wife.'

April's gaze fluttered over to the sideboard behind Jack's right shoulder. She cursed herself for not having noticed the picture sooner. There was a photograph of him holding two little girls, and laughing intently into the camera. He noticed her eyes were on the photograph, and smiled to himself. So, the girl was curious about him.

'My nieces,' he said softly.

'Sorry?' said April, looking blankly at him for a moment.

'I said, those are my nieces,' he repeated, amused by the relief flooding April's expression that she was unable to suppress. Suddenly, her face clouded over, and she turned to him.

'Are you married, Jack?' she asked, superstitiously crossing her fingers beneath the table.

'Yes,' he replied. April's heart was in her mouth.

'Oh,' she forlornly murmured. 'You must be very happy.'

'Not always, but I do find it very stimulating and satisfying at times, although at others, I'd like to just walk out and never come back.'

'Oh, I'm sorry to hear that,' April muttered politely, sorry that she had ever brought up the topic in the first place.

'But the money makes up for the misery, part of the time,' Jack added, enjoying the consternation that he was causing to this beautiful freckle-faced young woman.

'Pardon?' asked April, completely baffled by the turn that the conversation had taken.

'My career,' he said smiling. 'I am completely married to my job.'

'So you're not married in the church sense of the word?' asked April, determined that there be no misunderstandings.

'Being Hindu, I don't go to church. I assume you mean am I married to a woman, or any other living creature?' He cocked his head to one side and waited patiently for April's reaction.

'Right.'

'Correct, I am merely dedicated to my work and my welfare work in the community.'

'Are you a misogynist?' asked April bluntly. Subtlety had never been her strong suit.

'No,' he replied, quite at ease with her questions.

'I love women. They give an ugly and cruel world tenderness and beauty. Now how could any man hate something that important?'

'That's rather nicely put Jack. You should set yourself up as a university of flattery and charm.'

'Thank you,' he replied, bowing his head in mock deference to her statement. 'But you, on the other hand, are engaged,' he stated. April smiled at him.

'Since you told me that you know everything about me, I refuse to rise to the bait. Go on, give it your best shot.'

'Oh, please, you misunderstand my sources of information. They were very vague indeed about that side of your personal life. So, as you can see, you have me at a disadvantage.'

April suddenly felt uncomfortable discussing her love life with this man. He was so suave and sophisticated, and he must have had hundreds of woman falling at his feet. She felt like a silly schoolgirl talking about her fiancé, who was probably a decade older than Jack Nathan.

'Let's not talk about Parker. Now, tell me how you see my role in the Indian community from your point of view.'

'Permanent, I hope,' he responded frankly.

'Besides permanent, how do you…'

'April, drink your orange juice. You talk too much,' said Jack. April's indignation rose at this treatment of her when she had been trying to bring some semblance of professionalism to the discussion. She was just about to retort, when she heard the light step of someone behind her.

'Your juice, Mam,' said a tiny little black woman, holding out a tray to April. 'And here are those papers, sir,' the tiny woman said to Jack, holding them out to him.

'Thank you, Sarah. Cheers, April,' he said, raising his glass to her.

'Should I turn on the light on my way out, sir?' asked Sarah politely. April had not noticed that the office was dimly lit, the only light coming through the darkened window from the factory floor below.

'Yes please, Sarah. I'd like to be able to see my lovely guest properly, or else I might miss those flashes of fire in her eyes.'

Sarah chuckled deeply at his comments, and switched on the neon lights. April blinked as they flickered on. She had not noticed how dark the room had actually been. In the harsh neon glare, April found herself looking at a dark-skinned Indian man. In the dim light, Jack had looked Middle Eastern, but now she could see that he was darker than Yusef and Manilal. He looked exotic in that room of corporate trappings, and April fancied that he would look very good in a loincloth chasing tigers in the jungles of India. He was an incredible blend of European features in a dark setting. His nose was very large and Roman, and had he been short or squat, would have been his ugliest feature. But with his height and breadth, it was perfection. He could not have been called conventionally handsome, but his rugged chiselled features gave him a uniqueness that would be impossible to duplicate elsewhere. His almond-shaped eyes returned her stare unwaveringly as he in turn appraised her.

April tore her gaze away from him, deeply disturbed by the feelings that were churning deep inside her. This was definitely forbidden fruit, and went against not only her upbringing, but even the laws of the land. She suddenly felt an overwhelming premonition of impending doom, and shuddered.

'Are you cold?' asked Jack solicitously. 'I'll turn the air-conditioning down.' He stood up.

'No, no,' said April sharply. 'It's nothing. Like my mother always says, a goose just walked over my grave.

I'll be fine, really.' She smiled at him reassuringly.

'I've never heard that expression before,' said Jack with a puzzled frown. 'Your mother must be quite a colourful character.'

'She has her moments,' said April lightly, wanting to move off the topic of parents as rapidly as possible.

'Do you have your appointment book with you?' asked Jack, suddenly all brisk and businesslike.

'If you mean my diary, yes I do. I never leave home without it,' quipped April lightly.

'Let's see, today is what, Wednesday?' murmured Jack, speaking very much to himself. 'Perfect. What are you doing this evening?' April was startled by this question, and stammered inanely for a second or two.

'Why?' she finally managed to blurt out.

'Don't worry, despite what you may have heard about me, I can assure you that your virtue will remain intact. There is an open house session at the clinic building in Bloomsbury this evening, and I thought that it would be the ideal opportunity for you to meet some other community leaders and members of the general public at close quarters.'

'Yes, that would be lovely,' said April sheepishly, despising herself for her unsophisticated response. 'What time?'

'Be there at seven o'clock sharp,' he replied. 'Now I'm afraid that you will have to excuse me. I have another appointment. I'll see you this evening?' April nodded and made a note in her diary.

'Well, it was very nice meeting you, Jack,' she said politely, holding out her hand for him to shake. He stood up slowly, and she caught her breath. His sheer maleness screamed from every pore in his body, and April fleetingly wondered how it would feel to have those strong capable hands caressing her body. He took her hand and squeezed it firmly, but did not shake it.

'The pleasure was all mine,' he said softly. The moment seemed to stretch interminably, yet it was over in a second.

'Yes, well, goodbye then,' said April, a little shaken, retrieving her hand reluctantly. 'I'll see you and the rest of the leaders this evening. By the way, what exactly is an open house?'

'You'll find out soon enough. Until tonight, then, April. I look forward to your presence at our little gathering.'

'Your next appointment is here,' said Catlin sharply from the doorway.

'Send him in,' said Jack brusquely, annoyance at the interruption written across his face.

April sat quietly in her car in the car park, shaken by the emotions and thoughts that were churning through her mind and body. She seemed to have no control over where they were leading her. Annoyed at herself for her schoolgirl reaction, she started the engine, and drove smoothly out of the parking area.

Upstairs, in the office she had just left, Jack was aware of the lingering essence of April's perfume. He was having a very difficult time concentrating on what the desperate chemical salesman was saying to him. His mind was full of the visions of April as she had sat before him, demure and respectful, yet undaunted by him. He was used to women flirting shamelessly with him, and he found April's fresh young innocence refreshing. He smiled at the prospect of an evening in her intelligent company, chaperoned by at least 50 people.

April spent the rest of the day in a whirl of frenzied

activity. Exhausted, she arrived back at the office before 4 p.m.

'Where have you been?' asked Aneesa concernedly. 'I thought you'd been abducted or something.'

'No such luck, well not today anyway. I've been meeting all the people over at the National Department of Health and Population Development. I'll need as many resources as possible if I'm to even begin to make a dent in this community.'

'Never mind that. I've got great news. Guess what?'

'I'm too tired to even guess my own name right now,' said April, throwing herself down in her chair and swinging her legs up onto her desk She automatically reached for her handbag and her cigarettes. Jack's words came back to her and echoed through her mind. Surprising herself, she resolutely put the cigarettes back.

'I found you a place to stay,' said Aneesa, proudly. 'It's perfect, and it has everything that you wanted, so I hope you don't mind, but I put down a deposit on it for you.'

'Aneesa, you are a bloody marvel ... no a godsend. Have you actually seen the place?'

'Of course,' said Aneesa indignantly. 'How else could I have put a deposit down?'

'Of course,' said April, smiling.

'The agents fetched me to have a look, can you believe it?' said Aneesa excitedly. 'But I went in my lunch hour,' she hurriedly added, worried that April might think that she had been shirking her duties.

'Oh you goose,' laughed April. 'You are the very best thing that could have happened to me. Thank you.'

'I nearly didn't get let into the car,' said Aneesa seriously, her face clouding over at the memory. April sat forward intently on her chair, impatiently brushing the bouncy curls back behind her ears.

'What happened?' she asked quietly.

'Well, they were very friendly over the phone, but were not at all charmed when they arrived and found a little Muslim lady trying to get into a white neighbourhood. I had a devil of a job convincing them that it wasn't for me, or anyone like me. I had to take them into your office and show them your things. Luckily, you had left your identity book in the top drawer, so they could see by your photograph (which, by the way, is terrible) that you are white.'

'What a damn cheek!' exploded April, leaping up and storming from behind her desk. Aneesa retreated hastily to the opposite end of the office.

'I'm sorry, I didn't mean any harm by it,' she said, her lips quivering and her eyes pooling with tears.

'What?' snapped April testily, her mind full of the indignities suffered by people of colour in this country.

'I said that I'm sorry,' repeated Aneesa, a tear sliding down her cheek.

'Oh, Aneesa,' said April contritely, 'I'm mad with those insensitive estate agents that wouldn't take your word, and humiliated you. That's who I'm mad with.'

'Thank goodness,' said Aneesa, brightening perceptibly. She wiped the stray tear off her face with the back of her hand like a small child. The gesture touched April, and she went over and impulsively embraced her secretary. Aneesa stiffened in her embrace, then hugged her back. April looked into Aneesa's eyes and placed her hands on her shoulders.

'Now you listen to me,' she said firmly. 'This world is full of bigots and idiots, not that the two categories are separate entities mind you.' Aneesa laughed. 'How about a nice cup of coffee?' she added.

'I'll make it,' said Aneesa hastily, moving towards the kettle.

'You jolly well will not,' said April firmly, steering Aneesa to a chair. 'It's after four o'clock, we're off duty and are just two friends having a break. So, do you or don't you want coffee?'

'Yes please,' said Aneesa timidly.

'I met Jack Nathan today,' said April, busying herself with the cups and the coffee. She casually glanced around to see Aneesa's reaction. Aneesa regarded her impassively.

'Well? Aren't you going to say something?' asked April.

'It's your story, you tell me,' Aneesa replied impishly.

'Okay. I found him to be ... let's see ... all man,' she concluded triumphantly.

'What else?'

'Very intelligent, and professional. I could understand why Yusef didn't like him – he exudes authority and power, qualities that are envied by those who don't possess them.' April giggled at this description. 'Oh indeed, those qualities are far from Yusef's grasp.' Aneesa joined in her laughter.

'He phoned you twice today, you know,' she informed April.

'Who? Yusef? What did he want?'

'No, Jack Nathan. Looks like you may have made a conquest,' she teased.

'Don't be silly,' replied April, turning away to hide the blush creeping up her neck. 'It's all business. He doesn't know that I'm alive as a woman.'

'I have a confession to make,' said Aneesa, standing up and walking over to the window. Her hands fidgeted with the sunfilter curtaining as she gathered her thoughts together.

'All right, Aneesa, I'm listening,' said April gently.

'Shortly after Jusef's death, the building society phoned me to say that if I did not meet the repayments on the house within thirty days, they would foreclose. I was desperate, and did not know where to turn. I went and spoke to Hafez Nagoob and begged him to intercede on my behalf to the Muslim Council for assistance. But naturally, my father was involved in that organization, and I was turned away. Then one evening, I got a telephone call. It was the night before the building society were going to foreclose. The man refused to identify himself, and said that a benevolent benefactor had heard about my plight, and wanted to help me out of my predicament. I was very suspicious about the whole episode, as I was still grieving about Jusef, and knew that my father would stoop to any level to make my life unliveable. There was, however, no alternative. I had to trust the person on the phone.'

'What did they do?' asked April, unable to contain her curiosity. This secretary was turning out to be quite a storyteller, and fact was indeed turning out to be stranger than fiction.

'He told me that my benefactor would make the full arrears of the mortgage payment the next day, as he had only heard about my problem that day, but after that he was going to arrange to pay half the bond back in cash so that my repayments would be greatly reduced.'

'I'll say,' exclaimed April, her eyes wide with interest.

'To cut a long story short,' continued Aneesa, 'the payment was made, and within thirty days, I received a revised statement from the building society advising me that half my bond had been paid, and that my monthly payments would be nearly a quarter of what they had been. I could not believe that anyone could have done this for a stranger, and I had lost all my wealthy friends when my father disowned me as they were afraid of reprisals if they stayed friendly with me.'

'Right, that was wonderful, but what has this got to do with the confession that you wanted to make?'

'It's simple really,' replied Aneesa, turning and facing

April. No longer able to control her craving for nicotine, April reached for her cigarettes and rapidly lit one up. The smoke curled lazily above her head, making lacy patterns in the late afternoon sunlight that was streaming through the windows.

'I made a great deal of discreet enquiries, and eventually I was rewarded with the name of Jack Nathan.'

April stared at Aneesa incredulously. 'But you led me to believe that he was nothing special,' she said in surprise.

'I did not know you then, April. How could I tell you something that I had never told anyone else? This is surely the best-kept secret in Bloomsbury. Do you have any idea what it means in our community when a man pays for a woman's accommodation?'

'No, but I'm sure that you're going to tell me.'

'It means that she is kept by him for his sexual pleasure.'

'Are you telling me that you and Jack Nathan are lovers?' whispered April theatrically.

'That is precisely the assumption that everyone else would make. Do you now see why I could not talk about it?'

'Are you lovers?' persisted April.

'No. And we never will be. I went to see him after I found out who had helped me, to discuss why. He was furious that I had found out, because he said that he did not do things for public recognition, and that he had just tried in his small way to right the injustices that my father had committed against an innocent and defenceless woman and her children.'

'This guy sounds like Zorro,' said April, for once at a loss for any sensible words.

'He is a good man, April. He does many good deeds that are never recognized. You asked me the other day if you could trust him. Well, the answer is a definite yes. He asked me never to tell anyone else of his deed, and today is the first time I have broken that promise. But, today, it became very necessary.'

'Why?' prompted April.

'Because I sense that the two of you are one spirit.'

April drew deeply on her cigarette, and busied herself pouring the coffee. Presently, she handed Aneesa a mug and went and sat behind her desk. She felt as though she had been dealt a blow in the solar plexus.

'I see you are troubled by what I say, April. Do not be afraid, just let your instincts guide you with this man. It is right.'

'What are you saying?' whispered April, staring wide-eyed at the girl standing before her. 'Just what are you saying?' she repeated warily.

'Simple. I had the same feeling about you that I had when I was in Jack Nathan's presence. The two of you are one soul, and think with one mind.'

'You know nothing about me,' said April incredulously. 'How can you even begin to make these assumptions? It's just inconceivable.'

'It is true that I know no details of your physical life and your worldly past, but I was born with a great gift from Allah. I can sense a person's spirit if I am in the same room with them, and if I concentrate. An evil person is very easy to identify, and each person gives me a different sensation. But you and your Jack are one and the same.'

'He's not "my" Jack, for goodness' sake, and stop saying things like that. Even if I believed you, which I do not, by the way, the whole idea is preposterous and totally inconceivable.' April steadied her shaking hand on the edge of her desk.

'You are a very educated woman, and I am a simple one,' continued Aneesa, 'but please do not ignore what you know is the truth. It is what the Hindu people call

Karma – you will go along the right path because it was meant to be. I know these things. Trust me.'

April felt a peace stealing over her. Aneesa's words were having a hypnotic effect on her, and they felt so right although they sounded so strange to her Western ears. She had never encountered any genuine philosophers before, and Aneesa's simplicity was more convincing than any trappings of crystal balls and Tarot cards.

'Fine,' April responded. 'If what you say is true, what does this mean? For goodness' sake, I'm engaged to be married…'

'But you do not love him. It is wrong, and it is not meant to be,' interjected Aneesa quietly. April was astonished. She had never discussed her feelings about Parker with anyone, and here she had just heard her innermost thoughts voiced out loud by a virtual stranger.

'I see you are surprised. Please forgive me for being forward, April. But I want you to follow the path of your fate. It will bring you first great pain and suffering, alienation from things familiar. But these things will pass in the twinkling of an eye, as your Bible says. There is great happiness in store for you when the danger has passed.'

'Thank you very much,' said April flippantly, attempting to place some of the earlier lightness back into the conversation. 'Why can't you just say that I'll meet a dark handsome stranger, have three kids and be fabulously wealthy? But no … you go for the doom and gloom.'

'I am sorry. I should never have said anything. I made a mistake thinking that you would understand,' Aneesa hung her head dejectedly. April watched her closely.

'You're serious, Aneesa, aren't you?' she finally said. Aneesa raised her head and her eyes crinkled at the corners as she smiled broadly.

'What I say is true, April. Thank you for believing me.

It will all unfold to you as it should with time. I cannot tell you specific events in your life because I am not a soothsayer. All I can tell are impressions that I sometimes pick up, and it is just that these feelings have been very strong with you.'

'Fair enough,' replied April, putting out her almost forgotten cigarette in the ugly ashtray. 'But for now, let's concentrate on my immediate future, okay?'

'Okay,' agreed Aneesa happily. She was relieved now that this burden of sensing and knowing was off her shoulders.

'Let's go see my new apartment,' suggested April, snatching up her keys as she bounded energetically around her desk.

'I'm sorry, I have to fetch my children from Madressa. But here is the address. You will be happy there.'

'Is that an assumption or a prediction?' teased April.

'Both,' replied Aneesa emphatically, passing the piece of paper with the address to April.

Half an hour later, April stood entranced in front of a block of sea-facing brick townhouses. Behind her, the surf pounded onto Bluff Bay Beach with all the intensity and passion that it could muster. She climbed out of her car, her green floral skirt whipping about her legs. A passing jogger whistled appreciatively and waved to her as he jogged by. April bobbed a little curtsey of thanks, and smiled at his antics. Glancing at the piece of paper, she walked up to the solid wooden door of the caretaker's apartment, and knocked politely, having seen no bell. She winced as the hard wood bruised her knuckles. Taking her car keys, she rapped on the door with her large Taurus keyring, and was rewarded by the yapping of a small dog from within.

'Quiet, Killer,' came a gravelly voice, cracked with age and good use. The door swung open, and a wizened, ruddy little face peered at her from around the corner. 'Yes?' said the little old man whose appearance was more and more reminiscent of a well-intentioned gnome.

'Hello, I'm April Ross,' she replied, extending her hand politely. The door opened wider and a small bundle of white fluff hurled itself at April, barking ferociously.

'Oh!' she shouted, jumping back in surprise. The small dog launched himself into midair and landed squarely in April's arms, his pink tongue licking her cheek.

'Killer, mind your manners. This one's a lady.'

April laughed at this inappropriate name for this wagging ingratiating creature, who was doing everything in his power to kiss her to death.

'I calls 'im Killer cos 'es a killer with the ladies,' snickered the old man. His cockney accent was very thick, and strange to April's ears. 'You must be the luvverly wot's moving in to number one,' he said. April nodded, concentrating on avoiding the ardent licks of Killer. 'Your secretary was 'ere earlier. Nice lady. She said that you'd be very 'appy 'ere. I think you'd be 'appy anywhere, luv. Killer 'as taken a regular shine to you 'e 'as, and 'e's 'as fussy as they come. Taken a regular fancy to you 'e 'as.'

Laughing, April handed the dog back to the old man. 'Could I have the key please, Mr … er … what do I call you?' she asked.

'Just plain Sam,' he said, twinkling at her. ''ere it is lass,' he added, reaching for the key from behind his door.

'It's number one on the end there,' he said, coming outside and pointing down the lane of townhouses. April had to bite her lips painfully to stop herself from laughing. Sam must have been quite a hippy at one stage of his life. It was peculiar seeing a geriatric wearing a kaftan and beads with guru sandals.

‘Thanks “plain” Sam,’ she finally managed to say, returning Killer to his owner’s outstretched arms. She took the key, and walked resolutely towards her new home.

Crossing her fingers, she unlocked the large wooden door with the lion’s-head knocker, and pushed it open. The door swung effortlessly open on quiet hinges, and she walked into the Italian tiled hallway. Always aware of the possibility of muggers, she closed the door behind her. She looked around her in wonderment. The whole impression was one of space and light, with large french doors leading onto a small, enclosed and well-kept garden. The townhouse was much larger than it appeared from outside, and she stepped out onto the plush lounge carpet to explore further. Automatically slipping her sandals off, she let her bare toes dig deeply into the lush pile. It was like walking on marshmallows, a far cry from her present arrangement. She walked across the lounge area and unlocked the french doors, opening them outwards into the sunshine. They formed the windows of this room, framing a picture of riotous blossoms in the garden. April winced as her bare feet stepped out onto gravel where she had expected grass. Hastily retrieving her sandals, she slipped them on and ventured outside. The garden had been laid out like the Japanese gardens that she had seen in magazines, with beautiful flower beds bordered by gravel walkways instead of grass. Palm trees and oleanders grew and blossomed in terracotta Ali Baba jars near the bottom of the garden. She looked approvingly at the high brick walls surrounding the garden, keeping the eyes of curious passers-by at bay. She noticed a wooden gate flush with the wall, leading onto the road that separated the townhouse complex from the beach. The garden was not too large, and April breathed in the fragrances that hung suspended in the air. Setting the bass tone for the surroundings was the tangy and unmistakable salty smell of the warm Indian Ocean, crashing onto the shoreline only 500 metres away. Satisfied, April turned and walked inside.

She walked back across the lounge towards the ornate spiral staircase leading to the upper storey of the duplex. Her heels clattered metallically on the complicated trellis designs of the rungs as she ascended. The landing at the top of the stairs had the same Italian tiles that she had seen at the entrance hall, their soft cream colours blending in with the pale cream walls. She entered a bedroom that seemed to be almost as large as the lounge. The carpeting was the same beige as downstairs, and she walked silently across to the french windows that led out onto a small balcony. She caught her breath as she looked at the view. The entire Indian Ocean stretched out before her, rising and falling languidly in the fresh breeze. Throwing the doors open, delighted at this discovery that would make the long hot summer nights bearable, she stepped out onto the balcony. Already she was picturing long narrow window boxes, planted with a riotous arrangement of geraniums, placed along the walls of the balcony.

Returning inside, she noticed dark wood built-in cupboards stretching across the length of the room. Inquisitive as a cat, and hoping the previous tenant may have left something of themselves behind, she started opening the six doors. The first two were the traditional double doors to a hanging space, and the third being shelving. The greatest surprise lay behind the fourth and fifth doors. They formed the hidden entrance to the en-suite bathroom. Squealing with delight, April walked through into the small, functional green bathroom. Light streamed in from the frosted windows that faced the sea. The bath was round and sunken, and one wall of the room was entirely mirrored, giving the illusion of space and light. Closing the doors behind her as she left, April left the bathroom and went to investigate another door on the landing, supposing that it was a linen cupboard. To her delight, it led into a small room that could be used either as a study or a small second bedroom. The west-facing room was filled with warm afternoon sunlight. Looking out of the window, April would be able to see whoever might be ringing her bell. She left the small room and descended the staircase carefully. Satisfied with everything so far, she crossed the lounge towards the front door. On the right-hand side of the entrance hall, there was a sliding door. April pushed it open and gasped in delight at the small, compact kitchen. The silver window blind kept the room darkened and cool. The walls were covered with eye-level cupboards, all maintaining the theme of cream as set by the tiled flooring. April whirled around in delight. Aneesa had been right. This townhouse was perfect. The girl was a gem.

She walked out into the late afternoon sun, blinking at its orange intensity. A few feet away from the front door was the garage door allocated to her apartment. April felt as though she was walking on air as she stepped along the brick driveway towards Sam's door. Then she stopped short with the horror of a fresh realization. The price. She had never given Aneesa any indication of price, and from what she had just seen, this duplex was very upmarket. She felt as though cold water had been splashed into her face. With an impending sense of disappointment, she knocked on Sam's door, remembering to use her key ring. Of course, her key ring. She laughed aloud as she remembered her incredulity at Jack Nathan knowing her star sign. All he had to do was read.

'Now that's wot I like, a woman 'appy on me doorstep,' said Sam smiling as he opened the door. Killer launched himself at April again, and she caught him deftly in her arms.

'Oh Sam, it's so perfect that I could just die,' she said, breathlessly, 'but I'm afraid that it will be beyond my price range.' She ended on a melancholy note.

'Don't be so sure, lass,' Sam said enigmatically. 'Believe you me, it's well within your budget.'

'Now Sam, let's be realistic about this. My salary is not at all outstanding to make an understatement. I really don't think…'

'Lassie, lassie, it's done and all arranged. The deposit is paid, and you can move in right now if you like.'

'Just how much is it?' asked April, crossing her fingers behind her back.

'Only five hundred rand a month for you, luv. Now don't tell me that you can't afford that.'

April gasped involuntarily. She could afford that with ease. It just didn't seem possible though. 'Surely there must be some mistake, Sam,' she enquired shakily, hoping that she was not jinxing herself.

'No mistake, luv. So will you be sleeping 'ere tonight?'

'No,' she said laughingly, 'I'll have to give my creepy landlord twenty-four hours' notice and get some furniture in a hurry. I'll move in over the weekend.' She said it decisively, quite forgetting she had promised Parker she would be in Port Edward with him this weekend.

'Keep the key, luv. I've got me master copy to this whole block in case of an emergency. Ta ra then. I'll be seeing you.' Reaching for his little dog, he closed the door.

April's smile broadened until she felt as though her face would split clean in half. Turning sharply on her heel, she walked thoughtfully over to the Honda, her mind filled with the endless decorating possibilities that faced her.

# *Chapter Five*

April glanced uncertainly at her map of Bloomsbury in the evening light. It was that special time of evening that her Scottish grandmother used to call the gloaming, the precious minutes between day and night that were all the more spectacular in Africa where intensity of colour abounded. Frustrated with her inability to see properly, April pulled the Honda over onto the side of the road. Scratching her head thoughtfully, she studied the map intensely in the glare of the cab light. Then sighing with self-satisfaction, she folded up the map having pinpointed her route to the clinic in Freesia Drive. April drove confidently towards her destination, quite prepared for whatever this open house entailed.

Despite her anticipation of the evening's events, she was startled to find that she had butterflies in her stomach the size of Tiger Moth aeroplanes at the thought of seeing Jack Nathan again. She self-consciously patted her hair in a vain attempt to bring some order to the unruly curls, and cursed herself for not having allowed herself sufficient time to shower and change after the day's activities. But then, the acquisition of her flat - no, duplex - she mentally corrected herself, smiling, was well worth looking a little ragged around the edges for. She pulled up in front of a small brick building, and was surprised at the number of cars and people there. She noticed a police van out of the corner of her eye and felt a twinge of alarm that there may have been some trouble. Climbing gracefully out of the car, she looked alertly around. There was a murmur in the crowd as someone caught sight of her walking towards the clinic. Smiling a little self-consciously, April felt all her old schoolgirl insecurities flooding back. A deep male voice at her shoulder penetrated the fog of her feelings, and she jumped, startled at the unexpected intrusion. She whirled sharply around, her breath catching in her throat as she recognized Jack Nathan. He placed his large well-manicured hand reassuringly on her arm.

'Easy now,' he whispered, for only her to hear.

April smiled. She felt like a horse that he was trying to calm down before a race.

'Welcome to the real Bloomsbury. I hope you don't mind, but I organized a little welcoming crowd for you tonight. Also, the press is here.'

'The press?' asked April, thoroughly alarmed and convinced that something serious had happened connected to the police van.

'Of course. You're a celebrity you know.'

'Well, actually, I didn't know,' said April, flustered by this unexpected turn of events. Before her were a sea of dark, smiling faces, all curious about her and the world that she represented. Despite all the activity assailing her senses, April had noticed how handsome Jack Nathan was looking. He had changed, she felt herself noticing a little resentfully. His height and the breadth in his shoulders were accentuated by the short-sleeved white cotton suit he was wearing. Appreciatively she smelt the subtle woody tones of his aftershave lotion. She looked down at his dark hand on her fair skin, and noticed the close mat of black hairs on his forearm. The touch of his fingers gently yet firmly guiding her sent shivers of anticipation up and down her whole body. She felt a warm melting sensation in the pit of her stomach at the thought of him holding her in his arms.

'I'd like you to meet Major Donovan from the Bell Road police station,' he said. April pulled herself sharply back to reality, and nearly fell over as he relinquished her arm.

'Pleased to meet you, Major Donovan,' she said automatically, falling back on her years of good breeding.

'Major Donovan is here tonight to help us start a neighbourhood watch programme,' Jack explained as he moved forward through the throng. 'This way,' he said imperiously. April followed behind him in his wake as the crowd parted before him respectfully. April giggled as the irreverent picture of Charlton Heston as Moses parting the Red Sea came to mind.

She was led into a brightly lit and poorly ventilated room that could not possibly seat all the people milling about outside. Jack noticed the question on her face. 'The people stay outside and form a queue according to who came first. Then they come in one by one to discuss their problem in confidence with us.'

'Us?' April repeated, questioningly.

'Yes, the rest of the Civic Committee.' He turned around, and April noticed four men sitting behind a table talking amongst themselves. 'Gentleman, I'd like to introduce you to our new social worker, Miss April Ross.' April felt a twinge of resentment at the ownership of her person implied by the use of the word 'our'. The four men stood up and came around the table to greet her.

'This is Kris Naidoo,' introduced Jack.

'I'm so very pleased to meet you, such a vision of loveliness will now grace our community,' Kris said, his voice ingratiating. April shook his limp hand firmly, and turned to the next man. Out of the corner of her eye, she could see Kris Naidoo looking her up and down lecherously. He was not a physically unattractive man, and was nearly as tall as Jack Nathan, but there was a weakness about his chin that seemed to underline a weakness of character. April's father had always warned her that the more compliments a man bestowed upon a woman, the filthier were his thoughts.

'This is Mr Subrien,' continued Jack, introducing April to a small wizened old monkey of a man. April smiled as she thought of George Burns. The likeness was amazing.

'Hello, my dear. We are so pleased to have you with us on the team,' he said, extending his little hand like a paw. April was amazed at the strength in his grasp, and warmly reciprocated the greeting.

'This is Balu Bansda,' continued Jack. April was confronted by a tall very skinny whip of a man whose sharp features placed him firmly in the ferret family. She was taken aback by the thinly disguised hostility in the man's eyes as he reached out to shake her hand as though he was touching something very distasteful.

'How do you do?' said April politely, and was rewarded by a cool nod from the man.

'And last but by no means least, this is my good friend, Mohammed Hassim.' April found herself staring into intelligent light-brown eyes. Mohammed was her height, but was twice her size. This was a man who obviously enjoyed his food. His hair was silver grey, and his face was covered by a distinguished silver grey beard.

'Hello, my dear. Jack has told me much about you. Welcome to the sunny city. I'm sure that I speak for all of us when I wish you well here. I hope that you will be happy.'

'Thank you so much,' replied April, glancing surreptitiously at Balu. His expression was far from welcoming. It was obvious that he had a great many prejudices to work through.

There was a sudden bright flash of light that had April blinking myopically for a few seconds.

'It's just the photo-journalist being his usual hilarious self,' explained Jack reassuringly. April smiled weakly at the grinning red-headed young man with the large camera slung nonchalantly around his neck.

'Hiya,' he said breezily, grinning at April unrepentantly.

'April, I'd like you to meet Ginger Elliot, the photographer and photo-journalist for the non-white, or rather the so-called non-white areas.'

'Hello, Ginger. I hope that you aren't going to print that one,' said April cheerfully.

'Why not?' he rejoindered. 'You're a natural and I'm a first-class photographer. I'd even make a dog in curlers look stunning,' he said, a little undiplomatically.

'Thanks a lot,' said April laughing, amused by the young man's sense of humour.

'Okay, Ginger, enough dazzling of the ladies. Let's set up for the shot shall we?' said Jack, surprisingly sternly.

'Sure thing, Mr Nathan,' he replied good-naturedly, and busied himself, instructing April and the members of the Civic Committee on where to stand. April found herself between Jack Nathan and Kris Naidoo. They all had to stand slightly sideways for Ginger to line up the shot effectively, and April stood slightly tucked behind Jack's right shoulder, their bodies touching in the close proximity of the moment. Kris Naidoo pushed himself unpleasantly against her. She was hard-pressed to manufacture a sincere smile, and was relieved when Ginger stopped taking shots.

'Right, now let's get one of you and Mr Nathan alone,' he instructed. The others melted almost magically away, and April found herself looking deeply into Jack's eyes. Her heart lurched as his arm brushed her shoulder. She had never experienced emotions like those he provoked in her, and this discovery made her very uncomfortable. The whole situation was impossible, even if she wanted to pursue a relationship. Her breath caught in her throat at the ramifications of a relationship between the two of them. She shrugged her shoulders and shivered, and remonstrated with herself about how silly she was being. This man had no feelings for her whatsoever. They were from two totally separate worlds.

'Are you all right?' asked Jack solicitously. April suddenly realized that she had leaned heavily against him for support.

'Sorry ... it's the heat in here. Excuse me, I need some fresh air,' she ended weakly, and ran out of the building. The waiting crowd stepped back as she threw the door open. April gulped in lungfuls of air and nodded reassuringly to the people in front of her.

'It's okay, I just need a little air,' she explained, and turned around to go back inside. She bumped into Jack as he came rushing concernedly towards her She leapt back at the sudden contact like a scalded cat. 'I'm fine, I just needed a little air, that's all. There really is no problem.'

'Are you sure you want to go back inside?' he insisted. 'You're looking a little pale. Really, if you'd rather go home, no one's feelings will be hurt.' April smiled wanly up at him.

'Jack, please don't fuss so. I'm fine. Now let's go inside shall we?' she said firmly, walking ahead of him.

For the next two hours, April sat and listened intently as the people brought their problems to Jack and his committee. She was touched by the compassion he showed to the elderly and the dim-witted as they discussed problems ranging from not being able to get a house or be put on the waiting list, to things as obscure as the fact that their geyser was broken and they needed to know which repairman was the best. The other members of the Civic Committee sat silently watching the proceedings, with Mr Subrien nodding energetically at anything Jack had to say.

Kris Naidoo's eyes kept ranging over April as she sat towards the back of the clinic, but after a while she managed to ignore him, and then everyday life in Bloomsbury unfolded before her eyes. She was impressed by the humble mastery Jack brought to the proceedings, and touched by the obvious gratitude expressed by the people who had been helped, regardless of how trivial their problems appeared to be. She noticed Balu was writing everything down that was discussed, and assumed that he must hold the secretarial position on the team, but was puzzled by his dour expression and the continual shaking of his head as though in complete disagreement with everything that transpired.

'Well, that's certainly enough hard work for one Wednesday night,' said Jack, standing up and stretching as the last resident left. 'I hope we didn't bore you to death April,' he said, walking over to where she sat.

'I wasn't bored for one minute,' she replied truthfully, looking up at him as he towered above her. 'Is Balu the secretary?' she enquired.

'No. He's Hussein's lap dog,' he replied, grimly.

'Lap dog? I'm afraid I don't understand quite what you ...'

'There is nothing to understand. Hussein is in parliament, so we spend every Wednesday night here hearing the problems of the community, and Balu writes down everything I say to the people in case I get a little too generous with my advice,' he said grimly. His face had hardened, and April was aware of a mounting tension in him as he spoke.

'Is that legal?' she asked concernedly.

'In Bloomsbury, Hussein is the law,' he replied bitterly, his eyes flashing hatred and fire. Then his expression softened as he looked at her. 'April, I have one very important bit of advice for you. Stay away from Hussein and anything that he represents. He's ruthless and very dangerous. His greatest danger lies in his ability to charm. When he returns from parliament, he will be organizing a large welcoming party for you. I advise you to attend, but stay close to me whenever Hussein comes near you. Understood?'

'Aren't you being a little melodramatic?' replied April crossly, annoyed by his patronizing tone of voice.

'No,' he replied calmly, unperturbed by her adolescent retort. 'I'm not being melodramatic enough. Just remember what I said.'

'And what did you say, Jack?' asked Balu from behind him. April jumped. She had not seen him sidle close during her interchange with Jack.

'He was warning me about the Bloomsbury Romeos,' she quickly responded, flashing Jack a conspiratorial wink.

'Oh,' Balu replied dourly. 'Excuse me, good-bye.' He turned sharply on his heel and left.

'I'm pleased to see you can think on your feet, April. It makes me a little less worried about you after all,' Jack said, the respect in his voice heart-warming to her. 'It's been a very long day for me, so remember what I've said. Okay?'

'I had quite a day too, the best part being the discovery of the most perfect place in the world to stay,' replied April, her face brightening as she thought of the townhouse.

'That's wonderful. Well, thank you for coming this evening, April. Remember now, you're welcome any Wednesday night to the open house. If you don't come, we'll understand, and I'll just fill you in with the details on Thursday mornings.'

April felt quite disappointed that he had not been more interested in where she would be staying. She had the distinct feeling that cooking for him one evening would be a pleasure.

'Come, I'll walk you to your car,' he offered gallantly. Taking April firmly by her elbow, he steered her towards her car. 'Ah. I see that you have made a great improvement on the old rattletrap that Yusef used to dash around in,' he said, looking approvingly at the Honda in the moonlight.

'There was no way that I was going to risk my life, so I asked for a new car. I never expected a Honda,' she replied.

'Knowing a little about the pecking order in government departments, I'd say that you made a friend close to the top of the tree,' said Jack intuitively.

'You could say that,' replied April airily. 'Well, good night, Jack, and thank you for the escort to my car. Tonight has been quite a revelation, and I will take your warning to heart.' She quickly unlocked her door and climbed into the car, tossing her bag and briefcase onto the back seat. With a little wave she drove off down Freesia Drive.

Jack stood watching the disappearing tail lights of her car with a frown on his face. Thoughtfully, he walked back into the lit building.

April struggled with the lock on her apartment door, cursing like a sailor as she dropped her handbag and spilled its contents across the corridor with a loud clatter. She got down onto her hands and knees to retrieve the items, then the hair on the back of her neck rose as she heard the familiar click of her own door opening. Leaping to her feet, she whirled around, ready to die for her honour. Her face froze with astonishment. Standing sheepishly in her doorway was Parker.

'Hello, gorgeous,' he said. 'Surprised?' he asked, almost coquettishly. April was in no mood for coquettishness.

'Just what the hell do you think you're doing, Parker? You scared me half to death, man. And how did you get in?' she demanded angrily.

'First a kiss, then I'll tell you all,' said Parker coming towards her with his fat arms outstretched. April stepped back as a sudden wave of revulsion washed over her.

'Don't be silly, Parker,' she snapped, staggering as she stepped onto her tube of lipstick. She grabbed the wall to steady herself and held out her other arm to ward off his advances.

'Get inside. I don't want all the neighbours to see what an ass you can be.' Obediently, Parker turned around and went back into the apartment. Looking to the ceiling for inspiration, April squared her shoulders and followed him inside, leaving various items from her handbag scattered dangerously about in the hallway. Slamming the door behind her, she advanced on him menacingly.

'After the kind of day I've had, Parker, your timing stinks. And why did you just drop in out of nowhere like this? You nearly gave me a heart attack.'

'I'm sorry, sweet cheeks, I just thought that you would be happy to see me.' April felt guilty when she saw his hang-dog expression.

'No, I'm the one that should be sorry,' she replied. 'I'm just so jumpy that I'm seeing gremlins in every nook and cranny.' Leaning forward, she pecked him on the cheek.

Parker grabbed at her and pulled her into his strong arms, his fingers biting into her flesh. He stuck his tongue deep into her mouth, and she tasted salt as he cruelly bit her lips. Almost as suddenly as he had grabbed her, he let her go, and she staggered unsteadily, taken aback by this unexpectedly violent side of his nature. Wiping the blood away from her bottom lip, she sat gingerly down on the chair, the shock registering on her face. April reached for her spare packet of cigarettes and lighter as she struggled to regain her composure. She had smelt the acrid odour of whisky on his breath and was in no mood to antagonize him.

'You are my woman, and don't you forget it!' he snarled. She stared at him, open-mouthed in astonishment. Suddenly, she remembered that he had been attending assertiveness training classes in Port Edward as part of his sales technique training. He must have studied a little too hard, she thought to herself.

'Are you still so attached to that poisonous weed?' he growled. April's resolve to smoke intensified, and purposefully, she slowly lit up a cigarette and blew the smoke deliciously out.

'Does that answer your question?' she retorted.

'But you stink when you smoke,' said Parker petulantly. 'I can't bear to be near you.'

'Oh?' said April softly, watching him intently through the haze of smoke.

'Yes,' he continued recklessly, 'and your breath smells so terrible after you've been smoking. Even your hair stinks.'

'Really?' replied April pleasantly, watching the smoke as it blew sideways from a draft from the balcony.

'It cheapens you, April, and it makes you look like a slut.'

'A slut, eh?'

'Yes. A high-class low-life hooker that hangs around on street corners. I want you to stop smoking immediately,' he concluded, the spittle collecting at the corners of his mouth in his fervour to dominate her.

'Parker, why are you here?' asked April innocently, her eyes wide and enquiring.

'Oh, that was what I phoned you about, darling,' he said, his previous diatribe completely out of his mind. 'I've joined a movement that is based in Durban called CAN.'

'CAN? Can what?' asked April, genuinely puzzled.

'Yes, the Centre for Conscious Action,' he explained.

'Correct me if I'm wrong, but doesn't that spell CCA?' enquired April.

'Ordinarily it would,' replied Parker, warming to his theme, 'but we wanted it to be a catchy name that could be recognized by initials, so we chose CAN because it represents the positive aspect of the course.'

'Oh, so it's one of those "positive thinking will make you rich and famous" schemes?' asked April sarcastically.

'Exactly,' said Parker, beaming. 'I went to the first lecture this afternoon, and had a long encounter session with Lynette.'

'Lynette?'

'Yes. She's the lady who is running the course.'

'How many of you were there, Parker?' asked April.

'Well, actually, I was the only one that turned up,' he admitted defensively, 'but Lynette said that I wasn't to worry because now she could work more intensively with me.'

'I see,' said April. 'Tell me more about this Lynette person. She sounds fascinating.'

'Well, she's just so intelligent,' he gushed. 'She and I have so much in common. We're both divorced and...'

'Whoa there. Back up a minute. You say she is divorced. Doesn't that tell you something?'

'What?'

'It tells me that here is a person who has also failed at the most important relationship in her life, and now she is profiteering off a bunch of 'losers' who need to be told to stand up straight and act like men and not mice, based on her expert knowledge of what it takes to be rich and successful in six easy steps.'

Parker stared at April in horror. 'She told me that you were using me,' he responded defiantly.

April felt her temper rising. 'Using you?' she spat.

'Yes, Lynette said that you were too immature to commit...'

'Oh, I'll just bet she did,' said April, her mouth drawn into a thin line. 'Parker, at my tender and immature age, even I can see that this Lynette person made a big play for you. And furthermore, if I stink so badly that you can't bear to be near me, well then don't. There's the door. Use it. And don't slam it on the way out, okay? I'm leaving here tomorrow and I don't need trouble with the landlord.'

Parker stared at her. He had never dreamed that his assertive behaviour could have such devastating effects. April stared back at him impassively, the only indication of her rage being a muscle jumping in her cheek, and her unusual pallor. She was quite white around her mouth.

'Are you serious?' whispered Parker unbelievingly.

'Very,' she snapped, glaring.

'Oh please, I'm sorry ... I didn't mean anything by it. I'll do anything. But please don't end it this way, I beg you.'

April was horrified to see tears begin to course down Parker's cheeks. Where she came from, men crying for anything except death were considered sissies. And here he was, sobbing. She felt nauseated by the display, and was disappointed that he would resort to the oldest trick in the book that women would use to get their way.

'Parker, stop snivelling for goodness' sake. You're the one who was so insulting, and now you're trying to make me feel guilty. Well it just won't work, so please leave with your dignity intact.'

To her horror, he threw himself at her feet, sobbing uncontrollably, his massive shoulders heaving as he gasped for breath. She jumped backwards and got behind her chair.

'Parker, stop it,' she said sharply, gripping the back of the chair. 'I can't deal with this. Please just leave. Go away.'

Parker disconsolately picked himself up from the floor, and sat back on his haunches, his huge fat hands covering his face as he struggled to get himself under control. April stared at his sausage-like fingers, and shuddered inwardly as she compared them mentally with the well-tapered long fingers of Jack. He stood up like a lumbering bear and turned around. April watched him wordlessly as he ambled towards the door.

Turning around at the door, he faced her, his tear-streaked face a cruel parody of his manhood. 'April, please…' he whispered. 'I can't live without you. If you send me away I'm going to kill myself.'

April stared at him wordlessly, her natural compassion rising above her anger and indignation. 'All right, Parker, you win. We'll discuss this tomorrow morning after we've both calmed down. Will you still be in town tomorrow?'

'Yes, I've got a breakfast appointment with Lynette to discuss some issues that she would like to address.' His round face was now bright and filled with hope.

'Lynette is here?'

'Yes. We travelled together. Is there a problem?'

'No. Everything is just fine,' said April, suddenly bone weary after the long day. 'Then let's meet somewhere for lunch.'

'Here?' asked Parker hopefully.

'No. I've got a full day tomorrow, and I can't waste the time of driving all the way here. It will have to be at Luigi's in Riverways Estate. Say one o'clock?'

'It's a date,' replied Parker happily.

'No, it's not a date. It's an appointment where we will be doing some serious talking. I'll see you tomorrow.'

He lunged forward and caught April into his powerful arms, crushing her against his barrel chest, his lips seeking hers again frantically. She pushed him away with a strength that surprised even her.

‘Get out Parker! Now!’ she shouted, her chest heaving convulsively.

He closed the door softly behind him. April slipped the security chain onto the door as quickly as she could, her heart pounding with fright and revulsion at what had just transpired. She felt desperately tired and stumbled into the bedroom. Resolving to bath in the morning, she quickly got undressed, and pulled on her pyjamas that had seen too many summers, but were comfortable old friends. Within seconds, her eyes were closed, and she was fast asleep.

April was awakened by the insistent tones of her alarm clock. Dazed, she sat up in bed, unaware that she had even set her alarm. Its face registered 6 a.m. Feeling battered after the trauma of last night, she stood up slowly and walked into the bathroom to run her bath. Her lips still felt sore after the assertiveness ordeal with Parker. She walked through to the kitchen and switched on the kettle for a cup of strong coffee. April opened a cupboard door, and pulled out her packet of cigarettes that she always kept in her kitchen in case of an emergency. She lit the cigarette, and spooned the strong instant coffee into her largest cup. Uncharacteristically, she helped herself to two large spoons of sugar, then added the nearly boiling water. Splashing in some milk, she walked across the lounge and sat down for a few minutes to think. All of a sudden, there was a loud commotion from the corridor outside, and the unmistakable sound of someone falling.

‘Oh my God. I forgot the things from my handbag,’ said April, flying to her feet in her haste to help whoever had fallen because of her negligence. She threw open her front door, unmindful of the figure she presented in her short pyjamas, and gaped at the sprawling figure of her landlord in an ungainly heap, covered in roses and dripping water.

'Mr Sherwitz, are you hurt?' she asked concernedly, bending down to help the man to his feet.

'Only my dignity, my dear, and might I say that it was well worth it for the sight of you in those lovely little pyjamas.'

April dropped him unceremoniously as she ran inside to fetch a robe, seething with annoyance at his remark, yet relieved that no one was hurt. When she returned, he was on his hands and knees picking himself up off the floor. April lent over to help him and hoisted him to his feet. She hastily scrabbled around collecting the contents of her handbag that she had dropped the night before, and smiled with gratitude that some sweet little old lady hadn't fallen and broken her hip because of her forgetfulness.

'I'm afraid that I dropped your lovely roses. I'm sorry my dear.' Julius stared disconsolately at the shattered vase and the crushed flowers.

'Really, it was my fault for leaving that clutter in the corridor. I'm most dreadfully sorry,' said April, struggling not to laugh at the forlorn picture of Julius with a broken rose sticking out of his top pocket. He handed her the sopping wet envelope with the note.

'I put the flowers into water and in my best vase for you. I should have left them in the box, but I just wanted to make them look nice for you. My intentions were good.'

'Don't you know that the road to hell is paved with good intentions?' quipped April, determined to make light of the situation. 'And it was a very sweet gesture. Can I have the card please?' Tearing the sodden envelope open, April was not all that surprised to discover that she could not read a word of the note as the ink had run into illegible squiggles.

'What's that noise?' asked Julius.
'Hmmm?' responded April. 'Pardon, what did you say?'
'I said, what's that noise?' he repeated obligingly. 'Sounds like it's coming from your apartment.'
'Oh no ... the bath water!' shrieked April, flying into the apartment in her haste to reach the flooding bathroom. She groaned as she looked at the damage. The bath had filled, and the overflow pipe had been blocked, so the water spilled out onto the floor and was seeping into the carpet of her bedroom. She hastily pulled out the plug and switched the taps off.
'Oh dear, a bit of a mess, I see.' April whirled around. She had forgotten all about Julius Sherwitz.
'Oh Mr Sherwitz, I'm so sorry for this mess. I'll clean it up, I promise,' she wailed, forlornly.
'Nonsense, my dear. I am the landlord and it would never have happened if the overflow hadn't been blocked. I'll have it all sorted out by the time you come home this evening. Now I'll leave you to finish your morning ablutions in peace.'
April stared at his retreating back open-mouthed. She had never expected such understanding from a man like him, and she felt a little ashamed of herself that she had not seen his deeper nature earlier.
Giving herself up to the welcome lullaby of routine, April readied herself for work, thinking about the pending luncheon with Parker with trepidation. She had been horrified at his antics of last night, and had agreed to see him once more in a public place where he would feel too inhibited to make a scene. She was determined that the relationship would be ended today, for both of their sakes.

'Hello, Aneesa,' said April wearily as she walked into the office.

'Hi, I'm in here,' came the cheerful voice from her office. April walked in and stopped in amazement. There were no flowers this time, but there were hundreds of balloons, all different sizes and shapes.

'What on earth is going on? I just can't stand all this drama any more. Doesn't anyone in Durban just act normally?'

Aneesa shrugged her shoulders, mimicking April unconsciously. 'Nope. Sure doesn't look like it. Should I read you the card?'

'Please do,' said April wearily, pushing her way through the balloons to reach her desk.

'Ahem,' began Aneesa importantly as she cleared her throat. 'These tokens of my affection are to give your spirits a lift ... yours when you want me, Manilal.'

By the end of this recitation, both Aneesa and April were laughing uncontrollably. 'Oh goodness,' spluttered April amidst her laughter, 'he doesn't know about all his flowers having gone to the hospital yet. Boy, is he going to be mad.'

'I wonder what he will do?' said Aneesa, suddenly sober and concerned.

'Who cares?' said April. 'If he says one word, I'll just start redirecting his gifts to his wife. Right, same as last time, Aneesa, send all these over to the children's ward at the hospital.'

Aneesa busied herself sorting out the important matters of the day. The waiting room quickly filled with people and April lost all sense of herself as she delved into the problems of others. She glanced up with relief as Aneesa brought her a strong cup of coffee. 'That was the last client before lunch,' she announced. April glanced at her watch. She could hardly believe that it was nearly 1 p.m. Gathering her things together, she left and hurried down to the car.

* * *

The short journey to the restaurant was over all too quickly for April's liking, and she walked into the smoky ambience of Luigi's at exactly five past one. The brown tones of the restaurant were soothing and comfortable to her sensitive nature. The restaurant seemed to favour a Victorian theme with striped wallpaper adding to the intimacy of the room. There were no booths, and the open-plan nature of the restaurant suited her purpose today. She had no intention of being cloistered into a confined space with Parker if she could help it.

'Do you have a reservation, Mam?' came the cultured tone of the maître d' at her shoulder. She swung sharply around, startled in her present frame of mind.

'Er, no ... That is, I'm not sure,' she finished lamely. She had never even considered making a reservation. She cursed herself for this oversight.

'April. Over here.' She glanced towards the voice across a sea of heads, and saw Parker gesticulating wildly.

'It would appear that my luncheon partner made one, thank you,' she said. Winding her way agilely between the tables, she reached Parker at his place against the wall.

'I hope you don't mind, honey, but I ordered your favourite wine,' he said, pulling her chair out for her, and pecking her on the cheek. She noticed that there were several empty whisky glasses lined up in a row in front of him.

'Mmmmm. You smell really good.'

'For heaven's sake, Parker. You make me feel like a prime cut of meat that's cooked to your satisfaction. And you know that I can't possible drink wine in the middle of a working day. I have a hundred things to do this afternoon.'

'I thought you might have that problem, so I ordered you a soda water too, just in case,' he said, beaming proudly at her.

'My God, but you're so beautiful, April. I'd forgotten how lovely you can be.' He reached across the table towards her, and she quickly put her hands in her lap.

'Parker, please. This is not a social luncheon and we both know it,' she stated emphatically. 'We have to talk seriously about our future.'

'You know, this morning over breakfast, Lynette said that you were just acting out your newly discovered independence, and I really don't mind. Take as long as you like to come to terms with our marriage. I can wait.' He settled back in his chair and folded his arms smugly across his chest.

'Look, Parker, I don't need any of Lynette's pop psychology rammed down my throat. If you want psychology, I'll give it to you. You are rationalizing our problems away, and projecting your own desires onto me. Okay?'

Parker stared at her, taken aback by the quiet vehemence in her voice.

'Can I take your orders?' said the perky waitress. For the first time, April noticed the menus on the table. She was stunned to realize that she had no appetite whatsoever.

'Another soda water, pease,' she quickly said.

'And for you, sir?' the waitress asked, jutting her hips provocatively at Parker.

'I'll have snails in garlic as a starter followed by the roast pork with vegetables, please, and can I have an extra portion of chips?' He poured a generous glass of wine for himself as the waitress sashayed away, swinging her skinny hips almost ludicrously. April noticed that half the bottle of wine had already been drunk. Parker had never been one to hold his liquor, and was well on his way to oblivion.

'Are you driving back to Port Edward today?' she asked, as concerned for his well-being as she would have been for anyone. 'Yep. Straight after lunch. I've also got important things to do,' he said, grinning lopsidedly at her.

'Don't you think that you've had enough, Parker?' she said.

'One is never enough. Besides, I'm fine. Lynette and I had a marvellous champagne breakfast, so I'm just continuing the theme. That's all.' His voice had become louder as he spoke, and a few other patrons were turning around to see who was being so boorish.

'Sssh, Parker, people are staring,' April muttered frantically, embarrassed by the attention they were attracting.

'Let them stare,' he called out loudly. 'I'll give them something to stare at.' He jumped to his feet and emitted a loud bellow. 'There,' he said, falling back into his chair. 'That felt really good.'

'You are behaving like an absolute pig. I can't believe it. What the hell is the matter with you?' April hissed desperately.

'Nothing's the matter, love. Lynette told me that I was too inhibited, and that just isn't healthy for a man in my situation. She told me to "express myself" more.'

'Express yourself? For goodness' sake, this woman is positively dangerous. You're not supposed to express yourself in public. Right now, Mr Psychology Buff, you're doing nothing but behaving badly.'

'Don't you talk to me like that, you little bitch!' he shouted, rising to his feet again, and raising his hand to slap her across her face.

'I wouldn't do that, if I were you,' came a quiet voice from behind him. The man reached out and grabbed Parker's hand in mid-air.

'Jack!' exclaimed April, leaning backwards to get out of range of Parker's arm.

'Hey, let go of me,' shouted Parker, struggling to release

Jack's grip on his arm. In response, Jack deftly twisted his arm back and pushed his face forwards onto the table.

'Didn't your father teach you that you don't hit little girls,' he snarled. Parker struggled and squirmed to break free.

'Jack, please, let him go,' pleaded April, crimson with fury at the spectacle.

'Yes, let me go, you bastard,' said Parker, his voice muffled.

'Surely. But first, apologize to the lady.'

'Over my dead body,' Parker spat out.

'Suit yourself,' said Jack, calmly twisting Parker's arm a little further back.

'Ooww, okay, okay ... I'm sorry,' Parker gasped. Jack let him go so suddenly that he staggered and nearly fell. Turning around wildly he saw Jack standing behind him.

'You filthy Coolie, how dare you touch a white man.' He lunged out at Jack, who deftly ducked and landed a vicious jab to Parker's solar plexus.

'Mr Nathan, I'm so sorry for this lout's actions,' said the manager, bustling ever to their table. Parker lay groaning on the floor, clutching his stomach and gasping for air. Tears were streaming down April's face.

'Oh, Jack, I'm so humiliated,' she sobbed, falling back into her chair with her shoulders heaving. 'I just can't believe it. Oh, this is the worst day of my life,' she wailed.

'Here, Linden, this should take care of the damages that we've caused,' he said, pushing a wad of notes into the manager's hand.

'Mr Nathan, that's really not necessary, but thank you,' he said, sliding the notes into his pocket in a fluid movement.

'Come, April. You should select your dining partners more carefully in future,' he gently said, taking her elbow and helping her to her feet. Bending down, he said menacingly, 'Let this be a lesson to you, friend. Next time, you won't get off so lightly.' Parker just groaned in response, lying in the foetal position.

'Won't you get into trouble?' gasped April as Jack led her out of the restaurant under the inquisitive stares of the other patrons.

'Why should I get into trouble? Did knights get into trouble for slaying the dragons? Besides, I just over-reimbursed the manager for any damage caused. He'll be loathe to prosecute me, I can assure you, although I'm not so sure about your fiancé.'

April laughed despite her mortification. 'Hang on, how did you know that he was my fiancé?' she asked, suddenly puzzled.

'You don't strike me as the type of girl who dines with louts that try to hit you, so I just put two and two together and came up with four. Besides,' he continued, 'the whole restaurant was listening to your conversation, and it was obvious that he wasn't just a casual luncheon partner.' He smiled reassuringly at her. 'Here,' he said, reaching into his breast pocket, 'wipe your eyes and blow your nose.'

April stared at the silk handkerchief being held out to her. 'Oh, I couldn't,' she said, blushing.

'Come on, don't make me regret rescuing you, my dear,' he insisted, pressing the handkerchief into her hands.

'Thank you,' she murmured, gratefully accepting his offer. 'I feel like such a fool,' she said, her bottom lip quivering with shame at the memory of all those people's faces watching her.

'April,' Jack said firmly, stopping and turning April towards him, 'never regret throwing out a rotten egg. Okay?'

'Okay,' she sniffed, glad to have someone taking control for a while. Parker's accusations rang in her ears. She couldn't believe that she had misjudged him so badly. He had always appeared mild-mannered and pleasant, but then she had never had reason to provoke him before.

Jack led her to a sleek dark blue Mercedes and gallantly opened the door for her. 'Come along, get in,' he said.

'I can't just leave the car,' she began.

'I'm taking you to collect your own car at Government Garage, then you are going home, all right? I'll get one of my van drivers to collect the Honda and return it for you.'

'Yes,' April agreed meekly, dabbing at her eyes as a fresh batch of tears welled up at his kindness. Closing the door behind her trim heel, Jack Nathan smiled broadly and lifted his eyes to the heavens in thanks for this quite unexpected turn of events.

Settling down into the snug luxury of the leather upholstery, April pondered her good fortune that Jack had been there. She shuddered at the thought of what might have transpired had Parker been allowed to hit her unchecked. She nodded with grim satisfaction at how events turned out. She had been right all along in not being able to love him unconditionally. His vicious streak was quite an eye-opener.

'Are you still hungry?' asked Jack casually, whilst buckling up his seat belt.

'Pardon?' exclaimed April, startled out of her reverie.

'If you're still hungry, I know this great French restaurant at the top of the Port Rex Hotel overlooking the bay. I have a permanent table available to me any time I require one.'

April was surprised to realize that her appetite had indeed returned with a vengeance. 'Well, I really should be getting back to the office,' she replied, unconvincingly.

'Call them and say that you're taking the afternoon off,' he replied, handing her the car phone. April barely contained her gasp. Never in her life had she seen a car phone. Jack noticed her expression and smiled. 'I have connections in the post office,' he explained.

'Connections?'

'Yes. I did someone there a great favour some time ago, and seeing that he is aware of my weakness for gadgets, he presented me with this car phone as a gift. It's actually from America and not at all legal yet in this country. But he pulled some strings along the way.' April remembered a news item quite recently about the Minister of Posts and Telecommunications having done an extensive fact-finding tour of the States, but then dismissed the thought from her mind because it just couldn't be the same man. Reaching for the phone, she quickly dialled the office and told Aneesa of her plans.

'Enjoy, enjoy,' Aneesa cheerfully replied, 'and don't worry about a thing. I'll postpone your appointments to tomorrow. 'Bye.' The line clicked as Aneesa replaced the receiver.

April could hardly feel the motion of the car as it hummed along the roadway alongside the sea. The air inside the car was ice-cold on her flustered cheeks.

'What were you doing at Luigi's today?' she enquired.

'I had an early luncheon meeting with a customer that needed some gentle persuasion, and as we were leaving, I noticed your little problem with your "gentleman" friend.' He placed a subtle emphasis on the word 'gentleman'.

'But then you've already eaten?' said April despairingly. 'You can't sit and watch me eat.'

'Why not?' he asked lightly.

'Well ... because ... I'd feel silly, that's why,' she said weakly.

'The good news is that I only had a salad because my customer was a vegetarian, and I'm a meat and potatoes kind of guy, so I guess that this offer to take you to lunch is purely selfish based upon the aversion that I have to eating alone, and my rumbling stomach.'

The car filled with April's laughter. 'My idea of a perfect date is dinner and dancing without the dancing,' she laughingly related.

'Now isn't that a coincidence. Mine too,' said Jack, smiling broadly.

He parked the car expertly in a space that April would not have attempted with a Mini, let alone a Mercedes. 'Power steering,' he admitted, patting the steering wheel as he noticed her expression. They drew many curious stares as they walked across the parking area towards the lift doors. April and Jack were a striking couple. They were both dressed in light grey suits, almost as though there had been a conspiracy of the fashion gods that morning. Her long legs matched his strides as they neared the building. 'We look like twins, except for a few glaring differences,' he joked.

'Yes, isn't it strange?' she agreed. They were both silent as they took the lift up to the thirtieth floor. As the doors opened, April's sensitive nose was regaled with a barrage of subtle cooking aromas. They walked into a plush foyer carpeted with rich burgundy velvet floor and wall finishes. The blue sea sparkled far below through the floor-length picture windows. Soft instrumental music was coming from behind two solid-looking swing doors.

'This way,' said Jack, taking her by the elbow and leading her towards the entrance.

The ambience of the restaurant was overwhelmingly opulent. April bit her lip in her effort not to exclaim out loud at the beauty and symmetry that lay before her. 'Monsieur Nathan, 'ow good it is to see you again. It 'as been too long,' said the Maître d', bustling over to them where they stood framed in the doorway.

'Bonjour, Pierre. Yes, it has been a long time. Tell me,

do you have a table for myself and the lady without a reservation?'

'Monsieur Nathan, you never need a reservation. You should know that after what you did for me and my Michelle,' Pierre replied, his eyebrows lifting comically as his eyes widened with each word. April had never seen such a funny little man before. He was very short, and even his dinner suit and bow-tie failed to give him the status that he so obviously craved. His black hair was slicked down and parted in the dead centre of his round head, his thin pencil moustache giving more the impression of a gangster from an old film, than suave sophistication. 'Come, come, thees way,' he said as he led them to a private table at the window.

'Oh, this table is reserved,' said April in dismay, noticing the card propped up against the vase.

'But of course it is reserved, ma petite,' said Pierre incredulously. 'Look a leetle closer.' April peered at the card.

'Reserved permanently for Monsieur Jack Nathan,' she read. Jack pulled out a high-backed crushed velvet blue chair for April.

'Sit down and relax,' he said, pushing the chair deftly beneath her as she sat down.

'Monsieur, I have the perfect wine for you. Ah, unfortunately it does not come from France, but nevertheless, it is magnifique,' he said, kissing his fingers in a typical Gallic gesture.

'Please bring it to the table, Pierre,' said Jack. 'Now, April, could I make a few recommendations? Are there any particular foods that you don't appreciate?'

'Snails and pork?' replied April immediately. 'Seeing that the entire menu is in French, perhaps you could order for me?'

'It would be my pleasure. Pierre, please bring us two of my usual order please,' he commanded effortlessly.

Pierre hurried off to the kitchen to start organizing the meal. Almost instantaneously the bottle of promised wine arrived in an ice bucket at the table. The wine waiter proceeded to pour a minute helping into Jack's glass. He nodded, sipped the wine and slowly swallowed it.

'Excellent, please pour,' he said. April's glass was filled to the brim with the golden white wine, its fruity fragrance pervading the atmosphere.

'A toast,' Jack said as her glass was filled. 'To a brave lady and new beginnings,' he said, raising his glass and staring meaningfully into April's eyes.

'To a dragon-slayer, and new beginnings,' she replied enigmatically, clinking her crystal glass against his.

Pierre placed an aromatic seafood platter on the table for the two of them. April's eyes widened in delight. She adored seafood most of all. 'I thought ze platter would be better for you this afternoon,' said Pierre, winking at Jack.

'You're absolutely right as usual, Pierre,' said Jack. 'April, help yourself.' April leaned back in her chair.

'I'm full by just looking at this huge thing,' she laughingly replied. 'But hey, if I can't conquer a little seafood, then I won't be able to look myself in the eye any more.' Leaning forward, she helped herself with gusto. Jack laughed at her obvious enjoyment.

'You know, that's the first time that I've heard you laugh,' said April seriously. 'You should do it more often.'

'I'm afraid that I am a very serious man who seldom finds himself in situations worth laughing about,' he replied soberly.

'I'm sorry. Would you like to talk about it?' asked April, her natural instinct for wanting to help troubled people coming to the fore.

'Today you are my dinner guest, not my analyst,' he gently replied. 'Now, how do you like the platter?' he asked, deftly changing the subject.

'It's wonderful,' replied April sincerely. She had never tasted such juicy succulent prawns before.

'Shouldn't you be getting back to your office, Jack?' she asked concernedly, catching sight of the time on the grandfather clock, whose pendulum swung ponderously in its casing of glass and mahogany.

'I have plenty of time, don't worry. Just eat and enjoy at your leisure,' he responded.

'I'll be living very close to this spot by the weekend,' said April conversationally.

'Oh?' he replied noncommittally.

'Yes, I'm moving in to Ocean Vista townhouses. You know, those duplexes that are opposite Bluff Bay Beach?'

'Yes, I think I know where you mean,' he said, appearing quite disinterested.

'They're very private, you know,' she continued, not even sure why she was regaling him with these details. 'Each duplex is staggered slightly sideways so that you can't overlook your neighbour's garden or front door.'

'I see,' he replied, intent on crushing the claws of his crayfish.

'I can even have pets,' she ended lamely, a little deflated by his obvious lack of interest in her movements.

'Are you an animal lover?' he asked her, looking up at last. He appeared quite taken aback.

'Oh yes, I'm crazy about all sorts of animals. Except snakes,' she hastily added. 'I hate snakes. They paralyse me with fear.'

'I should imagine most people detest the creatures,' he responded.

'I shall get a dog and a cat when I move in,' she declared emphatically.

'On the same day?' he asked, his left eyebrow raised in mock surprise.

'Perhaps,' she airily replied. They continued eating their

meal in a companionable silence. April noticed that he was left-handed, and recalled that it had been his left jab that dealt Parker the crippling blow to the solar plexus. She giggled aloud at the memory of what had transpired earlier.

'Do I amuse you?' asked Jack, looking up at her from under his eyebrows.

'Actually, you do a little,' she replied. 'I was remembering how you floored Parker without even wrinkling your suit. The look on his face was quite something, I'll tell you.'

'April, I hope that you do not think that I go around hitting people all the time,' he said seriously. The grin faded from April's face.

'I know that, Jack,' she replied softly. 'You don't strike me as a physical man at all. More cerebral I should think. You outsmart your opponents with your intellect, don't you?' she replied, surprised at her own intuition.

'How perspicacious of you,' he said, taking a little bow in her direction. 'But seriously, April, I only stepped in because he was about to strike a woman, and my code doesn't permit that at all.'

'So you would have done the same for a stranger?' she asked, inexplicably deflated. It had been flattering to think that she alone had evoked such a protective element in this man's nature.

'It wasn't a stranger. It was you,' he replied diplomatically, his eyes sparkling as he smiled warmly at her. April felt a flush begin to suffuse her face with heat. She quickly turned away to the window, hoping he wouldn't see the effect he was having on her.

'This view is magnificent,' she desperately enthused, gazing at a passing container ship that was ploughing a snowy wake in the azure blue ocean.

'Yes, this view is magnificent,' he agreed, looking at the

arch of her neck as she struggled to bring her blush under control.

'Ees everything to your satisfaction, Monsieur Nathan?' asked Pierre, hovering at their table like an expectant father penguin. April glanced down at her plate, pleased for the respite.

'Delicious, Pierre. I do believe we're ready for the main course now?' Jack said enquiringly, looking towards April.

'Er, yes ... yes, thank you, it was delicious. But I feel so full, I honestly don't know if I'll manage another mouthful.'

'Ooo, but mademoiselle must not say that. I bring for you now the speciality of the 'ouse. I 'ave prepared it myself. Delicious Kingklip fish in a lemon butter and almond cream sauce stuffed with mushrooms. I would be devastated if you would not eat it.'

April laughed at Pierre's mournful expression. 'Oh, Pierre, I would hate to be responsible for your devastation. Please, bring me your speciality before my mouth runs to the kitchen in search of it.' Pierre's face lit up like a Christmas tree on Christmas Eve, and he scurried off to do her bidding.

'What a quaint little man,' she remarked casually to Jack.

'Don't underestimate that quaint little man, April,' he replied. 'He's a tough-minded little businessman beneath all the bowing and scraping. He owns this whole hotel, you know.'

'What?' replied April incredulously. She could not see Pierre in the role of rich tycoon at all. 'So why does he serve in the restaurant, for goodness' sake?' she asked.

'Like most truly wealthy men, he's a little eccentric. And you should see how agitated he gets when someone doesn't tip him. It's quite funny.'

'He doesn't need tips if he owns the Port Rex Hotel lock, stock and barrel,' said April. 'I may not have been in town long, but I've heard that this is the most exclusive hotel on the Natal coast, and that overseas tourists do their bookings months in advance.'

'That's true, and you can thank Pierre for the high standards. He snatched this deal away from underneath that shark Hussein's nose, and it was a happy day indeed for this town when that happened.'

'I hope Pierre's insured against arson,' said April thoughtfully, thinking of Aneesa's tearful face.

'I see that you have heard about the darker side of our illustrious leader,' said Jack, the dislike on his face twisting it into an uncharacteristic hardness. 'April, if I ever only give you one piece of advice, let it be this.' He lent forward and gripped her hand painfully in his enthusiasm. She struggled not to wince because she found herself wanting to be touched recklessly and intimately by this man. Shivers of sexual excitement ran up and down her body. 'Don't go near Hussein – not for any reason at all. He is to be avoided like a contagious terminal disease. Do you understand?' His eyes burned into her in their intensity. 'Promise me!' he demanded.

'I promise,' she whispered, a little afraid of the intensity of this man's passions. The woman that he loved would know that she was loved completely, she found herself thinking.

'Pardon, excuse me but the plate ees very 'ot,' said Pierre, putting down April's dish with a clatter. Jack quickly released her hand and leaned backwards in his chair, tilting it slightly. He dug his thumbs into the slit pockets of his silk waistcoat and regarded April with a level stare.

'Bon appetit,' trilled Pierre as he left them. Watching him, April had great difficulty in believing that this man was anything else but a waiter with a bad haircut. He looked like a crab rushing from table to table on his way to the kitchen.

'Bon appetit,' repeated Jack. April looked at his grim face, and nodded. This was one man whom she did not want for an enemy at any stage in her life. She sensed his barely controlled power, and had observed the effect that he had on people in all walks of life.

''ere is yours, Monsieur Nathan. Bon appetit,' Pierre said, placing Jack's meal in front of him more gently than he had done for April.

'Merci, Pierre,' he responded absentmindedly.

'Isn't the Port Rex a white concern?' asked April curiously. 'I mean isn't there some silly rule that says only whites can buy the land in white areas?' she ended lamely, hoping that she had not embarrassed Jack by her comments.

'Ah, yes, the famous Group Areas Act and the White Settlement Land Act,' he said between mouthfuls. 'April, there are more so-called non-whites owning important properties because they simply get a white man to front the concern for them. There are loopholes in every system.'

'Oh,' said April, feeling very naive. She had never really given much thought to these issues till now.

'Eat your fish and enjoy the atmosphere. It's not every day that a girl nearly gets assaulted in public,' he gently teased her.

'No problem,' she said, grinning as she tucked into Pierre's speciality, nodding as her tastebuds applauded his culinary skills.

'Pierre, can I have the bill please? I'm in a bit of a hurry to get back to the office,' said Jack, standing impatiently at the counter.

'What bill?' asked Pierre innocently. 'There is no bill.'

'I'm serious, Pierre, come along please.'

'Mon ami, I too am serious. It is on the 'ouse today because this ees ze first time that you bring such a beautiful lady to my 'umble establishment. I grow so weary of all the fat lazy businessmen that are usually your dinner partners.' He sighed and shrugged his shoulders dramatically, and April laughed as she noticed that it was Jack's turn to be embarrassed.

'Pierre talks too much,' he finally said as they were in the Mercedes driving towards Government Garage. 'Take no notice of what he says. He's just a Continental flatterer.'

'Oh, I have every intention of taking him seriously, Jack. I like what he has to say.' Just then, Jack pulled to a halt in front of Government Garage.

'Well, April, it was really delightful. We must do it again some time.'

'Jack, thank you for today. You restored my faith in human nature, and the food was *great*.' He laughed as she rolled her eyes heavenwards to underline her point. 'Well, thanks again. I'll be seeing you, goodbye.' She quickly leaned over and kissed him gently on the cheek, then she jumped out of the car and bounded laughingly away. Jack put his hand on the place where her lips had brushed his cheek, and smiled knowingly to himself. In his rear-view mirror, he watched her turn and watch him as he drove from sight.

# *Chapter Six*

The early morning rays of sweet sunlight brought out the red lights that danced in April's hair as she stood knocking insistently on Julius Scherwitz's door. Behind her, the same sunbeams picked up the dust motes that hung in suspended animation in the air. The high polished finish of the decorative parquet flooring gleamed as it embraced the warmth of the day's first rays.

'I'm coming, I'm coming,' grumbled a sleep-filled voice from inside the apartment. 'Yes,' he snarled as he flung the door open. Catching sight of April's apologetic face, his voice immediately became contrite.

'Oh, good morning my dear, it's you. Come in, come in why don't you.' He opened his door wider to let her in.

'Hello, Mr Sherwitz,' she said. 'I'm terribly sorry. Did I wake you?'

'No, no, of course not,' he lied unconvincingly yet gallantly, rubbing his eyes sleepily like a small boy.

April entered his apartment curiously. The air smelt musty and old, as though his windows were never opened. The furnishings were identical to those in her apartment, and the impression was one of zero individuality.

'Coffee?' enquired Julius, eagerly walking towards his kitchenette.

'No thanks, really,' she hastily interjected, anxious to get out of the cloying atmosphere as quickly as possible 'Again, I'm really sorry about coming in so early, but I have to be at the office by seven this morning.'

'Please don't apologize my dear,' he enthused, 'I wish that I could be greeted every morning by a fresh young nubile beauty such as yourself.' His little pig eyes travelled suggestively up and down April's body.

'Yes, well … I've come to tell you that I'm giving you twenty-four hours' notice according to your specifications,' she snapped, her prior resolve to be gentle dissolving rapidly.

'Why?' he cried piteously, wringing his hands together dramatically. 'Didn't I clean up your bathroom satisfactorily?' he whined.

'You cleaned it up beautifully, Mr Sherwitz. It's just that I've decided to move into a bigger apartment that I can furnish myself, so here is all the rent that I owe you,' she said handing him an envelope and walking towards the door.

'Not even a goodbye kiss?' he asked hopefully.

'I'm afraid that I'm not in the habit of kissing landlords, Mr Sherwitz,' she deftly replied, slipping fluidly out of the door.

'Goodbye, and good luck,' he said, watching her retreating figure with sincere affection.

'Goodbye, I'll be leaving first thing tomorrow morning,' she called back over her shoulder as she hastened outside to her car.

Aneesa was astonished to see April hard at work when she arrived at 7.30.

'Goodness, but you're early today,' she said.

'Hi,' said April, looking up from her report writing. 'I have to do so much today because I'm moving into the new townhouse tomorrow, and I still have to go out and buy furniture.' She groaned and rolled her eyes heavenwards at the thought of the daunting day ahead of her.

'Do you want me to reschedule your afternoon appointments for Monday?' Aneesa asked, ever mindful of her superior's comfort.

'No, no, I already took yesterday afternoon off. It's pay-back time,' April replied, losing herself in her work again.

'Where do you intend to shop?' asked Aneesa.

April looked up from her work again, a worried crease wrinkling her brow. 'Gosh, I never really thought about it,' she replied thoughtfully. 'I guess I just intended to rush from shop to shop in Main Street and hope that I got everything.'

'No, no. You're a very unprofessional shopper,' said Aneesa, shaking her head disapprovingly at the haphazard plan April had formulated. 'I'll tell you how to do it efficiently, speedily yet thoroughly,' she said firmly.

April laughed at Aneesa's adamant expression. 'You sound like a shopper's home guide commercial.'

'You have to select a place that is one-stop shopping,' Aneesa continued, warming to her theme. 'The parking has to be right and they have to be reputable and ensure delivery early on Saturday morning.' Suddenly, her face lit up. 'Leave it to me,' she said, delighted with her own thoughts.

'Okay,' said April, 'but you can't choose my things yourself you know. That would spoil all of my fun.'

'I'm not going to spoil anything,' Aneesa replied indignantly. 'I'm just going to arrange a few things. When will you be leaving the office?'

'I intend leaving at 3 p.m.,' April replied. 'Why? Is it a problem?'

'No problem,' replied Aneesa. 'In fact, it's perfect.' She swung on her heel, her long plait whirling in the air at her sudden movement.

Smiling to herself, April settled down and continued writing quickly.

* * *

'Lunch time,' said Aneesa, standing in the doorway to April's office.

'Not for me, it isn't,' she replied. 'I'm working right through, remember?'

'Right. Oh, by the way, I've set up your shopping. Would you like your itinerary?'

'Fire away,' replied April, marvelling afresh at her secretary's ingenuity.

'Have you heard of Seacres shopping centre?'

'Of course. It's practically the biggest shopping centre on the continent of Africa,' she replied.

'I don't know about that, but I do know that it's got every shop that you could possibly need. I've phoned the furniture manager of Green Bazaars to help you find all your furniture in an hour, and then you're expected at 4.15 p.m. at Pots And Pans And Things to buy everything that you could possibly need in a kitchen. They'll deliver too, as a special favour. You can spend thirty minutes there. Then Michael from Designer Fabrics is expecting you to come and choose your ready-made curtains. Do you know how many windows you have?' she asked April.

April was staring at her open-mouthed. 'My God, you've thought of everything,' she whispered reverently.

'Do you know your window sizes?' asked Aneesa impatiently. 'If not, I'll go and measure up for you quickly.'

'No, that's okay,' April replied, a little giddy from being dazzled by all this efficiency. 'I remember how many and I'll be able to judge the sizes when I see the curtains in the shop.'

'Good,' said Aneesa, consulting her list. 'After you've been to the curtaining shop, right next door, you'll find a boutique that specializes in linen. I've told Vera to expect you just after 5 p.m. to select your sheets and bedding goodies.' April was feeling a little flustered and pressurized by all that she still had to do.

'Then you'll have to go to Georgio's delicatessen,' said Aneesa firmly.

'Georgio's?' repeated April.

'Yes. You will need groceries won't you? Or are you planning on not eating?'

'But isn't a supermarket a better idea?' asked April.

'Trust me, Georgio's is cheaper, and you get real quality for your money. He also treats his customers like they're royalty. And, he's promised me that as a special favour, he'll deliver your whole order tomorrow morning to the townhouse.'

'Aneesa, you're a priceless gem and I love you dearly for it,' said April, rushing around her desk and hugging her secretary.

For the rest of the day, April concentrated furiously on her work.

Her telephone rang shrilly, startling her in her concentration. 'Jack Nathan on line one for you,' said Aneesa's voice sweetly over the phone.

'Hello,' said April, her voice shaking a little.

'Good afternoon, Miss Ross.' His deep tones set her skin tingling, and the fine hairs on her arm rose. 'How are you today?'

'Fine thank you, and you?' she politely replied.

'Very well, thank you. As you know, I'm also the Chairman of the Natal Welfare Committee, and I thought that you may not yet have had the opportunity to read the file and acquaint yourself with your duties.' His tone was brisk and businesslike.

She felt a lump forming in her throat, and swallowed hard to keep the tremble out of her voice. 'Actually, I have read the file,' she replied, her voice as cool as she could make it.

'Good,' he replied. 'Then you know how to set up a meeting for two weeks' time.'

'Yes. I have the list of all the representatives to invite,' she replied, trying to match his efficient tone.

'Don't forget Professor Dullabh from Port Edward.'

'If he's on the list, then I won't forget him,' she snapped, annoyed at his assumption that she was incapable of reading an address list.

'I doubt if Yusef put him on the list,' he calmly replied, apparently unmindful of her ill temper. 'Just check quickly and see.'

'Just a moment,' muttered April, placing the receiver on her desk with a purposefully loud clatter. She smiled as she thought of how it must have made him wince. She quickly checked through the filing cabinet and found the file. Paging to the relevant section, she scanned the page. Then she read it a second time more slowly. Professor Dullabh's name appeared nowhere. Slightly abashed, she sheepishly returned to the telephone.

'I'm dreadfully sorry, but you were right,' she haltingly admitted. 'Yusef didn't write his name down after all.'

'Fine, his address is PO Box 13007, Port Edward,' he supplied.

'He must get teased a great deal about the 007 part of his address,' said April softly, concentrating as she wrote it down. To her surprise, Jack burst out laughing.

'You know, you're absolutely right,' he said. 'I never made the connection before. I realized that the number looked familiar, but until now, I just didn't think why that was. When you see him, you'll realize why it is so ludicrous for him to have such a powerful number.' Jack chuckled to himself.

April found her body relaxing as she listened to his

mirth. Impulsively, she said, 'Jack, I'd like to thank you properly for rescuing me and feeding me yesterday. Would you like to have dinner with me at my new townhouse tomorrow night?'

Almost as soon as the words were across her lips, she regretted having issued the invitation. It sounded so brazen, even to her own ears.

'New townhouse? Oh yes, of course, I'd quite forgotten.' So much for worrying about my movements she thought, peevishly.

'Have you applied for a telephone yet?' he asked.

'Uh ... no,' she replied, startled by the unexpected question.

'Then that will be my house-warming gift to you. When are you contemplating moving in?'

'Tomorrow,' she replied.

'Perfect. The technicians will be there at 8 a.m. sharp to install your phone.'

'But that's impossible,' she squealed, 'the waiting period is at least a month.'

'Not for me it isn't,' he mysteriously replied. 'What time?'

'What time what?' she said, uncomprehendingly.

'What time would you like me for dinner?'

'Oh,' she said, feeling foolish. This man always seemed to have her at sixes and sevens. 'Is seven o'clock all right for you?' she asked, recovering rapidly.

'Perfect. See you then. I'll bring the wine. What is the address?'

'Number one, Sea Vista, Ocean View Drive, Bluff Bay Beach.'

'Right. Got it. Thank you. See you tomorrow night. Goodbye.'

The phone clicked in April's ear. 'Goodbye,' she softly murmured into the lifeless mouthpiece, and replaced the receiver gently.

'Oh my God!' she shouted, as the thought struck her. 'What on earth am I going to cook?'

'Seeing that he's Hindu, I'd suggest seafood or lamb,' said Aneesa from her office. April blushed as she realized that Aneesa had heard the entire conversation.

'Thank you,' she remembered to say.

April entered Green Bazaars eyeing the range of furniture that lay before her.

'Miss Ross?' enquired a tall thin man with spectacles. His bright green jacket was a beacon in the subtle tones of a sea of furniture.

'Yes,' she replied.

'How do you do. I'm Graham Noble, the furniture manager. Mrs Abdullah phoned and told me to expect you. I must say that the description hardly did you justice.'

'Thank you,' April responded, unsure of how to reply wittily. She was too down-to-earth to indulge in word games with strangers.

'I believe that you'll be requiring a lounge suite, dining room suite and a bedroom suite?'

'Yes, that's right,' she said.

'I've got the perfect items if you'll just follow me,' he said, turning on his thin heels and striding away. From behind, he looked just like the pictures of Ichabod Crane that she had seen in a children's story book.

When he stopped in front of a deep blue lounge suite, April gasped.

'It's absolutely wonderful,' she said, picturing it in her lounge.

He pointed to a light wooden dining room table, its high-backed chairs upholstered with the same fabric as the lounge suite. April nodded in mute agreement.

'And for your bedroom. I believe that this will do,' he

continued, walking her over to a four-poster bed framed by billowing grey chiffon hangings.

'Finally, might I suggest this exquisite Cheval mirror instead of the ordinary dressing table?'

April stared at herself framed in the floor-length oval mirror, its oaken tones blending in with the bed and the tables.

'Mr Noble, I'll take it all,' she said decisively.

'Are you sure that you don't want to look at anything else?' he asked, a little surprised by the determination in her voice.

'No, and could it please be delivered first thing tomorrow morning? I'm having company for dinner.'

'What about a stove and all the usual kitchen equipment?' he asked, determined to press his advantage. 'Fortunately, everything is all built in, but I would like a television set and a music centre.'

'Certainly, walk this way,' he said. April obediently followed him to the technotronics department and chose them.

'Now you'll need a cabinet to place these items in. We have one that will match the wood of your dining room suite.'

'Perfect,' replied April.

He shook her hand. 'This way for the paperwork.'

Glancing at her watch, April smiled in self-satisfaction. She was well ahead of Aneesa's rigorous schedule. She walked smiling into Pots And Pans And Things, jammed with racks of everything one could possibly use in a kitchen. A bell echoed in the back of the shop.

'Be with you in a jiffy,' said a muffled voice from behind one of the shelves. April looked around curiously.

'Drat all the dirt. Hello darling, can I help you?' The high-pitched effeminate tones and mannerisms that were emitted by the man walking towards her were positively mind-boggling. The man patted his head of well-styled blond hair self-consciously.

'Er … hello,' said April, recovering. 'I believe that you're expecting me? I'm April Ross.'

'Ooh you little beauty. Naughty Aneesa for not telling me how stunning you are, darling. Now tell David the secret of your beauty regime. I can't bear being so butch, you know.' April stared at David open-mouthed. She had never seen a man look less butch. His flowing dramatic purple and red batik kaftan did little to add to his delusion of overwhelming manliness.

Struggling not to laugh, April seriously replied, 'Soap and warm water, morning and night?'

'No,' he squealed, throwing his hands up, and bringing them to rest on his narrow hips. 'Darling, you should never bombard your wonderful complexion with the poisons found in soap. Anything that tastes so bad must be simply disgusting for you.'

'Tastes so bad?' she asked, her eyebrows lifting in puzzlement.

'Why yes, I always taste my facial products before I buy them,' he replied. 'That way, I know that little bunnies didn't die for my vanity. If I don't keel over poisoned, and if the product tastes good, then I buy,' he finished proudly.

'I see. Well, I guess that I never thought of it that way before,' she politely replied, seeing how earnest he was.

'Oh darling, I hope that a wonderful creature like you supports the Beauty without Cruelty campaign, and saves the whales and the seals and dolphins?'

'I certainly always buy products that are labelled Beauty Without cruelty,' she replied hesitantly.

'Good. A Bunnyhugger after my own heart. Now let's shop until we drop, okay?' He marched her over to the dinner services. 'Aneesa told me you were very partial to blue, darling.'

April's eye was caught by a deep blue set.

'That's rather lovely,' she said, pointing.

'Rather lovely? It's absolutely divine, my angel. What simply divine taste you have.' David's voice grew more high-pitched as his excitement increased. 'And I insist that you take this coffee service as a gift from me,' he said, firmly pushing a box into April's hands.

'But I couldn't,' she replied, staggering at the unexpected heaviness.

'You can and you must. I insist. Aneesa is a wonderful friend, and any friend of hers is a friend of mind. Take it. It's the same as your dinner service. Now let's choose your pots and pans.'

Before long, David had piled up boxes full of everything that April would ever need in a kitchen.

'Do you have a coffee percolator?' David asked, breathless after his exertions.

'No, I don't. Just an ordinary kettle.'

'Don't lie,' squealed David, a horrified expression on his face. 'Do you mean to tell me that you serve your guests that instant poison?'

'Er … yes … I guess so,' she replied.

'Well, not any more, sugar lips. I'm scandalized you would do such an uncivilized thing. So here is a coffee percolator as a gift to go with the coffee service.'

'But that is ridiculously extravagant,' she replied. 'There will be no profit left over at all from my purchases.'

He smiled knowingly at her. 'You're breaking my heart,' he said light-heartedly, far from heartbroken. 'I'll deliver all these goodies myself tomorrow, darling.'

'Let me pay you, now,' she began.

'Not on your life,' he interrupted. 'What if I break everything in my haste to get to your front door? No, whatever isn't broken, you can pay for later.'

* * *

April was a little late reaching Michael's curtaining place. He was the exact opposite of David, looking as though he would be more comfortable treading the dusty Karoo farmlands chasing sheep. His dark brown curly hair was springier than April's soft curls. Deep blue eyes regarded her coolly from his suntanned and weather-lined face. As with most big men, his voice was surprisingly soft and high-pitched, but by no means feminine.

'Right. Let's get you sorted out for curtains.'

April, frowning at the strain of remembering everything clearly, stepped out what she estimated the width of her window to be, as Michael wrote everything down in small neat figures in his book.

'Right, now let's talk colour schemes,' he briskly said.

'Blue lounge, grey and yellow bedrooms and green bathroom,' supplied April.

He led her over to each colour-coded section of his large warehouse, and in no time at all she had selected soft pastel pin-stripe designs for all the rooms.

'Right, we'll deliver tomorrow and hang for you.'

'Thank you,' said April, exhausted by this whirl of activity.

When April reached into her handbag for her chequebook, Michael waved it away, accepted a 100-rand deposit, and insisted he would bill her for the rest over six months.

'That's what I do for all my customers.'

Shaking hands and leaving her address on a buying slip, April left.

After whirling breathlessly through Vera's boutique for her linen, Georgio's was a welcome gourmet's delight. His delicatessen was as large as a supermarket, but the atmosphere was decidedly Continental. April grasped a food trolley and started to comb the aisles.

Within no time at all, her trolley was bulging. A tall white-haired gentleman with a large white moustache and watery blue eyes came out of the manager's kiosk as she neared the till.

'Hello, I'm Georgio Hannowa,' he said in a loud booming voice with a strong Austrian accent. 'I have not before seen you in my humble shop. Welcome and I hope you shop here all the time.' Reaching out a surprisingly large hand, he grasped April's fingers and squeezed them with a bow of his head and a Prussian heel-clicking movement.

'Good afternoon, I'm April Ross,' she replied.

'Ah yes, Mrs Abdullah's friend. And how is she today? Such a tragic little woman, tsk tsk tsk,' he said, shaking his head mournfully.

'She's fine,' replied April, touched by this man's caring. 'She mentioned something about you assuring delivery of my first order?'

'Of course. You are the one who is moving in tomorrow. No, you could not leave your perishables in an empty house overnight without electricity.'

Suddenly, the realization hit April that she had not made the arrangements to have the electricity connected, and the relevant department would be closed over the weekend. Tears sprang unbidden to her eyes.

'Meidschen, what is wrong? Have I upset you?' asked Georgio, horrified at the effect that his words had had on her.

'I'm such an idiot,' she wailed, stamping her foot in anger at her own stupidity. 'I forgot to go down to the electricity department and have the lights connected. And I'm having a guest for dinner tomorrow night. I can't serve him raw food.'

'Don't worry, I fix,' he said, turning around and walking towards his office.

Scurrying after him, April said, sobbing, 'It's no use, they're closed already. There's nothing you can do.'

'That's what you think,' replied Georgio, picking up his telephone. 'What is the use of having brother that is hot-shot in municipality if he can't help out a friend?'

April collapsed into the well-worn chair that adorned Georgio's minute office. She watched him with bated breath as he bellowed in German down the receiver. Every human emotion imaginable flitted across his face over the next five minutes as his tone of voice see-sawed between threatening and cajoling. Wiping the perspiration from his brow, he violently replaced the telephone receiver with a barrage of unintelligible words that sounded distinctly vulgar.

'Well?' asked April, hesitantly.

'Oh, he'll do it, no problem,' replied Georgio. 'I was fighting with him about the horse races tomorrow.'

April burst out laughing and threw herself into the astonished old man's arms. 'Thank you, thank you,' she repeated, kissing him on both cheeks.

'Er ... yes, well, don't mention it,' he said gruffly, disentangling himself rapidly. 'My Frau Anna she is madly jealous,' he said, pointing with his chin towards a fat short lady with her plaits coiled regally above her leather-like brow. April followed his eyes. Anna sat operating the till like an automaton. April watched his features soften as he looked at the shrunken old woman. Clearly, he was seeing her as she had been when they married at age 18.

'Do you take cheques?' asked April, still a little gun-shy from her experience with Michael.

'Ja, ja, of course. Anna will tally it for you. Just remind her that yours is the special delivery okay?'

'Okay. And thank you again, Georgio. I'll never forget your kindness,' she said, leaving a heady fragrance of her perfume in her wake. Georgio's tired blue eyes twinkled as memories of Anna's firm young body came flooding back to him. Rapping sharply on the glass partition, he attracted Anna's attention and blew her a resounding kiss. She rewarded him with a tender smile and crimson cheeks.

April was awake and dressed long before dawn broke. She was checking the cupboards one last time to make sure that she had left nothing of herself behind. Satisfied that all her belongings were packed, she settled down with her cup of coffee, one of Georgio's delicious cheese croissants and her first cigarette of the day. She was anxious for the time to pass so that she could drive out to her new home. Her head jerked upwards as her doorbell chimed. Through the frosted glass, she made out the bulky figure of a man.

'Who is it?' she called, getting to her feet and walking carefully across the lounge.

'It's only me,' came a familiar voice.

'Parker.' Her heart leapt to her threat. She slid the security chain into place and opened the door a crack.

'What do you want?' she asked, sounding a lot braver than she was feeling.

'Can't I come in, April?' he wheedled. 'I don't feel like baring my soul in the presence of your neighbours.'

'No, you damn well can't come in. Now what do you want?'

'Firstly, I want to apologize for being such a boor at lunch the other day,' he began, 'and then I wanted to ask you to please forgive me. Let's go back to the way things were.'

April closed the door, and unlatched the chain. 'Come inside if you promise not to slug me,' she said.

'I said I was really sorry about that, April. It was unforgivable.'

'Yes, it was, Parker,' she replied icily. 'Please sit down.

I'll get you some coffee and we can talk like two civilized adults.'

She disappeared into the kitchen as he sat lumberingly down on the couch. Looking around, he noticed her suitcases and a few boxes on the floor near the bedroom.

'Going somewhere?' he casually asked, his face speculative.

'Yes, I'm moving,' she called from the kitchen.

'Really? Don't you know that you will be breaking the law sleeping with him?' he snarled unpleasantly.

April walked slowly out of the kitchen, her face a mask of white fury. 'I beg your pardon,' she said, deceptively quietly.

'Haven't you heard of the Immorality Act of 1949,' he said. 'It's against the law for you to sleep with blacks. That's where you're going, right? To move in with the black avenger who punched me in the restaurant? Oh, I saw the way you looked at him. I'm not blind, you know.'

'No, Parker, you're not blind, just incredibly stupid. Here's your coffee,' she said, turning the mug upside down in his lap.

Screaming as the hot liquid splashed over his genitals, Parker leaped to his feet, wiping his fly area with a cloth he had grabbed from a nearby table.

'And don't try to hit me this time, Parker, because if you lay a finger on me, I'll kill you, so help me God.'

Looking into April's fearless stony grey eyes, the coward in him reared its yellow head.

'Don't worry, I'm going, you cheap slut. I hope that you and your nigger lover rot in hell.'

'Get out!' she screamed, her self-control slipping.

'With pleasure,' he retorted, picking up his keys. At the door, he turned spitefully back to her, his eyes narrowing to slits in his fat face. Absently, a detached part of her registered that he had put on a great deal of weight over the last month. 'Your life will be hell, now,' he said viciously, 'because I'm going to report you and your filthy swine lover to the security police. They'll raid you in the middle of the night and humiliate you in public like you deserve.' He grinned, very pleased with his plan. April looked him straight in the eye, and spat in his face. He stumbled backwards, and she slammed the door. Turning around, she slid down the door, her legs unable to steady her much longer, her breath coming in sobs of disgust and anger. Her whole body began to shake uncontrollably as she kept hearing his evil words echoing through her mind.

Struggling to her feet, she wiped her left hand across her trembling lips, getting rid of the remnants of the spittle. Her engagement ring caught on her bottom lip. She regarded it in disgust and wrenched it painfully from her finger, ripping her skin in her haste. She did not even flinch, so great was her determination to get rid of the offensive object. Rushing over to the window, she saw Parker's head bobbing as he left the building.

'You forgot your disgusting thirty pieces of silver,' she shouted, tossing the ring up into the air. He looked up towards her, and she had the satisfaction of seeing the ring hit him squarely in the eye, before it bounced off him and went rolling into the gutter with a metallic clicking sound.

Parker got down on his knees to retrieve the ring. After all, diamonds were diamonds. He covered his sore eye with one hand as he frantically searched through the filth of the gutters with the other hand. April watched him, finally able to smile about the whole situation. He stood up, grasping the ring triumphantly between his fat little fingers.

'Go and give it to Lynette,' April called down cheekily from the security of her upper-storey window. Parker glowered at her, and stalked off to his car without even replying. Gathering the remainder of her dignity, April waved a cheery hello to the early morning milkman who had been watching the exchange with huge bulging white eyes in his full-moon shaped black face. Breaking into a little jigging dance step he grinned up at her and doffed his cap respectfully.

April stopped her little red car in front of her new apartment with a sense of wonderment. It was nearly 8 a.m. and the summer sun was shining directly into her eyes. Picking up a variety of boxes, she struggled to her front door, her key poised to unlock it.

'Mornin', lassie,' said Sam close behind her. She jumped and dropped the boxes in her fright. Her experience with Parker had frazzled her nerves.

'Easy now, or you'll 'ave me jumping out of my skin too,' Sam said, grabbing April's arm. He hastily bent down to pick up one box. It was then that April noticed the familiar white box in his other arm.

'What's that, Sam?' she asked, already knowing the answer.

'I believe they're flowers for you, luv, and they got 'ere bloomin' early too, if you'll pardon the pun,' he said, doubling over with laughter at his own joke.

April joined in his laughter and unlocked the door. Between the two of them they managed to drag everything into the townhouse.

'Cor, wot are you gonna do for furniture?' he asked, looking around at the empty interior.

'It's all on its way,' said April, feeling very grown up and independent all of a sudden.

'That's good, cos you can't show your flowers off with no vase and a table to put them on, 'ey?' Again, his cracked laugh rang out.

'Good morning, Mam, we're from the telephone department. Where would you like your phones?' April swung around to the open door.

'Good morning,' said April. 'What do you mean, phones? I thought I was getting one just like everybody else,' she asked perplexed.

'The boss said to install two jacks where you needed them, and more if you so required,' the sandy haired young man replied.

'Wow,' said Sam, truly impressed by the preferential treatment April was receiving.

'One in the lounge, and one in the bedroom and one for when you're on the throne,' he said chuckling.

April showed the technicians through and pointed to the wall where she wanted the telephone fixed. Then she led them upstairs and showed them where her bed would be positioned so that the phone could ring right next to it. Her doorbell chimed. Running lightly down the spiral staircase, she saw the big green truck parked outside her front door from Green Bazaars. Her furniture had arrived.

The next few hours were spent in a frenzy of activity for April and the many people that came and went delivering all her items. David even plugged her percolator in and made her a delicious cup of filter coffee, better than anything she had ever drunk in a restaurant.

Finally, when all the people had left, April sank down into her new rocking chair with a sigh of relief. The morning had sped by, but she was very satisfied with its results as she looked around her. The place still needed pictures for the walls, odd coffee tables and knick-knacks, but all that would come with time. She looked across, and saw the white box still lying on the floor. Guiltily, she got up and slowly opened it. The roses were still fresh, their fragrance gently assailing her heightened senses. She opened the note, keen to read her next cryptic message, regardless of who the sender was. She knew now that it was not someone who wished her any harm.

'Welcome Home,' she read aloud. That was all. As usual, the note was unsigned.

'Welcome home,' she repeated dreamily to herself. Very very appropriate.

She quickly placed the roses in a crystal vase, and put them on her dining room table. She walked indolently over to her couch and stared at her new telephone. They had even managed to find her a blue phone that blended in to her decor unobtrusively. She picked up the receiver and hastily dialled her parents' number in Cape Town.

Her father answered on the second ring. 'Hello, the Ross residence. Bill Ross speaking.' Her eyes filled with sentimental tears as a powerful wave of homesickness and nostalgia washed over her.

'Hello, Daddy, how are you?' she managed to say, the tremor in her voice all too apparent to her father.

'Hello, my darling,' he whooped joyously. 'Inge, quickly, it's April,' he called. 'How do you like it in Durban?' he asked.

'It's wonderful, Daddy. I have been treated like royalty.' April continued to regale her father with all her news, her mother chirping questions in the background.

'Daddy, I know how you despised Parker,' she said, a serious tone creeping into her voice.

'Yes?' he cautiously replied.

'Well, I hate to admit it, but you and Mommy were quite right. He was a big loser.'

'Was? Is he dead?' asked her father, unable to disguise the hope in his voice.

April laughed. 'Daddy, you should be ashamed of yourself,' she responded. 'No, he's not dead. We had a disagreement, and I gave him back his ring.' April was loath to describe what had transpired between her and Parker.

'Wahoo!' shouted her father, making April wince and pull the phone away from her ear. 'That's the best news I've had in my whole life.'

'What is? What is?' April could hear her mother calling peevishly in the background.

'Here, you tell your mother yourself, darling. I love you, look after yourself, all right? Here's Mom.'

'April, what's going on? Your father is dancing around like a Russian bear and he looks just silly.'

'I called off the engagement,' said April, stunned at the effect her news was having on her parents.

'Thank heavens,' said her mother, giving her husband a thumbs up sign and a big wink. 'I'll tell Daddy to put you back in the Will.'

'Mom!' said April, scandalized by her mother's statement.

'Don't worry, darling, I was only joking,' her mother replied.

April found herself telling her mother about her dinner guest, and held her breath, waiting for that so-familiar disapproving tone.

'Well, that's wonderful, darling,' replied her mother sincerely. 'Just don't burn the man's dinner.'

'Oh, Mom, don't be silly. You know that I can cook you right under the table at any time with both hands tied behind my back and one leg chopped off.'

The cooking issue was a long-standing friendly feud between mother and daughter, both being excellent cooks. April's father had grown very portly after years of rival cooking sessions between her and her mother. He was always asked to judge which one was best, and diplomatically always told April that she had won hands down. At night, lying in one another's arms, he would tell Inge that he just pandered to his daughter to encourage her, and that *she* was still the queen of his kitchen.

April told her mother about the scene that Parker had made at the restaurant, and how Jack had rescued her.

'The bastard! If I see that Parker again, I'll kill him with my bare hands.'

Having had first-hand experience of the stinging repercussions of Inge's German temper, April had no doubt that Parker would be well and truly fixed.

She gave her parents her new number, and wistfully replaced the receiver after a tearful goodbye from her mother. Pulling herself together, April ran into the kitchen and started preparing the dishes for the evening meal. It was still early afternoon, but it was her nature to have everything finished, including the washing of pots and pans, by the time that dinner came around.

# *Chapter Seven*

April glanced at herself one last time in the Cheval mirror, nodding approvingly at the result of her hasty grooming. She appeared almost swan-like in the light blue dress that hugged her body snugly, and flared out softly from her hips. The swell of her breasts was just discernible at the softly clinging V-shaped neckline. She wore no necklace, giving her throat clean and graceful lines. Her make-up was light and skilfully applied, giving her grey eyes a soft velvety depth. Swirling on her high heels, she spun around like a ballerina, laughing child-like at the way her dress flew up around her hips, showing off her long and well-shaped legs. Giving her curly hair one last pat, she walked slowly and regally down her spiral staircase, pleased at what she surveyed. She frowned thoughtfully as she thought of all the money that she paid over the past two days from her hard-earned salary earned waitressing over the past four years. April was like a pack rat with her money, and had scrupulously saved every penny for the eventuality of making her first home comfortable and stylish. She was startled out of her reverie by the chiming of her doorbell. Suddenly, butterflies of panic took flight in her stomach, and she raced into the kitchen for one last spot-check on the roast that was browning in the oven. Wiping her hands nervously on the back of her dress, she breathed deeply and opened the door.

'Good evening,' Jack said admiringly, smiling approvingly at the vision of ethereal beauty that April presented. Her heart leapt in her breast. His cream suit and blue silk shirt contrasted elegantly with his bronze skin.

They both laughed simultaneously as they realized that the blue of his shirt was identical to the blue of her dress. April felt all her anxieties about the evening melting away as she stood aside and bade him enter.

'As my first guest, welcome to my first real home,' she sweetly said, blushing slightly under his admiring scrutiny.

'I'm honoured to be your first guest,' he replied, struggling with two baskets that he was carrying.

'Here, let me help you,' offered April, taking the larger of the two baskets from him.

'That one goes into the kitchen,' he said, 'but this one stays with me for the time being,' he added mysteriously, striding into the lounge. He settled himself elegantly down on the rocking chair, placing the basket gingerly at his feet, and smiled enigmatically at her. Realizing that she was gaping at him, April snapped her mouth closed and took the basket into the kitchen. Inside was a very expensive bottle of champagne, well chilled, a paté of a yet unknown variety, a dozen tiger lilies, and a container of chocolate-covered strawberries. She deftly opened the champagne and poured them both a glass of the frothing golden liquid.

Throwing the tiger lilies hastily into a glass bowl, she placed the cargo on a tray and entered the lounge. Jack reared up guiltily from the mysterious basket placed so carefully at his feet, and smiled a little too widely. An inquisitive frown puckered April's brow as she handed him a glass of champagne. Putting the flowers down next to her roses on the dinner table, April turned towards him.

'Okay, why all the mystery surrounding that basket?' she enquired, her tone of voice much lighter than she had anticipated.

'I brought you a little house-warming present,' he replied. 'But now I'm not so sure that you will like it,' he added, a crestfallen note creeping into his voice.

'I'm sure that I will love whatever gift you've brought me,' she replied diplomatically, picturing some monstrosity of an ornament.

'Well, you will have to love this gift, or I will be forced to take it back,' he replied.

'Indian giver,' she retorted, and her eyes widening with the realization of what she had just said. As she opened her mouth to apologize, Jack's laugh boomed out, filling the room with his male presence.

'I have no intention of giving you a gift, and then taking it back. Western women are very witty,' he stated, chuckling on.

'Er yes ... sometimes,' April replied, suddenly aware again of all the differences between them, Parker's mocking voice filtering through into her consciousness.

'Well, the moment of truth has arrived,' said Jack seriously. 'Come and open your gift.'

April walked towards him and reached out to pick up the basket.

'No,' he said firmly, his arm snaking out to grasp her wrist. She could feel the power in his fingers as they pulsed warmly on her arm. She was well aware of the fact that he could quite easily hurt her, if he so desired.

'All right,' she replied, kneeling down on the floor at his feet, her released hand pulling at the red bow that tied the top of the wicker basket together. Putting down her glass of champagne, April applied herself solemnly to her task. She sat back on her haunches and looked up at Jack. She was surprised to see the soft light that had come into his eyes as he watched her. He was so close that she could feel the heat his body was generating. She smelt fresh soap and a woody fragrance surrounding him. She had noticed that his hair had been curling in damp tendrils in his neck when he arrived, and images of his naked body in a shower sprang unbidden into her mind.

He held her gaze unblinking and, as though he had read her mind, reached out a hand to tuck a tendril of her unruly hair back behind her ear. She shivered as the palm of his hand traced a trail of fire across her cool silken cheek, and her eyes closed in ecstasy.

The basket gave an unexpected lurch under her hands, and April leaped back with a scream of fright in her haste to get away. Jack leaped to his feet and helped her up from her unladylike sprawl.

'What the hell is it?' she shrieked, pushing his helping hands away from her. To her annoyance, she saw that he was struggling to keep a straight face as he sat down again. Turning herself onto her knees, quite aware of the undignified picture that she must present, she hastily clambered up and faced him belligerently.

'Thank you for scaring me to death,' she stated, her voice shaking indignantly as she glowered at him.

'So, the kitten has claws,' he replied, smiling broadly now at her obvious discomfort. 'Come on, kitten, open up your present.'

'Not on your life,' she replied, retreating to the safety of the other side of the room, visions of snakes and creepy crawlies ranging unchecked through her imagination.

'All right then, I will open it for you, but I must say that I am a little disappointed in your lack of faith,' he replied, watching her reaction under lowered eyelashes.

Rising to the bait, April walked defiantly back to him and flung open the top of the basket, staring him squarely in the eyes. A rustle from the basket drew her attention away from him as she peered apprehensively inside. Her face lit up with delight.

'Oh, he's beautiful, Jack! I adore him!' April carefully placed her hands inside and picked up the warm and sleepy ball of white fur that wriggled in her palms. It was love at first sight for her and the puppy. His tiny pink tongue stretched out as he yawned, and regarded her with sudden interest. Holding him against her breast and rocking him gently, April could feel the familiar tears of sentiment welling up inside her lids.

'Oh, Jack, thank you, thank you,' she whispered. 'How did you know?'

'I told you once before. I've made it my business to know all about you, April,' he replied softly, his hand again stroking her hair as she stroked the puppy in her arms.

'Business? What do you mean?' she enquired, fully alert for his reply.

With a sigh, he settled back into the rocking chair. 'April, you are placing me at a disadvantage if I answer you now,' he replied enigmatically.

'All right, after dinner then,' replied April, lost again in the wonder of her first pet that she would have to be 100 per cent responsible for.

Leaping to her feet and rushing to the kitchen, she rummaged through her cupboards to find a suitable water dish and food dish for the dog. Grabbing a carton of milk from the fridge, she poured him a generous helping and ladled Jack's paté into the other dish. The dog was soon snuffling in the bowls.

Satisfied that all his immediate needs had been met, April took the two chilled seafood cocktails from the fridge, and placed them on the dining room table. Lighting the two blue candles on either side of the flowers, April pulled a chair away from the head of the table and beckoned Jack closer. As he settled down, April remorsefully told him about the fate of the paté.

'If we are dining in style, I don't see why the little fellow shouldn't either. By the way, what are you going to call him?' he asked, his mouth full of April's delicious seafood starter.

'What is he?' she replied.

'What is he?' he repeated, a little puzzled. 'A dog, of course.'

'But what type of dog? Will he be a Pyrennean Mountain Dog or a toy Pom?'

'Oh,' he said, his face clearing in comprehension. 'The fellow at the pet store said he was a Maltese.'

'That's wonderful,' she replied happily. 'Shakespeare!'

'Pardon?'

'I'll call him Shakespeare,' she replied firmly.

'That's an imperious name for such a little fellow,' he replied, smiling at the pleasure he had brought to her face. In the flickering shadows of dark and light that were being cast by the flickering candle, April appeared to be part of the dance of light and shadows. His breath caught in his throat as he watched her pale face thrown into planes of shadows and mysteries at the whim of the breeze that moved the flames.

'He's an imperious dog and so deserves something a little more original than Fido. Don't you think so?'

'Whatever you say, April. He's a lucky little fellow to have you as his life companion.'

The meal progressed in pleasant and light banter between the two of them. April felt as though she had known Jack all her life, and perhaps even longer. She listened, enthralled, as he spun her tales of Hindu history and philosophy, and felt that she had been a spectator at the great gatherings in royal palaces in India with his ancestors. His deep velvety voice had an almost hypnotic effect on her, and she felt herself wanting to be closer to him than his skin.

Later, on the couch over steaming cups of David's filter coffee that Jack had ended up making, April tucked her bare feet underneath her and sat silently and contentedly listening to him talk about his life and the colourful suburb of Bloomsbury. She laughed with him about the nosy neighbours that presided over all neighbourhoods, and found herself telling him about her stormy confrontation with Parker earlier that day.

'He wasn't all that wrong, you know,' said Jack softly as she finished her story.

'What do you mean?' she replied.

'I mean, that if you would let me, I'd like to get closer to you.'

April stared deeply into his eyes, unfathomable pools of mystery in the darkened room. Shakespeare had already staked his claim on the rocking chair, his fluffy little body reflecting ghost-like in its shadows. She felt as though time had stopped. Slowly, almost as though swimming underwater, Jack leaned towards her, his lips gently brushing her cheek. April gasped as an electric thrill of pleasure coursed through her body, seeming to light her up inside. The blood rushed to her head with a roar as loud as the pounding surf across the road. He moved closer to her and took her forgotten cup of coffee out of her hands.

Unable to move for fear of breaking the spell, April sat perfectly still, content to be touched by this man at his pace and according to his whims.

'April,' he whispered into her ear, his lips softly tracing the outline of her ear and cheekbone. She closed her eyes and felt herself arch towards him as though her body had a will of its own. She gasped as he softly kissed her on the throbbing pulse in her throat, and felt herself carried towards him on a tide of sweet desire and passion. His lips clamped down on her slightly open mouth, their cool strength conflicting with the rush of heat that his caresses brought to her body. His arms went about her in an embrace that felt as though she had come home.

She nestled into the warmth of his shoulder and felt the desperate need to return his kisses overwhelm her. His hands traced lazy circles on her bare shoulder where her dress had slipped back to reveal creamy skin. His breath was coming in short gasps as he rained kisses hungrily on her face, neck and shoulders. April was no longer capable of distinguishing where she was being kissed as her whole body melted beneath his skilled caresses.

'I'm sorry, forgive me,' he said, his voice strangled. He pulled sharply away, and April nearly fell over at the sudden removal of his strong embrace. 'I have to leave,' he said shakily, clearing his throat and automatically smoothing down his immaculate hair. He stood up sharply.

'What?' said April unbelievingly, her body still tingling from his touch.

'I am sorry. I have taken advantage of you. The champagne, the ambience...'

'Damn the ambience. You can't just leave, Jack. I know that you felt the same feelings I did. Please, don't leave,' she begged, holding onto his arm as though she would drown if she let go.

'If this was another country, another time, then we would have a real chance of a life together. Can't you see that this is an impossible situation, April? I'm a public figure. People will talk, and it will only be a matter of time before you crack under the pressure,' he said huskily.

'Crack? Just who do you think you are dealing with, Jack Nathan?' she replied indignantly, stomping her foot with frustration. Shakespeare lifted his sleepy little head, saw that his mistress was quite safe, and promptly went back to sleep, his little puppy breaths making him sound like a wheezing old man.

Jack stared at April in genuine surprise. Her face was twisted with fury at the thought that he was under the impression that she was a weakling who always took the easy way out.

'April, darling, please don't upset yourself so,' he replied, the term of endearment slipping naturally off his tongue.

'Then don't provoke me unfairly and unnecessarily,' she retorted, beginning to calm down, her dignity in shreds as reason started prevailing.

She started to pace up and down the room like a caged tiger. Jack sat down again and watched her quietly, waiting until she was ready to speak.

Choosing a chair a safe distance away from him, April sat down, her spine straight and her resolve to do battle firm. 'Jack,' she began firmly, clasping her hands tightly in her lap as though she did not trust them. 'We are two consenting adults with no commitments to other partners? Am I right so far?' She looked at him quizzically, challenging him to contradict her.

'Yes, but ...'

'Please let me finish,' she interrupted, holding her hand up stop street fashion. 'We are both mature, and know where we are going in life.' She watched him intently as she spoke, feeling as though she were standing accused before a hanging jury and had to speak in her own defence. She noticed that a smile lurked at the corners of his sensuous mouth, and his eyes were ranging over her face as she spoke. 'Furthermore, if I wanted a conventional and ordinary romance, I would no doubt still be with Parker, which I am not, thank God.'

'Thank God,' Jack repeated under his breath, sincere in the sentiment expressed in the statement.

'If you are after a little fling with the little white girl, then you can go to hell in a handbasket. But if you think that something meaningful can develop between us, then please give us a chance. Let this be my decision.'

April sat quietly waiting for his reaction, scarcely

breathing. Jack picked up his coffee mug and sipped slowly, watching her over the rim. April felt a muscle in her cheek begin to twitch with anxious anticipation as the silence stretched on seemingly endlessly.

'All right.'

She jumped as he spoke, surprised that his tone could be so normal after the diatribe that she had just subjected him to. 'All right what?' she falteringly enquired, afraid at what his answer might be.

'I have the greatest respect for you, April, and have loved you from the first time I ever laid eyes upon you.'

'At the factory? Not exactly my idea of a romantic meeting place,' she quipped, unable to comprehend the magnitude of his statement.

'No, my love, not the factory. Latiefa's garden.'

'Latiefa's garden?' she repeated, uncomprehendingly.

'Yes. My house overlooks their side garden which is where you were sitting under a bower of flowering bouganvilleas. My heart melted when I saw you, and even though I realized that our situation was hopeless and that it would bring you great pain, I fell in love with you,' he stated simply.

'But you were on a business appointment, Catlin said,' stammered April, confused as she tried to remember all that had happened over the past few days in the correct sequence.

'I went home for lunch. My housekeeper always prepares me something and leaves it in the fridge. That day, I was looking out over Bloomsbury thinking about some business problem, when you walked across their lawn and made even the flowers look shabby next to your beauty.'

'Oh please,' said April, laughing embarrassedly.

'Don't you know how beautiful you are my love? You turn heads in the street, and cars nearly collide when you walk by. You have an incredible modesty.'

'How do you know that cars collide, Jack? You have never seen me anywhere else except indoors.'

'I think that now would be a good time for my full confession,' he admitted, looking sheepish and incredibly handsome at the same time.

'You're married!' gasped April, ready to believe the worst.

'No, no, not yet, I…'

'You are engaged. That's it. You are engaged to marry some Indian princess or something,' retorted April, a hysterical note creeping into her voice.

Jack was laughing now, despite the seriousness of the topic. 'Are you going to condemn me for all crimes against humanity, too, or will you listen to me?' he asked.

'Sorry. I get a little nervous when things get this intense. Please, continue.'

'I first saw you in the garden, and, I repeat, I fell instantly in love with you. I then made a few very hasty and discreet enquiries, and found out who you were and where you lived.'

'Where I lived?' she repeated, startled.

'Yes. I had to know where I could send the roses,' he replied.

'The ro… that was you?' Her eyes were round saucers of amazement.

'Don't sound so surprised. Yes. I sent you two dozen red roses a day like a lovesick schoolboy. I'm sorry if I frightened you. That was never my intention,' he stated contritely.

'Frightened? Who, me? Never!' declared April bravely.

'Anyway, I discovered that snake Manilal was interested in you and he is really bad news. So when I found out that you would be at a meeting with him that could possibly last until very late, I followed you. All the way home and even as far as the ice-cream place – which was a crazy and foolish thing for you to do by the way.' He looked at her sternly, his brow furrowing with concern at her foolhardiness.

'Ah, yes, now it all begins to make sense,' she replied. 'But surely, bumping into me at the restaurant was a coincidence? You had already eaten and were with a client.'

'Sorry. I deceived you again. I knew that you would be there, so I decided to sit unobtrusively in a corner. I wanted to see if Manilal was making any unsavoury advances towards you, so I set up the appointment with a good lawyer friend of mine, Jon Smith, who thinks that I am crazy, incidentally. He says that anyone as beautiful as you and on the wrong side of the colour line is very dangerous.'

'Remind me to sort Jon out when I meet him,' replied April, a little testily, concerned that Jack's friend had already made up his mind about her.

'I was relieved to see that your date wasn't Manilal, but my heart sank when I realized that you were lunching with your fiancé. By the way, what on earth did you see in that fellow? Not only is he gross and ugly, but he has a nasty disposition as well.'

'Let's just call him an ill-chosen port in a storm, and leave it at that, shall we?' replied April, determined to shut that chapter of her life.

'I then knew that I had to protect you from yourself and your good nature,' he continued, making a careful mental note of her comment.

'So you took me to lunch.'

'Yes. I couldn't get you out of my mind. You were like a drug that had got into my system from the very first moment that I laid eyes on you. I couldn't believe it when I saw you running away across that factory floor the other day before I had even had a chance to hear your voice. Poor Catlin got it in the neck, I'm ashamed to say.'

'Well, that certainly explains her rudeness to me the next day,' said April.

'Anyway, your voice turned out to be as lovely as the rest of you, and I could not believe my luck when you agreed to have lunch with me. I had you all to myself for that entire afternoon. That was when I started loving you.'

'But I thought that you fell in love with me under the bower,' teased April lightly.

'Oh, I did,' he replied. 'But being in love with someone is nothing compared to actually loving them. In love is the champagne, but love is the water on fertile soil. I love you, April Ross, and I am so sorry about it because now I am going to ruin your life.'

The silence hung heavily suspended between them.

'More coffee?' asked April, at a loss for sensible conversation when all she could think of was Jack's lips on hers.

He burst out laughing. 'Ah, April, always the practical one.'

'So where do we go from here, Jack?' she whispered, her fears crowding back.

'That is up to you, April. The ball is in your court.'

'Cut the clichés, Jack. I need a little guidance here. This is definitely the start of something big and I don't want to screw it up.'

The tremor in her voice was the only indication of how nervous she was. She sat quite still in the shadows, scarcely breathing. Her craving for a cigarette overwhelmed her, reminding her that she had not smoked all evening. 'All right, April,' Jack emphatically stated, making her jump at the sudden rending of the silence, 'this is how it is.'

'Wait. I need a smoke,' she said, jumping to her feet and rushing towards the stairs, the craving now overwhelming. Shakespeare lifted his head again as he was disturbed by the antics of his mistress. Yapping, he jumped off the chair and fell in a small untidy heap at Jack's feet, rolling over and running after her as fast as his little legs would carry him. He tried valiantly to follow her up the stairs, but he was just too small. He whimpered piteously until she returned, swooping him up in her arms with soft words of reassurance. Content to be with her, he yawned widely, his little pink tongue curling out with the effort. She held him close to her as she sat down and waited for Jack to finish the conversation that she had interrupted earlier.

'April, have you heard of the Immorality Act?' he asked softly.

'Vaguely,' she replied, frowning with concentration as she listened carefully to his words.

'I won't bore you with the details,' he continued. 'The bottom line of it as it affects us is that we cannot officially be in love and get married, because it bans making love, and marriages across the colour lines between whites and all other races.'

'Yes ...' she gently prompted.

'And that means that we will not be able to have a relationship yet.'

'Yet?' she asked, her interest peaking at this sign of optimism.

'My friends and others in parliament assure me that the whole situation is about to change in this parliamentary sitting, with these issues being repealed. It should take until June or July to be made official.'

'June? But it's only January now,' wailed April in dismay. For the first time in her life, she regretted being a South African. She felt waves of frustration roll over her at this predicament. Life was so complicated when one least expected it to be.

'Yes, my darling. I know,' he replied gently. 'Now do you see why I was filled with such despair? I don't want to subject you to the indignities and humiliations that are bound to follow.' April could see his features were set in a grimace of pain.

'Jack,' she said, standing slowly up and replacing the sleeping Shakespeare on the chair that she had just vacated. 'We can do this. It will be fine.'

She walked gracefully across the room and stood before him with her arms outstretched. He took her hands in his and turned them palm upwards as he softly kissed the soft flesh at her wrists. She felt her senses heightening again, and dropped down onto her haunches in front of him. She felt as though a weight had been lifted off her shoulders as she peered intently into his ponderous eyes, and saw the love reflected there. With an anguished sob, he pulled her body towards his, his embrace crushing her in his desperation to ward off the realities of their situation.

'I love you and I will do everything in my power to protect you,' he murmured desperately.

April's arms went around his neck and she leaned back to look at him as she spoke. 'Where do we go from here?' she whispered, fearful of his reply. He gently kissed her nose, and tucked her straying curls behind her ears as he returned her gaze.

'From here, we take it cautiously, my darling. I don't want you to be persecuted in any way by your involvement with me.'

'Why should anyone want to persecute me?' she asked, alarmed at his intensity.

He leaned back on the couch, and pulled her up beside him. She snuggled into the warmth of his shoulder and sighed, content for now to just be near him. Beneath her fingers, she could feel the strength of his forearms as she absently traced patterns on the flesh that had been exposed by his rolled-up sleeves.

'April, you are basically good, but many people out

there are basically evil, and would go out of their way to make you unhappy about our involvement. Will you be able to deal with people staring at us and talking behind their hands as we come into a room? Will you be able to deal with owners and managers of a restaurant that is empty telling us that we can't sit down because they are full? And what about the possibility of a police raid in the middle of the night? Can you cope with the strain of keeping a relationship a secret for many months? Are you strong enough? Do you want to put yourself through all this unnecessary aggravation and heartache?'

'Sticks and stones,' she replied lightly. April had never been afraid to fly in the face of convention for a worthy cause, and she definitely found Jack a very worthy cause.

'Sticks and stones?' he repeated disbelievingly.

'Yes, you know ... "sticks and stones may break my bones but words will never hurt me" – surely you've heard it?' she said cheekily.

His laughter boomed out and he hugged her with delight. 'No wonder I love you, you saucy thing.'

'No wonder,' she replied dreamily. His whole presence engulfed her as she sat quietly next to him, their bodies softly touching with comfortable familiarity in the safe cocoon of the couch.

'April?'

'Mmmm?' she replied, lulled into complacency by the train of her thoughts.

'I am not entirely without influence you know.'

'What do you mean?' she asked, alert now.

'I mean that we are quite safe here in your apartment. Sam is a friend of mine, and he will see to it that you are never disturbed by anyone here, or else they will be quietly and quickly evicted.'

April sat up sharply and pulled away from his embrace. 'Sam is a friend of yours?' she quietly asked.

'Well, actually, he's more than a friend. He's my employee and is very loyal to me.'

'An employee? Does he work for Beckensuds,' she asked, puzzled by the situation.

'Not exactly,' he replied, choosing his words carefully.

'Well, then, what exactly are you talking about?' she asked impatiently, a note of exasperation creeping into her voice.

'I own Ocean Vista,' he replied.

'You own … but that's not possible,' she spluttered.

'Because I'm not white?' he completed her thoughts out loud.

'April, do you honestly believe that the Group Areas Act stops people of colour from owning properties and businesses in so-called white areas?'

'Well, honestly Jack, I never had much cause to think about it till now, did I?' she loftily replied.

'No, I guess that you didn't,' he replied, smiling at her youthful indignation.

'So tell me, how do you own Ocean Vista?' she asked pertly.

'The company is in Sam's name, with me as the person standing surety for him.'

'Isn't that dangerous?' she asked.

'Not at all. Jon drew up an agreement listing all my conditions, and all Sam had to do was have the building registered in his name.'

'How strange that I managed to find the most suitable apartment in Durban, and it happened to be owned by you,' she teased lightly.

'Ah, yes, confession time again. I'm afraid that I took advantage of Mrs Abdullah and asked her a few innocent questions about you in passing. I was very pleased that I owned what you were looking for, so I naturally just happened to mention this place in passing to her.'

'I see,' replied April. 'You are a devious so and so, aren't you? And what would you have done if I hated you? Would you have evicted me?'

'Never. You can say here until you are old and grey if you want to, and you can kick me out right now.'

'You know something, Jack, I am really impressed by all the trouble that you took to engineer this whole event in our lives. Are you always so relentless and thorough in everything that you do?' April began to feel twinges of apprehension at the extent of this handsome man's influence and power, and the irresistible web that he was spinning around her. However, the female in her could not help but be very flattered at the obvious lengths he had gone to, to win her affections. She smiled as she mentally compared Jack with all the other men that she had ever known, especially her latest disaster, Parker.

'I see that I amuse you, April. That is good, because as long as I can bring a smile to your lips and eyes, my life will be full. And, to reply to your question, I always do my homework very carefully before I commit myself to a business venture, so naturally the same principle applies doubly so for my private life.'

He lifted her chin with his hand, and bent slowly over her. April could feel the force of his energy even before his lips touched hers. Her senses swam with the pure sensual pleasure that his touch aroused in her. She felt as though a lightning bolt had shot through her, rendering her powerless and omnipotent at the same time. His lips moved over her face, as light as butterflies, and yet seeming to throb with a pure sexual energy. Her arms tightened around his neck as she arched her throat back for him to kiss. His kisses became more insistent as he felt her rising passion mounting to meet his in her responses. She whimpered as he tore his lips away from her neck. He took her face in his hands and looked into her swimming eyes, brimful of emotions she had never felt before, and a fragile elation. 'I started to live the minute I saw you April,' he murmured, his breath sending shivers of pleasure from her ears to the very tips of her toes. 'I'll never let anyone harm you, I promise,' he declared huskily.

'I know that, Jack,' she replied, surprised at his serious tone and thoughtful expression. She had always yearned for romance and adventure, and Jack certainly provided a great deal of both. 'I know that,' she sighed, in that instant trusting him completely. Her intuition told her that he was her man, and that she had come home. A tear slid silently down her cheek as the emotions overwhelmed her with their frightening intensity. Jack brushed away the tear with the tip of his tongue, rocking her back and forth in his embrace as a parent would pacify a frightened child. His mouth took possession of hers again, her lips opening to him in sweet surrender. The kiss seemed to last forever, and yet only for a moment. Sensing the depth of the sensations he was rousing in her, he pulled away with difficulty. April stared at him, confused by his actions.

'I have to leave now, April, or else I will throw all caution to the wind, and I might compromise you.'

April laughed at his elegant phrases. She had every intention of being 'compromised' by this tall man whose inner strength was surpassed by his sensitivity.

He kissed her chastely on the cheek and stood up. With three large strides, he put the distance of the entire room between them. Saluting her with one hand whilst pulling on his jacket with the other, he looked like a general readying himself for battle. Feeling very mellow and contented, April watched him make his preparations to leave.

Turning at her front door, silhouetted in the moonwashed

entrance hall, he said, 'Do you know your history, my darling?'

Startled by this question, April stared at him blankly, at a loss for words. This was the first person who had ever had her at a loss for words, and she delighted in the sensation. 'Why?'

'Because, my darling, I am about to make a grand exit that will be wasted unless you know a little World War Two military history.'

'Try me,' she responded mischievously.

'I *shall* return,' he stated imperiously, blew her a kiss and then closed the door resoundingly behind him. Shakespeare grumbled indignantly as he was once again woken by the peals of merriment from his mistress.

'Yes, General Patten,' she whispered, breathlessly.

# *Chapter Eight*

The next few weeks seemed to drift by like a sweet dream for April. She had to keep reminding herself that she was not going to wake up and find it had all been a figment of a spinsterish imagination. She could hardly wait for the days to end so she could rush home and prepare for Jack. She felt like a heady schoolgirl with her first serious crush, and savoured every moment of the feeling. Her life was complete. Her job was fulfilling and kept her busy with meetings, interviews, reports and seminars. Her professional reputation was growing, and she was asked to be the speaker at several elite women's groups meetings. Her head was spinning at her good fortune, and Jack's love was like an all-enveloping embryonic blanket that protected and nurtured her at the same time.

Shakespeare was growing rapidly, and his devotion to April was touching. The little dog followed her wherever she walked, and sat primly on the back window ledge of her car whenever she drove around. He went with her to work, his obedience absolute. He was disdainful of anyone else's advances of friendship towards him, except for when he saw Jack. His whole body would wag with delight, and his lip would lift back in an almost human grin.

The chill of autumn was in the early morning air and April's breath steaming before her. Her cheeks were red from running up the stairs, and her hair had grown to shoulder length and bounced around her oval face. She was making an all-out effort to grow it, and was quite surprised at the change it made in her appearance and her personality. She looked more sophisticated, and the security of Jack's love gave her an added edge of confidence that was carried over to colleagues and clients alike. She was smiling broadly as she reached the office door, and since she had stopped smoking, she no longer gasped and wheezed when she ran.

Barely glancing at Aneesa, April whirled through the outer office on the way to her door. Her cheerful morning greeting was met by a hardly discernible reply. Looking back in surprise, April was startled to see how pale and nervous Aneesa was looking as she stared, mesmerised, at an unopened letter on her desk as though it would bite her.

'Good grief! What on earth is the matter? You look like you've seen a ghost!' said April, concernedly.

'I think that I have,' replied Aneesa, her voice quivering.

'Here,' she continued, pushing the letter towards April. 'A letter for you.'

Puzzled by Aneesa's attitude, April picked up the letter and looked at the back to see who the addressee was. Suddenly, she understood what had happened. On the back of the expensive envelope were the following words, 'Honourable Minister Abdul Hussein', followed by his postal address. The lettering was gold and heavy. April ripped it open with the letter opener and quickly read aloud the card inside: 'You and your partner are cordially invited to attend the birthday party of the Honourable member of parliament, Mr Abdul Hussein, on Saturday 31st May, 1985 at 19.00. The venue is to be his residence, situated at 1 Clearwaters Drive, Bloomsbury. Attire: Gentlemen – black tie. R.S.V.P. by 23 May to the aforementioned address. Miss April Ross and partner will/regret that they will not be able to attend.'

The two women's silence hung heavily in the air as April let the card slip out of her fingers. Bending quickly, she scooped it up off the floor where Shakespeare was sniffing it suspiciously. They both jumped as the telephone shrilled.

'Indian Affairs, good morning,' said Aneesa automatically in her clipped telephone tone.

Her face relaxed, and she smiled. 'Good morning, Mr Nathan, I'm fine thank you. I'll put you through to Miss Ross immediately.' Aneesa gave April a broad wink and transferred the call as April flew into her office, her tweed coat billowing out behind her.

'Hello, darling,' she crooned into the receiver, as she absentmindedly played with the invitation that was still in her hand.

'Hello, my love,' Jack replied. 'Did you get the invitation?' he abruptly asked.

'What? Oh you mean the Hussein invitation. Yes, it came with this morning's mail.'

'Well?' he said impatiently.

'Well what?' she replied uncomprehendingly, perplexed by his brusque tone.

'Are you going?'

'Jack, I honestly haven't had time to stop and think about it. Why is it so important? And what could have possessed him to invite me? I've been a regular nuisance to him about all those crooked housing allocations that have been going on. I've never even spoken to the man.'

'Precisely,' Jack snapped, triumphantly.

'Jack, for goodness' sake, stop talking in riddles. What's going on?'

'It is simple, my beautiful, brave and sometimes brainless lady. This is a command performance where he is going to sum you up and see what sort of an adversary you really are.'

'Oh, come on,' said April laughing. 'You are more than a little paranoid, wouldn't you say?'

'I'm very paranoid, and with good cause, too. He phoned me first thing this morning as soon as I had got home from my jog to tell me that he had invited you precisely to sum you up and see what kind of a nuisance you might turn out to be. At the moment he is amused by your "voice of conscience" approach, but his undertones are very serious.'

'Jack, don't! You're scaring me,' replied April, shivering a little at the pictures her imagination was conjuring up.

'Good!' said Jack adamantly. 'Be afraid, because that way at least you'll be careful and wary of his every gesture, nuance and move.'

'But you'll be there beside me, love,' she crooned placatingly.

'Yes, but only as another guest, and not as your protector and partner, April. There is a very big difference. You know that at this stage, it is very dangerous for anyone to know about our involvement. They would arrange for life to be unbearable for us from a legal and social point of view.' His tone was stern and final.

'I know, I know,' she sighed, frustrated by the tangled web of deceit that her life had become. She wanted to shout her love for Jack from the rooftops. She was tired of fielding the awkward questions about her private life. She always retreated behind her standard answer: 'I prefer to keep my personal and professional lives separate,' she would say loftily, annoyed that men of her age and standing would never be asked these things.

'Write back and accept the invitation, April,' Jack said.

'But I have to take a partner,' she said sweetly, a mischievous grin lighting up her eyes.

'You are taking a partner,' he rejoindered. 'Me.'

'Ah, yes, but I cannot acknowledge it, so I will appear to be coming alone. That makes it open season by any standards, isn't that so?'

'Well, I guess the same applies for me,' he replied airily. 'Those matchmaking Mamma's of Bloomsbury will be delighted that I will be attending yet another community activity alone and very eligible.'

April felt a prick of jealousy and resentment. 'I don't find that particularly amusing, Jack,' she snapped.

'Darling, calm down,' he murmured. 'I love you, and only you, so never worry about me being eligible. You are the woman for me, now and forever, and I'll never let you go.'

April smiled into the receiver, picturing his earnest expression as he reassured her of his love. 'Anyway pet, have a good day. I'll see you at the townhouse tonight as usual?' she asked.

'No, I'm afraid that I can't make it this evening, darling. I'm having a business meeting that can't be postponed,' he replied.

'Oh,' said April. 'And who with, if I may be so bold as to enquire?'

She was curious as Jack and she had established a routine over the past few weeks that she had grown comfortable with. She was always ready for any show of spontaneity, but not when it involved exclusion.

'Oh, you don't know him, my love,' replied Jack, a little too hastily for her liking.

'Try me,' she insisted. Jack always discussed business with her and she had got to know all his associates by name and nature, although she had never met any of them in person.

'Look,' he said, his tone implying a resentment that she had never experienced before. 'I said that you don't know him, and let's just leave it at that, shall we?'

She rankled at his patronizing tone of telling the little woman that she was not up to important business secrets. Sometimes, and always unexpectedly, he would become very Eastern. But this was the first time she had felt as though she was being shut out of any aspect of his life.

'Fine, fine,' she said placatingly, suppressing her anger in an attempt to avoid an argument. They had never argued, and knowing their strong characters, it would be an awe-inspiring display of fireworks that could possibly leave them reeling in its aftermath. 'You can at least tell me where you are meeting this "business" friend,' she asked.

'No, I'm afraid I can't do that either,' he replied, mysteriously.

'But Jack, we always know exactly where the other one is at all times,' she wailed, hating herself for the needy tone that had crept into her voice. She felt a flood of all her original insecurities flooding back.

'I know, April, but it's simply that we haven't decided yet where we should meet.'

'Well, will you stop by afterwards, then?' she asked, hopefully.

'It might be very late when we tie things up, so I'd rather not bother you at an ungodly hour. All right?'

'All right, but for the record, Mr Nathan, I am not impressed,' replied April testily.

'I promise that I'll make it up to you, my love. Tomorrow night, I'm taking you out for dinner and a show. Okay?' He seemed almost desperate to make up for his secretive business assignation.

'Dinner *and* a show? Be still, my heart,' replied April, a little note of excitement creeping into her voice. 'But we can't do that. What about the people?' she said, her bubble of childlike joy bursting.

'I'm way ahead of you, my darling,' replied Jack warmly.

'We are dining in Amanzimtoti, and then we'll pop up to the Starlight Theatre for a charming evening of classical music. Happy?'

'Very,' she replied, already planning her wardrobe for the unexpected evening out. The fact that Amanzimtoti was an hour away only added to the delight.

'Till tomorrow, then, my love,' he softly crooned, pleased that she was so willing to lead this furtive life for his sake.

'I'll pick you up early at five. The curtain goes up at eight so we'll have plenty of time to get there and dine out. I love you very much, April Ross. You are my life, so don't ever forget that.'

'Darling, of course not,' she replied, a little taken aback at the passion in his voice. 'I'll see you tomorrow. 'Bye.'

Jack's brow wrinkled in concentration as he replaced the receiver. 'Catlin,' he called out sharply, 'get Minister Hussein on the line immediately, please. And then phone up the club and confirm the reservation for dinner tonight for two.'

'Sure,' she replied, not at all impressed by his curt instructions. He hadn't even noticed that she'd cut her hair and had been receiving compliments from everyone within his earshot.

'Dining out with Miss Ross?' she enquired, the lightness of her tone belying the urgency of the question.

'No, I'm not,' he replied brusquely, 'and I would appreciate it if we kept this dinner reservation strictly between us, all right?'

'Fine,' she replied, feigning disinterest, but perking up at the prospect that there was a secret to which just the two of them were privvy. She smirked with glee at the thought that he might be two-timing Little Miss Wonderful. Although she could not prove anything was going on between them, she had noticed the electricity in the air whenever April came to see him at the office on some pretext or other. Yes, this might be an instrument of sweet revenge. Her grin broadened to Cheshire Cat proportions as she quickly dialled the club's number.

'Hello, George, how are you?' she said sweetly into the receiver as the restaurant manager's voice came wheezing over the line. George was old enough to think that any woman under the age of fifty was young, available and desperate.

'Catlin, my dear. Long time no hear, and even longer time no see or touch.' She shuddered with revulsion at his syrupy tone.

'Yes, dear. It has been a long time. George, dear, I'm phoning to confirm Mr Nathan's reservation for two for dinner tonight.' She listened as he thumbed through the reservation book.

'Ah, yes, here it is. I see that he has reserved the private dining room and has requested the key for the private entrance.'

'Oh?' enquired Catlin, feigning a calmness that she was not feeling. This was definitely big news that Jack wanted kept quiet at all cost.

'George,' she continued sweetly, 'would you be a pet and fax me written confirmation of this reservation?'

'That is hardly regular practice,' replied George, all bristling self-importance.

'Darling, I know, I know,' soothed Catlin, 'but you know how strange Mr Nathan's requests can be, and we both know that he does not enjoy being crossed.'

'So he wants it confirmed in writing, does he?' asked George, feeling more comfortable.

'Yes, of course, silly,' she said with a schoolgirl giggle.

'And what's in it for me, Kitty Cat?' asked George, pictures of naked flesh filling his mind. He fondled his erection as he spoke, imagining an eager and ardent Catlin in his bed as she had been ten years ago before she was an important hot-shot's secretary. Of course, he had had to pay for the pleasures that her young flesh had yielded to him, but it had been well worth the expense. Her mouth had been hot and moist as she had explored every part of his body with her quick, darting professional little pink tongue, just like the rough and warm tongue of a kitten.

'Well, George. I guess you'll just have to fax me and wait and see,' she replied coquettishly, shivers of disgust going up and down her spine as she recalled his fetid odour and his pinching fingers bruising her nipples. She hated to be reminded of the days when she did sexual favours for money and drugs, but at least her experiences had given her a wide base of old customers to call up favours from with subtle hints of what she could tell their wives and girlfriends. And today, she was calling in a favour for services rendered a decade ago.

She smiled knowingly as she replaced the receiver with a firm click, and started dialling Minister Hussein's private home number. 'Ah, Jacky boy, what are you up to?' she softly hummed beneath her breath as she waited impatiently for the call to be answered.

April's excitement at the evening that lay ahead for her and Jack had almost reached fever pitch. This would be their first real date in public, and even though the weather had been cold and blustery all day, her spirits were sunny.

'Well, Shakespeare, how do I look?' she asked the little dog as she twirled around in front of the mirror. He cocked his head to one side and barked in reply. She laughed at his apparent understanding of her question.

Her hair was glossy and thick, and bounced on her

shoulders with all its freshly washed brilliance. Her cheeks were rosy with anticipation as she applied the finishing touches to her make-up. Shakespeare barked excitedly as he heard Jack's keys grating in the lock, and beat April as they both ran down the steps towards the door.

'Gosh, a hero's welcome,' laughed Jack, as Shakespeare and April both flung themselves on him. Bending to pat the dog, Jack smiled up into April's eyes.

'Come here, you,' he said hoarsely as he gathered her into his arms and kissed her soundly. She could feel his hardened manhood pressing against her as his desire for her mounted. Breaking away from her breathlessly, he assumed a cheery air and smacked her bottom. 'Come on, lovely, we'll miss the opening curtain.' He turned away and held the door open for her.

'Bye, Shakespeare darling. Be a good boy. Mommy will be home soon.'

The door shut on the disgusted little dog who had had every intention of going along. Resigned to his fate of an evening alone at home and watching the television that April always left on for him, he jumped onto her chair and breathed her scent.

'How was your meeting last night Jack? I missed you terribly,' April said as she nestled back in the comfort of the warm car's leather interior.

Jack's face remained impassive as he concentrated on the early evening traffic. 'Fine,' he said airily, reaching over and switching the radio on.

'So, where did you go?' she asked doggedly.

'To Pierre at the Port Rex,' he mumbled. 'Darling, you look ravishing tonight,' he said, slipping her a quick smile as he turned to admire her. 'You are the only woman I know who would give a paper bag class if you put it on.'

April was ridiculously pleased by his admiration. She had learnt over the last few whirlwind weeks that Jack was not effusive with his praise as most other men appeared to be.

'What, this old thing?' she laughingly replied, tweaking the collar of the cream trouser suit modestly. The emerald green blouse beneath the snugly fitting jacket gave green lights to her grey eyes. 'I must say that you don't look too shabby yourself,' she rejoindered, looking at the trim figure that he represented in his white turtleneck jersey and black suit.

Jack wore his clothes with casual simplicity, affecting none of the mindless vanities that previous suitors of hers had always exhibited. She breathed in the tobacco-scented and woody aroma of his aftershave lotion, her sensual nature rising to the fore.

April leaned her head over on Jack's shoulder as they drove in companionable silence towards Amanzimtoti, the radio crooning lilting melodies of romance and promises of things better yet to come.

'We're here, darling,' said Jack softly. April sat up with a start, realizing she had nodded off to the hypnotic sound of the tyres on the tar, eating up the miles. She looked around her, surfacing quickly.

The sky was a riot of reds and oranges as the sun was rapidly setting. Jack leaped out of the car and came around to open her car door in the unassuming and natural display of Old World manners that were an integral part of his personality. She stepped gracefully out of the car, stretching like a cat as she arched her body against the strain that her back muscles had taken from her twisted position.

Unlike other women, April hated to have a handbag, and even more so now that she wasn't smoking. She carried her tube of favourite lipstick in a pocket, and never felt as though she really needed much more. The cavernous handbags that most of her sex carried were an anathema and an enigma to her. She liked to feel free and unencumbered by additional appendages, however practical they might seem to others. She looked around her with interest. Jack had brought her to a beautiful stone inn that nestled comfortably in a grove of tall palm trees.

'This way, my love,' he said as he automatically took her hand and tucked it through his arm.

'Jack, what will people say?' she said half-heartedly.

'Tonight I don't care what the world says. I'm out with the most beautiful woman in the world, and am sure to be the envy of the male species.'

'I don't know about that,' she replied lightly. 'You may very well end up being the focal point of the security police for laying your hands on white flesh.' Her face grew serious as the reality of their situation hit her again full force. It was one thing being alone together at the townhouse, or seeing one another at meetings, but she was unsure of the rules out in a public place.

'Don't worry, darling,' he reassured her, squeezing her hand firmly and reassuringly. 'Tonight is a magical night, and no one here will bother with us. They'll take us for being two people from another country in love in the evening.' Turning her towards him in the gathering darkness, he leant over her and kissed her lightly on the lips. 'Come on,' he said, as she meekly followed him into the light that was spilling from the open doors of the inn.

The red wine glistened in April's glass as she stared at the dancing firelight shimmering behind it. She watched Jack over the rim as he tackled his roast dinner with gusto. Catching her watching him, he flashed her a brilliant smile. The dining room of the old hotel was practically empty, as it was still early for dinner, and she felt comfortable and at home there. No one had even afforded them a second glance in this busy tourist town. Her mind drifted off along avenues of comparisons as she watched the roaring fire that dominated the room.

'More wine, darling?' he asked lightly, filling her glass anyway. 'A penny for your thoughts,' he said lightly, as he caught the faraway gleam in her clear eyes. He found everything about April clear and fine – her complexion, her aura, her sweet nature, her clarity of purpose, her willingness to save the world at her own emotional expense. She was unstinting in her loyalty and he felt lucky to be in this relationship with her, as troubled as it was.

She smiled warmly at him, leaning back in her chair against her jacket. The fire had brought a rosy glow of health and vitality to her cheeks, picking up the natural red lights in her hair.

'You are so beautiful,' he said earnestly, covering her hand with his own as he stared into her eyes. 'You look like the fire goddess sitting there in that reflection, with the firelight dancing in your eyes and shining off your hair.' April was alarmed to see Jack's eyes fill with unshed tears as his voice quivered with emotion. He quickly let go of her hand and started attacking his food again with feigned enthusiasm.

'Jack, darling, I love you,' she whispered hoarsely. He looked up at her, his eyes now clear, and April found herself wondering if she had imagined the tender moment.

Jack fumbled in his inside pocket, twisting himself nearly completely around as he struggled to retrieve the little box from where he had nonchalantly thrown his jacket. April watched his antics with an amused and curious expression.

'Ah, there you are,' said Jack triumphantly as he retrieved the box. Leaning forward across the table, Jack put the box down on April's empty plate. 'For the woman I love and wish to spend eternity with,' he said.

April's eyes were riveted on the box. 'What is it?' she whispered.

'Open it,' he said softly. 'But wait,' he suddenly commanded her, capturing her seeking fingers in a bruising grasp. 'First, I'd like to ask you something.'

'Yes?' said April, looking at him through lowered lashes, smiling at his nervous tugging at the collar of the polo neck jersey that suddenly seemed to be depriving him of air.

'April Ross,' he began solemnly, and broke into a paroxysm of coughing.

A waiter came hurrying over with a glass of water and Jack gratefully glugged it down. Clearing his throat, he began again. 'April, darling, I loved you from the moment I first saw you in that garden, and as I've got to know you, I've realized that my first impressions were accurate, but not nearly deep enough. I have never yet met a woman that I have wanted to share my life with. At least, not until now,' he hastily added, looking into her eyes for the first time since his monologue had begun. April was smiling broadly at him.

'Yes, go on,' she said lightly, her heart racing. Jack saw the pulse throbbing in the base of her creamy throat as she held his hands tighter and tighter.

'I was wondering if you would do me the great honour of becoming my wife?'

'Oh, Jack, I was wondering when you were going to ask,' she squealed, and unmindful of the curious glances of the waiters and the other patrons, she stretched across the table and kissed him fiercely.

'Aren't you going to open the box?' he said laughing, and disentangling her arms from around his neck. 'And I take it your answer is yes?'

'Yes, yes, yes, a thousand billion times yes,' she whispered theatrically. Her fingers trembled as she pulled open the black velvety box. Her breath caught in her throat as she looked down at the most beautiful diamond and sapphire ring that she had ever seen. Three magnificent diamonds and two perfect sapphires twinkled back at her, set next to one another in a solid bar of gold.

She picked the ring carefully out of the box. 'It's square and I love it. Oh put it on for me, Jack, please! Let's do this right!'

He reached across for the ring and willingly obliged. It slipped on to her finger without any exertion. Twisting her hand this way and that so that the stones caught all the light in the room, April stared at the ring in speechless delight.

'Do you like it?' he anxiously asked, watching her intently.

'Hmmm?'

'The ring, darling. Do you like it?' To his consternation, April burst into tears.

'Oh my God, what's wrong?' His voice was quivering with concern for her obvious emotional state.

'I'm so happy,' she wailed through her tears.

'Then why are you crying?' he asked, genuinely puzzled by this unexpected reaction. He had steeled himself for rejection, a slap in the face, or happy acceptance, but this reaction was quite unexpected.

'Oh Jack, you really don't know women very well, do you?' she said, wiping ineffectually at the tears that rolled unheeded down her cheeks. Her eyes took on a green shimmering brilliance as she cried, Jack noticed irrelevantly.

'Obviously not,' he said, a little embarrassed by such a public show of raw emotion.

'I'm crying because I am so happy. I finally know where this romance is leading us, and I'm so very happy,' she sobbed, smiling at him through her tears.

'Ah, I think I understand,' he said, putting his silk handkerchief into her hands.

'Jack, if you love me so much, then why have you never tried to make love to me?' she asked curiously.

'Because I knew that I was going to marry you come hell or high water,' he firmly replied.

'But in this day and age, surely that didn't matter? I thought that there was something wrong with me,' she ended, staring rapturously at her ring.

'April, I can get sex from any Bimbo on any street corner,' he patiently explained. 'But only you could give me love. I respect you so much that I would feel like a thief if I had taken advantage of you.'

'Advantage?' April replied, a little hysterically. 'I have wanted to "take advantage" of you since the first day I met you.' Then the cold reality of their situation engulfed her.

'What is it, my love?' asked Jack, concerned by the unhappiness that was spreading across April's face.

'How can we get married, Jack? It's against the law,' she softly said, fear nagging behind the unspoken plea for him to make it all better.

'April, it's May now,' said Jack comfortingly.

'So?' replied a despondent April.

'So,' he continued, 'by June, that law will be a thing of the past.'

'How can you be sure?' she said fearfully, waiting for the bubble of her happiness to burst in a cold sobering splash.

'Believe me, I'm sure. I have it on the highest authority straight from parliament. Do you think I would ever have asked you to marry me if there was no future in this country for us?' He waited patiently for her reply.

'No, I don't suppose you would have,' she replied slowly, brightening to the truth of what he had just said.

'But what about the engagement? What will the community think?' She stared at him, fearful again.

'Darling, for the time being, this will just be between you and me. No one else needs to know. It is my private commitment to you.'

'Oh no. Can't I at least tell my parents?' she wailed, the little girl in her reaching out for family approval.

Jack regarded her silently for a moment, then shrugged his shoulders in resignation. 'Of course you can tell your parents, April. Would you like me to ask your father's permission?'

April's laughter at this old-fashioned gesture pealed out across the room.

'Of course not silly,' she replied. 'I'm a big girl now, and I get to choose who does or does not marry me. Good heavens, when Parker asked my father for my hand in marriage, he was told "no" in no uncertain terms. I certainly don't want to run that risk with you. Not that he would say no to you,' she quickly added, noticing the vulnerability at the corners of his mouth.

'He said no to Parker?' asked Jack disbelievingly.

'Yes. Oh it was the funniest thing, really. My father hated Parker on sight but was polite to him for my sake. Anyway, I was turning twenty-one and I'd always thought it would be kind of romantic to get engaged on my twenty-first birthday. Besides, all my friends were doing it. Haven't I told you this story before?' she said quizzically, interrupting herself.

'Go on,' he said, smiling and glancing surreptitiously at his watch. There was still another half an hour to curtain time. He settled back in his chair, enjoying the animation that lit up her face when she was telling a story. April had a God-given talent for making the characters of any story that she told come alive, as her face changed expressions with her voice.

'Okay,' she continued, delighted to have such an enraptured audience. 'Anyway, Parker got to the point where he thought that it might be a good idea if we got married so that he could borrow money from my father to buy a deserted farm in the Gazankulu district.'

Jack's face mirrored all the contempt he could feel for such an obvious fortune hunter. April carried on breathlessly. 'I told him that I wanted to get engaged on my twenty-first birthday, so he had better ask Daddy for permission. He hummed and hahed, but finally agreed. He was so weak,' she spat out, disgusted with herself afresh for ever having got involved with someone like Parker.

'Carry on,' prompted Jack.

'The evening before my birthday, he took me to a jewellery shop and asked the shop assistant for a tray of the cheapest diamond rings.'

Jack couldn't help gasping at this obvious insult.

'Anyway, the shop assistant obliged and he nearly hit the roof when he saw how much even the tiddly piddly rings were. So do you know what he said next?' She waited dramatically for Jack to respond.

'What?' he said, obliging her.

'He told her to bring out the fake diamonds.'

'No, he didn't!'

'Yes he did, and I was so eager to get that ring on my finger that I just nodded my dumb head. I suppose I was superstitious that if I didn't get engaged before I turned twenty-one, I would stay on the shelf for ever.'

'My darling, why would you have thought such a thing?' he asked her, puzzled at her obvious lack of confidence.

'Because Larry told me that I was stupid and no one would ever want to marry me because I was fat and ugly,' she said, shrinking into herself at the memory.

'Who the hell was Larry?' asked Jack, furious that

anyone could ever be so cruel to a fellow human being, let alone one as vulnerable and as naturally lovely as April.

'He was my first love,' replied April, pulling a funny face as she tried to make light of the situation.

'First love? He sounds like a real cad to me,' said Jack vehemently.

'That he was,' agreed April, nodding vigorously. 'Well, after Larry brushed me off for a nurse with a lot of bedroom experience, safe Parker appeared on the scene, blah blah, and then asked me to marry him.'

'For what he could get,' Jack added, angrily. He felt fiercely protective towards her as he watched her tenderly.

'To cut a long story short, he bought me a pretty ring with cubic zirconiums and then proceeded to go and ask my father for my hand in marriage. It was actually quite funny,' said April, giggling at the memory. 'I was in the kitchen with my mother, listening at the serving hatch in the wall. He must have talked rugby with my father for at least an hour before he got around to asking. He asked if my Dad would mind him marrying me, so my father replied as follows, "Well, yes actually, I would mind." When Parker asked him why he minded, he told him that there were a number of good reasons which he did not wish to go into.' April stopped talking, her eyes twinkling with merriment.

'Go on,' urged Jack, a little impatiently.

'Anyway, Parker came running into the kitchen and said that Daddy had said no and he didn't know what to do. What a wimp!'

'Definitely,' agreed Jack, despising Larry for hurting April so deeply that she had turned to a pathetic weakling like Parker with a penchant for hitting women to make himself feel like more of a man. Her self-image must have really been damaged.

'I told him to go back and say that we were getting engaged, whether he approved or not, but he said that he couldn't do it. So I went marching into the lounge and soft-soaped Daddy until he grudgingly came around. Daddy's parting words to me were that he wasn't too concerned, because he knew that I had sense enough to realize that I had made a mistake. Wise old owl.'

Jack found himself respecting Bill Ross immensely for his breadth of vision and insight into his daughter's real needs and her good sense in the long run.

'Hey fiancé, let's go. We've got a symphony concert to go to. Who is playing tonight, anyway?' April interrupted Jack's train of thought as she jumped up and slipped into her warm jacket.

'The Cape Town Symphony Orchestra are doing a tour and they're playing a collection of works by Mozart,' he replied, taking out the cash for the meal and leaving it nonchalantly on the table. Taking her elbow, he steered her out of the dining room towards the car.

'I adore Mozart,' she said delightedly, clapping her hands together with spontaneous joy. 'Gosh, what a night. I get to spend it with my two favourite men – one, a very talented but very dead composer, and the other, a very alive and sexy you.' April put her arm around Jack's waist as they walked through the dark, icy cold car park.

'Oh darling, I can't wait to be Mrs Jack Nathan,' she said breathlessly.

'And this time, are you doing it for love, April?' he asked laughingly.

'Only for love, my darling. Nothing will ever come between us,' she said, crossing herself superstitiously so that fate would not hear her and intervene to spoil her happiness.

# *Chapter Nine*

April drove her car slowly up the winding driveway towards Abdul Hussein's house. He had arranged valet parking for this evening, and she gracefully relinquished the keys to a capable-looking young man in a bright red uniform. He quickly placed a ticket into her hand so that she could reclaim her car at the end of the evening.

She looked up at the impressive three-storeyed mansion towering above her in the darkness. Minister Hussein's home was built along Greek lines, and sat imposingly on a hill overlooking Bloomsbury to the north and the ocean to the south. The front door was standing wide open, and April heard laughter and music coming from inside. Light spilled out of every window, and lit up the immaculate green lawn. Breathing in deeply, she gathered her long skirt in one hand and ascended the stairs quickly.

As she entered the marble hallway, she gasped at the sight of the beautiful crystal chandelier dominating the area. The mirrors made the entrance hall seem twice its size, and she caught sight of herself as she walked languidly across the delicately veined floor. She smiled briefly at her reflection, pleased with what she saw. She looked like a sea sprite in her aquamarine full-length gown. The dress was cut in very simple lines, and clung elegantly to her body, rippling like the ocean as she moved. The neckline was cut low so that her shoulders and cleavage were shown to her best advantage. Around her neck she wore a short single strand of creamy pearls that matched her earrings and bracelet perfectly. The evening shoes peeping out from below her hem were the identical colour and fabric of the dress – a warm velvet to contend with the cool and almost wintry air.

'Miss Ross, I presume,' said a deep and slightly sing-song voice from behind her. It was a statement, not a question. April swung around and stared up into the glittering black eyes of Abdul Hussein. He was a ruggedly handsome man, but his lips were thin and cruel. His face was dominated by his large hawk-like nose. His brown head gleamed in the lighting as his hair had receded rather far back on his forehead. He was much taller than she had imagined from having seen him on television. He was the picture of self-assured elegance in his impeccable black tuxedo, his starched white collar almost blinding in its purity. He had a cigar in his hand, which surprised April as she had never thought of him as a smoker. He held out his right hand to shake hers, and she was struck by its largeness, and the power in his grip. His grasp was cool and firm, for which she was grateful, having found that large men frequently have moist, soft hands.

'Happy birthday, Mr Minister,' she politely replied, self-consciously holding his gift out to him.

'Why, how charming,' he responded, taking the present eagerly from her, much like a child would. 'I shall open the gifts a little later in the evening,' he said, taking her firmly by her elbow and steering her purposefully towards the open double doors leading off the entrance hall. April felt anger welling up inside her at the opulence that this man possessed whilst his daughter and grandchildren had to survive on a pittance.

'I see that you are alone,' he said glibly, his admiration for her apparent in the way he was looking her up and down.

April sucked in her stomach self-consciously, feeling like a contestant at a cattle parade needing to pass inspection before the slaughter. She smiled brightly at him, determined not to be intimidated by his presence.

'Yes, I chose to come unescorted, Mr Minister. I am, after all, here in a work-related capacity, am I not?'

He looked at her intently, then his laughter boomed out across the room as he nodded his head approvingly.

'A worthy comment indeed, Miss Ross. I admire intelligent women who are sharp-witted.' He moved her expertly onto the dance floor. 'May I have the pleasure of this dance?' he asked, mockingly gallant. She looked around in alarm, and spotted Jack elbowing his way across the room towards them. As he was about to reach them, she saw him intercepted by one of the prominent Bloomsbury Mammas that they had frequently joked about. She looked up and saw Abdul Hussein staring at her intently, his sharp eyes glittering jet black and expressionless in his face. She felt like a rabbit mesmerized by the Cobra.

'I'd be delighted,' she lied convincingly. He swept her into his arms and started twirling her dizzily around the dance floor. She was surprised at his lightness and grace.

'How do you like Bloomsbury so far?' he asked her conversationally.

'Well, I've enjoyed getting to know a new culture,' April replied cautiously, wondering where the conversation was leading to.

'You know, you've been giving me and my team a little trouble regarding the housing allocations, my dear.' His hand in the small of her back was exerting just enough pressure to make her wince. April stiffened in his embrace.

'Oh?' she enquired, with a calmness that she was not feeling.

'But I told the boys not to take the matter too seriously. After all, you are all fired up with the idealism and enthusiasm of youth. Besides, how could a young woman as beautiful as you pose a threat to us?'

April looked up sharply into his face. It was devoid of any emotion, and unreadable. 'Mr Minister, I am merely trying to do my job as best I know how,' she countered softly.

'Ah, Miss Ross. You have to realize that housing is not a matter that really concerns you, so perhaps it would be better for all concerned if you concentrated your considerable talents on other matters?' Beneath the charm and gentility, she sensed his implied threat.

'Mr Minister, everything that happens in Bloomsbury is my concern, and when families are forced to live in cars because they have not been allocated homes when they were next on the list, then it definitely becomes an issue of welfare.' Her expression was adamant, defying further argument.

He laughed loudly, as though she had made an incredibly funny joke. 'Miss Ross, I really admire a woman with as much fire and sparkle as you. We must get together for some serious dialogue one of these days.' As quickly as he had grasped her waist for the dance, he let her go. She staggered slightly to maintain her footing.

'Please excuse me, my dear, I must not neglect my other guests. Thank you for the honour of the dance, and enjoy your evening. I look forward to having another little chat with you in the not too distant future. I have the feeling that you are a wonderful verbal sparring partner for me.' He bowed, kissed her hand before she could snatch it away, and quickly disappeared in the crowd.

April walked over to the side of the large ballroom, and grabbed a drink off a passing tray. She took a deep swallow and nearly gagged as the searing whisky burnt her throat. She looked wildly around for a potted plant where she could spit out the remaining mouthful without being noticed, but was suddenly aware of many eyes on her. Smiling a little weakly, she held her breath and swallowed the remaining liquid as though she had always been an avid whisky drinker.

April's hair had been swept up off her neck into an elegant chignon, held securely in place by a pearl-encrusted slide that had belonged to her grandmother. With her height and poise, she cut a striking figure, and was receiving longing glances from the men in the room, and envious glares from their overdressed and over-made-up wives. Most of the guests at the affair were Indian, and the women were all decked out in bright satin and silken saris. Her very simplicity made her the outstanding attraction. Through the crowds, she noticed that the State President was one of the guests Hussein was talking animatedly to. Over to the left of the ballroom, she noticed the handsome Minister of Foreign Affairs and his slim wife.

'Hello darling,' said Jack softly, reaching her at last across the crowded jostling room. 'How did your little tête-à-tête with the warlord go?' He was watching her intently as she replied.

'Well, the man dances like an angel,' she replied lightly.

'The Angel of Death, perhaps,' said Jack seriously. April was hard-pressed not to launch herself into Jack's safe arms.

'Actually, he was rather charming. But he did warn me to mind my own business, in no uncertain terms.'

'Oh? And what did you say?'

'Naturally, I told him that I just couldn't do that,' said April with a smile. She was quite unprepared for Jack's vehement reaction.

'You little idiot! I told you *not* to antagonize him! He's quite capable of having you eliminated. Why don't you listen?'

'Jack, let go of my arm, you're hurting me,' said April. Jack quickly released her.

'I'm sorry, darling,' he quickly said, remorsefully. 'I love you and I'm concerned about you, that's all.'

'It's all right,' she said brightly, rubbing the angry red welt that his hand had left on her arm. 'I didn't say anything to antagonize him. He actually laughed at me, so how much of a threat can I be?' She stared earnestly into his eyes, willing him to reassure her.

'Just stay away from him, that's all,' said Jack, after an interminable silence.

'No problem,' she quickly replied. 'Which one is his wife?' she asked, scanning the room with curiosity.

'None,' replied Jack, quietly. 'She does not appear at these glittering functions.'

'I thought he had two wives,' said April with a little frown.

'Yes, but they stay out of sight at all times. The entertainment is always arranged by his social secretary. That's her over there,' he said, pointing discreetly. April looked in the direction that he was indicating, and saw a striking young blonde woman standing next to Hussein, deep in conversation with the State President and his wife. Hussein was watching her with a decidedly proprietorial air.

'I see,' said April, winking at Jack in acknowledgement of the true state of affairs that existed between Hussein and his secretary.

'She is actually thirty-four,' said Jack in her ear, as the music had stopped and there was a lull in the buzz of conversation.

'But she only looks twenty,' said April in amazement. As if sensing that she was being spoken about, the woman looked up and directly at April. She was struck by the iciness of her blue eyes. They looked as cold as the ice floes in the Antarctic. Her features were finely chiselled, and the colour of her eyes was repeated by the shimmering blue gown that would have looked in place at an Oscars evening.

'She's Hungarian,' said Jack, witnessing the interchange between the two women.

'So what is she doing here, and in an important government position?' asked April, her eyes wide with surprise.

'She alleges that she escaped across the border in a coffin,' said Jack, his disbelief apparent in his tone of voice.

'Why don't you believe it?' asked April, turning back to look at the woman. She had disappeared in the crowd.

'Let's just say that I have my reasons for thinking that there is more to Eva than meets the eye,' he said mysteriously.

'April, darling,' whined a familiar voice at her shoulder. She spun around to see Manilal slobbering into his drink. Her eyes flew heavenwards in an attempt to make him disappear.

'Beat it, Mooljee,' growled Jack. 'You're drunk and the lady wants nothing to do with you.'

'Really? I don't see the lady objecting.' Without warning, he lurched into April and tried to pull her onto the dance floor. Without even thinking, she kneed him sharply in the groin, and was satisfied to see him double over, paralysed and breathless with pain. His glass fell, tumbled across the floor and smashed as it hit the french doors.

Jack quickly picked him up and put him into one of the brocaded chairs lining the wall.

'How about a dance, my darling?' he asked April, smiling at her self-preservation tactics with admiration.

'I'd be delighted,' she responded, and drifted into his arms on the wings of a Strauss waltz . Glancing over to the stage where the musicians were seated, April gasped in recognition.

'But there's Antonio Felluci, the first violinist of the Cape Town Symphony Orchestra.'

'Yes,' replied Jack. 'And if you look a little closer, you'll notice that half of that orchestra is playing here tonight.'

'Mr Hussein must be quite a big boy down at parliament,' whispered April. 'I've never heard of anyone hiring the CTSO, for goodness' sake.'

The evening passed in a whirl of colour and activity for April. She was always aware of Jack hovering within earshot of her as she danced and spoke with the many important guests present. Her head was whirling from the countless waltzes the orchestra had played, and the countless glasses of champagne she had unwittingly consumed in her thirst.

The ballroom was oppressively hot, and the noise level had risen to almost fever pitch proportions. She suddenly became aware of a pressing need to use the bathroom. Looking around her, she spotted a door swinging open and shut that only women seemed to be using. Setting off determinedly, she quickly negotiated her way across the room. She was dismayed to see that the queue was seemingly endless. Being enterprising, she walked out and recrossed the ballroom. Coming into the empty entrance hall was refreshing. Looking up the imposing mahogany staircase, she lifted her skirts in her hurry to ascend and reach the confines of an unoccupied bathroom.

The stairs were covered in a thick pile deep crimson carpet that was echoed by the first floor. Walking carefully down the corridor, she tried door after door, and was finally rewarded with a bathroom of Cleopatra proportions.

A few minutes later, a refreshed and relieved April walked back into the corridor. She headed back in the direction of the noise but stopped, her curiosity to see how this man lived overcoming her common sense. All the doors she had opened to reach the bathroom had appeared to be impersonal guest bedrooms. Heading stealthily back towards the interior of the silent house, she felt a thrill of danger running through her body like an electric current.

Her senses heightened, she heard a repetitive thudding sound coming from a room further down the hallway. Eager to see what was making the peculiar sound, she crept towards a door that was slightly ajar, its white light spilling out into the darkened passageway. As she got closer, she could hear muted voices, interspersed with the thuds. Thinking that she would be intruding on a secret assignation between two lovers, she turned away, but stopped sharply as her ears caught a muffled scream of terror and agony. Walking softly but determinedly back towards the source of light and noise, April felt her heart pounding unpleasantly in her chest. Carefully, she peered through the crack in the door, totally unprepared for what she saw. The room was obviously some sort of a den, the walls lined with bookshelves and hunting trophies. To one side was a large ebony and yellow wood desk, stacked with papers and stationery. But what held her gaze riveted to the centre of the room was the sight of the man tied to the wooden chair by cruel-looking ropes. His face was an unrecognizable bloody pulp, and leaning over him, talking softly and intently, was Abdul Hussein. April started in horror as Hussein quickly lashed out at the man with the back of his hand. To her disgust, April saw a piece of flesh fly across the room.

'Clean that up,' barked Hussein to one of the two men standing nearby.

April had not noticed them earlier. They were all dressed in tuxedos, except for the victim who appeared to be wearing what had once been a white dhoti. It was now splashed crimson with blood and vomit. She found herself gagging as a wave of revulsion and nausea threatened to overcome her. She remained rooted to the spot, unable to move even a muscle.

'Sign over that property now, you fool,' growled Hussein, not even looking in the man's direction. His reply was inaudible, but caused Hussein to bark with laughter. 'You idiot, there is no point in giving it to the Muslim foundation for a new madrasah. I'm going to build that townhouse complex there, even if I have to use your scrawny chicken bones for the foundations.' His voice was deep and menacing.

April could hardly believe this was the same man who had been charming and cordial at the party. She shook her head disbelievingly, convinced that this was a product of her champagne-fuddled brain. As her vision cleared, her head cleared too, and she felt more sober than she had ever felt in her life.

'Well?' Hussein said menacingly. 'Are you going to sell me that property at my price, or do I have to make your wife a widow?' He asked the question as calmly and as reasonably as if he was asking whether the man would like one lump of sugar or two in his tea.

April was aware that she had been holding her breath. She looked up and down the corridor, unsure of what to do. Another thud and a groan from the room drew her attention back to the drama that was unfolding before her eyes.

'Throw water on him,' Hussein brusquely ordered one of his burly henchmen. 'The fool has fainted.' He walked over to his desk and calmly lit a cigar as his orders were carried out. The man in the chair was sobbing and groaning as he regained consciousness. Hussein icily picked the flesh gouged from the face of his victim out of his heavy ring, and flicked it at the man as though it were a grain of dust. Squaring his shoulders, he strode purposefully over to the lolling man and stood in front of him, pulling his head back by the hair as he forced the man to look at him.

'Right, Hafez, let's have a last little talk. Are you going to sign the property over to me or not?'

'Rot in hell you filthy pig,' came the surprising answer. For a man in his weakened condition, April could hardly believe the vehemence in his voice. He then spat accurately and violently into Hussein's face. Without even blinking, he wiped the blood-flecked spittle away, then Hussein brought his fist around and crunched it into the man's temple with all his might, his head snapping sideways with a sickening crunch. The man jerked spasmodically for a few seconds, then hung limp, supported macabrely puppet-like by the ropes that bound him.

'Get rid of the body,' snapped Hussein, taking a silk handkerchief from his pocket and fastidiously wiping his face and his hands.

April's hand flew to her mouth and she tried to stifle her cry as the full impact of what she had just witnessed hit her like a blow in the solar plexus. All three men's heads swung around to the doorway.

'Get whoever that is!' shouted Hussein. April didn't wait. She picked up her heavy skirts and ran with the full speed of adrenalin pumping through her body. She leaped down the stairs three at a time and raced outside into the fresh air. Gasping convulsively, bile rising in her throat, she dived down the front stairs, and tore across the lawn into the spinney of trees. From her darkened hiding place, she watched the house in a state of near hysteria. Unable to control herself, she vomited repeatedly, gagging in her efforts to keep quiet. Suddenly, she saw the two henchmen saunter almost nonchalantly out of the front door. All her instincts for self-preservation came to the fore as she nimbly climbed up into the highest branches of a tree. Its foliage seemed to cover her like a fellow conspirator, as she shut her eyes and tried to make herself as small as possible, squeezed up against the bark. She listened in terror as she heard the two men coming closer. They had almost reached her tree when Hussein's voice boomed out across the lawn.

'The intruder couldn't have got outside so quickly. Come and search the house. He must be still hiding in one of the rooms.'

April nearly fainted with relief as the men turned away. It was obvious that they hadn't seen it was her, listening at the door. In the moonlight, she saw that they carried guns. She had seen enough films to recognize silencers, and she started shivering as the shock of what had happened set in. Trembling, she managed to clamber down from her safe perch. She brushed herself down and felt in her hair to see if there were any tell-tale twigs that could cause suspicion. She had to go back into the house and tell Jack what she had seen. Looking fearfully at the windows on the upper storeys, she made her way across the lawn, grateful for the clouds that kept crossing the moon. She felt a warm trickle down her right leg and was horrified to see that she was bleeding from her shin where she had grazed herself scaling the tree. Quickly grabbing a handful of grass, she rubbed at the blood frantically. Spitting on her hand, she wiped the graze in an effort to staunch the flow.

She ran lightly up the front stairs and sidled through the entrance hall as quietly and as unobtrusively as possible. There was no sight of Hussein and his goons. She quickly slipped into the ballroom, and only when the hot blast of air hit her did she realize how cold she was. She stood, ashen and shaking against the side of the ballroom, happy to play a wilting wallflower. She could see Jack's head bobbing up and down as he danced with a large Indian woman who was intent on stepping on his toes as often as possible. As he danced past, she managed to catch his eye as unobtrusively as possible. As though on cue, the orchestra stopped playing and announced a 15-minute recess.

Jack walked casually over to her. As he got closer, he saw that she was trembling, and her gown was torn on the knee. 'What the hell happened?' he asked, concernedly. April followed his gaze and blanched as she saw the tear. Sitting down quickly, and covering her knee with her hand to hide the torn gown, she motioned him closer.

Placing an artificial smile on her face as though she was making light conversation with him, she quickly told him about what she had just witnessed.

He stared at her open-mouthed. Finally, he said, aghast, 'April, are you crazy? How could you get involved? I warned you about him. Why on earth did you ignore me?'

'But I only wanted to use the bathroom, for goodness' sake. How was I to know that he was busy murdering someone in the next room?' Her voice had risen in her indignation.

'Sshhh!' hissed Jack sharply, smiling for the benefit of any interested passers-by. This was one conversation that he wanted kept very private.

Just then Hussein entered the room with his henchmen in tow. It sickened her to see the way he acted – as though he had just stepped out to have a discreet smoke. His sharp eyes scanned the room, and finally alighted on her and Jack sitting together. He walked over to them. April's heart seemed to freeze in her chest, and she felt the nausea returning.

'Oh my God, he's coming,' she hissed in panic through gritted teeth and a fake smile.

'Just relax,' said Jack, turning his head so that Hussein couldn't hear what he was saying. 'Let me handle this.' Without waiting for April's reply, he stood up and walked over to intercept Hussein. April breathed a sigh of relief as Jack entrenched himself firmly between her and the murderer.

'Hello Abdul, great party,' began Jack cheerily. Suddenly, he dropped his voice to a conspiratorial whisper. 'I don't know what is going on, but a man just came running down the stairs like a scalded rabbit. Was he stealing something?' Jack's face was a study in innocence. April struggled to lip-read what was being said, but it was no use. Jack kept his head averted away from her, drawing Hussein's attention entirely to himself.

'Oh?' enquired Hussein, his tone casual, but his eyes glittering malevolently.

'Yes,' continued Jack, warming to his theme, 'I couldn't see his face, but he was dressed in a dinner suit like the rest of us, and he upset that tray of champagne glasses as he raced out through the french doors onto the terrace.' Jack improvised as he saw the broken glass that Mooljee had dropped near the exit.

'Yes, the beggar was stealing,' said Hussein. 'Thank you, my boy. You don't know how helpful you've been. Benji, Kader, this way,' he called over his shoulder as he made his way to the doors. The henchmen ran after him like trained pit bull terriers.

'Right, now let's get you the hell out of here,' said Jack, practically lifting April bodily out of her seat. The orchestra started playing, and the milling guests quickly filled the dance floor again. He steered her out through a side entrance that she had not noticed earlier.

'Have you got your car ticket?' he quickly asked her, his eyes darting around the darkened grounds.

'Yes, it's in my ... Oh no. I don't believe this. I must have left my bag in the bathroom.' April started to shake as the sobs stuck dryly in her throat.

'Which bathroom did you use?' asked Jack impatiently.

'The upstairs one,' she whimpered.

'April, this house has eight bathrooms upstairs. Now think, which one did you use?' His fingers were biting into her flesh as he willed her to remember.

'Umm, it was the fourth door on the right,' said April.

'Stay here, and don't move. Do you understand?'

'Yes, darling. Oh that poor man. I swear I heard his neck snap like the wishbone of a chicken.' Her face became ashen as the memories flooded back .

'Hush, my darling,' soothed Jack, kissing her lightly on her troubled brow. She nestled into the safety of his arms for a moment before he moved back towards the building. April hugged herself to stop from trembling in the frosty air, the shock of what she had seen beginning to seep through to her bones. She froze as her ears picked up a foot tread nearby on the gravel. Moving back into the shadows, she held her breath with fright and anticipation.

'April,' came Jack's voice, calling softly out of the darkness. Sobbing with relief, she flung herself at him.

'Oh Jack, I thought it was them. Why did you come back a different way?'

'To avoid suspicion, silly. Don't you watch the James Bond movies?' He gently tucked a straying curl behind her ear. Her chignon was looking a little the worse for wear.

'Right, here is your purse. Get out your ticket stub, then walk around the corner. The valets are sitting there having coffee. I love you. Now don't worry about a thing. It will all fall into place.'

April looked at him quizzically. 'What do you mean, "it will all fall into place"?' she asked sharply.

'Nothing, baby, I just mean that once you've slept on it, it will all gain a little perspective.'

Irritated with his condescending tone, April pulled away from him.

'Jack, one never places murder in perspective. I watched him brutalize another human being, and then take his life as though it were worthless. How can anybody be that cruel?' She walked away from him, her face full of shadows as the clouds passed by overhead. The wind had risen and was biting and cold.

Coming up behind her, Jack put his arms around her and pulled her towards him. 'I know, my love. I'm sorry that you had to witness this terrible tragedy. Trust me when I say that he will he punished. But don't tell anyone what you saw tonight.'

She spun around so fast that he nearly lost his balance. 'I have to tell the police, Jack. I can't just ignore what I saw.'

'Right, and then what do you think will happen to you? Didn't you see the police chief here tonight? Hussein has them in his pocket, April. You breathe one word, and you'll be signing your own death warrant. Now I said leave it to me, and I mean it. Understand?' She stared at him open-mouthed, disbelieving that he could be so stern with her.

'April, don't look at me like that,' he said, softening as he saw the tears of frustration running down her cheeks. Nothing touched him more than the silent and heartfelt tears of a woman.

'All right, Jack, I'll trust you. I love you. But tell me what's going on. I have to know.' She wiped at the tears as she tasted their saltiness trickling over her lips.

'I can't tell you. Not yet. It's just too dangerous. But believe me when I tell you that Hussein will be getting his just desserts sooner than anyone thinks.'

Jack pulled April against his chest, crushing her with the intensity of his embrace. 'I'll never let anyone hurt a hair on your precious head,' he whispered, his voice thick with emotion. She could sense the tension in his body as he held her in his warm and safe arms. Releasing her reluctantly, he playfully patted her on her shapely behind. 'Come on, girl. You had better get a move on before Hussein and his trained apes come looking for the "mystery man" in this direction.'

April smiled up at him in the darkness, feeling her panic subsiding. She felt like a little girl and a woman at the same time when she was with Jack. She felt as though he could keep all the evils of the world at bay with the purity of his love.

'Will I see you tomorrow for breakfast, darling?' she enquired, beginning to feel the warmth that his touch had initiated spreading through her tired body.

'Of course. I'll stop by after my jog and pile all those kilograms back on with your good cooking. Deal?'

'Deal,' she laughingly replied. 'Oh, and bring all the newspapers that you can lay your hands on, will you? I want to see what is said about tonight's little drama.'

She couldn't see the frown that played across Jack's face in the disappearing moonlight. 'If I remember,' he replied offhandedly. 'Now get moving, darling. It's way past your bedtime.'

April glanced at her watch, its luminous hands showing that it was already half an hour past midnight.

'Crackers!' she exclaimed. 'Shakespeare is going to sulk for a week. I never realized just how late it was. Goodnight my love, and thank you for being my rescuer on a white horse.' Standing on tiptoes, she placed a smacking kiss squarely on his cheek. With her silvery laughter still floating on the air, she disappeared wraithlike into the shadows.

Jack stood, rubbing his chin thoughtfully in the darkness. He watched until he saw the red tail-lights of April's car disappearing down the long driveway. Turning, he sprinted back up the stairs and entered the ballroom again. The warmth hit him like an oven door opening. Across the crowded floor, he saw Abdul Hussein playing Lord of the Manor to the hilt, with the Ice Maiden on his arm. Elbowing his way through the teeming dancers, Jack made his way across to where the pair were standing.

'Of course, you will have to lay your bets on my horse in next Saturday's race, Sir Errol. My filly will definitely be winning. Take my word for it.' His jovial and ingratiating tone made Jack wince.

'I say, old chap. What is her name?' replied the British Ambassador, taking an expensive leather-bound notepad out of his jacket pocket.

'Swift Revenge,' replied Hussein, looking at Jack meaningfully as he joined the group.

'I say, what an extraordinary name for a horse. Oh, hang on a minute. Didn't she win the Metropolitan Gold Stakes last month?'

'Yes,' replied Hussein smugly. 'That is why I bought her. I only interest myself in the winners of this world. Don't you think that is a good philosophy for life?'

'Oh, indubitably, old man. Well, I shall jolly well make sure that my secretary places a sizeable bet for me. But we mustn't let the old ball and chain know, hey? What?' Sir Errol snickered at his own joke like a feeble parrot. His thin red lips were pulled back from his protruding teeth in a grimace of humour. Jack watched Eva as she quietly whispered the meaning of 'ball and chain' into Hussein's ear. He smiled politely at Sir Errol, despising the little man at the same time.

'Well, you will have to excuse me, Sir Errol, I have to see to the other guests.' Turning sharply away, he fixed his glittering cold eyes on Jack.

'Shall we go upstairs to finalise our "business" arrangement Jack?'

Nodding in mute agreement, Jack followed Hussein and Eva out of the room. He did not notice Hussein playing absently with the scrap of aquamarine velvet fabric that he had found fluttering on the lowest branches of one of the trees.

# *Chapter Ten*

April rubbed her eyes sleepily as she awoke to the insistent chiming of the doorbell. Shakespeare was yapping excitedly, and was already halfway down the stairs, as though he was capable of opening the door. Grabbing her comfortable old yellow floral robe, April slipped her feet into her slippers and lurched sleepily towards the door.

'Okay, okay, I'm coming,' she called out, a little irritated at being woken up so early on a Sunday morning after a late night out. Glancing at her wall clock in the passage, she was surprised to see that it was barely 6.30 a.m.

'Oh good grief, this is a bit much.' In her annoyance, she uncharacteristically opened the door without first checking to see who was there.

'Good morning, Starshine,' said Jack breezily, as he pulled her into his arms and twirled her around, her hair flying. Shakespeare was jumping up and down excitedly, so overcome with emotion at seeing his hero that he was no longer barking.

'Jack, for heaven's sake,' gasped April, the very breath squeezed from her lungs at his intensity. 'Put me down. Someone will see us.'

'Let them,' he replied recklessly, planting a resounding kiss on her up-turned nose.

Laughingly struggling to free herself, April pulled him inside. 'Are you crazy, disturbing my much needed beauty sleep so early on a Sunday morning?'

'Yes, I'm crazy about you, and besotted with you, and I can't sleep and can't eat unless I'm with you, and I can't think or breathe unless you are right next to me telling me to breathe in and breathe out.' His bantering tone had become very serious, and he clasped April to his broad chest in a desperate hug. She could hear the pounding of his racing heart.

'Jack, is something wrong?' she asked, feeling a flutter of fear at his obvious state of agitation. Above her head, his face was pinched, and his brow was creased with frown lines. Suddenly, he let April go, and she staggered as the absence of his embrace left her reeling.

'April, listen to me.' He turned away from her and sat down heavily in the rocking chair. Shakespeare immediately launched himself onto his lap, determined to be as close to Jack as he would be allowed. He absentmindedly stroked the little dog. 'Sit down, my love, I need to talk to you.' Puzzled, April lowered herself onto the couch.

'April, no matter what might happen over the next few weeks, please trust me, and know that I love you and would never do anything to harm you, neither would I let anyone else harm you. Do you understand me?'

'Well, I understand the words, but not why you are saying them to me. Why?'

'No questions, my love. I cannot give you the answers right now. Just promise me that you'll trust me and believe in me, no matter what rumours or stories you might hear?'

'Of course I trust you, Jack, but you're frightening me. What's wrong?' Her eyes were bright with unshed tears.

'Darling, please don't cry. I never meant to hurt you. I simply wanted to make sure that you understood how much I loved you.' Jack stood up and came and sat next to April, taking her comfortingly into his warm embrace.

'There is something wrong, Jack. What is it? Please tell me. I can't bear not knowing.' She lifted her head from his shoulder and scanned his face to see if there were any answers to be found. His face was impassive, but she could see the tension in his jaw as a muscle twitched beneath his cheekbone. He looked into her eyes, his gaze warming her and melting the ice of fear that had started squeezing her chest.

'I'm sorry that I stopped by so early, sweetheart. You were expecting me at nine, weren't you?'

'Actually, yes, but I'm thrilled that you're here now. Let's go back to bed,' she added impishly, her eyes twinkling with mirth.

'One of these days, young lady, and I'm going to take you up on your offer. Then you'll be very sorry.'

'Oh, I doubt that,' she said softly.

'I can see that all I can do to save you from yourself is to make an honest woman out of you, April Ross. As soon as possible.'

'I think that you will find the "dishonest" woman infinitely more exciting darling,' she replied huskily in a theatrical whisper. He laughed at her fluttering eyelashes.

'What about some of David's good coffee to wake us both up?' he said, pushing her playfully away from him.

'Sure, I'd love some,' she replied, settling back comfortably on the couch with her eyes closed.

'No Eastern woman would send her man into the kitchen to make coffee or wash dishes or anything else,' he replied.

'Ah, Mr Neanderthal caveman, guess what? I'm thoroughly Western, and we Western woman make slaves of our men. So how about that coffee?'

Sighing resignedly, Jack dragged himself to his feet. 'Come on Shakespeare, let's go and do our mistress's bidding.' Shakespeare bounded delightedly after him, quite prepared to walk into the fires of hell with this man.

* * *

With the aroma of freshly percolated coffee and cheesy croissants wafting through the townhouse, April and Jack read segments of the *Sunday Times* in companionable silence.

'Jack,' said April sharply, flinging down the last page.

'What?' he asked, preoccupied.

'There's absolutely nothing in it about that man who was killed at Hussein's place. There is an article about him and his guests, but nothing else.'

'Darling, this is a national newspaper. They don't report about local crimes. There would be no space for anything else.'

'I realize that,' she replied, a little impatiently. 'But someone of Hussein's high visibility would definitely feature in local and national papers, wouldn't he?'

'April, just drop it! All right?' His voice was sharp, the unmistakeable tone of authority making Shakespeare prick up his ears.

April looked at him in surprise. 'You can't pretend that it never happened,' she replied in surprise.

'No, but I want you to stop talking about it. Just forget it. The matter is being dealt with.' His face looked thunderous, and she felt a cold shiver as she looked into the face of this familiar stranger that had transformed before her eyes.

'But how is…'

'April, stop this,' he exploded with rage. She jumped, thoroughly taken aback by this uncharacteristic temper outburst. She felt the anger rising in her to meet his.

'Listen, pal,' she said venomously, too angry to be afraid. 'I put up with a great deal of nonsense from Parker, and I am not about to do the same with you. You have complicated my life unbelievably, so don't push me now. I simply will not take it.' Her face was red and her breath was rasping in her chest. Jack stared at her in surprise. To her consternation, he burst out laughing.

'Well, well, so the little maiden is made of iron after all,' he said. 'You are quite right, April. It was wrong of me to lose my cool and I am most abjectly sorry. Please forgive me?'

She watched him suspiciously, convinced that he was making fun of her. He sighed, and turned back to his newspaper as though nothing had happened. April was a little shaken, as she was slow to anger, and even slower to calm down. She began to realize that there were sides to Jack that she knew nothing about. Putting on her best smile, April nodded mutely. Jack put his hand over hers and squeezed it reassuringly. Their fingers entwined and he pulled her towards him, crushing the newspaper. Jack traced a trail of fiery kisses across the base of April's throat, and gently slipped her satin robe off her creamy shoulders. April's breathing quickened as her passion mounted. She clung close to Jack. Her nostrils were filled with his woody fragrance, and his woollen jersey made patterns on her skin. Its texture was pleasingly coarse. As though the elements were in tune with their rising emotions, the day perceptibly darkened outside the windows as the full force of the storm that had been threatening hit the shores with ferocity. April jumped as the lounge was lit with the fierce white flash of lightning. A few seconds later, thunder rolled across the roof and set the ornaments tinkling with its roar. April gasped and clasped Jack tighter, having always been in awe of the savagery of the elements. He felt her shaking beneath his firm hands, and soothed her, much as one would a frightened child. April felt all her feminist ideas fading as she let herself be comforted by him. She felt secure, and safer than she had ever felt before in her life. The heavens opened and the violent rain came tumbling out of the leaden skies.

‘How would you like to go for a walk?’ Jack suddenly said, raising his voice so that she could hear him above the shrieking wind that had gusted in off the sea only moments earlier.

‘Walk? In this weather? Jack, you have to be out of your mind.’

‘Why?’ he asked her, an excited smile lighting up his face.

‘Why? Because we could get struck dead by lightning, that’s why,’ she pertly replied, confident that he had been joking.

He leaped to his feet, towering above her like a Greek God, his dark good looks enhanced by his cream cabled jersey, and his long legs encased in his faded fashionable denims. The corporate Jack and the private Jack were two very different animals, and April was continually delighted at how different he was away from the workplace and in their private world.

He pulled her to her feet. ‘Go on,’ he said smiling down at her, ‘go and dress for the rain and the wind. We’re going for a walk on the beach.’

‘Sure, where we will first be struck by lightning and then drowned in a tidal wave rolling in off the Indian Ocean. Thanks, but no thanks.’

‘Scared?’ he teasingly enquired, throwing her the timeless challenge.

‘No, but perhaps a little cautious,’ she replied.

‘That is the little bull in you my love. Why don’t you challenge the storm with a big bad Scorpio. Besides, there won’t be anyone else on the beach, and you know that I’m forbidden by law to go onto it because I’m a little too suntanned for this country.’

April heard the pain behind the banter in his voice. ‘Okay, Mister, let’s go to the beach. You and I are definitely going to be the only fools out in this weather. See you in five minutes,' she laughingly shouted over her shoulder as she raced Shakespeare up the stairs.

The icy wind whipped April's hair about her face, but she felt snug and safe in her olive green and cream padded windbreaker. The icy rain squall seemed to have passed, and although the clouds were low and threatening, there was no sign of the earlier thunder and lightning.

The white expanse of the sandy beach stretched interminably in front of them. The grey ocean slapped the shoreline frenziedly as the wind whipped the white horses into white foaming peaks of power and energy. Shakespeare skipped around their feet, snug in his little red winter jacket. He had no desire to run away from them and explore unknown territories. Jack had been quite correct. They were alone on the beach, their footsteps looking lost and lonely in the flat sand near the water's edge.

'I always go to the beach at night and in storms,' said Jack softly, his breath warm and familiar on her ear, their hands entwined in the pocket of his big waterproof jacket.

'What does it feel like, Jack?' asked April gently, her grey eyes echoing the leaden sky and molten ocean pounding at her feet.

'What does what feel like, my darling?' he asked her, hugging her warmly against his side.

'Not to be allowed to live anywhere you would like to, or not to go onto the prime beaches, not to go to the schools and universities of your choice and capabilities?'

He remained silent for a long while. Presently he slowly replied, and his answer made April's heart heavy in her chest. 'Imagine being treated as a hostile stranger in your own home. I'm one of the lucky ones in that my parents could afford to send me to private schools, so I was always integrated from an early age, and my friends were from all races and walks of life. But we could never all go to one beach together as children. We would have to split up into the white group and the others, and then try to act as though this was all normal. But we survived those childhood years relatively unaffected by the realities of South African life. Things became complicated as we reached adolescence, and started falling in love. Then parents who had previously been friends of the family would turn on one another and forbid the youngsters to see one another out of a school environment. That was the first really hard lesson in life, and it created a great deal of confusion and heartache for us.'

April felt an unfamiliar twinge of jealousy at the thought of Jack ever being in love with anyone else. He had stopped walking, and he turned around to face her on the cold wet sand, pulling her tightly against him to shield her from the wind. His warmth reached right through her clothing and she felt as though he was touching her bare skin. Her cheeks flamed red at the sudden wantonness that overwhelmed her whenever this man touched her. She suddenly realized he had begun speaking again, and she did her best to concentrate on his words.

'When I left school, I discovered that what we had gone through was just the tip of the iceberg. Discrimination in the workplace was incredible. I had started my correspondence studies in commerce through the University of South Africa, and had years of experience from my family's factory, yet the only position available for me was a shift worker's job keeping the machinery functioning. There was a lovely bathroom facility for the white office staff, but I was expected to use the filthy broken toilets assigned to the black staff. I used to get into my car and drive all the way home to use my own Italian-tiled bathroom.'

Jack's voice was as hard as a razor's edge as he told her these stories, but there was no bitterness at all. April found herself seething on his behalf at the incredible indignities that he had experienced, endured and weathered.

'How could you put up with this Jack?' she burst out.

'Simple, darling. That was just the way things were, and in some places, they still are. At least today there are fewer restrictions than there were.'

'But for goodness' sake, there shouldn't be any restrictions. What's the matter with these people?'

'Darling,' crooned Jack in her ear, 'did any of this really bother you before you go to know me?'

'I'm ashamed to say that I never thought about anybody suffering,' April admitted sheepishly. 'It isn't because we didn't care, or didn't want everyone to live a full and productive life. It's simply that it was never close or real. My parents were often shunned by some of their friends for their acquaintances with people of other races, or their unpopular views that all men were created equal. But even so, I have never come close to the suffering that you must have gone through.'

'Until now?' asked Jack softly.

'Until now, my love. What on earth are we going to do, Jack? It all feels so bleak right now.' Unwillingly, tears oozed out from under April's closed eyelashes. She buried her head deeper into Jack's shoulder so that he would not see her weakness.

'The future has never looked brighter, my darling. Next month, the Mixed Marriages Act will go, and then we will live normal and free lives … or at least as normal as we can until they also abolish the Group Areas Act,' he hastily corrected himself.

Laughing through her tears, April had to agree that being able to marry one another but then being forced to live in restricted areas was the ultimate irony. She felt Jack stiffen in her arms.

'Come on, let's get back to the townhouse quickly,' he

said, an unusual edge to his voice. April turned her head but could see no one at all on the beach. She looked up and noticed that Jack was staring at the road that separated them from the townhouse. Looking again in that direction, she saw a large BMW cruising slowly past, the driver looking towards her building and not noticing the two of them on the beach.

By this time, Jack was literally pulling her along behind him, and they reached the pedestrian crossover point at breakneck speed, Shakespeare never very far behind. Scooping the small dog into his arms, Jack bustled April over the road, looking worriedly to his left. Peering around him, April saw the large car doing a leisurely U-turn and heading back towards them, but then they were through her garden gate, and it was lost from sight.

'Quickly, inside!' ordered Jack, bolting the gate behind him.

'What on earth is going on, Jack? I can't breathe properly from that mad race to get here.'

'That was Hussein outside,' he snapped. 'I have to leave before he spots my car here.'

'But he can't see your car unless he drives into the complex, Jack. And he doesn't have the card to open the boom anyway.'

Jack did not even seem to be listening as he hastily grabbed his keys off the dining room table.

'I have to go now, my love!' he exclaimed. 'Hussein must never know that you and I are seeing one another. That could be very dangerous.'

'But why, for heaven's sake?' wailed April despondently.

He looked flustered and opened his mouth as though he was going to tell her. April could see the decision to remain silent flit across his face as he hastily embraced her. 'Goodbye my darling. I love you very much. Never doubt that, no matter what happens.'

'There you go again with all your cloak and dagger stuff, Jack. Tell me, what is going on?' She stamped her foot angrily.

'What is going on is that I love you madly, and I am going to marry you come hell or high water, and nothing is going to stand in our way. Fair enough and clear enough for you? Now goodbye!' She caught sight of him blowing her a kiss as the door closed in her face. April stood flabbergasted in her entrance hall, the whole morning having been mysterious and dissatisfying.

Resigning herself to a Sunday alone, April walked upstairs and changed out of her heavy rainweather clothing. She was pulling the brush through her thick glossy hair when her doorbell chimed loudly in the Sunday silence.

'Hmmm, wonder who that could be,' she said to Shakespeare, who had made himself comfortable on her bed. After his experience in the wet outdoors, he was not even interested in ringing doorbells and unexpected visitors. His main priorities now were warmth and sleep. April ran downstairs and remembered to stop before opening the door.

'Who is it?' she called out merrily.

'A message that has to be delivered in person,' said a man's voice, heavily accented in German.

April opened the grill in the front door. A man in his early thirties stood before her. His eyes were a piercing blue, and his hair was so fair it was almost white. He was well dressed, and he smiled reassuringly at her.

'Please, Fraulein, if I do not deliver this message properly and give you the item, my employer will have me served for breakfast.' His expression was wide-eyed and guileless as he regarded her with friendly anticipation.

'I'm afraid that I cannot pass it through the grill to you or it would be badly damaged.'

'Who sent you?' asked April cautiously, her sixth sense screaming that all was not as it should be.

'All will be revealed to you when you open the gift. I assure you of that, Fraulein.'

Deciding to test him, April laughed although she was feeling far from happy.

'Oh I know, it's that thing that Jayson said he was sending some time this week. I thought that he'd forgotten when nothing arrived. Am I right?' She watched him carefully.

'Ah, now you have spoiled the surprise! I was supposed to keep you in suspense until you had opened the parcel.' He smiled back at her, yet the smile never reached his cold eyes.

'I'm afraid that you just painted yourself into the proverbial corner,' she replied sweetly. 'I don't know any Jayson, so you, sir, are a liar, and I would rather go straight to hell than open this door. Get lost or I'll call the police.' With a bravado that she was not feeling at all, April stared at him through the grille, willing him to leave.

'You are too clever for your own good, little girl,' he hissed venomously, his pale face suffused with colour. 'But one day, when you least expect it, we will get you. Then we will see how brave you really are before you die.'

April gasped and slammed the grille shut, her legs shaking so much that her knees could no longer support her. His mocking mirthless laugh pounded her ears relentlessly.

'As they say in the movies, I know who you are and I know where you live.' He laughed uproarously, very pleased at his witticism. April listened as his footsteps faded away.

Struggling to regain her composure, she scrambled to her feet and raced upstairs. Parked outside her garden gate on the street that was empty of all other traffic was

Hussein's car, glistening malignantly in the feeble rays of sunlight that were trying to force themselves through the clouds. She saw the blond man walking towards the driver's door. With the keys in his hand, he looked straight up at her window as though he had been expecting her to be there. She involuntarily stepped backwards, but held his gaze determinedly. He mockingly saluted her, then unlocked Hussein's car and got confidently into the driver's seat. The message had been clearly delivered, and April knew with dreadful certainty that Hussein had known it was her who had seen him last night, snapping that man's neck as though it were a chicken bone. She felt her body reacting involuntarily to the stomach kick of fear that twisted her, and barely made it her bathroom where she was violently sick.

She jumped as the phone rang. Wiping her mouth with the back of her hand, she raced into the bedroom, convinced that it was Jack calling.

'Hello!' she said breathlessly.

'Hello, Fraulein, I'm calling from the car phone. Hope I didn't scare you too much?' The mocking concern in his voice was obscene.

'Leave me alone, you filthy bastard!' April screamed, her final vestiges of control slipping away from her.

'Do not put this phone down!' he snapped harshly. Shivering with fear and rage, April's grip on the receiver tightened. 'Are you there?'

'Yes, I … I'm here,' she said softly, willing herself not to be sick again.

'Good. Good girl,' he crooned gently. 'Now listen carefully if you want to stay alive.' There was a silence as she waited.

'Yes, what is it?' asked April weakly.

'Here's the thing, Fraulein. You are a beautiful woman and I would hate to have to use my considerable talents on your lovely face so that you could be discovered dead in a compromising situation. You are going to be a good little girl and you are going to tell nobody about our little call. All right?'

'All right,' she weakly responded.

'I will know if you have gone to the police, Liebling, because my boss owns them, do you understand?'

'Yes,' she replied, clenching her teeth in terrified frustration. Her mind was racing. Did they know about Jack? Was he safe?

'Er … can't I even discuss this matter with my fiancé?' she said, testing the extent of this man's knowledge.

'The fat slug would have a heart attack my dove,' replied the German. 'Besides, you need a real man in your bed, not a loser like him. And I know that you and he are not presently on very good terms my dear. Do you take me for a complete idiot?' His tone was so polite and gentle that April was having great difficulty reconciling the man with his vile threats. To her relief, he did not seem aware of Jack at all.

'What is it that you want?' she finally managed to blurt out, overcoming another wave of nausea.

'I want you to go and take a look on your front porch. I'll call you back a little later.' There was a click and a buzzing as he severed the connection.

She peered through the grille at her front door but could see no one. Cautiously, she opened the door a crack. On the mat outside her door was an innocent-looking white shoebox. April bent down to retrieve it, and nearly fainted as another wave of nausea gripped her. Clenching her teeth, she scooped up the box and carried it inside. Thoughts of bombs and snakes filled her mind as she placed it on the dining room table and watched it. There was no movement, and she could hear no ticking. Slowly, she lifted the lid off with a ruler and looked over the edge. At the bottom of the box was a scrap of the green material from the dress that she had worn to Hussein's party the night before. Her heart pounded painfully in her chest. She raced upstairs and snatched the dress out of her wardrobe. She frantically examined it for any damage, and was about to sigh with relief, when her eye caught the jagged tear that she had noticed before, not realizing that the fabric was missing. She jumped as her phone rang shrilly next to her.

'Yes?' she said shakily.

'See, Fraulein? I told you that I had a delivery for you.' The now familiar voice was expressionless and matter-of-fact. The lack of emotion in his tone sent chills up her spine.

'What is it that you want?' she asked breathlessly, feeling drained and frightened at the same time.

'Nothing, dear lady,' he replied. 'The boss just wanted you to know that he knows that you know.' He giggled insanely at his play on words.

'I don't know what you are talking about,' April said, grasping desperately at feigned innocence.

'Tsk tsk, Fraulein, you disappoint me greatly,' the man replied, mock concern and patience oozing across the wires. 'Do not think we are fools, dear lady. It will be a mistake that can easily cost your life.'

'Really!' snapped April, her outrage finally overcoming her fear of the situation. 'Get to the point, whatever your name is, you rotten stinking bully.'

His laughter was loud in her ear and she grimaced in agitation. 'My dear lady, and you can call me Hans by the way, although we both know that it is not my real name. Your courage impresses me although it is as ineffective as a flea shouting threats at an elephant. It is a mere irritation, and is losing its charm rapidly. Now, let's get to the point shall we?' His voice became crisp and decisive.

'Yes, let's,' replied April, thoroughly annoyed by the whole situation.

'This dress scrap was found in a tree in the area that we were searching last night. Now what else would you be doing up a tree except hiding?' He waited, as though he expected her to reply. April bit her lip in her effort to retain her composure, and could hardly hear his voice above the sound of the blood that was thundering in her ears.

'The point being this, my dear,' he said, his tone silky. 'He knows what you saw last night, and he is giving you the opportunity to live if you keep your pretty little mouth shut. If you don't, my special services will ensure that your death will look completely like an ugly and rather unfortunate accident.'

'I see,' she said, at a loss for a more sensible reply.

'We shall know if you tell anyone, do you understand me? Anyone! You are to keep your mouth shut and take this with you to the grave, which will be your next port of call if you fail to listen to reason.'

By now, April expected the dry mirthless cackle that followed Hans' evil humour. Again, the receiver went dead in her hand. April immediately began dialling Jack's number, but froze in mid-dial as the horror of what the man had said hit home. Her phone could be tapped by this stage, and dialling Jack would be a dead giveaway. She slammed the receiver down and stared at the telephone as though it was a snake that could strike any minute.

April sat curled up in front of her fire, sipping a scalding hot cup of cocoa, absentmindedly rubbing Shakespeare's head as he rested it on her stomach. Her mind was in turmoil. If she pursued her relationship with Jack, then Hussein would know for sure that they were involved, which would put his life in danger. There was no way that she could still see Jack and not tell him about what had happened. April had kept no secrets from him since the day they had declared their love for one another, and she was not about to start lying to him now. Shakespeare lifted his head as she sighed out aloud, perplexed by his mistress's silence and stillness that whole day.

She started as her phone shrilled in the late Sunday afternoon silence. Walking across to the table, she put her hand out, but could not bring herself to answer it. Presently it stopped ringing. She slumped down into the rocking chair, her head in her hands, sad to the very core of her existence. That call could have been from Hans with more vile threats, in which case she would have fallen to pieces. Or it may have been Jack, so she was glad that she had not answered it, because she did not know who might have been listening. Jack had been acting rather strangely lately about Hussein, which convinced April even further that he should not know about her being threatened. Nothing made sense.

'I have to end this relationship,' she said out loud. Then she began to sob as the full impact of the day's events crowded in on her, and the realization that her being a witness to a senseless murder had changed her life inexorably. She felt the loss of innocence as her tears flowed unchecked down her cheeks. Aneesa had been right about her devious and manipulative father. Jack had been right to warn her against Hussein's evil machinations. Her regret that she had ever gone to the party was overwhelming. April sniffed and resolutely blew her nose. This constant 'if only' pattern was going to drive her insane unless she took some form of action. Grabbing her windbreaker and her car keys, she headed for the door, whistling softly for Shakespeare to follow her. He needed no second invitation.

* * *

Standing in the telephone booth at the nearby supermarket, April leaned her head against the cold glass and clutched the coin convulsively in her hand. Dialling slowly, her face hardened as her resolve strengthened to do the only thing she could do. Her heart was pounding as the phone rang.

'Hello, Nathan speaking.'

She nearly dropped the phone as Jack's voice came across the lines. She had been praying that he would not be home, so that the moment could be put off. 'Hello. Is anyone there?' She could hear the annoyance in his tone of voice. April quickly inserted her money and listened to the hollow sound as the phone accepted the coin.

'Hello, Jack,' she said in an uncharacteristically small voice.

'April? For heaven's sake, darling. What are you doing calling from a pay phone? Is your phone broken? I called earlier and there was no reply.'

April felt relief that she had not answered her telephone's insistent ringing.

'Er ... yes, there does seem to be a problem,' she quickly said, grateful that he had provided so plausible an excuse.

'Darling, I love you. I'm so sorry that I took off like that and left you. I was sure that I saw Hussein's car cruising past.'

'Oh, I understand, Jack,' she replied. 'It probably wasn't even him, as you say, but I know that we can't be too careful.' She was surprised to find silent tears coursing down her face. She felt as though her heart was slowly seeping out of her tear ducts.

'Is there something wrong, darling? You sound a little strange.' Jack's voice was warm with concern.

'No ... no of course not, darling,' she quickly replied. 'I'm just a little inhibited by all these late Sunday afternoon shoppers. I just wanted to hear your voice, that's all.' She wiped her eyes on her windbreaker sleeve, conscious of the inquisitive stares of passers-by who could not help but notice this lovely woman's obvious distress.

'I'm glad you did phone, darling. I've been thinking about you all day. I can't wait to see you again. I'll have your telephone fixed first thing tomorrow morning.'

'No!' retorted April quickly, 'I mean, don't worry darling. It's already reported and taken care of. Thank you.'

'April, are you sure that nothing's wrong? You don't sound yourself at all.'

'Jack, don't be silly. I'm fine. I just woke up from a nap, that's all. Really. And I just wanted to phone you to ... to ...' She floundered as she searched for the right words.

'To what, sweetheart?' prompted Jack gently.

'To ask you to come and see me at my office tomorrow morning, darling. There's something important that we need to discuss, and I can't do it over the phone.'

'Sure. I'm free at ten o'clock. Will that do?'

'Yes, of course,' replied April, making a note to cancel her meeting with the housing department.

'April?'

'Yes?'

'I love you, honey, no matter what. Understand?'

'Yes.'

'Yes? Is that all?' he playfully teased. 'I bear my heart to you on a silver platter, and all you can say is "yes"?'

'As long as it isn't your head, Jack. I couldn't bear that,' she replied, aware of how easily that comment could come true if Hussein knew about their involvement.

'Come now, love. Why so serious? I'm really becoming worried about you, April. Are you sure that everything is all right?'

'Darling, of course,' replied April, forcing a lightness that she did not feel into her voice. 'Now I've got to run. I'll see you tomorrow at the office, all right?'

'All right. What are your plans for this evening? Should I perhaps pop around and bring a light supper with some nice mulled red wine?'

'I'm very tired, Jack,' she quickly replied. 'Can I take a raincheck?'

'Sure. I understand. Be good and dream sweetly.'

Fat chance, thought April to herself. 'Bye, darling.' She replaced the receiver lightly, unwilling to sever the connection, but knowing that this was just the first of many connections to this man that she would have to sever. With a heavy heart, she walked slowly back to her car, unmindful of the drenching rain that was soaking her hair and mingling with the steadily flowing tears on her face.

# *Chapter Eleven*

'Mr Nathan to see you, April,' said Aneesa, puzzled as to why April had cancelled her appointments for the day, and had barely spoken two words to her. She was racking her brain to try and remember if she had done anything that could have offended her in some way.

'Thank you, Aneesa. Come in, Mr Nathan,' said April, feigning an outward calm that she was far from feeling.

As the door closed, Jack covered the distance between them and pulled April urgently into his arms. She gripped him tightly, swallowing to keep the tears at bay as she held him for the last time. Disengaging himself, Jack kissed her upturned nose.

'Now, why so serious, Miss Ross?' he asked playfully, his face becoming grave as he noticed the unhappiness in her eyes. 'What's wrong, darling? You look so pale this morning.'

April had not slept at all, tossing and turning as she thought about the empty days that were ahead for her without Jack. In such a short space of time, he had become the centre of her universe, but her own hand was about to sever their connection inexorably.

Nervously, she cleared her threat. 'Coffee?' she asked, quickly spooning some into two cups.

'Please,' he replied, sitting down and watching her closely.

'Here,' she said, handing him a cup. His eyes widened as she pulled a cigarette out of her cigarette box, and lit it with a shaking hand. He did not comment at this lapse into one of her former bad habits. April grimaced as her mouth filled with the bitter taste of an unfamiliar cigarette. But today, she needed this crutch.

'Jack, I asked you here today because ... I ...' she stopped, trying to find the words.

'Relax, darling,' Jack replied gently. 'You can say anything to me. You know that. Just let the words come.' He sat back, sipping his coffee and watching her intently over the rim of the cup.

Clearing her throat, April crushed the unsmoked cigarette in the ashtray with great attention. She could hardly bring herself to say the words that she had been practising in front of her mirror the whole night.

Standing up, she restlessly began pacing the room. Finally, she came to rest with her back to the windows so that her face was hidden by the light streaming into the office from behind her. Jack's face was in clear daylight.

'Jack, I asked you here today for a special purpose.' She strengthened as she continued, falling into the safe pattern of a well rehearsed speech. 'I'm sorry to have to tell you this, Jack, but I can't see you any more.'

'What?' he exclaimed, leaping to his feet in amazement, unmindful of the scalding coffee spilling over his hands.

'Please, let me finish what I have to say,' she beseeched desperately, afraid that her composure would shatter. Silently, he sat down again, watching her expressionlessly. April knew that expression well. It was his poker face for when he was brimful with emotion, but controlling it so that he could assess his adversary. She felt weak at the thought that she had become his adversary.

'I let our relationship go too far too soon, and I'm not ready to settle down and make a commitment quite yet,' she said, hating herself for hurting him like this. He sat quietly, watching her implacably.

Nervously, she continued. 'I mistook my feelings for you

for love when in fact they were curiosity to see what is was like to be close to someone er ... different.' She winced as she saw the sudden pain in his face as his mask slipped for an instant. Like an iron door clanging shut, she saw him master his emotions, the only indication of his distress being the muscle that jumped in his cheek.

'I'm sorry that I led you on in any way,' she continued, determined to see this through to the end. 'I thought that I loved you, but I was wrong, so it would be pointless for us to see one another personally again, although I realize that we will still be dealing with one another professionally. I hope that this will not interfere with our business relationship at all?' She held her breath as she waited for him to be angry at her, or take her in his arms and tell her that he loved her. Her resolve would have willingly crumbled.

'Have you finished?' he asked her quietly.

'Yes ... yes I have,' she replied, nonplussed by his reaction.

'I'll bid you good day then, Miss Ross. Thank you for the coffee,' he added politely, standing up and putting his half-empty cup on the nearby tray.

Not even glancing back at her, he strode out of the room, leaving the connecting doors open. She heard him exchanging pleasantries with Aneesa and a few clients in the outer office, his deep laughter ringing in her ears. She could not believe the lack of impact that she had had on this man. Shakily, she went behind her desk and fell into her chair. She was in a state of shock, and everything around her seemed unreal. Suddenly alarmed that she was going to faint, she shook herself and breathed deeply. The room stopped spinning, but she still did not lose its sense of unreality.

'Well, he was certainly devastated,' she said grimly to herself, her pride wounded that he had not even tried to convince her otherwise.

'Oh stop it,' she scolded herself. 'You got exactly what you wanted, even though nothing will ever be the same again.' Despite all her efforts, the tears rolled down her face. She was surprised to see them as they fell onto her arm. She had thought it impossible to cry any more tears after last night.

'Aneesa, please tell the clients that I'll see them tomorrow. I'm going home soon. I don't feel well,' she said into her desk intercom. 'And please shut the interleading door for me. Thanks.'

Aneesa's brow creased as she heard the exhaustion in April's voice. 'Sorry everyone, Miss Ross is unavailable for today. Let's make appointments for tomorrow.' There was a mumble of dissatisfaction from the waiting people.

'Listen, you ingrates,' said Aneesa firmly, taking them all by surprise, 'I would suggest that you be reasonable. You should know by now that appointments need to be made in order to see lawyers, doctors, bank managers. So why is it so difficult to make appointments with the social worker? You are all thoroughly spoilt by the man who was here before who never planned his days to help you constructively. So make appointments now!'

The crowd quickly surged forward to do her bidding, and Aneesa felt the dizzying rush of the power of standing up to situations, just as April had told her would happen.

'Minister Hussein's office,' said the well-modulated tones of an impersonal secretary.

'Good morning. Could I please speak with the Minister? It's Miss Ross here from the Welfare Department.' April's hand shook as she held her phone as firmly as possible.

'May I ask what it is in connection with, Madam?' asked his cautious secretary.

'It's personal,' replied April, frustrated by the girl's efficiency.

'One moment, Madam, I'll see if he is available,' she quickly replied.

Taped music piped soothingly in April's ear as she was put on hold. Wishing that she had told the secretary that this was a long-distance call, April drummed her fingers impatiently.

'Hello, Miss Ross. How are you? So sorry to keep you waiting.' April started as Hussein's cultured tones echoed hollowly in her ear.

'I got your message,' she snapped, ignoring his polite enquiry after her health.

'Message?' he asked, sounding almost genuinely confused.

'Yes, the scrap of material? The "I know you know" cloak and dagger bit? Am I ringing any bells yet?' April heard anger creeping into her voice, and fought to control any outbursts that she may later regret.

'My dear lady, I really don't know what you are talking about,' insisted Hussein, his voice painstakingly patient and polite. Suddenly April understood. If she was having their conversation taped, then he would be compromised as blackmailing her and threatening her with bodily assault.

'Minister Hussein, I...'

'Please, dear lady, do call me Abdul. I feel that we will be getting to know one another so much better in the future.' April froze as she detected the unmistakable leer in his voice.

'I'd rather not, if you don't mind,' she snapped.

'Very well, April, I certainly will not force you to do something which you find distasteful. But I am sure that once we have had our little person-to-person chat, you'll understand me so much better, and be comfortable with a few little familiarities.'

'I doubt that. I phoned to tell you that I got the message, and I understand the terms. That's all. Your German friend made the implications clear enough. I find your behaviour on Saturday night despicable and, quite frankly, reprehensible, and you will be punished somehow. I certainly don't know how, but the day will come.' She was shaking as she concluded her last sentence. His laughter was mocking.

'My dear, you amaze me with your wit,' he said, chuckling amiably as he spoke. Anyone listening to their conversation would find her side of it confusing and rude, whereas Hussein was careful to not mention anything that might later be misconstrued. He sounded like a genial old flatterer having a little harmless fun with a young girl.

'Consider yourself warned, Minister,' she concluded, sounding feeble and weak to her own ears.

'I will be back in Durban in three weeks' time, April. I'll get my secretary to set up a meeting with you to discuss your obvious dilemma.'

'That won't be necessary,' said April quickly, a stab of fear shooting through her as she thought of the prospect of having to see this man again, let alone having to see him by herself without Jack's protection. She found herself regretting her impulse to phone him and let him know that she was aware of his evil actions.

'Oh, but it will, my dear, it will indeed be necessary. Now I have to go. Parliament awaits and I cannot keep the country waiting. I will see you in three weeks' time give or take a week or two, I'nsha'Allah. Good-bye.' Before April could say anything, he put the phone down.

'Dammit!' shouted April, slamming her phone down. Shakespeare looked up at her in surprise, and quietly slipped off the chair, slinking away before she could turn her wrath on him for the chewed-up report that lay as yet undetected beneath her desk.

* * *

April dragged herself to work for the next two weeks, hardly conscious of what was going on around her. She functioned automatically and went through all the motions that her job required, but the spark that had made her so unique was dead. The weather had been continually blustery, and icy squalls threw themselves at her home and office windows.

'April, Jack Nathan on the line,' said Aneesa. April felt as though her heart had stopped beating in her chest. She gasped as she struggled to breathe, her thoughts whirling frantically around in her head.

'Put him through,' she managed to say, surprised at the normality of her voice.

'Hello, Miss Ross, Jack Nathan here.' His voice was cold and distant, as though they had never shared any closeness or intimacy.

'Hello, Jack, how are you?' she replied, every fibre in her being screaming for her to make things right again with him. She wanted to let all the fear, loneliness and misery spill out, but knew that she couldn't let it happen.

'I thought that I had better remind you of the next welfare committee meeting as the minutes haven't been circulated as yet, and we are nearing our fourteen-day deadline.' His tone was brusque and businesslike. Her heart felt like a cold lump of metal in her chest.

'Aneesa will be posting them later on with this afternoon's mail,' she replied, the atmosphere heavy with unspoken emotions.

'Fine,' he replied. 'Well, I just thought that I'd remind you. Have a good day. Goodbye.'

'Goodbye,' she replied softly.

'Okay, what's going on?' April looked up in surprise as Aneesa stood in the doorway, a quizzical expression on her face. April slowly replaced the receiver, and motioned her closer.

'April, you look ghastly. What's been happening for the past two weeks?' asked Aneesa, concerned for her friend's well-being. April had black rings under her eyes, and her clothes were hanging loosely on her angular frame.

'I think that I need to go home for a while,' she replied, wearily.

'Home? To the townhouse? Yes, maybe you should take some time off,' she replied.

'No, I mean home to Cape Town,' said April, her mind full of her loving family, magnificent mountains and oceans extending for as far as the eye could see in every direction. Aneesa's eyes were large in her face as she stared at April, aghast that her friend was thinking of leaving.

'Why? What happened, April?' Her brow was furrowed with frown lines.

'Let's just say that I wasn't quite prepared for the realities of life in the big bad world, and that I'd like to go home to lick my wounds for a while.' April smiled gently at the older woman, appreciating her concern.

'Will you be coming back?' asked Aneesa fearfully.

'I hope so,' replied April enigmatically. 'Please phone head office for me, Aneesa. I need to have the leave approved. I'll be wanting to leave as soon as possible. I'm due to have ten days' leave anyway, so there shouldn't be a problem.'

Aneesa nodded pensively and returned silently to her desk. She had never seen April so dull and lifeless before. And it obviously had something to do with Jack Nathan. It was highly unusual for him not to call at least twice a day. She smiled as she thought of the times that he had made feeble excuses to talk to April, and the way that April's whole being would light up when she heard that it was him on the phone. But today had been different. For the first time, April had seemed defeated after the telephone call. It was as if something inside of her had died.

'Head office has confirmed your leave, April,' said Aneesa from the doorway. 'And I have taken the liberty of confirming a flight for you for Cape Town for eight-thirty tomorrow morning. Will that be in order?' She waited as April checked her diary and nodded in agreement. 'I've booked your return flight for ten days' time, but I have made it provisional so that you can change it at any time. Will that be all right?' April smiled wanly at the concern in Aneesa's voice.

'That will be wonderful. Thank you so much for organizing me so efficiently. What would I do without you?'

'I honestly don't know,' replied Aneesa light-heartily, delighted that she had brought a smile to April's face. It felt like an eternity since she had last smiled.

'I have to go to Amanzimtoti for a late afternoon meeting today. Why don't you come with me for a change? I'd really love the company,' said April.

'But I have to make arrangements for the children, and ... and ... oh yes. Why not?' replied Aneesa emphatically. 'Why should you have all the fun?'

'Quite right, my dear. Why should I have all the fun?' said April, laughing gently.

'What time are we leaving?' asked Aneesa quickly, already making a list of all that she had to do first.

'Mmm, let's see,' mumbled April, glancing at her wristwatch. 'It's ten-thirty now, and the meeting is scheduled for three o'clock, so we have to leave here by one forty-five at the very latest.'

Even as she was speaking, Aneesa was rushing to her office to make all the necessary cancellations, phone calls and attend to the last-minute typing that needed to be done.

'You won't believe this, but I have never been to Amanzimtoti before,' said Aneesa, as excited as a child as they drove into the town. This city was a living monument to the 1820 British settlers who had come to South Africa to tame the wilderness. April turned left and drove smoothly up to the civic building's car park. The large brick building was certainly no artistic masterpiece, but demanded respect as it clung precariously to the hill, overlooking a small dam and the whole of Amanzimtoti.

April smiled to herself as she remembered the Eisteddfods she had participated in here in the winter school holidays. Every year, Amanzimtoti hosted an arts festival in July as local talent was afforded the opportunity to sing, dance, act and perform in general to an international audience. The town would be bursting with all the artists and members of the public that would be attending, and the streets would be filled with mime artists and other colourful personalities. She smiled as she remembered one young woman she had seen who carried her pet white rat around on her shoulder, regardless of whether she was in the audience, performing or eating out in one of the restaurants. She had attended all the festivals April had been present at.

'Come on, then,' she said, her heart lifting with her memories as she climbed lithely out of the car, 'let's go and get cultured, shall we?'

Aneesa stared at her uncomprehendingly, but obediently followed April towards the imposing building, feeling that she was at last part of the maelstrom of professional life.

April's rapid loss of weight had given her an ethereal appearance, and for the first time in her life, she was pale and interesting-looking, although she was totally unaware of her appearance. Her face had lines and angles to it that had previously only been hinted at, and her suntan had faded so much that even her freckles were no longer apparent. Her brown dress hung loosely on her, where before it had clung provocatively to her figure, but instead of detracting from her appearance, it enhanced her beauty and increased her seeming vulnerability. Her face looked fresh and natural without any make-up, and her lips seemed rounder and fuller than ever before. Women looked at her enviously as she walked unconcernedly past them, and men turned and gaped after her long stride, the afternoon sun shining through the thin fabric, outlining her sharply against the backdrop of the fresh blue winter sky. Aneesa nodded approvingly to herself as she noticed the attention April was getting, pleased that her self-esteem could rapidly be restored, if only she bothered looking around to see the impact that she was making.

'Good afternoon, gentlemen,' said April, as she pushed open the double doors of the committee room, all the men present rising politely to their feet as she and Aneesa entered. 'I hope that you don't mind, but I brought Mrs Abdullah along today as representative of the Muslim Cultural Society.'

Aneesa's eyebrows rose in surprise at this ostentatious introduction. She caught April's wink and smiled brightly to the assembled gathering, feeling a part of the proceedings.

'Hello, Miss Ross, you look stunning as usual,' responded Gerald Bekker, motioning them to chairs near by him. 'We are delighted to meet you, Mrs Abdullah, and are looking forward to your input regarding the Muslim community.'

Aneesa stared wide-eyed with fright at April, who smiled innocently back to her. 'All will be revealed,' she silently mouthed.

'Right, I'd like to call this meeting to order. Thank you all for attending this meeting of our cultural planning committee for festival arrangements. We are especially delighted to have representation from the Indian community in the persons of Miss Ross from the Natal region, and Mrs Abdullah from the Muslim Cultural Society.' Aneesa glared at April, who smiled innocently back at her.

'Gosh, but I'm starved,' said April as they walked out of the committee room.

Aneesa was surprised to see that it was already six o'clock by the large wall clock that hung before them. She was feeling exhilarated from the meeting. Never before had people listened so raptly as she discussed possible events that the Muslim community could participate in. She felt her timidity evaporating like mist before the morning sun as the discussion was lobbed back and forth across the table, and had surprised herself most of all at her eloquence when discussing something so familiar to her, and so foreign to others. April beamed at her, very proud that she had stepped out of her traditional role as a quiet homemaker with no other talents. Now, she had stepped into the organization of an event as important as the Amanzimtoti Festival, and she had taken to it like a duck to water.

'Do you want to get home right away, or would you like to have some dinner with me here in Amanzimtoti?' asked April, feeling the need for prolonged company. For literally the first time in weeks, she was feeling hungry.

'I've arranged for the kids to be with a friend for as long as it takes,' replied Aneesa, enjoying her new-found sense of freedom from daily chores and the worries of single parenthood. 'Let's go out to dinner, before you fly away to Cape Town,' she added, smiling broadly.

'Good! Let me think ... ah yes. I know the perfect restaurant which is nice and quiet, and tucked out of the hustle and bustle. And it's Halaal,' she added, seeing the question forming in Aneesa's mind. 'Come on, let's go to Bruno's. You'll love it. Do you like Italian food?'

'I have no idea,' replied Aneesa sheepishly. 'I've never had it.'

'What?!' exclaimed April in mock horror. 'You haven't lived until you've tasted Bruno's lasagne.' Grabbing Aneesa by the arm, she set off at a run for the parking place, leaving Gerald Bekker staring wistfully behind. If she had been alone, he would have taken her to dinner, and who knows what else might have happened. Turning around in the gathering twilight, April impishly waved at him, aware of what his intentions had been. She sighed to herself as she thought of Gerald's unsuspecting pregnant young wife sitting faithfully at home, whilst her husband amassed the dubious honour of being the most desperate hunter of female flesh since the harem owners of the Arabian Nights.

'This is beautiful,' said Aneesa in awe as she settled back into the plush brown velvet of a cosy booth.

'Mamma Mia, two beauties to grace my molte disgusting establishment tonight,' said a large Italian man, bustling over to their table. His suit was very expensive under the expert scrutiny of April, the tailor's daughter.

'Buena Sera, I am Bruno, and it will be my personal pleasure to serve you two lovelies tonight!' His handsome face was not masked by his considerable size, and April detected that the bulges beneath his jacket were more likely muscle than fat. She smiled as she noticed Aneesa blushing under his scrutiny, and he was obviously finding her very attractive. Suddenly, to Aneesa's intense fright, he swooped down and dragged her unsuspecting hand to his lips, kissing it soundly. Ah, you are so beautiful, like the sky of Venice at the height of the harvest time. Tonight, I prepare your dinner with my own hand. No nincompoop will serve you the slop that they like to call food.' He glared towards the kitchen area, and let a torrent of Italian pour out at the little chef that stood there. He was rewarded by an equally agitated torrent of heated Italian words, several of which April recognized as being distinct swear words. The tirade was concluded with some expressive finger signs that left her in no doubt as to how little the chef respected his employer. Knowing Italians and their volatile temperaments, she was sure that these two men were the very best of friends, as only friends could be so happily rude to one another without blood being spilled.

'I … er … thank you,' replied Aneesa shyly, looking up at his bulk from under her eyelashes.

April was delighted by this unexpected turn of events, and felt the typical female urge to play Cupid.

'Hello, Bruno, I'm April, and this is Aneesa, the director of the Muslim Cultural Society.' She twinkled innocently as Aneesa glared at her in despair. Turning away from April as soon as it was polite to do so, Bruno beamed at Aneesa, who was blushing deeply.

'Such beauty, and a brain to match. How rare in this terrible old world of ours,' he gushed, still gripping her hand tightly in his. April smothered a laugh as she noticed Aneesa wriggling her fingers in a vain attempt to extricate herself.

'I must go and cook for you,' he stated, releasing Aneesa's hand with a final kiss.

'Er ... may I have the lasagne, please,' said April.

'Yes of course,' he replied briskly. 'Would you like my lasagne too?' he asked, turning back to Aneesa.

'Um ... I don't know. Yes,' she replied, nonplussed by all events of this strange and very different day.

'Bellisima. I go now to cook,' he replied, with the severity of a world-famous heart surgeon.

'My, my,' teased April mercilessly. 'Quite the little heart-breaker aren't we?'

'I don't know what you mean,' replied Aneesa airily, smiling innocently, her eyes following Bruno's progress to the kitchen. Suddenly, her face set in a mask of horror.

'What? What's wrong?' asked April, unable to see what had riveted Aneesa's attention so suddenly.

'Oh God! I don't believe it,' stammered Aneesa.

'For heaven's sake, what is it? You look like you've seen a ghost!'

'Not a ghost ... a nightmare.' Her previously flushed face had been swept clear of all colour, and her pallor frightened April.

'Aneesa! Stop it! You're frightening me. What have you seen?' April resisted the urge to lean across the table and shake her.

'My father. It's my father,' she finally stammered.

'What?' said April disbelievingly. 'It can't be. He's in Cape Town. What on earth would he be doing in a restaurant in Amanzimtoti, for goodness' sake?'

'It is him,' insisted Aneesa, shrinking back into the booth as though she would evaporate if he looked at her. 'And he's not alone.' She stared wide-eyed at April, who was now just as pale, as the threats came crowding back into her brain. She could hear echoes of the German's mocking laughter as he jokingly threatened her life.

‘He’s not alone?’ said April softly, her fears increasing.

‘No.’

‘Do you know the person he’s with?’

‘Yes.’

‘Yes? Who is it?’ asked April, surprised by her friend’s monosyllabic answers.

‘I can’t believe it,’ whispered Aneesa in reply, obviously dazed.

‘Oh, for goodness’ sake,’ said April, thoroughly exasperated. She stood up in their booth and turned to see what had so transfixed Aneesa. She caught her breath as she recognized the unmistakable bulk of Hussein in the gloom of the restaurant. Her vision was still a little blurred from the candle on her table having been so fascinating. She focused on the figure sitting opposite him. Just then, Bruno ambled over to Hussein’s table and with some jovial chatter, lit the candle. She felt faint as the murky figure came to life, and found herself staring at Jack Nathan.

‘Oh God, I don’t believe it,’ she said, falling back into her seat, perspiration beading her forehead although she felt ice cold inside.

‘It’s not possible, it’s not possible,’ she muttered in a daze.

‘April! Snap out of it,’ hissed Aneesa, quickly snuffing the candle on their table so that they would not be immediately apparent to the two men.

‘What is he doing here with that animal?’ wondered April out loud, her head spinning. Why hadn’t Jack said that he would be in Amanzimtoti today. Oh, why should he tell me, she thought. We are no longer of concern to one another. But that was not true. April felt her concern for his safety rising. Here was a man who had always warned her to stay away from Hussein, and here he was cosying up to him in a restaurant far away enough from Durban that they would not be seen by anyone familiar.

April's eyes widened as she realized the full implications of what she had just thought. Spinning around, she carefully peered over the high back of their booth. She couldn't hear what was being said by the two men, as the restaurant was too large, and they were stuck towards the back. Their heads were bent towards one another as their discussion intensified. She watched Hussein reach into his pocket and hand Jack a buff envelope. In turn, Jack put his attaché case on the table and slid it towards Hussein. Her mind was reeling. It was obvious to her that some deal was going down right in front of her that was highly suspect.

Feeling the nausea return, she turned back to face Aneesa. Both women's faces were ashen. 'Did you see that?' asked April quietly. Aneesa nodded, unable to speak, her gaze transfixed on her father like an animal cornered by very dangerous predators.

'We have to leave as quietly and as quickly as possible, all right?'

'All right,' she replied, her voice small and reedy.

Just then, Jack and Hussein stood up and moved across to the salad bar. The two women cringed back in their seats. Jack and Hussein were deep in conversation, and didn't notice them.

'They look very chummy, don't they,' said Aneesa, echoing April's thoughts exactly as she watched the men laugh and slap one another on the back like long-lost friends. Chatting like two old schoolfriends, they moved back to their table. Bruno went bustling over to them, and deftly opened a bottle of champagne, laughing uproariously with the men as the white froth poured out over the napkin he was holding.

'Congratulations, it's a boy,' muttered April, peeved at the obvious bonhomie that they were displaying to one another.

'What?' asked Aneesa, looking at April in puzzlement.

'Nothing. They just look as though they have something very special to celebrate. And I get the distinct feeling that they would be most unhappy if they knew that we had seen them. Come on, let's go.' April slid out the other side of the booth, and walked nonchalantly towards the doorway. She didn't stop until she reached the car, where she leaned against the parking meter taking gulps of fresh air. Aneesa came flying out of the restaurant, and breathlessly joined April.

'Where were you?' said April, worried that she may have been seen by Hussein.

'I just left my name and phone number on the napkin for Bruno,' she admitted sheepishly.

Despite her nausea and displeasure, April couldn't help laughing at her. 'Still waters *do* run deep, don't they?' she said.

'Oh, you don't know the half of how deep they run,' replied Aneesa, looking youthful and exhilarated in the moonlight. 'Now let's see Bruno put his money where his mouth is.' Their girlish laughter tinkled in the crisp evening.

Shivering, April quickly unlocked the Honda and they jumped into the warmth and security of the car, glad to be on their way.

'That was too close for comfort,' said Aneesa, watching the road ahead as only a nervous passenger could.

'Indeed,' agreed April, her mind racing as she digested what they had seen.

# *Chapter Twelve*

April stared unseeingly at the flickering images on the television set. Suddenly, her whole being focused on what the late-night newsreader was announcing.

'History was made in South Africa today as parliament amended the Immorality and Prohibition of Mixed Marriages Act of 1949. The Act is now known as the Immorality and Prohibition of Mixed Marriages Amendment Act No. 72 of 1985, which now makes it legal for people of various racial groups to marry one another. This decision was vigorously opposed by the Dr Treurnicht's official Opposition Conservative Party, but was carried convincingly by the rest of the House of Assembly. Very favourable comments were made by the spokesman of the White House as well as No. 10 Downing Street.'

April stared at her calendar. The nineteenth of June 1985. Her eyes filled with tears at the irony of her situation. The greatest hurdle of her relationship with Jack had been obliterated a few short days after their relationship had been severed. The tears fell down her flushed cheeks as images of Jack and Hussein in the restaurant that day marched relentlessly across her mind.

Oh stop it! she admonished herself, angrily brushing away the tears of self-pity. Shakespeare nuzzled her gently, placing his head in her hand and offering her the comfort he instinctively knew that she needed. Burying her face in his soft white fur, she let the sobs rack her body as her anguished soul sought relief from so many pent-up emotions.

Tonight, she could have been celebrating with Jack.

Instead, she was unhappier than she had ever been before. Today, her faith in Jack had been shattered, and today, the greatest hurdle separating them had been removed. Her mouth twisted with pain and bitterness at the losing hand that fate had dealt her. Wiping her tears away with the backs of her hands, like a small bewildered child, April stood up wearily, and climbed the stairs to her bedroom to start packing for her trip home.

Outside in the darkness, the howling wind whipped the waves into a frenzy of frothing white seahorses, and dust devils tore destructively across the sand and the road, coming to rest against the wheels of the large blue car. Unmindful of the hostility of the elements, Jack stood against the passenger door, staring blindly up at April's illuminated bedroom window. He watched unflinchingly until her light clicked off, plunging the window into darkness. Expressionlessly, he climbed slowly into the car, his shoulders slumping with weariness, started the engine, and drove smoothly off into the turbulent night.

April was hardly aware of the turbulence of the plane as they crested the Hottentots Holland mountain range in their descent to Cape Town International Airport. The steel wing-tips of the aircraft reflected the blinding silvery light of the snow that capped the highest peaks. Looking out of her window, she saw the glittering waters of the Steenbras catchment area beneath the plane's left wing-tip. The earth suddenly fell away before her eyes as the large Boeing lumbered out of the mountain range, and dived giddily downwards across the wine farms of Stellenbosch far below. The turbulence stopped almost immediately, and the large plane shuddered as it responded to the slowing mechanisms of the flaps being lowered. Looking back towards the mountain range, April could see the large white anchor of rocks and the large 'GB' in capital letters on the hillside of Gordons Bay. The plane banked sharply out over the sea, and she caught a panoramic glimpse of a lopsided Table Mountain as they descended into the strong north-westerly wind.

'Darling! Over here.' April smiled as she saw her mother leaning dangerously over the rail to attract her attention. Inge was attracting a lot of attention as usual, waving wildly so that all nearby people were forced to duck for cover. Her umbrella had become a potential lethal weapon as she wielded it with ferocity and skill in her determination to reach her daughter before anyone else could reach their arriving family members. Clutching April to her in a smothering embrace, she smiled to herself, pleased that her daughter was safely home.

Then she suddenly frowned and pushed April away from her. 'Where have you disappeared to? I've never seen you so thin. Are you ill? Is that why you've come home so suddenly? Oh my God. You're dying, aren't you? I don't think that I can deal with this. Why didn't you let us know you were sick? I...'

'Mom, just relax,' interjected April hastily. 'I'm fine. Really. And we are all dying a little each day, but no ... I do not have any terminal disease that I am aware of. Okay?'

'If you say so, darling,' said her mother, her usually smooth brow creased with the worried lines of a frown. An innocence and sparkle had left April's face, and her pallor was shocking in one who was usually so sundusted and carefree.

'Let's get the luggage and get home, Mom. I'm really tired and I can't wait to see Dad again,' she said, turning self-consciously away from the scrutiny that only a mother or jealous lover could give.

'You are skin and bone,' persisted her mother, poking April in the ribs.

'For goodness' sake, Mom, stop poking me like the witch in Hansel and Gretel. I am only visiting, not planning on being your next meal,' she snapped.

Inge burst out laughing, her good nature and sense of humour triumphing over her concerns for her daughter's well-being. Hooking her arm into April's, they set off resolutely towards the crowd that had already gathered around the baggage carousel.

April sat pensively next to her mother on the scenic drive home, hardly registering the familiar landmarks as they whizzed by. Inge's favourite Mozart tape was playing quietly in the background. For the first time in months, April felt herself regaining a wholism and serenity that had been lacking in her life in Durban, although the pain of Jack's betrayal still throbbed agonizingly in her chest.

'Will I ever forget?'

'Pardon, darling?'

With a start, April realized she must have spoken out aloud. 'I just said that nothing has changed and I'll never forget,' she replied smoothly. Inge glanced sharply sideways at her daughter's impassive profile, the upturned nose emphasized by her gaunt cheeks. She had sensed April's pain, and was uncharacteristically biding her time for her daughter to share the problem. Frowning, she returned her concentration to the winding road that twisted sharply into Hout Bay. The small fishing village nestled between high mountains fringed with green forests and vineyards. The Ross home overlooked the valley, and the harbour full of brightly coloured fishing boats manned by cheerful and jaunty dark-skinned fishermen. April breathed in the familiar smells of home as they drove up the winding gravel road that led to the tall white gates of the driveway. The air was damp and cool on her skin, the storm of the dark night having passed with only traces of small pools of water to bear witness to its ferocity. April smiled as the house came into view. One always expected to see a Gothic masterpiece after such an impressive entrance. Instead, the white bungalow sat securely in the carefully maintained wilderness of the garden, dwarfed by the mountain that rose up imperiously and timelessly above them.

'Daddy's at work but he said to give you his love and that he couldn't wait to see his "baby" again.' Inge rolled her eyes comically upwards at the use of the word 'baby' and April laughed good-naturedly. April carried her suitcase into the familiar cosy interior of the welcoming house – the refuge and sanctuary of her growing years. Proteas and heather adorned all the brass and earthenware containers, filling the air with their unique fragrance of wildness tempered with satin that was soothing and very familiar to any CapeTonian.

'Gosh Mom ... been robbing the nature reserves again?' teased April lightly.

'Just the garden this time, Puss. Maybe I'll invade Kirstenbosch the next time you make a triumphant homecoming,' she lightly rejoindered.

April smiled at the unlikely scenario. Inge was the most militant conservationist she had ever met or was likely to meet. Memories of her mother dragging her along to protest rallies for rights for dolphins, seals, whales, rabbits being experimented on, the extinction of a wild flower, flooded her mind with crystal clarity. She laughed out loud as she remembered how her mother had arranged the dumping of two tons of garbage on the sweeping front lawns of a powerful and environmentally unscrupulous industrial magnate. The day that her mild-mannered and genteel father had to bail Inge out of jail still provided grist for the family conversational mill.

'What's the joke?' asked her mother lightly, pleased to see some merriment and life coming back to her daughter's unusually sombre countenance. April affectionately hugged her mother.

'I was just remembering what a firebrand you used to be about the really important things in life.'

'Used to be!' exclaimed Inge indignantly. 'I'll have you know, young lady, that I am still as much of an embarrassment to your sweet father as I ever was, thank you. Now go and unpack. I have a million things to do before I fetch that father of yours.' She gave April a playful shove into the cool interior of the tiled passageway.

April unpacked her suitcases slowly in her room. Looking around her, she felt as though she had been living here yesterday, and at the same time, in another lifetime. So much had happened to her in just six months. A light breeze lifted the floral green and pink curtains, issuing in the heady fragrance of the winter garden, and the salty tang of the Atlantic Ocean. April grimaced guiltily as she unpacked the small photograph album of snapshots of Shakespeare that she had brought for her animal-crazy parents to sigh over. He had looked so reproachful as she left him at the SPCA kennels that morning. Sam had offered to take care of him, but she was taking no chances with his forgetful habits of leaving doors and windows open.

'Guess who's coming to dinner, darling?' said Inge from the doorway. April started, her heart pounding in her throat like a trapped butterfly. She had forgotten how silently her mother moved.

'Mom, you startled me,' she lightly admonished, picking up the fallen photograph album.

'Sorry, Angel,' replied her mother unrepentantly. 'Oh he's adorable!' she crowed as she swooped down on an errant photograph of Shakespeare that had fluttered loose. Shakespeare's angelic image grinned mischievously back at her. 'Let me see them all,' she enthused, snatching the album from April's unprepared hands.

'Mom, don't grab like that!' she snapped, unreasonably irked by her mother's familiarity with her life and her possessions. There were pictures in there that she had wanted to keep to herself for a while.

'Is this Jack, the famous love of your life?' asked Inge playfully, concentrating on the photograph of the man holding the dog and smiling boyishly into the camera. April felt as though a hot knife had been thrust through her heart, and gasped involuntarily at the rush of pain. Inge looked sharply up at her daughter's sudden intake of breath, her smile fading rapidly on her lips as she noticed April's struggle to regain her composure.

'Darling, what is it? Have I said something wrong?' she asked, dropping the album and embracing April.

'Nothing, Mom. Let it rest, okay?' she replied, the strain in her voice very apparent.

'No, it's not okay,' her mother insisted, tucking a straying curl behind April's ear. 'I've known your every movement and expression since you were born, and I have never seen you so wiped out before. Now, for God's sake tell me what on earth is wrong so that I can help you to begin to make it right!' Inge's pedantic Teutonic nature never lurked far beneath the surface, and April smiled involuntarily at her mother's adamancy in facing a problem square on, and putting a band-aid on a broken heart.

'Mom, this is one sore place that not even your talents will be able to heal,' she gently replied, disentangling herself from her mother's embrace, and walking elegantly across the room to gaze out of her window at the vista of flowers, forests and sea.

'Try me, darling. A mother's love is powerful medicine,

you know,' Inge persisted, joining her daughter at the window.

Standing next to one another, the similarity in their posture was overwhelming, and they could have been two pearls from the same oyster. April sighed resignedly, and perched herself precariously on her windowsill as she had done a million times through her growing years.

'Very well then.' She leaned her back against the sun-warmed window frame, and swung her long legs up with the soles of her now bare feet pushing against the opposite side. She looked like a painting framed in the late warmth of the winter afternoon sunshine, with the vista stretching endlessly on behind her. Keeping her face averted towards the view, she tremulously began telling her mother the reason for her return to the refuge of her family's bosom.

April's voice rose and fell for an hour, uninterrupted by her mother who listened carefully to every word. 'Now you know everything, Mom. I fell in love with a man who was charming, sincere and honest, and at the end of the day, I discovered that he was just another of Hussein's pawns, and he endangered my life in the process. Because of him, I never reported that murder to the police, and now it's just too damn late. They'll never take my word against such a respected politician, and there is no body to prove the story. It could be just another missing husband who bailed out on a nagging wife.'

'Have you finished?' asked her mother quietly.

'Yes, I guess I have,' she replied, sighing deeply.

'So you have effectively run away to come home and lick your wounds without even giving Jack a chance to explain what you saw?' April stared at her mother in surprise. She had expected sympathy, not recriminations.

'What…' she stammered.

'I thought I had taught you to never believe the obvious my darling. To seek for the true and hidden meaning behind things. Why haven't you applied it in this case – perhaps the most important case of your entire life?'

'Because it's so obvious, that's why,' retorted April angrily, stung by her mother's attitude. 'Besides,' she continued, 'I have decided to put a little distance between us so that I can gain perspective,' she added defensively.

'How can you possibly gain perspective if you don't have all the facts?'

'I have all the facts I need. Whose side are you on anyway?' April's voice had risen sharply.

'Don't shout, darling. I'm on your side as always. Isn't it obvious?' replied Inge disarmingly.

'Quite frankly, no, Mother! It isn't the least bit obvious. Why do you always try to complicate matters? Can't you ever accept anything at face value?'

'Face value, April? Since when is face value good enough for a Ross? I'm surprised at you. With your qualifications and people skills, I would have thought that face value would be the last thing on your bright little mind.'

April stared at her mother, flabbergasted, and at a complete loss for words.

'Close your mouth, dear. You'll be catching flies if you aren't careful.' Her mother stood up and smoothed the non-existent creases out of her skirt. 'I must fly, darling. If I'm late fetching your father tonight, there will be all hell to pay. He is so excited that you are coming home.'

'Mom, wait,' said April, swinging herself out of her window.

'Yes, darling?' she replied from the doorway, her eyebrows lifting in exactly the same manner that April's did when she had a question.

'Who is coming to dinner?'

'The Capshaws, sweetheart. You know, Samantha and Dennis of the Capshaw diamond house in Cape Town. Their son Jonathan is the political correspondent for the

Houses of Parliament. We see him on television whenever anything dramatic happens within the seats of power.' Inge's face took on mock reverence for an institution that had never impressed her. 'Samantha and I are involved in Greenpeace, so we have oodles in common. Dennis and your father have always been friends since their school days, and Jonathan will be good company for you,' she added innocently.

'Wait a minute, Mom. You aren't trying to set me up with this man are you, after all that you've said about Jack, are you?' demanded April suspiciously.

'Don't be ridiculous, April. I would never dream of doing anything as unsubtle and completely transparent. However, if you could use your charms on him to soften him up on the importance of reporting green issues as well as the blood and guts politics that he usually spits out, I would be delighted. Samantha and I have had absolutely no influence on him whatsoever. But she did tell me that he's a sucker for a pretty face.' She twinkled mischievously at her daughter. Despite her indignation at her mother's amazing ability to manipulate, April couldn't help laughing at her ingenuity in finding new ways to fight for everything that couldn't fight for itself.

'Okay, Mom. I'll soften up Jonathan if you back off about Jack. Fair?'

'Deal, darling. Besides, Jonathan is a total frog compared to your dark prince.' Her laughter echoed down the hallway as she ducked youthfully out of April's room, the shoe that April had playfully tossed at her mother striking the bedroom wall harmlessly.

'Where's my baby?' thundered Bill Ross exuberantly from the tiled entrance hall. People found it most peculiar that he refused to drive a car despite his dexterity and heavy duty driving licence. He was a mountain of a man with a heart as soft as butter. Feeling ten years old again, April raced down the passage and flung herself into her father's waiting arms. Inge smiled as she watched her family. There had been a time, long ago, when she had felt like an intruder, and was jealous of the close relationship that Bill Ross shared with his daughter. But those pangs had been laid to rest when she and April had discovered the kindred spirit that bound them comfortably together like mirror images of one another. They had an uncanny ability to complete one another's sentences, and would often sense what the other was thinking.

'Did your mother tell you what she's gone and done, darling?' teased Bill, smiling fondly at his wife over April's shoulder. They had become closer in the time that they had had alone together, than they had been for many years.

'What, Daddy?' asked April, disentangling herself from his embrace and struggling to retain her dignity and air of sophistication.

'Invited a group of Yahoos over for dinner, and on your first night home too.' The family moved into the lounge, and Bill walked over to the liquor cabinet for the nightly ritual of pouring sundowners. Smiling broadly, he aligned a third glass for April.

'I invited the Yahoos, as you so elegantly put it, dear, long before I knew that your daughter was coming home. More ice for me, please, I'm boiling hot. I can't understand why it is so hot this time of the year. Must be the effect of the depletion of the ozone layer.' She collapsed dramatically onto the large three-seater couch next to her daughter. Both women sat with their feet tucked up under them.

'Here's your drink, darling,' said Bill, giving his wife a tall glass full of clinking ice cubes bobbing around in a white wine spritzer. 'Do you want the same, precious?' he asked April, looking at her quizzically.

'Yes please, Daddy. My tastes haven't changed in the last six months, you know.'

'Well, you've certainly changed,' he replied seriously, handing her a drink whilst he snuggled comfortably into his favourite recliner. 'You went away a "boy" and you've come home a "man".'

April and her mother guffawed simultaneously into their glasses, splashing one another in their merriment.

'God, Daddy. I haven't sprouted chest hairs, have I?' asked April, laughing wildly at his little joke.

'No, darling, no chest hairs, but you're skin and bone. And I don't think I have ever seen you looking so pale.' Inge cleared her throat to stop him putting his foot squarely into his mouth.

'But it suits you, darling,' he hastily added, smiling broadly for her benefit. 'Well, Inge, why don't you go and finish off the dinner arrangements while we discuss father–daughter stuff?' He gave his wife a reassuring wink that convinced her he wouldn't touch on any of the sensitive subjects they had been discussing about their daughter on the way home from town.

Inge happily complied, her agile mind already concentrating on last-minute hostess details. The six Border Collies that she had rescued from a spirits drinker frisked happily about her long legs as she swept out of the room.

Chopin played softly in the background as they all sat down to the meal. The firelight from the large hearth in the dining room reflected off the crystal glasses at each person's left hand. The smell of fragrant candle wax hung pleasantly in the air. April smiled self-consciously at the fresh-faced young man who sat opposite her. Jonathan Capshaw had been most attentive since he had taken one lustful first look at her, elegantly clad in a figure-hugging simple black dress that hung just above her shapely knees. The neckline was enhanced with the glitter of small multi-coloured rhinestones that twinkled in prisms of light as her breath rose and fell, affording him tantalizing glimpses of her still abundant cleavage, despite her dramatic weight loss.

'Ah, thank you Maria,' said her mother as the dignified Malay woman carried in the starters on a highly polished silver tray. She set each avocado cocktail in front of the six diners with a cheerful smile. April squeezed Maria's hand affectionately as she walked past, and Maria dropped a quick kiss on the shining curls of the beautiful young woman that she had helped to raise.

'I would like to propose a toast,' said Jonathan, awkwardly scraping back his chair as he leapt enthusiastically to his feet. Bill Ross stared at him in amazement. It was seldom that he was pipped to the post of proposing a toast to his daughter, especially in the confines of his own home. His parents smiled adoringly up at their son. It was still a constant source of surprise to them that they had managed to raise such an extraordinary human being from their very plain and ordinary selves. Samantha was a short and very matronly blonde, who overcame her dowdiness with her sunny disposition and wide uneven smile. She and Inge were physical foils for one another, but in spirit, they shared the same beliefs. Dennis was even shorter than his wife, and just as rotund, with watery myopic blue eyes that peered owlishly over his black-rimmed glasses as they slid continuously down the fat bridge of his nose. Regardless of the weather, Dennis was always sweating and mopping his brow with a sodden handkerchief. Thanks to his friendship with Bill Ross, he was always immaculately dressed. They were long-standing rugby buddies, season ticket holders who had sat next to one another on the grandstand at the Newlands rugby grounds for 18 years. They had remained firm friends, who always backed the same teams.

'To the homecoming of the most beautiful girl in the whole of Cape Town. Let's raise our glasses to April.' April shook herself out of her reverie, and smiled weakly at Jonathan as he towered above their dining room table, beaming pontifically down on her. There was a clink of glasses as everyone joined in the toast, and Bill gave his daughter a conspiratorial wink that indicated just how much of a buffoon he found Jonathan Capshaw.

'Thank you,' responded April meekly. 'But I'm afraid that you made a slight error, Jonathan,' she continued, her voice gaining in strength as she warmed to her theme. The Capshaws stared at her in puzzlement, and Bill gave Inge an encouraging squeeze on her still shapely knee under the table. 'This is not a homecoming for me, simply a temporary return. I will be holidaying with my parents for about a week. My future lies elsewhere ... of course, where precisely it lies eludes me for now. But thank you for the kind thought, Jonathan.'

Smiling smugly at his taken-aback expression, she leaned comfortably back in her chair. She did not notice his expression harden as he glared malevolently at her turned head. He smiled wanly, his thin lips pinched tightly together as he sat heavily down on the chair. Only his mother noticed how white his knuckles had turned as he gripped the stem of his glass.

The chill that had escaped the warmth of the day had returned with the swift setting of the sun, and there was a distinct smell of rain in the air. The dining room was pleasantly heated by the fire that Bill had lit himself, despite this not being one of his particular talents.

'April, could I talk to you for a minute?' April spun

around. She had been standing on the patio looking out over the twinkling lights of Hout Bay. Jonathan Capshaw stood towering above her. He was at least six feet seven inches tall, and was almost sinfully handsome. His looks were swarthy and distinctly Italian despite his fair parents. He was also the only child, and had grown up to be wilful and self-centred with his parents doting besottedly on him and everything he did.

'Sure, Jonathan,' she replied, the annoyance at his presence swiftly suppressed. 'Shall we sit?' She disliked his proximity and bulk towering above her, and moved deftly to a single chair. He lowered his lanky frame into the recliner, and she was thrilled to see that it diminished his height considerably.

'I can't believe that you grew up into such a beautiful woman, April. You were the fattest, ugliest teenager on this side of the planet when I last saw you.'

'Thank you,' she replied sardonically.

'Now you are absolutely stunning. I would like to see more of you during your stay here. Would you mind?' His voice was professionally groomed for television, and the words oozed out of his mouth like thickened syrup.

'You are seeing me now, aren't you?' she replied, unable to check the gall from rising in her. For some inexplicable reason, she had always disliked him, and nothing had changed.

'Are you seeing anyone romantically? Because if you are, I'd like to challenge him to a duel at sunrise and claim you for my own. And if not, you will be saving a great deal of innocent bloodshed.'

He chuckled self-confidently at his delivery of his standard line to any pretty girl that would look his way. In the dark, April made a gesture of sticking her finger down her throat, and grimaced at the idea of this smooth-talker coming within 20 miles of her.

'Jonathan, I haven't seen you in a million years, and we have never had anything in common, so why should now be any different?'

'Because now I see what a fool I have been. I should have locked you up in a castle until you ripened just for me.'

'Ripened? How dare you?' April demanded, jumping to her feet indignantly. His hand snaked out faster than she had ever believed possible, and he grabbed her wrist with a painful twist.

'Sit down, you pompous little piece of cheap arse,' he snarled, forcing her back into her seat with the severity of his vice-like grip. April gasped in pain and shock, and fell back into her chair. 'Now you listen to me very carefully, or else I am going to snap your scrawny little neck like a twig and blame it on a fall after the considerable amount of wine that you swallowed at dinner time. Do I make myself clear?' His tone was conversational and controlled, and a passer-by would have thought they were sharing intimate thoughts with one another.

'How dare you speak to me like this, you filthy bastard,' she hissed, arrows of red hot pain shooting up her left arm as she twisted to try and free it from his grasp.

'I dare because I am being paid well to do so, bitch, that's why,' he softly replied. 'Now listen carefully.' April froze, her whole being flooding with dread. 'I was very talented, but no one at the SABC was intelligent enough to see that until my benefactor saw me at an interview that I went to at the Houses of Parliament – to become a messenger boy, of all the lowest things imaginable.' His grip on her tightened in his remembered anger.

'Your benefactor?' whispered April softly, sitting perfectly still.

'Yes. He came along, saw me, asked me for my CV, which was totally fictitious of course, and saw right through me to the truly rotten self-serving person that I really am.'

'At least you got that right,' retorted April angrily.

'Stop twisting, you nigger-loving little whore, or I'll break your arm,' he hissed, jerking her to her feet and down again like a helpless rag doll. 'And don't scream, because what I have to tell you is very important, understand?'

'Yes. Just let go of my arm for God's sake. You're hurting me,' she replied, fighting tears of fright and pain.

'If you promise to shut your mouth like a good little girl,' he taunted, twisting her arm further until she thought it would surely break. She slapped ineffectually at him with her free hand, but he only laughed, and twisted her wrist more savagely.

'I promise,' she gasped, helpless. Her arm was turning numb from the pressure he was exerting.

She gasped as he let her go, the blood supply hurting her more than his grip had done.

'The only reason that I am here tonight at this sickening little display of domestic bliss is because I have something very important to tell you.'

'But my mother invited you,' stammered April uncomprehendingly, rubbing her wrist mechanically as she stared at the glittering pits in his face where his eyes were. His laughter, as it echoed across the patio and was swallowed by the cold night air, was hollow and mocking.

'Ah yes, your animal rights activist mother. What a laugh. She and my mother are two similar idiots. They sicken me.' Even in the chilled darkness, April could see how his face twisted with hatred.

'For God's sake, Jonathan, she's your mother,' she snapped, her moral outrage at his insensitivity overcoming her fear.

'Oh, didn't you know that I'm adopted, darling?' he replied.

'No, and frankly, I couldn't care less,' she angrily retorted.

'Yes. That is the best-kept secret in the entire country. I am someone prominent's unwanted bastard. At least, unwanted until now, that is,' he hastily corrected himself, smiling broadly in the black night. April felt an icy pocket enveloping her heart as she stared at him, mesmerized like the snake by the mongoose. Her breath caught raggedly in her throat, and her pulse throbbed painfully in her temples.

'Yes,' he continued inexorably, 'I am the result of a deliciously sinful liaison between a very ruthless and rotten to the core politician who raped my "mother", an eighteen-year-old debutante from a prominent old Cape Town family who promptly sent her away to France while I grew insidiously inside her. Am I fascinating you, dear sweet little April, the vestal virgin of Hout Bay?' His voice was dripping with sarcasm as he leered at her, and April gasped in pain and shock as his hand snaked out and tweaked her left nipple viciously. She reacted on reflex and slapped his face with a resounding crack. There was dead silence. Even the crickets stopped chirping. In the distance, April could hear the strains of a Strauss waltz coming from the lounge accompanied by a buzz of their parents' indecipherable conversation. Sebastian the largest and most protective of her mother's six Border Collies, came padding out onto the patio, his patches of white fur seeming to float in the weakening moonlight. He loped over to April and pushed himself between her and Jonathan, putting his wet muzzle in April's shaking hands. The large dog growled uncharacteristically as Jonathan made a move towards April, and he swiftly withdrew. Like all bullies, Jonathan Capshaw was a coward at heart.

'Get that mutt out of here,' he snapped, nervously pushing himself further back in his chair.

'You have to be joking,' replied April, bravely.

Sebastian's head rested reassuringly on her lap. Her

long fingers stroked the animal gently, as he stared up lovingly into her face. 'I suggest you leave, you spineless toad,' she spat vehemently at him, sickened by his cowering attitude.

'Not before I deliver my message you…'

'Careful what you say now, or I'll set my dog on you,' she bravely replied. She smiled as he pushed himself even further into his chair. Almost as if on cue, Sebastian turned his head towards Jonathan and growled menacingly.

'Call it off,' he pleaded, his voice reedy and terrified. 'I won't touch you again. I promise.'

'Shhh, Sebastian, you can eat him later,' teased April lightly, stroking the animal's nose. The dog sat down and watched Jonathan carefully. 'Now you were saying that your incredibly, famously wealthy, debutante mother went to France to have you … please continue.'

'Er, yes … well, anyway she went to France…'

'So we have established. Anything else that you feel compelled to share with me?' she asked sarcastically, despising him for his cruelty and his weakness.

'*Ahem.*'

He cleared his throat nervously. 'My father had her followed, and used a go-between to arrange for my adoption. He paid off the doctors and had me placed with the Capshaws here in Cape Town without my mother's parents knowing about it. They thought I had gone to some childless couple in Italy where my dark complexion would blend right in.'

'Dark complexion? I don't understand,' said April uncomprehendingly.

'My father is an Indian, so my arrival would have caused awful complications for my grandmother and grandfather who were loyal supporters of the conservative section of the Nationalist party.' April gaped at him, taken aback by his revelation.

'So why are you telling me this?' she asked, puzzled by his candour.

'Haven't you figured it out yet?'

'Obviously not, Jonathan. Stop being so theatrical.'

'My father is my benefactor, and he asked me to give you a message. Are you ready?' He paused, and watched her smugly as her confusion ranged across her lovely face. 'The message is, and I quote, "You can run but you can't hide. I know where you are and I know what you saw." End of quote. Figured it out, yet, Miss Smarty Pants?' Hatred dripped in his voice like malodorous honey. 'Hold that dog while I take my leave of your extremely middle-class bourgeois parents. So long for now.'

April stared after him as he walked elegantly through the french doors into the light and warmth of her family environment. April shivered as she suddenly detected the shadow of Abdul Hussein following his poisonous illegitimate son.

# *Chapter Thirteen*

'Darling. What on earth are you talking about? You just got here. Why on earth would you want to return so soon?' Bill Ross stared at his daughter, dumbfounded. The watery winter sunlight streamed across the breakfast table, causing red lights to dance in April's curling tresses. She looked like a pale porcelain doll, the blue veins translucent in her throat as her pulse beat rapidly at the base of her neck. Her hand was shaking as she gripped the glass of orange juice Maria had just poured. The six dogs lay around the dining room floor like breathing shaggy carpets, hoping some tasty breakfast morsels would fall from the plates of their loved ones into their never-satisfied pink mouths. Sebastian lay with his head on April's feet under the table, and growled a warning whenever any of his brothers and sisters got too close to her.

'Honestly, Daddy. I simply forgot about an important meeting that is scheduled for tomorrow morning in Tongaat. I have to get back tonight at the very latest. It just slipped my mind when I came home, that's all.' She played nervously with a tendril of hair a sure sign to her father that she was lying. He had learnt to know all the signals that she gave ever since she was a little girl.

'Funny how it just slipped back into your mind again,' he grumbled, very unhappy at the prospect of losing his daughter again so suddenly. He was puzzled by her lack of trust in him, why she wouldn't tell him the truth behind the reason why she was in such a hurry to go back to Durban.

April's knuckles were pinched white as she squeezed the glass in her hand. Jonathan's words kept ringing in her ears over and over … Hussein's son right here in the bosom of her family like Cleopatra's asp. She had to get away so that the danger for her parents could dissipate.

'I'm really sorry, Daddy. I know that you had all kinds of things planned for us to do, but it just isn't on the cards for now. Anyway, I hate the Cape Town weather in June. I'll be back again in the spring. How's that for a compromise?' She stared remorsefully at him, meeting his gaze fully for the first time that morning. His grey eyes peered into her soul, and she knew he was aware that she was lying. Quickly, she looked away, blushing red with shame, and with anger at the man who had changed her life forever by snapping a man's neck like a dry twig. Unconsciously, her hands clenched into tight fists that she would gladly have put straight into Hussein's evil eyes. His aura hung around like a pervading toxic substance that was invisible, but paralysing.

'What compromise is this?' asked Inge from the doorway, the collies bounding uninhibitedly about her warmly clad legs. She looked like a Scandinavian earth goddess in her brown corduroy trousers and autumn-toned Fair Isle jersey.

'The child is leaving. Just like that,' replied her father indignantly.

'What? Why ever would you be doing such a thing, April? That is the most ridiculous thing I've heard in a long while. You only got here yesterday.' April felt 12 years old again as her mother scolded her while she helped herself to breakfast. Flushing with guilt and annoyance, April stood up, staring meaningfully at her mother's bowed head.

'If you'll excuse me, I have to pack,' she said, and swept out of the room, leaving her parents staring open-mouthed at her retreating back, Sebastian padding loyally at her heels.

'Damn him! Damn him! Damn him to hell and leprosy!' April cried as she flung her clothes onto the bed for packing. Sebastian stared at her with his head to one side as she pounded her pillow in frustration, imagining that it was Hussein's head that she was bashing. 'Oh God, I'm no better than he is,' she cried as she flung the pillow away from her.

Barking vociferously, and delighted by this game that April had begun, Sebastian sprang onto the pillow and with one shake of his mighty head, feathers went flying around the room.

'No! Mom will kill us,' she cried as she tried to rescue what was left of her pillow, but Sebastian hung on grimly, determined that this was a fight to the death. Suddenly he sneezed as the feathers flew into his nose. April landed flat on her back in the middle of the room as the dog let go. The feathers covered her like drifting snowflakes, and she thought of Jack's favourite saying, that you could carelessly toss the feathers out of a pillow, but you could never put them back again. All the pain, fear and misery came swelling out of April like a boil that had been lanced as she sobbed and spat feathers out of her gasping mouth. Sebastian whined at her misery, and conscientiously licked away any tears that he could find. Embracing the warm and comforting dog like a friend, April sobbed out her frustration into his shining black and white fur. She felt as though her heart would leap right out of her heaving chest as warm memories of the Jack she had trusted came rushing at her from the hidden recesses of her mind, crippling her emotionally with their intensity.

'I can't have been so wrong about him,' she wailed as she remembered all the tenderness and concern that he had shown her. But he had lied every step of the way, and the final betrayal had come in the restaurant in Amanzimtoti, as he socialized with the murderous Hussein right in front of her very eyes. There was no reason on earth that he should have been there that day that would have justified his actions to her.

Finally, her shuddering sobs stopped, and she lay curled up in the feathers like a forsaken rag doll. Sebastian had withdrawn to the comfort of her bed, and lay peacefully snoring on her quilt. There was a tentative knock at her door. April sat up quickly and wiped her face, trying to remove the evidence of the ravages of her weeping.

'Who is it?' she asked querulously, sweeping the feathers under her bed in a desperate attempt to hide Sebastian's handiwork from a vengeful mother.

'It's Maria, April. I've come to help you pack.' Sighing with relief, April hastily stood up and went to unlock the door.

'Are you alone, Maria?' she asked rather unnecessarily, as her mother always left Maria to carry on with her work unsupervised, being practically a member of their family. April had no idea how old she was, as she only grew stouter as the years passed. Her smooth black hair was always in a neat bun in the nape of her neck, and she wore her black uniform with a lace collar that she had crocheted herself when April was a baby. 'Oh Maria, I have missed you so,' said April, throwing her arms around the stately Malay woman.

'I can see that,' she replied tartly, poking April in the ribs. 'You haven't eaten a single thing since you left here. Why are you so thin?' She stared at April accusingly, pushing her away from her sternly, and patting her uniform self-consciously.

'Because nothing compares with your cooking, darling Maria, that's why,' she smartly replied.

'Lands sakes. What have you and that mutt done to

your pillow? Your mother is going to throw one of her famous hissy fits when she sees this.' April laughed at Maria's outraged expression. She had shielded April from many of Inge's 'hissy fits' over the years, and had often taken the blame for broken crystal and chinaware. Maria advanced on Sebastian menacingly, and he scampered out of the room with his ears flat and his tail between his long legs. He and Maria were old and loving adversaries, and she protected him on many accounts of grand theft in the kitchens when no one was looking.

'So. What is this that I hear that you are leaving so soon, missy? The only reason could be a man,' she added wisely, watching April with her traditional element of careful calculation and old-fashioned romanticism.

'As usual, O wise one, you are right in a round-about kind of way.' April's face grew grim as she turned towards the bed, and she absently started picking up clothes and folding them untidily for the suitcase.

'Give that here,' snapped Maria as she snatched the dress out of April's hands. 'I thought I done teaching you better than that.' In her agitation, she lost the use of the Queen's English that she had prided herself on from her convent school days, slipping her back into the Malay quarter of her origin.

Within minutes, she had packed April's suitcase so professionally that there was actually room to spare. April sat in her window, huddled against the cold north-westerly wind that carried the bite of coming rain, and watched Maria affectionately.

'What's the matter, child?' asked Maria, placing her hand on April's furrowed brow. 'You are not yourself at all. Ever since you came home, I've smelt fear around you. Are you running from someone?' April sat quietly under Maria's smoothing touch.

'How did you get so wise, Maria?' she softly asked.

'You know that I was born with the sight, child. What a question. Do you think that Maria is too old to still be able to see things? I know that you are fearful and very troubled and you have also misjudged someone that is very important to your survival.' Maria's face grew blank as she looked into the distances of her mind. April paled. She had often listened to Maria talking this way to friends in the kitchen, and even once or twice to Inge, who swore by her sayings, but this was the first time that she had spoken to her like this.

'What do you mean, Maria?' asked April, swinging her legs out of the window, her long green slacks rucking up above her ankles. Absentmindedly, she pushed her straying hair out of her eyes as the wind tugged and pulled at her. She felt cold inside the very core of her being, and it had nothing to do with the weather.

'You have a powerful enemy, child. A man of my faith who walks with Satan. He has a dark soul, and wants to destroy the goodness and purity that he sees in you. He uses people, and hates you because you are strong and won't submit to his wrong-doing. Great danger lies in wait for you, but you have to face it, because if you don't, it will follow you everywhere and swallow you whole. You can beat him. If you chop the head off the snake, the body will be harmless.'

Maria sat down heavily on the bed, beads of perspiration dotting her forehead. Her skin had a yellow tinge to it, and she looked more exhausted than April could ever remember seeing her. Taking her familiar lace lavender-scented hankie out from beneath her watchstrap, she mopped her face quickly, and breathed deeply. Under her breath, she mumbled an Islamic prayer, her face contorted by her fervour.

Suddenly, her eyes flew open, and she smiled at the startled April. 'God is with you child. Do not be afraid.

Now, I have work to do, so goodbye, and I will see you again very soon, I'nsh'Allah.' With that, she bustled out of the room, duster in hand.

April stared thoughtfully after her, breathing in her lavender-scented wake as she absorbed what Maria had said.

April's stomach churned as the large Jumbo lumbered over the high-rise buildings of Durban in its cumbersome approach to the airport. It never ceased to amaze her that the airport was built so close to the affluent suburbs, and that the rate-payers were prepared to put up with the whine of jet engines at all hours of the day or night simply to be associated with living in the good suburbs. Her reverie was interrupted by the bumpy landing, and with a sigh of relief, she unbuckled her seat belt as the large plane glided to a standstill outside the large terminal building.

'Here I am, April. Hello!' She glanced over to where Aneesa stood waving madly from the baggage carousel.

'Hello there. Miss me after my frightfully long holiday?' she lightly teased.

'I couldn't believe my ears when you phoned me this morning. Why on earth are you back so soon?' Aneesa's eyes widened as April quickly told her about Jonathan Capshaw and his relationship to Aneesa's father.

'A brother. I don't believe it. That rotten bastard for cheating on my mother like that.' Aneesa was white with fury.

'And let me tell you that Jonathan is the evil twin of your father. He threatened me, and enjoyed doing it too.' April quickly picked up her luggage and headed for the parking area. The wind whipped their hair around their faces as they walked out of the automatic doors. 'How did you get here by the way?' asked April, remembering that Aneesa couldn't drive. She had asked her over the telephone to arrange something, and hadn't expected to see her there in person. Aneesa smiled shyly, and stopped next to a green BMW.

'Here we are,' she said, opening the back passenger door for April, grinning like a mischievous schoolgirl. Even in the darkness, April could sense her blush.

'Bueno Sera Signorita. Com e'sta?' Bruno's booming voice filled the plush interior of his car.

'Bruno! Ciao...' stammered April, delighted that her friend was happy.

'I couldn't stay away from this beautiful Bellisima girl, so I drove from Amanzimtoti to throw myself at her feet and to serve her in any way that she would allow.' He playfully stroked Aneesa's face as she clambered self-consciously into the car next to him. His huge hand looked like a gentle bear's paw as he held Aneesa under her elfin chin. 'She tell me that we fetch you from the airport, so here we are.' His laughter boomed out, echoing his happiness. The two women couldn't help laughing as his infectious chuckle filled their ears. Aneesa turned around and gave April a knowing wink and the thumbs-up sign of international thanks and gratitude.

'Oh, I fetched Shakespeare for you from the kennels this afternoon. I thought that you could do with a friendly homecoming. I hope you didn't mind?'

'Mind? Oh Aneesa, I'm thrilled. I can't believe how much I missed him, even though I saw him just the other day.'

'I left him at the townhouse so that he could settle down a little before you came home. I also left him a little bowl of steak. I thought that he would enjoy a little treat after kennel food. Hope he eats Halal steak!' The two women laughed at the prospect of the fussy little dog refusing steak on religious grounds.

'We'll drop you off at the door, and then be on our way. We have … er … plans for this evening,' Aneesa added shyly.

'Si. She will teach me about Islam, and I will teach her about love,' said Bruno, turning to watch her and driving recklessly fast in his haste to deposit April at her doorstep.

'That's fine,' she replied, shutting her eyes tightly. If she was about to die in a twisted scrap of metal, she had no intention of seeing it coming.

'Bye!' shouted Bruno, exuberantly as he drove away in a cloud of dust. April feebly responded, smiling to herself at the power love had to overcome all obstacles. Sometimes. Her expression grew wistful as she thought of her and Jack's relationship that had not withstood deceit, lies, betrayal and treachery. The townhouse loomed darkly and coldly above her, for the first time it did not appear inviting and safe. Admonishing herself for her flights of fancy, April jiggled her key in the lock. Frowning, she twisted it again. The lock appeared to be sticking. 'Damn sea air,' she softly cursed as the lock finally clicked open. Picking up her valise, April opened the door with a flourish. 'Shakespeare, I'm home,' she called out, pleased that she would not have to spend the night alone. There was no answering bark. April frowned. Usually, the small animal set up a rumpus from the moment he heard her key in the lock. April screamed with fright and jumped as the door slammed behind her, pushed by the rising wind that was whipping the trees and the sea into a frenzy. 'Shakespeare, here boy, come on,' she called coaxingly, making kissing noises with her lips. Her hand moved along the wall in the darkness to find the lounge switch and she recoiled in fright as a spider scuttled away from under her touch. Laughing nervously to herself,

April felt again for the light switch. She sighed with relief as her fingers closed over the switch, and she pressed. Nothing happened. The clouds scudding across the night sky threw eerie shadows around her as she peered intently at the switch. She pressed it again several times, but all she was rewarded with was the exasperating clicking sound. Inching forwards, she found the kitchen light switch and pressed it. The result was the same. Overwhelming all enveloping blackness. 'Damn, damn, damn!' she exclaimed, stamping her foot in frustration at the inconvenience of a power failure.

Suddenly, her blood froze in her veins as she became aware of an unfamiliar strong perfume. Squinting, she looked slowly towards her lounge.

'Hello, Miss Ross. I've been waiting for you.' April stifled a scream, as a shadow detached itself from her rocking chair, and stood silhouetted in front of her lounge curtains. She instantly recognized the clipped, precise tones of the blonde woman she had seen on Hussein's arm the night of his party.

'What are you doing in my home?' April stammered, her mind racing, 'And just how did you get inside?' She gasped involuntarily as a match flared in the Hungarian woman's hand, and she quickly lit April's candles, throwing the room into garishly romantic relief as the flames sputtered and danced.

'Please, do not be alarmed. Sit down and join me in a glass of wine,' the woman said conversationally, as though she were the hostess and April her guest. On the coffee table was a bottle of Bellingham Johannisberger, already opened and poured into two glasses. 'I think it would be best, don't you?' the woman said, sitting herself and making a sweeping gesture to the chair next to her. April found herself moving hypnotically towards the chair, the woman's voice soothing and unthreatening. Suddenly, she stopped short.

'Where's my dog?' she asked sharply. The woman stared at her for what seemed an eternity, then smiled coldly, baring her teeth in a predatory manner.

'Oh, he's in good hands, my dear. Now please, sit down.' Her tone sharpened and April moved to the chair resignedly.

'How did you get in?' repeated April, her voice stronger than she was feeling.

'Through the front door, of course. I do not enjoy scaling walls and trees like some of my colleagues, so I put my considerable lock-picking talents to use, and entered through the front door like any self-respecting visitor.'

April could see the woman clearly in her mind's eye as she had clung onto the arm of Hussein, and acted the hostess at the party. She was certainly more than his secretary. April felt a cold fist closing around her heart as she sat opposite the woman in some caricature of companionship, her eyes brimming with unshed tears, not for herself, but for her hapless dog. Clearing her throat in an effort to pull herself together, April reached for the wine glass, and took a large fortifying sip.

'Cheers,' said the woman, her Hungarian accent barely discernible. Her eyes had a Slavic tilt to them, and her platinum hair shone like the halo of an unholy angel in the candlelight.

'Why no lights?' asked April, realizing that the darkness was not because of any ordinary power failure.

'Candlelight becomes me,' replied the woman coldly. 'Besides, I certainly didn't want to advertise my presence by having lights on, and I don't think that I could have stood a hysterical scream from you the moment you snapped the lights on, quite possibly blinding me with their brightness, could I?'

Eva. Her name came back to April. Hussein's 'social'

secretary who was quite as dangerous as he was, maybe even more so. History was full of tales of the vengeful nature of evil women compared with their male counterparts. They were more ruthless and creative in their methods of cruelty. 'Let's chat, shall we?' she said, interrupting April's depressing train of thought. She nodded, watching Eva intently over the rim of her wine glass. 'I had a call from Jonathan last night. He says that you have quite a way with dogs.' She smiled the same predatory smile that lifted her full lips back from her perfect teeth, but never reached her eyes. Her gaze on April was unblinking, and unnerving. 'But I digress. Let me get to the point.'

'Please,' said April, sarcastically.

'We both know that you witnessed something unpleasant at Abdul's birthday party, is that not so?' She tilted her head to one side and waited for April to acknowledge her before she continued. 'We all know that it was you there that night, dear. So silly of you to get snagged on that tree like that. Tsk tsk tsk.' Eva shook her head in mock dismay.

'The point being ...' prompted April, bluffing her bravery.

'The point being that, if you keep your pretty little mouth shut, and join Abdul's team, your life can become very comfortable. Besides, as things stand now, you have absolutely no proof that a crime was ever committed, and certainly no self-respecting police officer would take your word over the word of a man who sees to it that their families are well provided for, if you get my drift. You do get my drift, don't you?'

Eva leaned forward, and placed her well-manicured hand on April's knee. Resisting the urge to slap it violently, April sat perfectly still, a muscle jerking in her right cheek. Eva rubbed her knee gently and caressingly, her eyes fixed warmly on April's mouth.

'I just know that you and I could be such good friends.' Her intentions were very clear to April, who felt a shudder of revulsion creeping up from the pit of her stomach.

'Oh?' she responded weakly, willing herself not to slap the woman's hand away, and then punch her in her sensuous mouth.

'Now,' continued Eva, rubbing April's leg in ever widening circles, 'you are going to be reasonable, aren't you? If you keep quiet, so many good things will happen for you.' Her voice became a little ragged as her passion mounted. Her nipples showed hard and erect through the sheer fabric of her silken blouse. Her hand crept slowly higher on April's thigh, and was now joined by her other hand that stroked April's other leg. April could feel the strength in the fingers even through the thick fabric of her trousers. Just when she thought that she was going to throw up or scream, or both, Eva sat back in her chair, her hands returning to her lap where they lay like twitching butterflies in their death throes.

'Good things?' April congratulated herself on how normal her voice sounded.

'Very good things. Like your life, money, power, the life of your dog and anything else that your heart desires.' She stared meaningfully at April.

'In return for ... what exactly?' asked April, feeling more in control of the situation now that Eva had her hands to herself.

'In return for your silence, and whatever Abdul expects from you, my dear. You will have to show him how grateful you are, of course. He is a man of great appetites, and needs variety frequently. I help him to obtain that variety, and so make his life, and mine, very pleasurable. A great beauty such as yourself is bound to give us both great pleasure.'

'Us both?' asked April uncomprehendingly.

'Abdul likes to watch me take my pleasure with his

women once he has finished with them. Voyeurism, I believe, is the psychological term given to his state?'

'Really?' said April calmly, although her flesh was crawling.

'We know that you have not been involved with anyone since your fiancé was struck off your list of favourite people, so I am sure that you need an avenue for the release of all your sexual tension, is that not so?'

April felt an overwhelming surge of relief that they seemed unaware of her liaison with Jack. Suddenly, she felt puzzled. If Jack and Hussein were such close friends and business partners, then why hadn't Jack told him about them? She started to feel uneasy about her quick assessment of Jack's lack of character.

'Well?' April became aware that Eva was watching her intently, waiting for an answer.

'I ... I'll have to give it some thought,' stammered April, at sixes and sevens with this awful dilemma. She sat back in her chair sharply as Eva stood up and leaned over towards her, giving April an unwilling eyeful of her white breasts. April could feel her breath on her face as Eva stared intently into her eyes. April returned her gaze unflinchingly, and even managed a weak little smile. With a caress on her cheek as light as butterflies, Eva trailed her fingers across April's face, kissed her lips briefly, and moved wraithe-like across the room. Her expensive perfume lingered in the air. Suddenly the lights went on as Eva threw the main switch outside the kitchen window.

April's nausea at the scene that had just played itself out overcame her in waves, and she raced upstairs, barely making it to the bathroom where she was convulsively and violently sick. Eva's heavy perfume brought on fresh spasms of nausea. Feeling weak, she wiped her mouth and gargled with mouth rinse to rid herself of the disgusting taste in her mouth. She let out a scream of alarm as her telephone shrilled in the bedroom. Racing to the side-table, she lifted the phone.

'Hello?' she asked, fearfully.

'Hello, Fraulein, how was your little "visit" with Eva? Are you excited at the prospect of sampling her delectable wares?'

The German's mocking laughter echoed down the line into April's unwilling ear. She felt a fresh wave of nausea threatening to engulf her, and swallowed distastefully to normalize her heaving stomach.

'How do you know about Eva's little visit?' she snapped, her queasy stomach finally under control.

'She is sitting right here. I dropped her off. Did you forget about the car phone?' His tone was almost polite and conversational.

'What do you want?' she asked wearily, the highs and lows of the past three days catching up with her on a tide of hopeless fatigue.

'You don't want your little doggy?' There was dead silence as the implications of his remark sank in.

'Yes, of course I do. What have done with him?' She couldn't stop a tear welling from her eye, and once that one escaped, it seemed to release an army of tears that poured soundlessly down her cheeks in a quiet deluge. She didn't even attempt to brush them way, her mouth filling with their saltiness. Never before had she felt so helpless and alone.

'Taken him for a little swim. If you hurry, you might just find him before the tide drowns him completely. He is under the pier.' The connection went dead, cutting off his hysterical laughter abruptly.

April sat holding the receiver in her hands, immobilized by shock. Suddenly, her body reacted with a surge of adrenaline, and she went racing down the stairs. She lunged at her keys on the dining room table, and sprinted towards her garden doors, nearly crashing through them in her haste to reach the beach. Finally, the doors swung open, and she raced out into the garden, tripping in the dark over one of the rockeries. A sharp rock gashed her leg, but she didn't even feel it, or the trickle of blood down her shin. Miraculously, the first key that she tried in her garden gate was the right one, and it swung open.

April dashed out and ran across the road without looking left or right, narrowly missing being hit by a truck as it swerved violently to avoid her.

'You bloody idiot! Are you blind?'

April was hardly aware of the man shouting wildly after her swiftly fleeing figure, her full concentration riveted on the pier about a kilometre away. She could hardly make out its shape in the inky blackness of the night. The moon had retreated behind a battalion of heavy rain clouds, and the only visibility she had was the light from the road behind her, and the reflections of the white caps on the water as the ocean surged and boiled in its frenzy to attack the beach. The surf was already pounding wildly at the pillars supporting the pier, the water rushing up the beach under the wooden structure. April was completely numb from the cold. Her hair was plastered to her head, and her blouse clung sheerly to her wet body. The rain ran down her face in rivulets, washing away the saltiness of her tears. Her breath burned raggedly in her throat as she gasped in sobbing lungfuls of air. Her feet were bare – she had lost her slip-on shoes. April sprinted towards the pier, feeling as if she were in a nightmare where the faster you ran, the further your destination retreated from you. Her feet guided her by instinct, and she leaped over large chunks of driftwood and colonies of stinging bluebottles. The elements were wild and furious, and the black night was illuminated by flashes of blinding lightning that seemed to streak out of the heavens and touch the ocean at the horizon. Her ears filled with the deafening crash of surf and thunder.

'Shakespeare!' she screamed, her words whipped from her mouth and tossed into the tempest-torn ocean. She gasped as she ran into the pounding waves, and their icy coldness, caused her to stagger. The pier loomed up in the darkness, and suddenly she was directly underneath, protected from the rain. The echo of the rising tide was amplified tenfold beneath the wooden girders, and she could barely hear herself as she screamed for the dog, The barnacle-encrusted stanchions cut her hands as she held onto the poles for support. Her nostrils were full of the cloying odour of old seaweed. Sobbing with frustration, she leaned against the large wooden pole, sliding inexorably down towards the water that was rising and ebbing to her knees. Her blouse ripped as her legs collapsed under her, and she fell to her knees, her head hanging in exhaustion and hopelessness. A large wave crashed over her, picking her up and rolling her along the sand, finally slamming her into the next stanchion. She was winded, bruised, and her hair hang in wet fingers that seemed to be clawing at her face. April coughed as she spat out the seawater. Suddenly, she was alert, hardly believing if she had heard a sound at all. The water raced back towards the large ocean, preparing itself for another hurling attack at the beach, and in the lull, she heard the sound again distinctly. A whimper. Jumping up, she looked wildly around her, and saw another large wave racing towards her. The roar became deafening in her ears, and she clung onto the sodden stanchion to stop herself from being thrown up the beach, or dragged back into the ocean. She staggered as the wet sand beneath her feet whirled away, leaving her off balance. The wave struck her mercilessly, attempting to pick her up and dash her against the wooden pillars. She clung on, her hands ripping further on the roughness of the pole, the salt stinging her wounds like burning fire. April screamed in pain, rage and frustration. The sea withdrew, and she screamed again. There was a sharp bark in answer to her cry.

'Shakespeare! Where are you?' she called, searching the gloom for him. Stepping out from her temporary shelter, she saw the white corner of a box protruding from behind the next stanchion. The dog barked again, sharply. April ran towards the box, racing the wave that was crashing behind her ankles. She swooped on the container and tried to gather it up into her arms, staggering under its unexpected heaviness. Pitting her last ounce of strength against all odds, she hoisted the sodden box up out of its nest in the sand where it had entrenched itself, and ran up the beach under the pier. The angry wave crashed harmlessly behind her fleeing heels, spattering her with its icy ineffectual spray. She dodged out from underneath the pier, and collapsed in the drier sand further up the beach. The whining coming from the box was pitiful, and seemed to grow softer. Ripping the string off the lid impatiently, April left scarlet smears of blood across the sides of the box. Sobbing in frustration, she finally managed to break it open. Sea water gushed out as its structure collapsed, and she reached inside for the huddled wet bundle that shivered beneath her touch.

'Bastards, bastards!' she sobbed as she gingerly lifted the miserable animal out of what was left of his intended coffin. A large rock was in the bottom weighting it down so that it could never have floated. The dog screamed in pain as she touched his back leg. It was twisted out at an unnatural angle away from his body. Her hand felt softly over his leg in the darkness, and she gagged as she realized that the hard protuberance that she had felt was his bone that was sticking out of the bloody pulp of his flesh. The broken leg was tied to the rock, ensuring the dog could never have escaped his watery death even if he had managed to jump out of the box. April bent over the terrified animal and gnawed through the string, releasing him from his prison. Shakespeare was soaked to the skin, his fur matted with sand and blood. April tore what was left of her blouse and gently wrapped it around his shivering body, making soothing little sounds to him as she worked. He quietened under her gentle touch, licking her hand weakly with his little pink tongue. It felt hot and dry on her icy flesh.

'Good boy,' she softly crooned, lifting him into her arms and holding him securely against her near naked body.

'Come on, boy, let's go home. Then I'll get you to the vet, and everything will be all right.' The dog shuddered in her arms as she began the long journey back across the beach, bruised, battered, bleeding and practically naked. The icy rain poured relentlessly down, increasing their misery.

Looking back towards the pier, April shivered with horror as she saw that the spot where she had found Shakespeare was now completely under water. He had come within a hair's-breadth of losing his life. Shaking with anger, she clutched the dog tighter to her breast.

'I don't know how, and I don't know when, but I am going to make you all pay for this! Enough is enough! Hussein, I'm going to get you!' She screamed her challenge into the wind as the sky lit up with violent lightning, and the heavens pealed thunder.

# *Chapter Fourteen*

April stared at her calendar in wonderment. She could hardly believe it was already early July. The past two weeks had been a flurry of activity and concern for her as Shakespeare made a slow recovery from his ordeal in the Pets' Hospital. His small leg was bound tightly in a plaster cast as the badly damaged bone knitted together. The vet had already told her that he would be left with a severe limp. And the dog had barely survived a bad chest cold that his experience in the cold winter ocean had left him with.

April walked over to her bedroom window and shuddered as she looked at the now placid ocean. The memories of her near death under the pier were still giving her nightmares – she would awake screaming in the night, the feel of seawater clogging her nostrils, her thin body drenched with sweat. She held a cup of tea in her bandaged hands, and sipped absent-mindedly at the hot liquid. The flesh on her hands had been badly ripped by the wood and the barnacles, and she had been unable to use a pen or cutlery of any description for two weeks. Rings of fatigue shadowed her eyes, and her hair hung limply and listlessly down to her shoulders. She was very close to reaching breaking point, and had stopped eating cooked food altogether. Her bones pushed out against the sheer fabric of her nightdress. Sighing tiredly, she turned back to her room and got dressed for work like an automaton.

* * *

'April, when are you going to pull yourself together?' asked Aneesa concernedly from the doorway. April looked up from the computer where she had been typing in a preliminary report.

'Mmmm? Sorry?' she said, her mind still on her report.

'I said, when are you going to do something about yourself? You are looking absolutely washed out and defeated.' Aneesa's gaze softened as she looked at her friend. All the sparkle and vitality had gone out of April since the incident with the dog.

'I'm fine. Don't worry about me. I'm just a little tired, that's all,' she replied, turning wearily back to her work, her fingers stiff and sore under the bandages.

'Hello, April,' said a deep voice from the doorway behind Aneesa. April stiffened, thinking her ears had deceived her. The door clicked softly shut as Aneesa retreated, smiling, and Jack Nathan strode purposefully to her desk. Turning herself slowly around in the swivel chair, April looked up into his dark and handsome face, his brow creased with lines of concern.

'Good Lord, what on earth has happened to you?' Jack stared disbelievingly at April's wan appearance.

'Your friend, Mr Hussein, happened to me,' replied April heavily, her heart skipping a beat as her body cried out for Jack's comforting embrace. 'What do you want, Jack? Didn't I send out the minutes in time for the meeting?'

'I'm not here on business, April. I came to see you as a friend,' he responded heatedly, sitting down in the comfortable chair opposite her desk as though it were a sofa in his living room. April winced at the use of the word 'friend'. They had been through so much together, and all he thought of her was as a friend.

'Oh?' she managed to enquire, watching him intently, absorbing every detail of his beloved appearance. Despite his betrayal, she still had very deep feelings for him.

'Come on,' he said, jumping to his feet again, startling April with the sudden movement. 'Let's go to Pierre's restaurant and have a decent meal and some peace and quiet. There are some things that I need to explain to you, and you have to give me your well-fed and absolute concentration. Okay?'

'No! Not okay,' replied April heatedly. 'Are you crazy? I'm not going anywhere peaceful and quiet with you so that you can peacefully and quietly slit my inconvenient throat for your buddy!' Her cheeks were flushed with annoyance. To her consternation, he burst out laughing. The room filled with the roar of his laughter.

'It's not funny, dammit!' said April, standing up and stamping her foot in anger. Jack moved swiftly around her desk, and before she could protest, gathered her hungrily into his strong arms and kissed her passionately on her still protesting mouth. April felt the familiar thrill of his touch rushing through her body from the pit of her stomach, leaving her dizzy. She pushed ineffectually at his broad chest, whimpering in pleasure and frustration. Tearing her lips away from him, she gasped and gathered in her breath for a full throated scream. Abruptly, Jack released her. She staggered against the desk, her mouth hanging open imbecilically.

'Just testing if you still loved me,' he teased.

'What? How dare you!' shouted April, incensed by his comment.

'And you do, my darling – you most certainly do love me almost as much as I love you. Now, are you coming?' He crooked his arm gallantly for her to take. April stared at his arm, and back to his face, in utter bewilderment.

'Well?' he prompted, watching her carefully from beneath lowered eyebrows.

'I … actually, no,' stammered April, pushing her hair back from her flaming face self-consciously, suddenly aware for the first time in weeks of how she might appear. 'I … have to finish this report,' she said weakly, her darting eyes fixing on the blinking computer screen. 'Yes,' she said, more firmly. 'I have to finish this report, now if you don't mind, I'd appreciate it if you left and let me get on with my work. I don't have the time or the inclination to rush off to lunch with you.' Sitting down, April began desperately typing gibberish.

'April, darling. I'm on to your little game. I love you. I need you by my side, and I will always want you as long as there is breath in my body.' His face was earnest, and his tone was gentle and sincere. April looked at him sharply, searching his face for clues to his hidden motives for the sudden show of interest and concern.

'Don't do this, Jack. It's beneath your dignity. You don't have to lie to me or pretend any more. I know all about you. What I can't understand is why you ever got involved with me in the first place.' She sighed sadly as she looked up at him. His face was puzzled as he returned her gaze.

'April. Look at me. Look into my eyes and tell me that you still see lies there. Please. I beg you. I do love you. I have never stopped loving you since the moment I first laid eyes on you. Let me explain …'

'There is nothing that I want to know, Jack,' she replied, interrupting him. 'I know all about your involvement with Hussein, and everything that he has done to me must have carried your knowledge and perhaps even approval. Now please … go away and leave me alone.' She looked back at the computer screen, turning away from his handsome face. Suddenly she let out a scream as she felt herself being lifted bodily out of the chair, and slung like a bag of potatoes over his shoulder. He kicked open the door to Aneesa's office, and she was surprised to see that the room was empty.

'Put me down!' she sobbed, pounding her fists into the small of his back with no effect at all. It was like a fly swatting at an elephant for all the notice that he paid her.

'Oh, by the way, I took the liberty of getting Aneesa to cancel all your appointments, and I gave her the day off too. I expected a little trouble from you.' Jack's voice was jocular and conversational – he appeared very casual about kidnapping her.

'Ouch! You're hurting me,' exclaimed April as her hipbone pressed into his shoulder blade.

'What? Me hurting you? That's a laugh,' replied Jack laughingly. 'You are the bag of bones that keeps stabbing me.'

'Put me down!' she snapped, hitting him again. April gasped as her head banged against his firm buttocks. 'Jack, please put me down. What are you doing?' she wailed tearfully, his nearness hurting her more than any physical discomfort.

Abruptly, she was standing in front of him in front of the dingy office building. She hadn't even been aware of the stairs that he had just galloped down. Gently, he wiped a tear away from the corner of her eye, then he pulled her towards him, crushing her in his fierce embrace.

'What I am doing, my darling, is fighting for my life, because if I can't have you, then my life is over and not worth living for another minute,' he softly whispered into her hair.

'Please, Jack,' she replied, unmoving in his familiar arms, 'please let me go. We'd only destroy one another. Things are just too complicated now.'

'Come on,' he said, pulling her towards his car and swiftly opening the door for her. 'Now get in and let's go to Pierre's restaurant to discuss this. All right?' April couldn't argue without causing a major scene in front of the inquisitive passers-by, so she graciously sank into the plush seat of the car.

She sat silently next to him as he drove speedily to the Port Rex Hotel, her mind racing with what might happen to her when he had her alone with no witnesses. She felt powerless to argue with him, and let herself be led meekly to the waiting lift that swooped them skywards to the Room at the Top restaurant. The lift music that was normally so soothing jarred on her frayed nerves, and having caught a glimpse of herself in the ample mirrors and bad lighting of the lift, April stared down at her feet to overcome the shock of her spectral reflection. Her lighting at home had been far gentler with her, and she began to realize why her appearance was having such an impact on her friends. She had become a shapeless shadow of her former self, hollow-cheeked and deathly pale.

With a resounding ping, the doors flew open, and April shrank back. 'I can't go out there and be with people,' she said nervously. Jack gently took her thin arm, shocked afresh at how painfully thin she had become, and led her slowly to the lift door.

'Come on, darling. There isn't anyone else here. I wanted to make sure we were quite alone when I explained myself and my actions of late to you.' April allowed herself to be led into the restaurant, and true to his word, the elegant room was empty. Her ears filled with the strains of a Strauss waltz coming from the expensive sound system ensconced in the plush walls. She smelt the light and delicious odours of French cooking wafting from the kitchen. Jack led her to a table by the window like a concerned parent feeding a frail child out into the sunlight. He quickly pulled out a chair so that she could sit and face the sea view.

'If you don't mind, I'd rather face the restaurant. I have

had enough of a sea view to last a lifetime,' said April softly, smiling to herself at the irony of her remark.

'Whatever you want my, darling,' he replied, complying with her wishes. He deftly opened a bottle of champagne that was nestling in its silver ice bucket next to the table. April shifted uncomfortably in her chair, watching Jack closely as he poured two generous glasses of the frothing golden liquid. Sitting down, he handed her a glass, and raised his in a toast.

'To Abdul Hussein. Cheers!'

April stared at him, horror-struck. She felt a rush of fear at the mention of her enemy's name. Slowly, she put her glass down.

'I can't drink to that, Jack. I'd rather drink nails,' she stated. Jack threw his head back and roared with laughter. He put his glass down and slapped his leg in his merriment. If April had not been so astounded and annoyed at the source of his merriment, she might have unwillingly joined in his laughter as his enjoyment was always so infectious.

'Would you care to share the joke?' she said stiffly, fidgeting with the stem of the delicately fluted crystal glass.

'My darling, that is precisely why I brought you here today. To share the truth and the joke with me. Now please, humour me and have a sip of champagne. It will put the colour back into your lovely cheeks.' April stared at him in consternation. 'All will be revealed, April. Now please, have some champagne, my love.'

'Stop calling me your love and your darling!' she finally exploded, dashing the glass off the table where it splintered into a thousand prismatic shards. 'You burst into my office after months of practically ignoring me, you change my whole schedule, you have the unmitigated gall to chase away my secretary, you ... you kidnap me and drag me here to this place where we are quite alone playing the mystery man, and now ... now you try and force champagne down my throat to celebrate something that that odious vile disgusting pig of a toad Hussein has done. How dare you, you bastard!'

She stopped, exhausted by her diatribe, and yet relieved. Her face was suffused with colour, and her eyes were sparkling in anger. Jack opened his mouth to speak, but stopped as she held up her hand imperiously to stop him. 'I haven't finished,' she snapped.

'I'm all ears,' he replied, settling back into his seat with a slight smile lurking at the corner of his mouth.

'Thank you,' she said, trying to drag her eyes away from the sensual lips that were smiling at her. 'Now ... where was I...?'

'I believe you were telling me what a bastard I am,' supplied Jack helpfully. April could feel her hands balling into fists under the table. Just then, she was distracted as she caught a movement out of the corner of her eye. Pierre came walking out of his kitchen, balancing a delicious platter of aromatic and steaming calamari on rice. Unwittingly, April licked her lips as her mouth filled with almost forgotten juices.

'Hello, cherie,' greeted Pierre warmly, diplomatically acting as though he hadn't heard a word of April's rather loud outburst.

'Hello, Pierre,' she replied sheepishly, flashing him a brilliant smile. 'It's nice to see you again. How have you been?' she enquired politely.

'Bon, merci,' he replied, placing the platter expertly on their table and managing to sweep her hand up to his lips in the same fluid movement.

'Ah, I see that you have had a small accident,' he said, looking at the remnants of the broken glass. 'Don't worry, I bring another. It is so good to see you back again with Monsieur Jack. When I do not see you, then I do not see him. Excuse me, I go to fetch a glass.' As he moved quickly away from the table, April sat silently looking down at her place setting, avoiding Jack's eyes.

'Please, April, help yourself,' he prompted, handing her the serving spoon and fork.

'No, thank you, I'm not hungry,' she swiftly replied, looking away from the mountain of tempting food that had awoken her stomach, which was now rather embarrassedly growling for some relief.

'Very well,' replied Jack, helping himself lavishly. April stared at him in surprise, and swallowed as she watched him take a mouthful of the lightly crumbed golden rings of calamari.

'Your glass, Mademoiselle,' said Pierre at her elbow. She had not heard his quiet approach. He swiftly poured her a glass, and then took an exaggerated double-take at her empty plate. 'You don't like my calamari?' he asked, horrified at the prospect.

'No ... no ... I mean, yes of course I like it,' stammered April helplessly, caught between her desire to make her point with Jack, and to eat up everything before her. Quickly, she made up her mind and reached for the serving utensils, piling the food untidily on her plate. 'I just let Jack start, that's all, while I ... er...'

'While she waited for her glass,' said Jack helpfully.

'Yes, that's it,' said April, hysterically grateful for the comment. 'I wanted my champagne before I started eating.' She nodded desperately like a nodding doll, and quickly took a sip of the champagne. Pierre smiled broadly, satisfied that his culinary appeal had not deserted him, and walked swiftly back to the kitchen.

April sat eating in stony and disapproving silence, torn between her longing to rekindle the flame with Jack, and her anguish over his betrayal. 'What is the time?' said Jack, looking at his watch.

'What?' stammered April. 'Er ... it's about five minutes to one. Why?'

'Just checking the time. My watch has been acting up a little lately. Incidentally, have you been watching much television, or reading newspapers or listening to radios recently?' April stared at Jack uncomprehendingly.

'No, actually, I haven't,' she replied, unwilling to admit the extent of her self-imposed isolation, and the endless nights of coffee, books and cigarettes.

'Excellent!' he exclaimed, smiling broadly, obviously very pleased with her reply. She sat, waiting for him to continue, to perhaps offer some explanation.

'Excuse me for a moment, will you?' he said, and walked towards the doors that Pierre had exited through moments earlier. April looked around the restaurant. The fact that there were no other patrons was most unusual for this time of the day, knowing the restaurant's reputation for fine cuisine. She looked towards the entrance and noticed that the doors were shut. Just then, Jack returned to the table beaming broadly at her. Pierre bustled busily over to the desk that housed the sound system, and flicked the dial from Viennese classics to the local radio station. The loud tones of its signature tune filled the restaurant.

'April, I am going to give you the biggest present of your life right now,' said Jack, reaching across the table and taking both her hands in his. He gently squeezed them and she felt the familiar dizzying rush of sensation that his touch always aroused in her. He gripped them firmly, as though he were afraid that she would snatch them away. She looked down at the familiar contours, the fine black hairs curling tightly against the olive-toned fingers.

'Jack, please don't do this to me,' she whispered brokenly,

shutting her eyes firmly to will away the tears that lurked, ever ready to roll down her cheeks.

'April, I want you to listen to every word that the newscaster is going to read. You will never forget this news, because today is the day that I hand you Hussein's head on a silver platter.' His expression darkened and turned inwards at the mention of the man's name, and she winced as his grip tightened painfully on her fragile hands. She noticed fine lines at the corners of Jack's eyes and mouth that had not been there all those carefree months ago. His dark hair showed a sprinkling of silver hairs at his high temples, that served to heighten his distinguished good looks, and somehow lend him an air of vulnerability. April felt breathless and dizzy. Suddenly, she realized what he had said. Pulling her hands abruptly away from his, she chided herself for letting her guard drop. She had been on the brink of surrendering herself to any fate that he had planned, but the mention of Hussein's name was like an electric shock. Putting his finger to his lips, Jack bade her to be quiet. She acquiesced, suspiciously, alert to whatever his next move might be. Apprehensively, she glanced towards the closed doors, expecting to see Hussein and his entire evil entourage come bursting through to violate her.

The nasal tones of the announcer bored their way into her consciousness. April could hardly believe what she was hearing.

> Good afternoon. Here is the news brought to you on Radio Natal at 1 p.m. The biggest scandal ever to break rocked the Houses of Parliament earlier today as the Minister of Cultural Affairs in the House of Delegates, Minister Abdul Hussein, was arrested on several accounts of fraud, extortion, and being found in possession of graphic pornographic material that

has been linked to several businesses that he was operating. When asked to comment, the Minister threatened members of the press with bodily harm, and a further two charges of assault have been laid. Police investigation into the extent of possible other crimes is ongoing at present. Minister Hussein has not been granted bail, and will await further prosecution in the Pollsmoor Prison in Cape Town.

The radio died down into silence as Jack motioned Pierre to switch it off. April sat in stunned silence, unable to believe what she had just heard.

'And you don't need to worry about Eva and the rest of his merry men either,' said Jack gently, reaching across the table to wipe away the silent tear that coursed down April's cheek. 'As we speak, they are being arrested, and will be tried for their involvement in his affairs.'

'I don't understand what's happening,' whispered April, her face creased with confusion.

'Let me tell you a story that started long before you arrived in Durban, April. It's not a pretty story, but at least it has a semi-happy ending. Would you like to hear it?' He looked at her quizzically, waiting for her reply.

April settled herself comfortably in the high-backed chair, her natural curiosity piqued. 'Sure,' she replied, nodding emphatically, 'I'm all ears.'

'Do you know what a sting is?' asked Jack earnestly.

'I think so,' she replied. 'It's when you set someone up and then catch them out or beat them at their own crooked game, isn't it?'

'Excellent description,' replied Jack, beaming. 'You are a smart cookie, aren't you, my darling?'

April stiffened at the use of the familiar term of endearment, still not ready to blindly trust him.

'Right, let's begin,' he said. 'The story starts exactly a

year ago when I was approached by a friend of mine from the murder and robbery squad. He knew that I was closer to Hussein than most men, and that the man respected me, and even admired me a little, although he knew that I was incorruptible. With me so far?'

'I think so,' she replied, her eyes widening with increasing interest.

'They had their suspicions about Hussein's crooked dealings because the tax inspector picked up a discrepancy on his taxes, and after very discreet investigations, it came to light that he was living well beyond his means on his declared income.' Jack's face was firm, his brow furrowed in concentration as he spoke. 'Naturally, there had been rumours around the area that pointed to a few shady deals, but there was never any concrete proof of crimes having been committed, and there were never any definite and reliable witnesses. The one reliable witness that they had was the man whom you saw being killed that night at his party. He was supposed to give some vital evidence about an extortion deal that Hussein was involved in, but he died before he could testify, and his body disappeared without a trace. Now you know that without a body, you cannot prove a crime, right?'

'Right,' agreed April, hanging on his every word and hardly able to believe what she was hearing. 'But what has this got to do with you, or me for that matter?' she asked.

'Patience, I'm getting there,' he replied, taking a sip of the ice-cold champagne, and clearing his throat softly. 'Now,' he continued, 'as I was saying, a friend in the Special Investigations Branch asked me to assist in investigating Hussein's personal affairs so that they could get some tangible proof of any crime that could have been committed.'

'But why you?' asked April interrupting his monologue.

'I already told you. He trusted me, respected me and

saw me as a challenge for corruption because I was always such a "good boy". Does that make sense?'

'Perfect sense,' she replied. 'Please continue,' she added, her need to know overcoming her urge to walk out of the restaurant and never see him again.

'I approached Hussein about a year ago, and told him that I was in a spot of trouble with a gambling debt, and that I needed to make some extra cash very quickly or face prosecution. The Special Branch set up a seemingly legitimate debt at the Wild Coast casino through the manager there, and to all intents and purposes, I owed Sun International the staggering amount of half a million rand. Naturally Hussein investigated my story, and was satisfied that I did owe this money.'

'But what has this got to do with the present situation?' asked April, shuddering at the memory of the pounding surf under the pier that night.

'Do you want the whole story, or not?' replied Jack, a little impatiently.

'Sorry. Yes, of course I do,' she replied, picking up on his tone of annoyance.

'Hussein set up a meeting with me, and cleverly had me frisked in case I was wearing a wire, which was something that they had expected of me. Fortunately, my detective friend bowed to my superior knowledge of the man and his deviousness, or else the game would have been up there and then.

'Hussein then took me for a walk in the rain, so that we couldn't be listened in on, or easily followed, and he told me that he regarded me as the son he never had.'

'That's a damned lie!' exclaimed April, her face flushing at the memory of Jonathan Capshaw and his threats. 'You do know that he has an illegitimate son in Cape Town, don't you?' she asked, wondering if she may know something that Jack didn't know.

'Oh, Jonathan's existence is common knowledge in security circles,' he replied. 'They just haven't done anything about it yet because he was never seen as having any value in the investigation.'

'Just how long has this investigation been going on?' she enquired.

'Nearly as long as Aneesa has been a widow,' he replied.

'Good grief! So they suspected him then already of murder?'

'Not quite. The tax investigation started about two months before her husband was killed, and because his dislike of his son-in-law was common knowledge, it simply became yet another suspicion, but with no proof. Anyway, let's get back to my role in this little drama, shall we?'

'Absolutely,' she agreed, nodding her head emphatically.

'During the walk in the rain, Hussein told me that I had to prove myself worthy of joining his followers by pulling my own brand of blackmail in order to raise the cash. I then arranged that one of the undercover agents become my mark, and…'

'Mark?' interrupted April, puzzled.

'Yes. My victim, in other words. We set up an operation that looked as though I was blackmailing this man with photographs of him and another woman in bed together. You have to understand that as an undercover agent he had to present a façade of ordinary respectability, so he was running his own business, very lucratively too, I might add. The man has a solid reputation as an upstanding citizen of this town. He served on the city council, was a deacon in his church, and was also the president of the local Rotary Club. He enjoyed a high public profile, which helped him greatly in his undercover work, because people thought no one so visible could possibly be involved in anything of a security nature. But what people didn't know was that his frequent business trips always coincided with intensive training in covert operations. His greatest speciality was disguises. He used to infiltrate the seedy night clubs, and was responsible for several cases where he unearthed drug and prostitution cartels. But always in disguise.' Jack stopped talking, and absently sipped his champagne, his thoughts turning inwards.

'And what happened next?' prompted April, leaning forward in her chair, aware of the familiar woody scent of his aftershave lotion.

'This man and a rather nubile and dedicated female police officer posed for some rather compromising photographs to be able to provide me with the ammunition I needed to launch a blackmail operation.'

'Who is this man?' asked April.

'That I can never tell you, darling, because you might inadvertently blow his cover one day, and we don't have any Witness Protection Programme where he could get lost in.' Unconsciously, Jack reached across the table and took April's delicate hands into his own, rubbing her knuckles with his thumb. She looked down, but could not bring herself to tear her hands away from him.

'I set up another meeting with Hussein, and showed him the photographs. He was thrilled with them because they suited his perversions perfectly, although they were so expertly taken that you could only see their faces and great expanses of flesh ... enough to compromise the man as his face was clearly shown, but certainly not pornographic at all. Hussein was delighted, and then proceeded to tell me how to use these photographs to maximum advantage and how to actually get money out of the man in return for the negatives and my silence. Naturally, he had me make another set of negatives so that we could use them again in the future for more capital. He also informed me that because he had taught me how to blackmail so well, his cut of every extortion would be twenty-five per cent. The first payment was for a quarter of a million rand. So Hussein made sixty-two and a half thousand rand for himself.'

'But where did you get the money?' asked April, bewildered by the amounts involved.

'Ah, that's the beauty of the operation. The only actual money that exchanged hands was Hussein's percentage which he received in marked bills as proof that he had accepted it. Also, my "debt" at the Casino was reduced on their books by the appropriate amount, making it look as though I had received the volume of cash, and paid off nearly half of the debt. The money was approved by the Special Security Division, and would be recovered later. This little deal was my test to get into Hussein's operation, and it gained me a whole lot of trust in the process. I was in a position to plant bugs in his study which was the one place where he felt the safest, and where he did his biggest deals.'

April recalled the victim's neck snapping in Hussein's study, and knew that Jack was telling the truth.

'Then something very unexpected happened,' he continued, looking at her wan face.

'Unexpected?' she prompted.

'Yes. You. You came into my life like an unexpected whirlwind and ended up being one of Hussein's prime targets. All my months of work were nearly ruined by my feelings for you. And you were my greatest secret. Hussein once asked me if I was interested in you, so I had to play the big deal and say that it was only for a quick screw, and nothing more. Why do you think I kept on warning you to stay away from him? He was evil and manipulative, and wanted to get you into bed by force or whatever it took to humiliate you and bring you to your knees.'

'But why? I'm nobody special, Jack,' she replied, horrified by these latest revelations.

'Oh, you were very special, my darling. Do you remember that girl he raped in Cape Town? Jonathan's mother?'

'Well, yes,' she replied hesitantly. 'But I never met her or knew who she was.'

'Hussein has a photograph of her in his wallet. And she looks exactly like you.'

'What?' she gasped, aghast at the prospect of looking like Hussein's main obsession.

'I couldn't believe it when I saw her picture. Hussein had taken me so into his confidence that he would share his personal thoughts with me. And one of them was you. The girl had eventually committed suicide, and Hussein's obsession with her started then. When you walked into this job, and he saw you for the first time, you were a marked woman. I had to do everything in my power to protect you, and that is why I didn't even question you when you called our relationship off. I thought that you had just fallen out of love with me, and by then I realized that Hussein was fascinated with you. Our relationship had become very dangerous for your safety. He swore that he would kill any man that came near you, and that he would then kill you very slowly. Not being involved with you was the best way for me to protect you, my darling, and if you had not ended the relationship that day, I would have done it myself very soon afterwards.'

'Why didn't you tell me this?' she whispered, her face ashen.

'I couldn't risk it, April. I was so close to nailing this creep that I had to keep you out of the picture, or else he would have eventually got his evil hands on you, and shaken the truth out of you.'

'But why didn't you have him arrested straight after the extortion deal?' she asked.

'Because they wanted to get him on more serious charges than simple blackmail. In any event, I had to get him to admit certain crimes to me on tape, or else he would only have been charged with tax evasion, and the whole operation would have been a massive waste of manpower and time.'

'What about that time that I saw you with him in the restaurant in Amanzimtoti?' asked April, probingly.

'That was the delivery of another cut in the blackmail operation,' he replied.

'Another cut?'

'Yes. Remember my gambling debt had to increase with interest added to it, and so he managed to squeeze a further eighty-seven and a half thousand rand out of the deal. The catch was that the briefcase I handed to him was bugged, and after he left me, he had another meeting that involved drug smuggling and increasing the prostitution he controlled, so they had this unexpected bonus. I must tell you that I nearly had heart failure when I saw you and Aneesa there that evening.'

'You saw us?' she asked in amazement.

'Of course I saw you, my darling. I would spot you anywhere even if you had a bag over your head.'

'Did Hussein see us?' she asked.

'No. I kept him occupied with disgusting jokes and the promise of another non-existent deal so that he wouldn't look in your direction. I even went so far as spilling the wine over the table when you people were leaving, so that he would be distracted.'

'Why didn't he have any bodyguards with him that evening?' asked April, determined to find out as much as she could about this evil man who had pervaded her life like the lingering odour of death.

'He never had bodyguards with him when he met with me, because he never wanted his left hand to know what the right hand was doing. Besides, he trusted me implicitly, and knew that if there was ever a problem, I'd protect him.'

'But you just left me to his mercy, Jack,' said April softly. 'He had me terrorized and threatened. He nearly killed the dog, and me in the process. Where were you then? He had my home broken into. He had me frightened out of my wits in Cape Town with Jonathan. I was terrified that he would do something to my parents. Where were you in all of this? I had to face it alone.' Her breathing was ragged as her feelings of anger came crowding back, crowding out her last vestiges of self-control. 'Where were you?' she shouted.

'I was always close by, my darling, and when I couldn't be close, then agents were. I couldn't rush in to save you every time that you were threatened, because it would have blown the sting. I also knew that he was trying to frighten you, and that your life was never in actual danger. I was the most dangerous part of your life. I was the only one who could have been responsible for your death.' April was horrified to see that his eyes had filled with tears. His voice broke, and he looked away to gain control.

She was instantly calm. 'I never knew, Jack,' she said softly, cupping his face in her hands and turning his head to face her. 'I'm sorry, I just never knew what you were going through. I should have known better. Please forgive me for doubting you so dreadfully.'

He held onto her hands tightly as they caressed his face. 'There's one more thing we'll have to do, April, before this is all over,' he said, gathering control of his emotions as he looked into her large grey eyes.

'Testify?' she replied, without hesitation.

'Yes. Can you go through the court case and all the publicity, and tell everyone what you saw that night?'

'Of course I can,' she replied, smiling broadly at him, her heart racing.

'April, I love you so much, my darling. Thank God this deception is all over. I need you so much in my life. My days have been empty without you.'

'And your nights?' she asked, impishly.

'My nights have been unbearable since the day that I met you,' he replied, his expression grave and earnest.

'We will have to do something about that,' she replied, batting her eyelashes theatrically at him. He threw his head back and roared with laughter at her antics.

'I can see that I am going to have to make an honest woman out of you, April Ross,' he said, still laughing.

'Fine,' she replied airily, pulling her hands away from his grasp. 'But first, I need food. I'm starving! I haven't eaten for about three months,' she said, picking up her knife and fork purposefully. Laughing at his incredulous expression, she threw the cutlery up into the air and whooped in sheer enjoyment. Jumping up, she planted a smacking kiss on Jack's forehead. Grabbing her, he pulled her down onto his lap.

'Miss Ross,' he said earnestly, gazing deeply into her eyes. 'Will you please do me the incredible honour of becoming my wife?'

April put her arms around his neck and pulled his head down to meet her lips. She kissed him chastely and gently, and nestled into his shoulder like a small child seeking comfort and protection.

'Oh, definitely,' she said softly, feeling the happiness welling up inside of her like a dam about to burst.

'What did you say?' teased Jack.

'I said Yes, Ja, Si, Oui, yes in all the languages in the world. I love you desperately, madly, gladly, badly...'

All further words were silenced and smothered by his lips crushing down on her ripe mouth, and for the first time in her life, April saw stars in the arms of the only man that she had ever truly loved. Little did they realize what fate had in store for them. The web was only half spun.